PRAISE FOR OF

"Pe ng."

Also by
Kristine Smith

CODE OF CONDUCT
RULES OF CONFLICT
LAW OF SURVIVAL

CONTACT IMMINENT

KRISTINE SMITH

An Imprint of HarperCollins*Publishers*

This is a work of fiction. Names, characters, places, and incidents are products of the author's imagination or are used fictitiously and are not to be construed as real. Any resemblance to actual events, locales, organizations, or persons, living or dead, is entirely coincidental.

EOS
An Imprint of HarperCollins*Publishers*
10 East 53rd Street
New York, New York 10022-5299

First Eos paperback printing: November 2003

Eos Trademark Reg. U.S. Pat. Off. and in Other Countries, Marca Registrada, Hecho en U.S.A.
HarperCollins® is a trademark of HarperCollins Publishers Inc.

Printed in the U.S.A.

10 9 8 7 6 5 4 3 2 1

Thalassa
Commonwealth Colony of Elyas
Summer, Year One

My name is Torin Clase, and I have been charged with writing the story of Jani Kilian. Who she is, and how she came to be.

A quarter century ago a Vynshà priest named ní Tsecha Egri prophesied that one day his race, the idomeni, and my race, the humanish, would blend in the fullness of time to form a single people. In his quest to promote his vision, Tsecha compelled his people to allow humanish to live on the idomeni homeworld of Shèrá, and to establish a consulate on the outskirts of the dominant city of Rauta Shèràa.

Tsecha also compelled the idomeni to allow humanish into their dominant educational institution, the Academy. That first class of six students learned documents protocols from the race that devised them, as tensions grew between those bornsect idomeni who feared the humanish presence within the Shèráin worldskein and those few who believed that Tsecha's blending prophecies defined the future.

When these tensions erupted into civil war, one of those six humanish graduates, Jani Kilian, had attained the rank of Captain in the Commonwealth Service. As she worked to mediate relations between humanish and idomeni, she learned of illegal dealings between them that would have given victory to the ultraconservative elements of the idomeni and bolstered repressive forces within the humanish government. But when she acted to expose this conspiracy, she was killed, murdered as the transport in which she rode exploded on takeoff outside the hospital-shrine of Knevçet Shèràa.

But killed and dead are two different things. Kilian was saved by a humanish physician named John Shroud, who refashioned her using idomeni genetic material. He believed he had inactivated what he considered the undesirable aspects of that material, but he had not.

As the war drew to its bloody conclusion, Kilian escaped with her life. For almost twenty years she lived a fugitive existence in the colonies, on the run from her past, each day growing more aware of the change that had begun to claim her. Last year, she traveled to the Commonwealth homeworld of Earth for the first time, to the capital of Chicago. There she investigated crimes that provided her with the links between her past and her future, and revealed to her the path she was destined to follow as the first of her kind. The first hybrid.

She lives in Chicago still, working with the idomeni embassy and studying the ways of a priest with ní Tsecha, whom she calls "inshah." Teacher. Doing that which she is bound to do, for she is, as ní Tsecha named her, the Kièrshia, the "toxin," the bringer of pain and change. She is also, as I have said before, the first.

And I so wish to meet her . . .

CONTACT IMMINENT

CHAPTER 1

"Chicago is a cold place. In every way."

Clase, *Thalassan Histories, Book I*

"*Coppélia* is a classic tale. In it, a doctor named Coppélius builds a clockwork doll and tries to give her life." Colonel Niall Pierce sat with his booted feet propped on the edge of the portable com–array console, hands folded primly in his lap. "A young couple, Franz and Swanilda, cross his path. Franz falls in love with the doll, named Coppélia, whom he thinks is a real girl. Swanilda becomes determined to find out more about this mysterious beauty who has stolen her lover's heart, and breaks into the doctor's house to find her." He leaned back, the harsh overhead light washing out his bronze Service burr to pale brown and casting his features in sharp relief. Narrow. Angled. The wolf in repose. "And it's a comedy, I'll have you know. Nobody dies."

"Imagine my amazement." Jani Kilian tucked her hands inside the sleeves of her field coat and huddled against the curved wall of the prefab bunker. Outside, freezing rain fell—she could hear it patter on the domed roof. Insets in the polyfoam wall and floor supplied the heat that made the space bearable—she pressed against the hard smoothness, soaking up all the warmth she could. "I thought someone had to keel over every five minutes for an opera to qualify as a classic."

1

"*Coppélia* is a *ballet*, not an opera." Niall tilted his head back and spread his hands palms up, begging the ceiling for respite. "I told you all about it at lunch last week, but it appears to have slipped your mind." He turned to look toward the figure who sat on the floor next to Jani. "Have you ever attended a ballet, ní Tsecha? Humanish dancing?"

"No, Colonel." Ní Tsecha Egri, the Haárin dominant, shook his head back and forth, his latest adoption of humanish gesture. "I have seen plays, and holoVee programs. Histories and such. No dancing." He pushed up the edge of his headscarf with one gold-skinned finger and scratched his scalp. "Nìa," he leaned close to Jani, his voice falling to a whisper, "ballet is leaping about to music?"

"Pretty much, inshah."

"I saw a dancing goat once. Is that as ballet?"

"It is quite similar, yes." Jani unfolded to her feet and walked across the shelter to join Niall at the console. She placed a hand on his shoulder, felt his warmth through his blue fatigue shirt, and tried to remember the days when she could feel warm under conditions like this. "Any change?"

Niall glared in injury, the scar that cut his left cheek from his nose to the corner of his mouth deepening as he frowned. "A dancing goat?" His eyes spoke to the frustrated patron of the arts that he was. Honey-brown and long-lashed, his only handsome feature, they were currently laced with aggravation and regret over missed performances and unappreciative students who ignored lunchtime instruction.

Jani offered a rueful grin. "I'm sorry you couldn't attend your ballet. I know you looked forward to it." She dragged a stool from beneath the console and sat next to him, then pointed to the display screen in the center of the flickering communications array. "Doesn't look any different than it did twenty minutes ago."

"Part of that's the fact that the pickup's malfunctioning. Our comtech should be back any minute with the replacement parts." Niall sighed. "The image straightens out every few minutes. From what I can see, they're still clearing snow. Marking out the cordon." He massaged the back of his neck. "Mine clearance is one of those dichotomous activities. Nerve-wracking to perform, but boring as all hell to watch. Especially when no one seems to be doing anything."

"I heard that." A male voice laced with annoyance emerged from the array's speaker system. "If you're both bored in that nice, warm, *dry* bunker, two hundred meters from all the stuff that goes *boom*, I'd be more than happy to trade places with you."

Niall and Jani looked at one another and smiled. "Hey, Pull," Niall said with a laugh. "How's it going?"

"Saturday night at the Haárin enclave—what a rip-roaring place." The irritation in Lieutenant Randal Pullman's voice was palpable.

Jani glanced back at Tsecha, who had risen and now walked across the bunker to join them. He stood taller than she by a head—the top of his headscarf grazed the light fixture as he passed beneath it, sending it swinging back and forth and casting his thin frame in weird shadows on the wall.

"Rip-roaring, nìa?" Tsecha stood over Jani, arms folded and hands tucked in his sleeves, his long face skull-like. "What is rip-roaring?"

No sound emerged from the speaker for a time. Then came a throat-clearing cough. "Is that you, ní Tsecha?"

"Yes, Lieutenant Pullman—glories of the night to you." Tsecha glanced at Jani and bared his teeth, cracked amber eyes bright with humor. "What is rip-roaring?"

"Rip-roaring? It's—it—" A long sigh rattled. "Ah, boy."

"Out with it, Pull." Niall's shoulders shook.

"Rip-roaring means . . . exciting, ní Tsecha. Thrilling." Pullman's voice grew softer with each passing syllable. "Electrifying."

"So you find standing in deep snow late at night an excitement? I learn more of you each day, Lieutenant." Tsecha's air of mischief faded. "What of the mine?"

Pullman's voice emerged more businesslike. "From what

I have been able to determine thus far, ní Tsecha, the mine is most likely a remnant from an old field exercise. The Service used to operate training facilities here before the land was leased to the idomeni."

"What sort of mine—have you yet determined such?"

"No. Ní Tsecha. That's still under investigation."

"It is a trainer, as you say? Or a dud? Such objects emit signals particular to their type, do they not? One simply identifies the signal, and thus the type of mine, and removes it accordingly."

"Yes. Ní Tsecha. We have not yet identified the signal."

Jani glanced at Niall to find him regarding her, his face set with concern. They had both sensed Pullman's reluctance to discuss the situation. *They've had two hours to ID that mine, and they haven't yet. What's the problem?*

She reached for the console controls and tapped one of the pads. The flat display shimmered, then the two-dimensional image pushed out from the screen, lengthening and widening to form a three-dimensional layout of the mine site. The casualty radius, centered by a black X and encircled by an orange ring two hundred meters in diameter, stared out like a huge bull's-eye. The image stuttered every few seconds as the relays miscued, but it remained steady enough to discern the movement of personnel and equipment, both human and idomeni. "There's the demolitions tech." Jani pointed out the lone figure standing within the cordon, operating the remote-control 'bot that cleared snow from around the mine. "He's still digging the thing out, but I can already spot it at this scale. Why's he still working?"

"Where is Dathim?" Tsecha leaned over the console and searched the miniaturized scene for the towering figure of his suborn. "I will contact him and learn what he knows." He walked to the far side of the bunker as he dug inside his coat for his handcom.

Niall leaned close to the speaker and dropped his voice. "OK, Tsecha stepped away for a while," he said, the sharp tones of Vynshàrau Haárin serving as background. "What's going on?"

In the three-dimensional image, a figure at the edge of the cordon raised a hand. Pullman, kitted out in grey and white winter camou topped with a layer of body armor. "The disposal tech thinks that some water got into the brain of the mine and is screwing up the thing's ability to respond to signals. I'd never heard of that happening, but your guy confirmed. Faber, your comtech. He's at the supply truck hunting for parts for your console."

Niall edged about in his seat as he studied the scene. "So if the tech doesn't know what kind of mine we're dealing with, how the hell is he setting up?"

"According to Ordnance, it's one of two types. Either a Slager that's live but sans detonator, or a Beekman trainer that's most likely a dummy but could be live as well. The Slager's casualty radius is the greater of the two at one hundred meters, so that's what we've gone with." Pullman-in-miniature paced a tight circuit on the edge of the cordon. "It's getting tense here, sir. The Vynshàrau have already gone nose-to-nose a couple of times with our folks. They're picking apart the fact that one of our demis detected the mine signal in the first place—they want to know why we were flying that far inland over their territory. Diplomats from both sides are weighing in with all kinds of questions and demands, and to top off this shitcream sundae, I don't think this tech could find his ass at high noon in the Hall of Mirrors."

Niall patted the front pocket of his shirt, the usual resting place for his nicstick case. "Who's handling the diplomats from our team?"

"Dubrovna. Problem is, everyone at this level is used to dealing with Cal Burkett. Hard to back down to a major when you're used to dealing with a general."

"So why the hell isn't Burkett there now?"

"He's with the PM, sir, back in Chicago. They're patched

in via the same live feed you have. It's my understanding that they're briefing Ambassador Shai."

Niall massaged the back of his neck in earnest. "Tell me about the tech."

Pullman muttered something foul under his breath. "Name's Wode, sir. Lance Corporal Rikki—two k's and an i. Supposed to be good, but you wouldn't know it from the way he's fartin' around out here. He's recalibrated his equipment four times already, and if he digs out any more around that mine, the entire forest floor is going to collapse."

Jani tried to imagine the thoughts going through Wode's mind—surrounded by testy soldiers and bureaucrats of two species, mindful that every move he made, or didn't make, would be examined under a dozen microscopes, each using a different filter. "A Slager would require one type of code to ensure disarm, a Beekman another. A cross-up in signals would precipitate a crisis I don't even want to think about. If the mine brain is malfunctioning and he's unsure about which type he's dealing with anyway, isn't it better that he take his time?"

"He has to make a decision sometime, ma'am, or hand it over to someone who can. We have to clear this thing and get these people and idomeni out of here before a fistfight breaks out." Pullman's image seemed to stride atop the console board from one set of touchpads to another. "Why can't we just clear the area and blow it up? Hell, we could have blown it up from Sheridan."

Niall hung his head. "We have to be able to show the intact device to Ambassador Shai and prove it didn't pose a danger to the Haárin."

"They're not willing to take our word for it?" Pullman asked.

"Over the last three months, four Haárin have been attacked and the enclave itself has twice been the target of vandalism. The newssheets are questioning the presence of the Haárin enclave so close to the Commonwealth capital, and the last time Ambassador Shai's skimmer floated

through Chicago unescorted, somebody heaved a brick at it."
Jani could sense Niall's stare, and avoided it. Sometimes she
felt as though he didn't want her to talk about the worsening
relations between the idomeni and humanish, as if doing so
made matters worse. "Given that," she continued more quietly, "I don't think they'd take your word for the time of day,
do you?"

Pullman-in-miniature kicked at the snow. "No, ma'am."

Jani sensed someone approach from behind, and turned to
find Tsecha standing at her shoulder. "Dathim has told me
that Shai has sent nìaRauta Elon to see to this matter, along
with her suborns, nìRau Ghos and nìRau Feres." Tsecha
turned his head to face his left, then brought up his left hand
chest-high, palm facing outward. It was a High Vynshàrau
gesture of dismay, of the sort he seldom employed since his
outcast to Haárin. That he felt compelled to express his con-
sternation in such a definite manner said all that needed to be
said about Elon. "I recall her from my time as ambassador.
The Council willed her as my security dominant; thus was I
forced to tolerate her." He broke off his posture and looked
to Niall. "I should attend this matter, Colonel. Your Lieutenant Pullman should not be left alone to deal with such as
Elon."

"No, ní Tsecha. Sorry." Niall shook his head. "While your
concern is appreciated, your assistance is not required. We
have Major Dubrovna to deal with nìaRauta Elon—Lieutenant Pullman is safe." He patted his shirt pocket again, his
longing for a dose of nicotine etched in every line of his
face.

"You have not dealt with Elon. She is as a mine whose
signal you do not know!"

"You stay *here*!" Niall's voice shook the air in the small
space. "Ní Tsecha. Please." He sat forward, hands dangling
between his knees, his gaze fixed on the floor as he struggled
to regain his composure. "To most Chicagoans, you are still
the symbol of the idomeni presence on Earth. That
presence . . . is being questioned by some humanish at the

present time, and because of that, both your dominants and mine feel that you should not be observed involving yourself in this matter."

"OK." Jani stepped between the two, man and idomeni, and felt the current of tension that flowed between them. "That explains why you're keeping Tsecha holed up here." She stared down at Niall until he raised his eyes to meet hers. "Why am I here?"

They studied one another—Jani sensed the time pass just as she discerned Niall's examination, just as she knew how she appeared in his eyes. The strange golden cast to her brown skin. Her long-limbed gangliness. Her eyes, dark green irises surrounded by the paler sea of sclera, eyes unlike those any human being ever possessed.

Niall took a deep breath. "You know damned well why you're here. Everywhere Tsecha goes, you're never far behind. You're as much associated with the idomeni presence here as he is. You're—" He reached into his pocket, then yanked out his hand as though it burned.

"I'm the hybrid. I'm what all those questioning humanish fear they'll see one day when they look in the mirror." Jani swallowed a howl of frustration. "I'm not contagious, Niall. It took months of medical intervention to get me this way."

"I know that."

"So why—" Jani fell silent as a sharp *thunk* sounded from outside. Another.

They all looked to the door of the bunker as the panel slid open. A young man decked out in Service raingear blew in, escorted by a gust of chill wind.

"I'll have those relays retimed in a minute, sir." He swept back his hood and undid his coat fasteners as the water dripped and puddled around him. The cold had bitten his ears and nose—they flared red against his pale skin and dark hair. "I spoke with the techs down at the truck—they said the sub-Misty's functioning normally. What we're seeing up here is what's really happening down there."

"Thank you, Faber." Niall's face lightened, his relief at

the interruption obvious. "What's the mood like down there?"

"Irritable, sir." Faber hung his coat in the gear alcove at the far end of the bunker. "Everyone's wet. Cold. Waiting for something to happen." He turned to face them and hesitated, his gaze passing over Tsecha and Jani before settling on Niall. "At the rate things are going, they're going to be there awhile."

"And every hour spent here translates to a month's worth of follow-up investigation." Niall shot Jani a questioning look. "Aren't you supposed to be going on a trip soon?"

Jani nodded. "Outer Circle. Day after tomorrow."

"Hmm. Looks like you may miss most of the fun." The flatness in his voice gave away nothing. "How long will you be gone?"

"Six weeks out, same back. Week or two to do what I have to. Close to four months."

"We'll be well into spring by the time you get back." Niall stood, then walked across the bunker to the gear alcove. "Probably about the time the first reports get issued." He dragged on his field coat. "I'm going to take a walk. See what I can see from out here." He activated the door panel and pushed through the gap without a backward glance.

"I do not believe, nìa, that he wants you to leave."

Jani turned back to Tsecha, who had cocked his head to one side, a gesture of curiosity more humanish than Vynshàrau. "He will have to get used to the fact, inshah."

"Yes. As will you."

Jani hesitated. "I'm going outside." She walked over to Faber, who stood bent over the console. "Excuse me."

Faber straightened, then slowly lifted his gaze to look Jani in the face. "Yes, ma'am." The top of his head only reached her shoulder, and the difference in height seemed to rattle him.

Among other things. Lance Corporal Micah Faber of Supreme Command Communication Systems, Jani decided, didn't like her. She'd run into it more and more often as of late, this sense from some humanish that they didn't want her to get too close. *If I kissed him atop his pointy little head, would he run screaming into the rain?* Given the tension around the place, maybe now wasn't the time to experiment. "Could I borrow your coat?" she asked, knowing full well that to him the request might constitute the same sort of invasion. "I need to talk to Colonel Pierce, and my coat isn't keeping me warm as it is."

"Ma'am." Faber led her back to the alcove. He lifted his coat from its hook, shook off the remaining droplets of water, then held it out for her.

Jani took the coat and flung it across her shoulders like a cape. "I promise I'll touch it as little as possible," she said, leaving him to redden like an alarm as she slipped out into the rain.

She found Niall huddled in the shelter of a nearby stand of evergreens. He turned when he heard her approach, but didn't speak.

"You want to go down there, don't you?" Jani wedged into the shelter beside him. The rain fell about them in a steady patter, but the canopy of branches slowed the flow-through to the occasional drop. "Go ahead—we're fine up here."

"I have been ordered to remain with you and Tsecha, and remain with you and Tsecha I will." Niall had already flipped open the top of his nicstick case and removed a long, white cylinder. He bit down on the bulbed end—the tip flared blue-white in the cold wind. "Tell me about this trip of yours." He stuck the other end in his mouth and took a long drag, then released a stream of smoke with a groan of relief.

Jani pulled Faber's coat more tightly around her shoulders. "I told you about it last week, during lunch. It crossed paths with *Coppélia*—they must have cancelled one another out."

"Humor me," Niall replied, not amused.

"I'll be paying a courtesy call on the Haárin at the Karistos enclave on Elyas. Their dominant, ná Feyó Tal, is a favorite of Tsecha's. He wants me to deliver a gift to her." Jani knew how inadequate the explanation sounded, but Tsecha had given her little more to go on.

Feyó requires an assistance, nìa.

"You're leaving at a time like this to deliver a *gift*?" Niall exhaled another cloud of smoke, which the wind sliced to nothing. "Haárin shuttles leave Luna once a week. Let one of them play errand boy."

"You just finished saying that I require protection to continue to work in Chicago. I think my getting away for a few months might be a good idea."

I cannot leave this damned cold place, nìa—Shai will not allow such. But you may go, and go you must.

Niall shook his head. "On the contrary—I think it will make matters worse. You'll be acting as the intermediary between two Haárin enclaves. How is that going to dispel the perception that you're not human anymore?"

"But I'm not human anymore."

"That's news to me."

"Only because you don't listen."

They lapsed into edgy silence. In the distance, dim illumination shown through the trees. Every so often a shout would carry. A flash of light from a piece of equipment.

Yes, it is dangerous here for Haárin. It is dangerous everywhere, nìa. You must go.

The bunker door opened a crack—Faber's head emerged. *"Wode's started to move the mine, sir!"*

"About damned time." Niall extinguished his 'stick against the wet trunk of a tree and shoved the spent cylinder in his pocket.

Jani followed him into the bunker, to find Faber sitting at the console, Tsecha looming over him. She returned Faber's coat to the alcove, then joined them.

"They just got started, sir." Faber glanced over his shoulder at Jani before switching his attention to Niall, who had dropped into the chair next to him. "Wode's decided to use a biobot to hoist it. He must be too worried about signal cross-up to use a standard comwave."

"Jack up the mag on this," Niall replied. "I want to see what's going on."

Faber worked comtech magic on the console. The outer edges of the image disappeared as the area of the cordon itself expanded. As if on cue, Pullman glanced up—Jani could see the droplets of rain that dotted his armor and ran down his face like sweat.

"Drop that face shield, Pull," Niall grumbled.

"Sir." Pullman flipped down the poly barrier. "Wode's ready to lift the thing."

"Will wonders never cease." Niall braced his elbow on the edge of the console and covered his mouth with his hand, his eyes fixed on the scene playing out before them.

Wode looked even younger than Faber. Colder, too. The wind had nipped his cheeks as well as his nose, so that he looked flushed with fever. He stood thirty meters from the exposed mine, his hands gloved with the translucent sensor web that enabled him to control the cylindrical biobot. He stood still, straight, his arms bent at the elbow and hands facing in as though he held a box by the sides. Every few seconds one finger would move, then another. Each time he moved, the biobot would edge closer to the mine.

The mine itself seemed a puny thing. A blank silver oval the size of a man's hand, it vanished like an eclipsed moon as the biobot rolled over it.

"The 'bot's hollow," Niall said, eyes still locked on Wode's every move. "Once it's settled above the mine, it will hoist it up inside."

"Then the bottom of the 'bot will close," Pullman added. "The mine will be encased until it can dry out. Wode figures fifteen minutes with some warm air circ, and he'll be able to identify the signal."

"Why's he standing so close to the mine?" To Jani, Wode appeared like a man entranced, eyes closed, shoulders slumped, fingers twitching. "Can't he do that from outside the cordon?"

"He says that the problem with bio signals is that they're weaker than standard comwaves." Pullman's voice held a skeptical edge. "He says he has no choice."

As they watched, one of the Vynshàrau broke away from the crowd and walked inside the cordon to stand by Wode. A young male, his thin frame padded by armor, his face covered by a shield.

"It is Feres," Tsecha said, "Elon's suborn."

Niall stood and bent over the console. "Pull, what the hell is going on?"

"Feres is a witness, sir. The Vynshàrau don't trust our transmissions. They want one of their own to watch the mine be contained."

"That's bullshit!"

"We tried to block it, sir, but Dubrovna overrode."

"Well, I just trumped her. Stop everything *now*! Get that Vynshàrau out of there *now*!"

"Yes, sir!" Pullman stepped inside the cordon. *"Wode, pull up now!"*

Wode and Feres both turned.

Light travels faster than sound. The flash filled the image space like a miniature sun. Yellow-white. Blinding.

Then came the thunder of the explosion. The bunker shook, the light fixture trembling as though a giant set down his foot.

They had all dropped to the floor. Now Niall bounded to his feet and ran for the door. *"Faber—stay behind and watch them!"* he shouted as he pushed through the gap.

Jani lay on her stomach, the echo of the explosion still sounding in her ears. "Ní Tsecha?"

"I am most well, nìa."

"Good." She boosted to a running crouch and headed for the door, then fell to one knee as a hand gripped her coat sleeve.

"You're not supposed to leave." Faber's eyes were wide.

His hands encircled her arm without clamping down, as though the thought of contact repulsed him.

"Stop me." Jani shook him off and bolted.

The rain fell harder now. Jani coursed through it, following the light and the equipment sounds. The cries.

Then she broke through a ring of trees, and the console image filled her eyes. The vehicles. The humanish. The idomeni.

She took one step. Another. Tried to avoid the shattered branches, the flecks of red in the snow. Watched medics hoist Pullman atop a gurney and cover him with a medblanket. *They're taking care with him—hurrying—*That meant he lived. *Please.*

"What the hell are you doing here!"

Jani turned to find Niall bearing down on her from the other side of the cordon.

"Who let her in here!" He waved toward a figure in body armor. "Morton! Get her out of here now! Carry her if you have to!"

"I'm going!" Jani held up her hands like a surrendering prisoner, two steps ahead of the advancing Morton. "I said I'm going!" She broke into a run, didn't stop until she stood amid the trees again. She looked behind her to find Morton had returned to the site. Emergency illumins flashed yellow and orange against the night sky. An ambulance siren wailed.

CHAPTER 2

Jani checked every room and alcove as she walked down the aisle of Service Medical's Trauma Center, keeping one eye toward collision avoidance as doctors and nurses darted around her and orderlies pushed past her with skimgurnies and carts bearing equipment.

She found Niall in a waiting area within sight of the main nurses station. He sat in a darkened corner, hunched over a spent nicstick, the floor in front of his chair wet and mud-streaked from the mess shed by his boots.

He looked up as she entered. A streak of mud coated his left cheek, smoothing over his scar, erasing his sinister air. Inde-finable dark stains spotted the coat he'd draped over the back of his chair, as well as the front of his fatigue shirt and trousers. They might have been blood, but it was impossible to tell in the poor lighting. "You made it out of the madhouse."

Jani lowered into the chair next to his. "I saw Tsecha back to the enclave, then hitched a ride on one of the equipment trucks. The last ambulance had just left." She glanced toward the hall in time to see two nurses break into a sprint. "How's Pull?"

Niall started to speak. Stopped. Licked his lips. "Some-thing hit his right side hard. Part of the biobot casing. A piece of Wode or Feres. Medical doesn't know for sure yet, but there may have been a fault in his armor." He patted his left side. "Kidney's gone. Liver's banged up. Even though his augmentation had kicked in, he bled . . . a lot." He exhaled with a shudder. "They got to him in time. They don't need to break out the brain boxes and make sure he's still hitting on all boards."

"So the tally is?"

"Two dead, Feres and that . . . *tech*." Niall slumped back. "Twenty-seven wounded, including two Haárin and three deputy ministers."

"I heard on the way in that Mako just left to see the PM." Jani tried to imagine the mood in that meeting, and found she didn't want to. She despised Admiral-General Hiroshi Mako, and though he preferred to deny it, he felt the same way about her. But a member of his Service had made an error that threatened to kneecap humanish-idomeni relations already crippled by recent tensions, and it fell to him to explain what had happened. Jani almost felt sorry for the man. Almost, but not quite. She ached for Niall, however. He was the A-G's man-on-the-scene, and even though it hadn't been his show to run, she knew he'd blame himself for every error and miscue. "So what went wrong?"

"Where do I fucking start?" Niall held up his closed fist, then raised his index finger. "We should never have let Diplo make the calls." The middle finger. "We shouldn't have allowed all those observers on-site." Ring finger. "Like Pull said, we should have cut all the crap off at the pass by doing a remote disinter-disarm from Sheridan, and told Shai to kiss our collective ass when she howled." He glanced at Jani sidelong. "In so many words." He let his hand drop and lay his head back. "Of course, none of this would have happened if whoever had been in charge of the initial land clearance had done their job. A lot of brass is going to go over the side before this investigation is signed off."

Jani rose and walked across the alcove to the vend machines, digging in her trouser pockets for tokens. "You're using some pretty nasty training mines now compared to what they used in my day." She found the coffee selector and ordered two cups.

"That was no trainer. It was a live and kickin' Slager with an intact detonator sensitive enough to respond to the biobot signal. Once Wode pulled it out of the ground and enclosed it in the 'bot compartment, a heartbeat could have set it off." Niall took the dispo cup of coffee Jani handed him, but instead of drinking it he just stared into the steam rising from the liquid. "I'm going to see his face in my sleep. Looked like a damned twelve-year-old. Should have been operating a remote control skimmer in his parents' backyard, not a mine removal device in the woods in the middle of the night."

"It's not your fault."

"Yeah."

Jani returned to her seat. Sipped her coffee, and winced at the taste of the sour machine brew. "So what was a live and kicking Slager doing buried on the grounds of the Haárin enclave?"

Niall tried his coffee. He swallowed it without a change in expression. Either he was made of hardier stuff than she or he was simply too numb to taste. "You remember the drill. Sometimes the demo techs play it too smart and put the real stuff out there to practice on." He scratched at the dried mud on his face, then stared at the dirt under his nails. "That's against procedure, however, because, well, people can get hurt. So they fudge the records, which then means that they can't always depend on them to tell them what's out there. The old hands know that. But they didn't send an old hand—fresh-out-of-the-box Wode got the call. By the time they got someone out of bed who realized what that could mean, it was too late." He rose and walked to the vend area, still scratching at his muddy cheek. He grabbed a dispo napkin from the dispenser next to the machines, then soaked it in the stream from the water fountain. "Not to change the subject, but what are you doing here?" He leaned against the wall as he cleaned his face. "I thought you'd stay with Tsecha."

"I wanted to find out about Pull." Jani peeled an advertising sticker from her cup, a pass good for two free tickets to a midweek showing at the base Veedrome. "Tsecha and Dathim are administering to the injured Haárin."

"I thought that was the sort of thing he'd been teaching you over the last few months. How to act as a priest."

Jani nodded. "I've learned some of the ceremonies and protocols. But there are a few Haárin who haven't adjusted to me yet. One of them was among the injured—Tsecha and I both figured that the last thing she wanted to see was my face bending over her, muttering prayers."

Niall finished cleaning his face, then checked the results in the smooth metal surface of one of the coolers. "I wouldn't have expected Tsecha to give in like that. He's a great one for shoving things down people's throats."

"He's starting to feel discouraged."

"Welcome to the damned club." Niall tossed back the last of his coffee, then crumpled the cup into a ball and banked it off the wall into the trash. "Not to change the subject again, but how do you feel? My augmentation's activated. People keep backing away when I try to ask them questions."

Jani watched Niall kick at the floor like a restless horse pawing the ground. She couldn't imagine backing away from him for any reason, but she nursed the same Service-made gland in her head that he did, and the synthetic neurotransmitters it pumped out had much the same effect on her as they did on him. "I feel—focused. Like I have things to do, and I can't rest until I get them done. Colors are sharper. Sounds seem louder. Everyone else moves too slowly. The usual."

"Started to come down yet?"

"No." Jani paused and tried to get a sense of herself. "Maybe a little. The hybridization has made it less predictable than it used to be." Or rather, less predictable in its unpredictability. At one time, her augie caused her senses to jumble. Sounds became aromas, while touch and scent sang to her in a range of tones. Now she simply grew tired and jittery as her brain and body said "Enough" and battlefield alert gave way to moody exhaustion.

"Sometimes I think I should take all that medical advice I've received over the years and have the thing taken out. I feel like hell." Niall gathered his coat. "If you contact Special Services, one of them can see you home. I have to check on Pull. Then I need to contact his parents."

Jani watched her friend move with the heavy-footed gait that spoke of exhaustion and the emotional bottoming-out that in his case went along for the ride. "Niall, stop hammering yourself. Pull will be all right."

Niall looked at her and nodded, his predator's face reddened from rough washing, his poet's eyes dull. "Yes. I can tell his folks with complete confidence that the Service is up the spout with the finest medical staff in existence anywhere." He walked out into the hallway in the direction of the nurses station, shoulders bowed. "And idiots aplenty to ensure they keep in practice."

Jani walked out into the night to find the rain had finally stopped. The sky had cleared as well; only some fast-moving clouds remained to obscure Luna, and hide the few stars that could be seen through Fort Sheridan's blaze of outdoor lighting.

"I'm not calling Special Services," she said to herself. She'd never tell Niall, but his regard didn't buy her much in the way of acceptance—except for Pullman, no one else on his staff liked her very much. A silent ride into the city lacked appeal under the best of circumstances. With humanish-idomeni tensions now thick on the ground, the word *best* did not apply.

Instead, she followed the walkways from the hospital to a less-traveled area of the base. On the way, she passed office buildings in the semidark of graveyard shift. Maintenance sheds. Rolling landscape buried beneath melting snow, broken up by stands of bare trees and winter-stripped shrubs.

Before long South Central Bachelor Officers Quarters came into view, a multistory cement block devoted to the housing of male officers in various stages of transition. Jani walked in the front entry, ready to avert her eyes on the off chance she encountered anyone in the halls or the stairwell. *I should have applied film to them.* But her identity as a human-idomeni hybrid was well-known—all of Chicago knew what her eyes looked liked. What good did it do to apply a film to make them appear human, when everyone knew what lay beneath?

She keyed into the stairwell, took the steps two at a time. Stopped at the fifth floor. Negotiated the familiar twist of hallways before coming to a stop in front of the door marked WEST-1, the name L. PASCAL etched into the metal nameplate.

Jani reached for the buzzer, but the panel slid open before she had a chance to press the doorpad.

Lucien Pascal stood in the doorway, a disheveled vision in Service blue pajama bottoms, white-blond burr diffusing the backlight to a pale aura around his head. "I've been trying to track you down for the last hour." He stepped back to allow her to pass. "You have a real talent for falling off the map."

"A talent I worked at for years. Nice to know I'm still in practice." Jani caught the barest whiff of cologne as she entered the spare three-room flat. A peppery scent, lighter than the throaty musk Lucien favored. She looked toward the bedroom. The door was open, the corner of the bed that she could see was rumpled. "How much have you heard?"

"Good morning. It is officially morning now." Lucien stepped in front of her, blocking her view of the bedroom. "I'm fine. I'm not hurt. Tsecha is fine. So is Dathim. Everyone you know is all right. If any of those comments are incorrect, could you tell me now so that I'm not caught by surprise later." He moved closer. The light fell across his neck and chest, accenting scattered red blotches, along with several fresh bruises that formed a characteristic pattern.

Jani touched a red mark near the hollow of Lucien's throat.

"I'm fine. Tsecha is fine. Dathim. Everyone you know." She pressed her fingertips against the bruises, gauging them—yes, they had been left by someone who had gripped far harder than they had to. "You, on the other hand, look a little roughed up."

Lucien gripped Jani's wrist and eased her hand away. In contrast to Niall, his face was the poet's, fine-boned and full-lipped, with just enough softness about the jaw to imply a vulnerability that in truth had never existed. Again in contrast to Niall, his eyes were the predator's, chill brown and calculating, windows to a mind that saw life as a gameboard and all others as pawns, to be played, or sacrificed, as the situation demanded.

"You want to know how much I've heard?" He backed away and walked about the sparsely furnished sitting room, picking up clothes, straightening couch cushions. "Demiskimmer on lake patrol flew too close to the Haárin enclave. Picked up a choppy transmission that spelled 'one of our mines.' They informed Ordnance, who said 'oops' and informed the world, who converged on the enclave. The demolitions tech they sent to pull the mine misread the signal, killed himself and a Vynshàrau." He stopped in mid-pillow fluff and looked at Jani. "Anyone you knew?"

"Feres. One of Elon's security suborns."

"One of the hardcore elite. That should play well back on Shèrá." Lucien resumed his housekeeping. "Have I missed any of the high points?"

"Not really. Except that they thought the mine was a trainer, but it turned out to be live and fully armed."

"Ouch."

"Yeah." Jani started her own walkabout, poking through the places Lucien had yet to straighten. "For someone who looks like he just rolled out of bed, you sure do know a lot." She arrived at a chair one step ahead of him, grabbing for the object that lay in a small heap beneath.

"That's not yours." Lucien bumped her and tried to pull the thing from her hand as she reached down for it.

"It's not yours, either." Jani held the article up for inspection. It proved to be a man's Service-issue T-shirt. "Wrong size." She sniffed the neck and detected the same spicy odor she had when she entered the flat. "Wrong scent, too. Besides, you don't fling your clothes around the room."

"Not unless someone asks me to." Lucien plucked the shirt from her grasp and folded it. "He works for the Public Affairs Office. When the first calls came in, his admin tracked him here. It's his job to head up damage control, which in turn means he has to know what damage needs to be controlled." He glanced at her beneath his lashes. "I can be very persuasive when I want to be." He lay the shirt over his arm. "Another memento to add to the others," he said as he smoothed his hand over it. "Are you even a little jealous?"

"Of what? Those lovely bruises?"

"Sometimes you have to give a little to get a lot in return."

Jani patted a chair cushion into place, then slipped off her coat and sat. The standard issue ergoworks braced her back and legs, but not well enough to ease the growing aches that signaled the need for sleep. "You played him. It's a talent you've worked at for years. You're still in practice, too." She tried to stifle a yawn and failed. "If we were both dropped in the middle of a strange city, I daresay we'd manage pretty well. But we're both in Chicago, and the natives know our footprints. We need to take care."

Lucien strolled to the couch and sat. "You're not making much sense, you do realize that?"

"I'm leaving for Elyas the day after tomorrow."

"I know."

"I'll be gone awhile."

"I know that, too." Lucien lay the T-shirt on the cushion beside him and stroked it like a cat.

Jani followed the smooth flow of his muscles, the play of light across his chest and stomach. An hypnotic sight, marred only by the bruises that had blued and darkened in the time since her arrival. *Mr. Public Affairs plays rough.* She toyed with the idea of tracking down the man and giving him a little of what he dished out, except . . . *It's none of my business.* Lucien lived most of his life outside her purview, and he never did anything without a reason. If he felt that what Mr. PA offered was worth the knockabout, the best favor she could do him was to stay out of it.

He does what he feels he has to. Circumstances had compelled Jani to live the same way once. Maybe it was the memory of that time that touched the anger in her now, a vein of hostility that opened more and more frequently as her hybridization advanced and the idomeni aspects of her personality emerged.

So much rage. Jani struggled to focus on the present. *What do I have to work with? Look at the situation as it is, not as I think it should be.* "Seeing as you're in Intelligence, how difficult would it be for you to attach yourself to the mine investigation?"

Lucien's hand stilled atop his souvenir shirt. "Officially, my spec is communications. Weapons interface falls roughly under that header, but there are people in Ordnance who know a lot more about the subject than I do, and they're the ones who will be called in to answer questions."

Jani examined the back of her right hand. She had cut it sometime during her run through the woods—a thin line of dried blood traced along her knuckles. "Unofficially, your spec is killing inconvenient people." She flexed her fingers, felt the wound sting. "Apply yourself in that direction for a bit."

Lucien's hand moved to his thigh, the T-shirt forgotten. "You think that mine was put there deliberately?"

"I heard a whole truckload of reasonable explanations during the return ride across the lake. Now I'd like to hear the unreasonable ones." Jani gazed at the sitting room walls, flat white and as bare as the day they were finished, without even a tacked-up holo to indicate the personality of the man who lived within their bounds. "The Haárin took up residence in the enclave four months ago. At first, things seemed peaceful. The Holland area wasn't populated by humanish, so no one lost their property. The Haárin had less reason to go into Chicago, so they didn't rattle the natives by turning up in odd places, as they had been wont to do when they lived on the embassy grounds."

"Dathim used to enjoy doing that." Lucien grinned. He nursed an infatuation for the Haárin that had led to the development of one of the Commonwealth's stranger friendships.

"Yes, he did. The people who looked up to find two meters worth of long-faced Vynshàrau looming over them didn't find it so enjoyable, however." Jani smiled anyway. The tales of Dathim's exploits had made for an evening's entertainment on more than one occasion. Then she sobered. "As I said, things seemed peaceful at first. The honeymoon lasted for about three weeks. Then one morning an Haárin security suborn found one of the enclave food repositories broken into and humanish excrement smeared over the bins."

"I don't need the recent history lesson." Lucien dragged the T-shirt onto his lap and picked at the hem. "I spend as much time there as you do, if not more. I know all about it."

"Did you know that whoever got in there destroyed kettles containing experimental media? Thanks to some urging by ná Feyó and the other Elyan Haárin, Tsecha had sanctioned research into synthetic foods. When Shai found out . . . my old teacher barely managed to talk himself out of a one-way trip on a fast cruiser back to Shèrá." Jani fought the urge to rest her head on the seatback. If she did that, she'd drift to sleep, Lucien's soft voice serving as lullaby. "Then came that sniper attack. Skimmer sabotage. Add the mine, and we've got people who not only know what they're doing but have access to very nasty things."

Lucien locked his hands behind his head and sprawled back, a pose that displayed his naked torso to its best advantage. No matter how serious a discussion turned, he never forgot what he considered the essential argument. "Do you think the Service is responsible?"

Jani admired the view, however calculated. "The mines and weapons are manufactured by Family companies. They fear the Haárin's economic competition just as the Service fears their impact on Commonwealth security. If you assume the Family supplied the means, then the question becomes whether they do the dirty themselves or hire it out. I'd say the field is pretty wide open."

"Given that, I'm surprised you're still planning on leaving tomorrow."

Jani shrugged. "I have no choice." She felt Lucien's stare, knew he expected her to tell him why she had to leave, and knew just as surely that the less she told him, the better. *That won't be difficult—I don't know much.* "Ná Feyó has told Tsecha very little—she doesn't trust the security of the Haárin communications linkages. All he can determine is that she's enmeshed in some sort of power struggle. An Haárin version of a bornsect fallout. He can help her by throwing his support her way—most Haárin still consider him their religious dominant even though he's no longer Chief Propitiator of the ruling bornsect. The ideal solution would be for him to visit the Elyan enclave himself, but he's afraid to leave Earth. He thinks he'll draw unwelcome attention down on Feyó. He also thinks that once he's left Earth, Oligarch Cèel won't allow him to return."

"So he's sending you as his emissary?" Lucien eyed her skeptically. "I've watched you train in bladework with Dathim. He's told me enough about your religious instruction to know that it will take years to learn all you need to. You've only been at this a few months."

"I know." Jani shifted in her seat. She nursed her own bruises thanks to Dathim's enthusiastic teaching. A sword in his hand worked like a metal-plated fist. "But I didn't come into this wholly unprepared, and I've helped the Elyan Haárin before. If Tsecha tells them, through me, to support Feyó, they will."

"Is she that important?"

"To him, she is." Jani fielded Lucien's smirk. "It's not just that he esteems her. Feyó's a radical by any measure, and she has a revolutionary's personality. She knows how to work idomeni and humanish alike. If she loses her position, there's no one of her caliber to replace her. Considering how thoroughly Haárin shipping lines and trade routes have integrated with their Commonwealth counterparts, her ouster could destabilize the entire Outer Circle."

Lucien lowered his arms and sat up. "If she's so magnetic, why has she lost influence?"

"That's what I have to find out." Jani once more fought the urge to close her eyes. Like Niall, she knew what she'd see when next she dreamed. Pullman's raw-boned vitality, reduced to pools of blood in the snow. Wode's slow fingerings as he maneuvered the biobot over the mine. "I don't want to leave now, but I don't have a choice. That's why I'm asking you to plug yourself into the mine inquiry."

Lucien stood, purloined T-shirt in hand. "Someone is going to wonder why I'm interested." He padded across the carpeted floor and disappeared into the bedroom. "The fact that I'm information-gathering for you isn't going to fly. I'm not supposed to feed classified data to Haárin intermediaries."

Jani listened for the sound of a dresser drawer opening, then closing, the sign that the T-shirt had joined its brethren in their very private display case. "Could you tell people you're doing a favor for an old Family friend?"

"I'm sure I'll think of something. I always do." Lucien stepped into the bedroom doorway. "I found a blue-bordered envelope in my paper mail yesterday. It contained a nice, thick sheaf of documents from the Office of Review, all signed off." He folded his arms and leaned against the jamb. "Effective last month."

Jani smiled, and meant it. "Congratulations, Captain. I know you were starting to feel anxious."

"I'm not sure how long I'll stay a captain if I have to keep the home watch. Things have a tendency to spin out of control when you're involved."

"I won't be here."

"You'll be here in spirit. That should prove sufficient to

upset the domestic balance of power." Lucien pretended interest in the condition of his hands. "So, now that's settled, any plans until the sunrise?"

Wariness worked through Jani's growing haze as the many possible replies to Lucien's simple question presented themselves. She'd visited his flat only a handful of times, and had never stayed the night despite his veiled, and not-so-veiled, invitations. As always, she felt that she intruded, that she had entered a place in which she didn't belong, the inner workings of which she didn't want to know. She stood and gathered her coat. "I should go home."

"I hope I haven't offended your delicate sensibilities." Lucien's voice sharpened, the soft French Provincial accent faded to nothing. "I have showered. Unfortunately, the bruises won't be healed before you have to leave—"

"*Lucien.*" Jani stopped in the middle of the room. The hand that held her coat felt gloved in lead. It hung at her side, leaving the garment to drag on the floor. "The psych job. Save it for someone who buys it."

"I would have done anything he wanted in order to find out how you were."

"Rough trade for information. You've done it before. You crave the power. The control. You like it. Your. Choice." Jani fixed on the image of Pullman being lifted from the snow onto the stretcher—the memory touched some deep place within her and released sensations she'd long suppressed, touch and smell and sound. "Well, there were times in my event-filled past when I didn't have a choice. So stop trying to make me feel guilty about all the awful things you've put yourself through on my account, because your primary consideration has always, *always*, been what's best for Lucien Pascal." Her breathing came labored—the sense of weight had moved up her arm and across her chest.

"Post-augie irritability, compounded by fatigue and the effects of hybridization. Aggravated by all those memories that bubble to the surface because you've lost the will to keep them locked down where they belong." Lucien left the doorway and walked to her, shaking his head. "I know the feeling."

Jani opened her hand and let the coat fall to the floor. "You are a liar."

"Yes, but I'm *your* liar." Lucien rested his hand on the open neck of her coverall, then waited to see if she'd pull away. When she didn't, he opened the top fastener, the second, the third, his fingertips brushing her skin with each slow movement. "Your spy. Your whore. Your whatever you happen to need at the time." He bent close, his lips and tongue tracing swirls of heat along her throat and neck as he slipped the garment from her shoulders. "All I want in return is the chance to make us both feel better for a little while. Is that too much to ask?"

Jani took Lucien's hands in hers and held them away from her body. Caught the chill that flashed in his eyes, the anger at a need denied. Pushed down his hands until they hung at his sides, then freed them. Counted the seconds as they stood, still and barely breathing, separated by a few scraps of cloth and a gulf of understanding wider than any sea.

"My choice." She leaned forward and kissed him.

CHAPTER 3

"If the mine *was* deliberately planted, how do you think the idomeni will react?" Lucien exited the Boul just as the early morning traffic slowed to the usual crawl. "Relations are tense now, but when haven't they been?" He steered the Service-issue sedan onto the deceptive quiet of the Parkway, a graceful seclusion of town houses and apartment buildings separated by parks and scattered shops and restaurants. "Besides, we lost one of ours in this mess, too. That must count for something."

"Not really." Jani took what she could from the beauty of the hour—the streaking of the eastern sky into bands of orange and indigo, the illuminated columns of the Chicago skyline that formed the Parkway's backdrop. "Ever since he became Oligarch, Morden nìRau Cèel's goal has been to turn back humanish-idomeni relations fifty years."

"Fifty years ago there were no humanish–idomeni relations." Lucien turned down the first in the succession of tree-lined avenues that led to Jani's house. "Isn't Cèel a little young to be that closed-minded?"

"Age has nothing to do with it. He was just as isolationist twenty years ago at the Rauta Shèràa Academy." Jani thought back to the Cèel she had watched from afar that lifetime ago, the green-eyed, slope-shouldered warrior who turned away whenever a humanish crossed his path. "If we find out that the mine was deliberately planted, I predict a proclamation from Cèel that all bornsect and Haárin must forsake the evils of the humanish Commonwealth and return to the godly confines of the Shèrá worldskein. I then predict that a certain percentage of the Haárin will tell him to go to hell. After that, things should get really interesting." She paused to yawn. She should have taken the opportunity while at Lucien's flat to grab a couple of hours' sleep. Needless to say, she hadn't availed herself of that particular option.

The trees that lined the narrow streets had been strung with colored illumins. Backlit by twinkling leaves, Lucien cocked his head like a young boy considering what he wanted for Christmas. "You're thinking civil war?"

"No, we enter uncharted territory with that one." Jani sat up straighter as the skimmer rounded onto the street she called home, a cul-de-sac of eight identical three-story houses, each built of tan brick and ringed by metal gates and hybrid greenery. "Civil war is the divinely ordained shedding of bornsect blood that may or may not lead to a regime change. A bornsect offensive against balky Haárin who refuse to toe the line hasn't occurred in recorded idomeni history to my knowledge. Cèel would have to have decided that the Haárin who disobeyed were no longer true Haárin, that proximity to humanish had degraded them to the point that they no longer merited his protection. It would prove an interesting point for the theologians to debate at Temple. I can see arguments for both sides."

"Can you?" Lucien eyed her doubtfully as he turned up the narrow drive that curved behind her house, then waited for the gate to slide open. "All that religious instruction has sunk in, has it?"

Jani tipped her hand in a back and forth motion that spoke more of the humanish bargaining table than it did any idomeni gesture. "It's just rules. Rules and order. I'm a documents examiner by trade, remember. A paper pusher. That's all we know, rules." She glanced at Lucien as he unfastened the top of his shooter holster, his gaze locked on the skimmer's dashboard array. "What's wrong?"

"Readings from the backyard. One skimmer. Two men. One of them is armed." Lucien tapped codes into touchpads—multiple views of the house and yard formed on a small display. "You have company." He relaxed, but only a little. "Your doctors make house calls, I see." He drifted up the drive and around the house, coming to a stop a few meters behind a silver sportster. Safety lighting activated, illuminating the yard and the two men who emerged from the sleek vehicle.

"So much for a little time to ourselves," Lucien muttered.

Jani alit from the skimmer just as John Shroud and Val Parini drew near. Val led the way, his stride clipped and his head high.

"Not that we were worried, mind." He circled around to Jani, high-boned face aging from boyish to middle-aged as he drew closer and the details came into focus. "How are you?" His examination took on a professional sharpness as he looked her up and down. "What happened?" A light brown forelock fell over his eyes, and he pushed it back with a curse.

Jani looked Val over as well. A blue pullover and dark green trousers peeked out beneath his brown coat. Mismatched clothes thrown on in haste. Not his habit at all. "What did you hear?"

"That's my one and only girl—never give an answer when another question will do." Val took a step closer. The safety lighting struck him full in the face, illuminating hazel eyes gone dull and bloodshot from lack of sleep. "Service Medical called our shop. They needed to borrow one of our De-Vries shunts. Neuro demanded to know why, and managed to pull a story out with pliers. Blown mine at the enclave. Thirty or so people hurt. People and idomeni, I should say."

"The shunt isn't for Lieutenant Pullman, is it?" John asked as he slipped in behind Val. Unlike his business partner's, his clothing matched—a pearl grey daysuit topped by a coat of the same color. "I understand he was one of the injured." He stopped near the front end of the Service skimmer, not too close yet not too far away, his monkish face a studied blank. Taller and rangier than Val, with the dour countenance of a period painting, he looked imposing even in the harsh lighting.

Snow wraith, Jani thought as she took in his white cap of hair and parchment-pale skin, his eyes filmed the same silvery grey as his garments. *Albino*, her less romantic side reminded her. *The sun is rising, and daylight isn't his time.* "It wasn't for Pull, no. He suffered abdominal injuries, not brain damage. He'll be fine, though."

John nodded. Paused. "Niall's all right?"

Despite the tension in the air, Jani hid a smile. *I know that one was a struggle, so we'll give you full points for effort.* John and Niall did *not* like one another. Niall felt that John had forced Jani's hybridization upon her, which was true, and John felt guilty enough over the situation that the criticism stung. *But he knows Niall and I are friends, so he tries.* It had been a difficult thing to witness as of late, John Shroud's laboring to be flexible. Like watching an oak trying to bend as a willow, with all the creaking and straining the image implied. "Yes, Niall's all right." She walked around Val to John's side. "You wouldn't happen to be carrying a shooter by any chance?"

The quick change in subject caught John by surprise. He blinked. Then the look in his eyes sharpened and the color rose in his cheeks. "We couldn't find out whether you'd been hurt or not, and we didn't know what we'd find here."

"John thought we might arrive to find ministry security stripping the place." Val sauntered past, his hands in his pockets. "He's been taking lessons." He freed one hand and raised it, forefinger extended, miming a weapon.

"And they'd have dropped him before he had a chance to sight down." Lucien paused to refasten his holster. "Speaking as ex–Ministry security, that's what I'd have done."

"And on that note." Jani herded the men toward the house, avoiding John's glower and Lucien's jaundiced glare.

The house was pleasant enough, three floors of white walls, trayed ceilings, and skylights, with enough old wood to imply an age it didn't possess. Niall had chosen it for the location, the stone in a ring of older Family dwellings, set in the geographic middle of the Parkway neighborhoods. He reasoned that with human-idomeni tensions increasing as they were, the security forces of the other houses would guard Jani as well as their own charges, if only to prevent any unpleasantness that might find her from slopping over into their jurisdictions.

Jani keyed her visitors through the rear entry and waited as they doffed their coats. Her own, she kept on. The number of humanish visitors she entertained prevented her from adjusting the temperature of the house to the higher setting her hybrid internal thermostat demanded, and she had resigned herself to feeling chilled until summer.

"You look beat." Val wandered over to her, his trousers and pullover now truly revealed for the mismatched muddle that they were. "I hope you managed to catch some sleep, at least."

"No, I didn't." Jani avoided Lucien's pointed look. She pressed a hand to her stomach, and felt as well as heard the grumble. "Some food would be good."

"I'll take care of it." Lucien strode down the hall toward the kitchen, neat in winterweights, his orange captain's bars bright against the dark grey shirt.

"I'll make coffee," John grumbled as he took off after him.

Jani watched the two men disappear through the kitchen doorway, then turned to Val, who eyed her in tired amusement.

"Lucky you. It's been a long time since I had two men fighting over me." He grabbed her sleeve and pulled her after him, stopping along the way to straighten a holo of a city scene that hung crooked on the wall. "I was afraid something like this might happen if we showed up unannounced. But after we got that first call from Service Medical, John spent hours twisting arms for word about you. No one he called knew anything, which did wonders for his mood. Lucien can say what he likes, but if I had the choice between battling a ministry security team or my business partner, I think I'd take my chances with the nominal professionals."

Jani leaned against Val and lowered her head to his shoulder. "I should have called him, I suppose."

"Yes, you should've." Val slipped an arm around her waist and steered her toward the kitchen. "That was the least you could have done."

"Thank you."

"You're welcome."

By the time they entered the kitchen, the aroma of brewing coffee had already staked its claim to most of the room. The scent of frying onions, however, had taken hold of the area near the stove and seemed destined to beat back any and all comers with the aid of a few more ingredients.

"Omelets, I think." Lucien removed eggs, cheese, and other items from the cooler and set to work mixing and chopping, revealing not only an enviable ease around the kitchen but also the fact that he'd visited Jani often enough to know his way around hers. This in turn wasn't lost on John, who shot Lucien looks of increasing sharpness as he scrabbled through drawers and cupboards in the hunt for coffee accessories.

"If anyone has any particular dislikes," Lucien said, "tell me now because I'm throwing in everything I can find."

"Hold the green pepper, if there's any green pepper to hold." Val held a chair for Jani as she sat at the square, four-person table, then took the seat next to hers. "Can't abide the stuff."

Lucien turned. Val never spoke to him if he could avoid it, and his surprise at the man's response informed his face with a teenage lightness. "No green pepper, it is." He held Val's gaze just a beat too long, then returned to his cooking.

"Christ." Val's face reddened, his voice dropping to a rough whisper. "Doesn't he even bother to hide it when you're around?"

Jani shrugged. "His is a continuing quest to make me jealous—it irks him that I never rise to the bait. Besides, he's going to be on his own for the next few months. He needs to lay groundwork for future conquests."

"I am not interested." Val watched Lucien chop and stir for a time, then shook his head and looked away. "I told you before that avoiding stuff like him has become a second vocation of mine. You sure as hell don't need his brand of trouble, either."

"And John, of course, is no trouble whatsoever."

"So sometimes he sticks his nose in where it doesn't belong."

"Try meddling and controlling."

"He's trying to learn to back off—give him a break. At least I don't see him getting you killed anytime soon. Or trying to hurt you so that he can relish some sense of power." Val paused to reload, but before he could continue his defense, the object of his labors joined them, a tray of cups in hand.

"I hear whispering." John had removed his suit jacket in the interim, revealing the white, band-collared shirt he wore beneath. "What are you two plotting now?"

"The usual mayhem." Jani accepted the steaming mug he handed her. "I should have let you know I was all right. I'm sorry."

"Not a problem." John sat down across from her, concentrating on his coffee as though avoiding her eye. "I daresay you were otherwise occupied."

Jani heard Val mutter "John" under his breath, thought of a score of cutting rejoinders, and voted down them all. Instead, she sipped her coffee, and as usual found it as rich, complex, and overbearing as the man who'd made it.

"Breakfast is served." Lucien carried a plate in each hand and two more nestled in the crooks of his arms, setting them out with the skill of a waiter from Gaetan's before returning to the counter for toast and other side dishes. "You're almost out of these," he said as he set a small tablet dispenser beside Jani's plate.

Jani shook out two of the brown digestive enzyme tablets and tossed them in her mouth, washing them down with coffee. "Should I just give Xenodietetics a call?" she asked, directing her question to Val.

"I'll take care of it." John shoved a forkful of omelet in his mouth, chewing with the stolid determination of a man dutybound to find something to complain about. He couldn't, though. Cooking was part of Lucien's toolkit, and like everything else in the set, the skill was flawlessly executed. For several minutes the sounds of cutlery clatter were the only ones to be heard.

Jani dredged a last corner of toast through a smear of cheese. "Loathe as I am to eat and run, I need to find out what's going on." She popped the morsel into her mouth, savoring the flavors as well as the final moments of relative peace in what promised to be a whirlwind of a day. "The *Trib-Times* morning edition is out by now, and the news services have had all night to patch together something lucid." She pushed back from the table and stilled, her hands braced on the edge, trying to work up the nerve to stand up and walk to her office.

John wadded his dispo napkin, tossed it atop his plate, then picked it up again. "I didn't realize you put that much stock in public information sources."

"I don't when it comes to fact. But as a gauge of public mood, of what the PM wants people to think, they're hard to beat." Jani watched him twist the corner of the napkin between his fingers until it shredded, then glanced at Val to find him staring down at his plate. "You know, I spent a few months of my life in a basement watching you two take turns not telling me things. This is Mealtime Ploy Number

Thirty-Seven—Studiously Disinterested in One Another."
She sat back and folded her arms. "What's going on?"

Val tapped his fork against his cup. "Could you spare us a
few minutes?"

"Even if this mine incident hadn't occurred, we still
would have arrived on your doorstep. We need to talk to
you." John's metal stare never left Jani's face. "Alone."

Jani looked at Lucien, who continued to eat as though un-
aware of the insult, a skill learned through years in Family
service. "I've asked Lucien to wangle a place on the mine inquiry team. If you know something that you think can help
in that regard, we both need to hear it."

John looked at Val, who held up his hands in a *Who
knows?* gesture. "We're not sure if it does or not." He
glanced around the small, brightly lit kitchen, then pushed
back his chair and stood. "Not in here. Someplace a little
less closed in." He circled around the table, plucked his
jacket from the drawer pull on which he'd hung it, and
headed out the door.

With Val and Lucien at her heels, Jani tracked John to the library. A shrine to paper, to information, the room was her favorite in the house, a two-story space topped by a skylight of
shooter-proof scanglass and lined from floor to ceiling with
filled shelves and storage niches. When alone, as she usually
was, it served as her office, her dining room and lounge;
when work claimed too much of her time, it served as her
bedroom as well. As she followed John to the semicircular
couch that served as the room's centerpiece, she harbored
the selfish hope that he didn't intend to deliver bad news,
since she knew it would affect her feelings toward the place,
and make her feel as though she'd lost something dear.

"How secure is it in here?" John had put his jacket back
on, and paced around the couch with his hands shoved in his
pockets.

"How secure do you need it to be, Doctor?" Lucien stood
with his back to a bookcase. His voice came sharp, the first

sign that John's animosity had started to grate. "I recognize the position Jani is in, as well as her penchant for privacy. I have adjusted matters accordingly."

"That's what worries me." John eyed the ceiling as though he expected a recording holosphere to float past at any moment.

"Before anyone says something I'll regret." Jani walked to her desk, which was located near the french-windowed rear wall. She opened a touchlocked drawer and removed a flat metal case. Opening it, she picked through various discs and cylinders until she found the object she wanted, a brushed silver tube that chirped when she twisted it about the middle.

"This is the newest block out there. Covers a fifteen meter radius." She placed the device in the center of the low table that stood in front of the couch, then fell into a nearby lounge chair. "What is said here will stay here."

Lucien hurried over to the table, his eyes wide. "Where did you get that?" He leaned over the device as he spoke, and flinched as his voice fractured and wobbled.

Jani set about getting comfortable. She slipped off her boots, then tucked her legs beneath her and covered them with her coat. "A street vendor on South Wabash." *By the name of Niall Pierce.* She looked from John to Val and back to John. "So?"

John walked to the couch and sat down, eyeing the block as though he didn't quite trust it to do its job. "Approximately two weeks ago I received a shipment of artwork from one of my colonial brokers." He reached into the inside pocket of his jacket and removed a metal case similar to Jani's. "My senior admin found this inside." He flipped open the case and removed a cylinder of his own. It was shorter and thicker than the block, and flared on one end like a tiny trumpet. "He almost disposed of it, thinking it was a catalogue. I took it from him, to peruse at my leisure. I finally opened it last night." He set the device on the table beside the sound block, then touched a raised dot on its side and sat back.

Light flickered around the device's mouth, then burst forth toward the glass ceiling. An image formed.

A young man—no more than eighteen. Slim. Attractive in a gawky yearling way. Dark brown hair, clipped short. A green pullover that bagged at the neck.

Jani stood. The hologram consisted of the young man's head and torso only, but it displayed at such a height that she could look it in the face. She leaned close and studied the stark bones, the long neck. She looked to Val, who stood off to one side, gaze fixed on the floor. Then she leaned around the image to question John, but he sat on the edge of the couch with his head in his hands and didn't answer when she called.

She returned to the figure, her heart pounding. Green eyes. Humanish eyes. Like hers had been before she changed. Strange, though. Too monotone. Too dark and lifeless. As though someone had painted the irises with a single color.

She felt someone move beside her, and turned to find Lucien at her elbow.

"You don't realize what you're seeing, do you?" He looked to the image and shook his head.

"We had nothing to do with it. Val and I." John's voice sounded far away. "I swear to you, Jani. You have to believe me. We didn't do this."

"We didn't," Val said. "You have our word."

The young man raised his open right hand, palm facing out, lips moving as though he recited something. Jani tried to decipher what he said, but she couldn't—the image chopped in places and his mouthings weren't emphatic enough. So she concentrated instead on his spindly fingers, which were so long that at first glance she thought they contained extra joints. *Arachnodactyly—I know you well.* Jani raised her own right hand and placed it against the image of his, matching his spidery fingers with hers, length for length.

She studied his skin and found it gold, studied his wrist and found the bird-boniness she saw every time she dressed or bathed or checked her reflection in a mirror.

"He looks enough like you to be your brother." Lucien looked from Jani to the image, his voice hushed. "He's a hybrid, too."

CHAPTER 4

The library had a bar. They all made use of it. Val took his usual gin over ice, and fixed a double shot of bourbon whiskey for John. Even Lucien, who generally avoided anything that could interfere with his self-control, opted for a shot of vodka.

Only Jani, on whom alcohol had ceased to have much effect, played the teetotaler. She made do with lemon tonic over ice, to which she added several slices of bitter orange as substitute for the ethanolic warmth and bite. "The most obvious question is," she said as she returned to her seat and propped her stockinged feet up on the table, "are you sure this thing is real?"

"I talked to several people—CapNet technicians, an actress friend of mine." Val dragged a wireframe chair beside Jani's and sat heavily. "Yes, these images can be faked rather readily. But even if this one was, why bother? Why make John and me think that someone out there has manufactured another hybrid if they in fact haven't?"

"Bait. To draw you out." Lucien had taken a seat on the couch on the side opposite John. He rested his head back, drink in hand, and surveyed the view through the skylight. "Someone wants one or both of you to visit wherever this thing came from."

Manufactured . . . thing . . . Jani thought of filmed green eyes, and wondered at the clarity beneath. Thought of a youthful face, and wondered how old he'd been when the change took him. *Did you have a choice, whoever you are, or did you have it thrust upon you? Do you even exist, or are you simply a trick of light and technology?* "Where did the image come from, by the way?" She sensed that she knew the answer, but asked the question anyway. "Where is this particular colonial broker located?"

"I wondered when you'd ask that." John had boosted his legs onto the couch and once more removed his jacket, but appeared more rumpled and tired than relaxed. "Amsun, the Outer Circle's most populous world. That's why Val and I would have come to see you regardless of other events. You're on your way to Elyas, another Outer Circle colony. You're acting for Tsecha in some diplomatic capacity. I wondered if there was any chance that your trip and our discovery could be related."

Lucien kept his sights fixed on the skylight. "It's possible."

Jani picked a slice of bitter orange from her drink and bit into it, savoring what to her hybrid palate tasted like pleasant astringency. Judging from John's wince, however, no humanish would have shared her opinion. "Tsecha hasn't been able to learn the whole story. All he's been able to piece together so far is that someone has challenged ná Feyó for dominance of the Elyan Haárin. Our feeling is that whoever the challenger is, they most likely don't possess Feyó's influence with the other Haárin or the colonial humanish. Given that, Feyó's loss could destabilize the region."

"*Our* feeling?" John's brow arched. "Have you adopted the imperial 'our' or are you speaking for Tsecha, too?"

"We speak with one voice. I am his suborn." Jani paused to drink. As she did, she became aware of a quality of silence, a tension that evidenced itself whenever she referred to herself as Tsecha's underling.

This time, Val issued the objection. "I thought your official position was human-Haárin liaison."

"It's hard to liase when one side isn't interested in participating." Jani tried to keep her voice low and even, but over the past months she'd explained herself more times than she could recall, and the idomeni half of her had long ago lost what little patience it possessed. "First the meeting notices stopped. Then I had my ministry security clearances pulled, one by one. If I hadn't turned over my documents business to Steve Forrell and Angevin Wyle, all three of us would have gone broke."

"You could have said something," John muttered into his glass. "I have managed to put a little aside over the years."

"Then you could have been criticized for involving Neoclona in an idomeni-owned business venture."

"You're *not* idomeni!"

"I know that, and you know that, but no one else in this city is interested in the distinction anymore!" Jani hesitated as her heart skipped a beat and a reenergizing warmth pumped through her veins. Her idomeni temper, which took hold lately anytime her blood rose. *Slow down—this isn't the time*. She pulled in a deep breath, another, and waited for her throat to unclench so she could speak normally. "I don't know if you've noticed, John, but your association with me has been coming under some heavy scrutiny lately."

"Is that all it is?" John's voice emerged softer as well, his gaze fixed on nothing. "An association?"

Lucien's head came up. "Could we please keep to the subject? We have an image of a hybrid that may or may not be real. If it isn't real, who faked it and why, and if it is real, how did that boy become a hybrid and who treated him?"

Time passed as the four of them practiced not looking at one another. Then Val raised his hand like an uncertain student in a difficult class.

"John and I have a guess as to who could have provided treatment." He looked at Jani. "You aren't going to like it."

"I don't like any of this so far. So it gets worse?" Jani met Val's bleary-eyed stare, and read his thoughts as though they were her own. "No. Not him."

"I bet I know who you're thinking of, Doctor." Lucien concentrated on the view above his head once again as he tilted his empty glass back and forth. "Eamon DeVries. The third man in the Neoclona triumvirate. He used to be my physician when I worked for Exterior Minister Ulanova. I think he's the one who augmented me, but I was never able to determine it for sure. He's been spending more and more time away from Earth these past few years. Some say he attends to Minister Ulanova when she's in residence at Exterior Main on Amsun, but I know for a fact that she's had another personal physician for the last two years because I ran the woman's security screening myself."

Silence fell once more as everyone pondered Lucien's information. He'd been Anais Ulanova's lover for over ten years, from his early teens up to the previous year, when he met Jani—no one felt inclined to argue with him regarding his knowledge of the Exterior Minister's medical issues.

"So what's Eamon been up to if he hasn't been seeing to Anais?" Jani twisted a length of orange peel into a tight knot, then dropped it back in her glass. "Don't you two check up on him?"

"Of course we do." John massaged his forehead. "We have a contract—call it division of labor—"

"We stay out of the gadget business, Eamon stays out of the gene business." Val got up, glass in hand, and walked across the room to the bar. "We felt it would be better for all concerned if we each stuck to our specialties." He saw to his own refill, then poured out a splash of bourbon and carried it over to John, all the while ignoring Lucien's empty glass.

Jani waited for Val to return to his seat. Waited for a frustrated Lucien to push to his feet and get more vodka for himself. Waited, all the while sensing John's eyes on her as she nursed the feeling that the past never died, but simply bided its time until it saw the chance to insert itself into the present. "There are people out there who felt you should have been imprisoned for the hybridization work you performed on me all those years ago. But if every person who broke the law during the last idomeni civil war was sent to the Lunar shipyards, we wouldn't have anyone left to run the government. Or the NUVA-SCAN business conglomerates. Or the Service. So, after the Commonwealth reopened relations with the Shèrá worldskein, a few deals were made to calm troubled waters. People went away, or went into other lines of work. Was this contract Neoclona's deal? Did Eamon officially take the fall for all of you?"

John tossed back his drink in a single swallow. Val ran his finger along the edge of his glass and stared at the floor.

"Looks like he may have gotten a little of his own back, doesn't it?" Jani stared across the room at John, who eventually raised his eyes to meet hers. "Am I correct in assuming that you'd like me to look into this while I'm in the area?"

"No." John swung his legs off the couch and sat up. "I want to accompany you." He leaned forward, elbows on knees, looking as gangly as the figure in the image. "If Eamon is involved . . . his dispute is with me, not Val. Matters have accrued between us for years. Now's as good a time as any to sort them out once and for all." He rubbed his chin. "And if he isn't involved, he may know who is. He always did have a nose for the nasty."

Jani hoped she didn't look as uncomfortable as she felt. *Just me and John.* In the close confines of a ship. *For the next six weeks.* "I don't see how it can work," she said too quickly. "It was hard enough getting the dispensation for me to travel on an Haárin craft, and you're not me."

"We can always travel on a Neoclona ship. We do have one or two to spare." John sat back slowly. "It does offer advantages. It's less official-looking—that should serve to keep the Commonwealth off both our backs. There would be more privacy for you—we have private slips at every dock between here and the Outer Circle, so you won't have to worry about being hounded by the press."

Jani had to give John credit. His ability to sustain an attitude of studied innocence had improved over the years. "You've been thinking about this."

"Not at all." John glanced at her, and the light in his eyes flickered, the first crack in the façade. "Well, perhaps just a little."

"It makes sense." Lucien still stood at the bar. He had finished his vodka and moved on to fruit juice, a sign that recess was over and the time for clear-headed thinking had arrived. "Everyone will be so fixed on trying to figure out whether or not you've resumed your relationship, they'll forget about all the other possible reasons for your being together."

Jani sensed John's surprise at an unexpected ally, Val's restlessness as he waited for what would come next. "The ones whose opinions count won't be so easily distracted."

"They will be if Doctor Parini and I drop a few well-placed hints." Lucien looked to Val, his smile brilliant. "I think we can come up with a story acceptable to all, can't we, Doctor?"

Jani stared at Lucien until she drew his attention away from Val. Then she raised her glass. *"Bravo!"* She savored Lucien's discomfort, the sight of his smile slowly fading. "You play the pimp for me and wedge Val into a corner, all in one masterstroke. John and I can't say no, because I need to get to Elyas, he needs to see to Eamon, and we both need to find out about this alleged hybrid. Meanwhile, you stay behind with Val and plan, and oh the planning you need to do. Hours and days and weeks worth, as all the while you work to wear him down."

Lucien had been leaning against the bar. He drew up straighter now, his free hand clenching into a fist. "I'm sure I don't know what you mean." His hand relaxed. "I'm merely suggesting a strategy for getting you off Earth with as little complication as possible." Clench. Relax.

"That would make two of us with an in at Neoclona. You're tallying the ill-gotten gains already, aren't you?"

"I really don't know what you're talking—"

"Hah! *Liar!*"

"Jani?" John rose. He pocketed the imager and the sound block, then edged toward her in a sideways shuffle, as though approaching an animal he didn't trust. "Did anyone in Service Medical examine you after you left the enclave?"

"No. Why?" Jani grew conscious of her pounding heart, the sing of blood in her veins. Her skin prickled, as though she sensed an approaching storm. "I feel fine."

"I'll get the bags." Val shot out of his seat and headed for the door, waving a dismissive hand at Lucien along the way.

Jani tried to bolt as John closed in, but his hand on her shoulder stopped her before she could rise from her seat. *"I'm all right."*

"Humor me," John said, his grip like a trap.

"Follow the lights." Val held a black cube the size of his head, dotted on one side with an array of pinpoint red illumins. "When I say 'Now.' "

"Do I have to?" Jani sat atop the kitchen counter, pounding out a beat against the cabinet doors with her heels. "It's just my augie experiencing a storm surge. It's been happening off and on for the past month or so." She gave the doors an extra hard kick—one jarred open under the impact, and she pushed it closed with a bang.

"Do what Val says, please." John set up the sound block, then stepped off to the side, arms folded. "If your augmentation is still firing, we may need to bring you down."

"Now," Val said.

Jani struggled to avoid looking at the lightbox Val held, even as she felt herself drawn to the flickering lights like an accident scene. "But I feel . . ." The first pattern splashed across the surface—she followed it like a cat tracking the flight of a bird. "I feel better than I have in months. My joints don't ache anymore. My back—" The patterns continued, irregular jumps and flutters, abrupt changes in speed and direction. "You know, those lights are really irritating."

Val shut down the box and shook his head. "Whatever's going on, it has nothing to do with her augmentation. If it still fired, she'd have gone under by now."

John walked to the table, on which Val had placed two

hefty carryalls. "You've felt this way for a month?" He scrabbled through one of the bags, and after a few moments' digging came up with a sensor stylus. "I wish you'd said something before now." He approached Jani, gesturing for her to hold out her hand.

Jani held out her right hand, feeling a tremor of warmth as John enclosed it in his and pressed the vibrating end of the stylus against the tip of her index finger. "The anger comes in a rush, like a drug. Once it surfaces, it needs to discharge somewhere, I guess." John released her—as always, she felt the pressure of his grasp long after the flesh had parted.

"While I couldn't think of a better target for your wrath than Captain Pascal, I can imagine times when it would be better for you to keep your mouth shut." John examined the stylus readout and frowned at Val. "Blood readings are normal, relatively speaking." He tucked the stylus into his trouser pocket. "Tact and diplomacy were never your strong suits, and now that idomeni mood swings have apparently entered the picture, it's only going to go downhill from here."

"Tsecha's idomeni, and he manages all right," Jani muttered.

"No, he doesn't—" John and Val replied as one. Then all three of them grinned.

Val walked to the table, lightbox in hand. "A full Neuro workup would be a good idea." He slipped the device into a padded sack, then zipped the sack closed and tucked it into one of the bags. "If we determine where the changes have occurred and to what extent, we could design an augmentation to act as a moderator."

"We don't have time." John drew up next to the counter and leaned against it, a move that brought him closer to Jani. "I could start the preliminary work on the ship if I took one of our neurologists along."

Jani shook her head. "Drag someone away from home for three months or more on a day's notice? Not on my account, please."

"It's an unwritten part of the job description," Val said as he slung one of the bags over his shoulder. "Neoclona offers classes. If you can't learn to pack for a twelve-week long haul in ten minutes flat, we kick you out to live amongst the heathen." He hefted the other bag and trudged to the door. "If you pass the test, the Commonwealth is yours to command."

"Ten minutes? Why not make it a month?" Jani called after him. "I can do it in less than five."

"Unfair." The sound of Val's steps receded down the hall. "Too much practice!" A muffled curse drifted back as he pushed through the rear door, followed by silence.

Jani stared down at her socks for a time, then looked up to find John regarding her with an odd mix of amusement and concern that it seemed he reserved lately for her and her alone. "Would a new augmentation help smooth out the mood swings?"

"Possibly." He boosted atop the counter next to her. "The problem is that it would need to function all the time, as opposed to your Service augmentation, which only has to operate at times of extreme duress. You'd experience many of the same issues—misfirings, over- and undercontrol, the risk of chronic bioemotional disorders, which may turn up that much more quickly because of the increased exposure to modified neurotransmitters. Then there's the fact that you possess the only hybrid brain in the Commonwealth. Even with advanced modeling, it would all be guesswork on the part of my Neuro group until we learned more about how your brain functions, and I'm really not anxious to see you become a test subject for every tweak and nudge that comes down the pike."

Jani thought back to the hybrid boy's image. A smile and long, thin hands like hers. "What if I'm not anymore? The only hybrid brain in the Commonwealth."

John smoothed a hand over the front of his jacket, then started fiddling with one of the fasteners. As usual, tension made him fidgety. "Like Val said, holo images can be very readily faked. I'm more concerned with who it is who's trying to attract our attention. And why." He forced a smile. The harsh kitchen lighting accentuated every line on his so-pale face. "I'll let you worry about whether it has anything to do with your little matter."

"I wish it was a little matter." Jani rubbed her stomach, where Lucien's omelet weighed heavily amid the growing churn. "A little matter at this stage in the game would be a positive delight." She held out her hand to John. "Are you still carrying that shooter?"

John's brow arched. Then he reached into his inside jacket pocket and removed a burnished C-curve of dull silver.

Now it was Jani's turn to act surprised. "Fancy." She took the graceful weapon from him and examined it, conscious at every level of the residual warmth the metal held. "A Beecham-Grenoble S-40. Strong enough power source to kick it up into the medium-range class. How long have you been taking shooting lessons?"

"About two months. A club I belong to has a range. One of our new staff members in Orthopedics is ex-Service." John looked down at the floor. "She's been showing me the ins and outs."

Has she? Jani's heart skipped, but not because of a flood of idomeni anger. No, this was more a humanish brand of emotion, unreasonable though it was. *He has every right—I showed up here with Lucien, and he knows we didn't spend the night sitting around talking.* "Just remember that if any-one who knows weapons sees this, they're going to assume you know what you're doing and react accordingly." She handed the shooter back to him, taking care not to touch his hand.

"Funny. Marya said the same thing." John's lips curved, an almost-smile that contained enough self-satisfaction to inspire violence.

I won't push him off the counter. What she wanted to do, against all reason, was push her hands through that silky mass of hair and pull him to her, shatter twenty years' sepa-ration with a single kiss. Wipe away the smile inspired by another woman and replace it with one inspired by her. *I love you, John Shroud.* She'd admitted the fact long ago, to him as well as to herself, and knew he felt the same. *But it would never work.* No matter how they tried, it always came down to her independence versus his desire to protect her. *There's nothing left to talk about. Nothing left to feel jealous over.* Yet jealous she was, painfully so. That meant it was time to change the subject. Time to stick to business. "Lucien was right, you know. Any ministry guard worth a damn would have dropped you before you'd sighted down."

John's smile died. "I still believe he exaggerated."

Jani shook her head. "Tensions are mounting. The bornsect Vynshàrau think they're losing their souls and their Haárin. The Families know they're losing money and their grip on the Commonwealth frontier. Everyone's trying to figure out a way to keep what they have, and that ozonelike odor you smell is the short, sharp scent of panic in the wind."

John sighed as he slipped the Beecham back inside his jacket pocket. "That misplaced mine didn't help, I'm sure."

"No, it didn't help one bit." Jani slid off the counter and walked to the table. Val had stacked the dirty plates and cutlery to one side in order to deposit his and John's medical gear. She picked them up and carried them to the cleaner. "I need to take a trip back across the lake. Break the news to Tsecha about the ship, find out what transpired at the enclave after I left." She inserted all the tableware into the appropriate slots and holders. "I thought I'd try to catch some sleep first."

"Are you going to tell him about our possible hybrid?" John pushed off the counter, then paused to fuss with his jacket.

Jani closed the cleaner, then activated it. "I have to, especially if it's possible that it may be entangled with Feyó's problem."

"How do you think he'll take it?"

"It's what he prophesied. What he prayed for all these

years." Jani yanked a dispo towel from a countertop dispenser and wiped her hands. "On the other hand, considering the current climate, he may wish our young friend had chosen a less tangled time to make his appearance." She crumpled the dispo and tossed it into the trash, followed the flash and the puff of smoke that signaled its demise, then walked with John into the hall.

"I don't know if I'll see you before we leave." He seemed subdued, as though the import of their upcoming journey had just struck home. "Seventeen-up is the usual departure time for an afternoon trip. I'll send a skimmer for you at about sixteen."

"All right." Jani felt his presence beside her, and tried not to think about it. "I should have called. I'm sorry."

John grinned weakly. "You have this knack for putting yourself in the middle of things. When I heard that a mine had exploded at the enclave, I thought the worst."

Jani touched John's arm, pulling away just as a look of surprise crossed his face. "I was in a bunker, 200 meters away, with Niall, Tsecha, and a comtech who didn't like me very much."

"More fool him." John hesitated at the door, as though he wanted to say more. Then he saw Val lower the skimmer boot lid and circle around to the driver's side. "Tomorrow," he said, his businesslike demeanor returned.

Jani took John's coat from the rack and handed it to him, feeling its softness long after she released it. "Tomorrow." She saw him out, watched him get into the skimmer, then watched the vehicle float out of sight.

She then returned to the library to find Lucien standing at the bar sink cleaning the glasses. He looked up when she entered, then quickly away. Jani walked to the couch and lowered onto it, yawning as the cushions swallowed her up. The remains of her augmentation, her idomeni nature, both had retreated, leaving her drained. She hoisted her legs aboard, lay back, and contemplated the square of blue sky visible through the skylight.

"You embarrassed me."

Jani lifted her head. Lucien had finished with the glasses and now wandered the room, straightening and adjusting. *When he's on edge, he needs to move. Just like John. Just like me. We're none of us comfortable enough in our skins to stay in one place.* "It's going to happen more and more often. My brain is changing. My bioemotional balances." She tried to inject some levity into her voice. "If you think you're getting the raw end, look at me. I'm going to wind up even more popular than I am now." Lucien ignored her as he continued his housekeeping promenade, and she decided that in this particular instance, surrender was the better part of valor. "I'm sorry." She tried to think of a bright side. "If it's any consolation, Val had you figured out before I opened my mouth. He doesn't fool easily."

"That's all right. I love a challenge." Lucien gave a chair one last shove-into-place. "I need to get back to Sheridan." He headed for the door, but at the last moment he slowed, then turned and approached the couch. "You want him to be real, don't you?" Sunshine streamed through the skylight, lightening his hair until it looked as white as John's. "The hybrid boy. You want him to be real and you're afraid that he's not."

Jani opened her mouth to protest, but no words emerged. As usual, Lucien got right to the heart of the matter, then grabbed and twisted. "It's a mistake to get one's hopes up," she said after a time. "I learned that the hard way."

"If it's any consolation, two hybrids would upset people twice as much as one." Lucien drew alongside the couch, then leaned over. "Even more than that, considering that one is you." He kissed her, softly at first, then not softly at all, leaving her breathless as he slipped away without another word.

"Au revoir, mon capitain." Jani regarded the closed door as the minutes passed, and gradually another sensation took hold. Less painful than love, less urgent than lust, yet in its own way as implacable, as undeniable.

She held up her hand, imagined the hybrid boy's still hanging in the air before her. Saw them meet, felt warm flesh instead of cool light. Pressed hard, palm against palm, finger against finger, each matching as though they mirrored one another.

"I always wondered what it would have been like to have a brother." She lay there, holding her hand in place until sleep claimed her.

CHAPTER 5

A muddle of images. Wode's face as he turned to the sound of Pullman's shout, melting into that of Feres, the dead Vynshàrau.

A sound. A name. Her name.

Jani.

Feres's face shortening. Widening. The eyes altering from gold to green, sclera paling, whitening, changing—

Jani?

—to a face she knew well though she'd seen it only once. A young face with filmed eyes, humanish films that covered, but not well enough—

"Jani."

Jani opened her eyes.

"Jesus, gel." Niall Pierce released a shaky sigh. "You weren't waking up and you weren't waking up. I thought I'd have to call Shroud." He sat on the edge of the low table, one hand braced on the couch cushion near Jani's head. "I've been jawing at you for five minutes—didn't you hear me?"

"I fell—" Jani stared above her head at the view through the skylight, and saw only dark slate grey where there'd once been sunlit blue. "Oh, damn."

"Oh damn is right." Niall sat back, his expression lightening as he realized she was conscious and aware of her surroundings. "It's a little after nineteen. You slept most of the day away." He offered a fangy grin. "Join the club. I called Pull's folks from the doctors' lounge, then sat back to take a breather. Too many hours later . . ." He shook his head. "One of the neuros ordered them to let me sleep. Damned augie. After I woke up, I shambled to the office. Far North Lakeside was a beehive, of course. Sat through nine meetings in as many hours, then decided the hell with it and bolted."

Jani tossed back her coat, which had served as a coverlet, and slowly sat up. "How's Pull?"

"Awake, but bleary." Niall reached into his shirt pocket and pulled out his nicstick case. "Doesn't remember the blast, which is a good thing, if you ask me."

Jani motioned for Niall to move down the table so she could swing her legs off the couch. "And the meetings?"

"The usual. How, what, when, why, and who can we throw to the dogs?" He pulled a 'stick from the case and crunched down on the tip with intent. "Everyone's poring over field exercise notes going back six years. Pulling in everyone from Spacers First Class to Ordnance chiefs, questioning them on every move they made during this or that night maneuver a year or more ago. If Service Investigative thinks people are hiding things, they're going to break out the truth sera, and won't that be fun for all concerned." He slumped, the smoke curling around his head like a free-form halo. "Mako's still with the PM. Couple of loons burned an idomeni in effigy on the grounds of the Exterior Ministry, which was as close as they could bloody get to the embassy, thank God. Shai's in special session with the Oligarch, or in as much of a special session as she can be via Misty communications. Could be the end of the month before they get all that back and forth sorted out."

Jani tried to imagine Morden nìRau Cèel's response when the news of the mine reached him. *Will you think past the end of your nose for once in your life, you chill bastard, or will you thank the gods for giving you the excuse you need to close the enclave?* "Any word from Tsecha?"

"He gave a short interview on CapNet this morning. Spoke English, and looked right into the cam. Sincere regrets for all lives lost. Said the word 'accident' three times that I counted. Wily old bird, trying to calm the whitecaps. Hope someone listens." Niall stood up and walked to the bar. "You still leaving tomorrow on your gift-giving excursion to Elyas?"

Jani watched Niall pour himself a drink. Scotch and soda, his usual. He'd switched out of his soiled fatigues for civvies, tan trousers, and a cream pullover that seemed too casual a choice for the man who wore them. *Niall doesn't relax well.* At the moment, he didn't appear relaxed at all. "Yes, I'm still leaving tomorrow."

Niall turned to face her, glass in hand. "I stopped by the kitchen on the way down the hall, thinking you might be in there. Quite a few plates stacked in the cleaner." He didn't look at Jani but at some spot above her head.

"You had to open the cleaner to find that out. Did you think I was hiding inside?" When Niall didn't reply, Jani sat up a little straighter. She'd been questioned in this same offhand manner countless times in her past. The best response was, of course, to tell the truth. At least regarding the facts that could be checked. "I went to see Lucien after I left you. He brought me back here. We found John and Val waiting for me. Service Medical borrowed some equipment from Neoclona, and they found out what happened. They came by to see if I was all right. We all came inside. Lucien made breakfast."

"John and Pretty Boy in the same room. That must have made for some fun." Niall set aside his drink, then wandered to Jani's desk and riffled through a stack of old newssheets. "That's the whole story?"

"Are you asking as my friend, Niall, or as Colonel Niall Pierce, Special Services, hatchet man-in-waiting to Admiral-General Hiroshi Mako?"

"Would the answer be different, depending?"

"You didn't think I was home. You thought I was at the enclave. You came here to search the place."

"Better me than anyone else." Niall circled around to the opposite arm of the couch and sat down across from Jani. "Two hours ago a Neoclona shuttle filed an O'Hare-Luna flight plan. Luna Station reported soon after that a Neoclona cruiser submitted GateWay requests from Mars through to Amsun. Elyas is a four day skip from there. John Shroud's going to take you to deliver your gift himself, isn't he?"

Jani shrugged. "He's rich. He can afford to be generous."

"Jani." Niall sat back and thumped his head against the couch cushions. "You can't shove things down people's throats. Tsecha tried that with his predictions of hybrids and a blending of the human and idomeni races, and where did that get him? He lost his position as religious leader of the ruling bornsect, along with all the power that went with it. The soapbox. The ability to persuade, to change from within. And oh, he's such a charismatic bastard—he could have charmed the birds from the trees, but he blew it." He took a last pull on his 'stick, then pondered the spent cylinder. "And then there's you, taking up where he left off. There's no one I'd rather have at my back with a loaded shooter, but so help me, if there's one person I wouldn't want arguing for my life before a judge and jury, it's you, with your 'my way or go to hell' approach to everything."

"I recall telling you once that I was not political." Jani concentrated on picking through the past, on uncovering the evidence to counter Niall's assertions. On countering the words themselves, without stopping to consider their meaning. "I recall you replying that politics had gotten us into the messes we were in, that the city needed someone with my point of view."

"I have been known to make mistakes." Niall hung his head. "You strong-armed Chicago into opening the doors for an Haárin enclave before they were ready to accept Haárin in their midst. We're paying the price for that now."

"Enclaves have existed in the colonies for close to half a century. Chicago is a tad behind the curve."

"It's the Commonwealth capital. The heart of humanity. It already had an embassy, just like we have our embassy in Rauta Shèràa. It didn't need anything else until it was prepared to accept it. It's a bigger step to take *here*." Niall snapped the 'stick in two and tossed it into a dish set out for the purpose. "It feels threatened. It's overreacting, falling on any hint of trouble and magnifying it a hundredfold."

Jani imagined Niall's speech in a voice other than his Victorian twang. A guttural baritone, Earthbound in accent, educated without sounding cultured. "Thank you, Colonel, for delineating the Admiral-General's point of view so well."

"It's mine also. To an extent." Niall rubbed his eyes. His skin appeared dull and sagged, as though he hadn't slept at all. "I'm a human being, Jan. This is my Service. This is my world."

"I am not a human being." Jani looked down at her hands, the hands that had matched so well those of a boy who odds were didn't exist. "Do you understand that now?"

Niall sniffed, kept his gaze fixed on the floor. "You're—" He took a deep breath and tried again. "You're leaving tomorrow at seventeen-up."

You ought to know. Jani bit back the words. She didn't want her farewell to Niall to consist of a fight. "Yes."

"You need to see Tsecha." Niall stood, worked his shoulders. "I'll take you."

Jani watched him move, his actions controlled and cadenced. *He's conserving his ammo.* Warming up, but not too much. Expending just enough energy to get him where he needed to go. *Oh, Niall. You still have another shoe to drop, don't you, me lad?* She rose, gathered her coat, and started for the door, then waited for him to join her.

The ride over the lake to the enclave proved more pleasant than Jani expected. Niall stuck to opera, ballet, and general Sheridan gossip. For her part, Jani talked about her parents and her youth on the colony of Acadia, since Niall had been orphaned at an early age and often hinted that he liked hearing tales of family life.

"They've gone back, your folks. To Acadia." Niall swore under his breath as lake chop struck the underside of the skimmer, sending a shudder through the cabin. "I thought things weren't safe there."

"They've improved. The PM installed a new governor, who happens to be someone the Acadians actually like. A few heads rolled in the Legislature. A few undesirables left in their socks." Jani looked out the window to the moon-dappled swell that stretched to blackness beyond. "Papa never admitted it, but he always felt that coming to Chicago was tantamount to running away. Maman didn't want to admit it, but she was homesick. When Oncle Shamus sent up the distress flare late last year that his resort business had grown too big for him to handle alone, I knew it was only a matter of time." She thought back to the day they came to break the news to her, their eyes alight. "Maman knows twelve ways to coax an obsolete dicad battery back to life. Not much call for that in Chicago."

"Aren't they worried about you?"

"Yes. They want me to join them. Shamus has enough work to merit keeping his own documents examiner on staff."

"Seems a ready-made job."

"It's too cold." Jani hunched deeper into her coat. "That's why the Haárin never tried to negotiate an enclave there. The weather's too rough, even for the Oà, and they're the northernmost idomeni. They've experience with harsh winters."

"That's why coats were invented." Niall eyed her askance. "What's the real reason you don't want to go back?"

Jani tried to glare him into submission, but as usual he met her straight on. "Some of those people form my first memories," she said finally. "I know them. I know how some of them would react if they saw me now. They haven't taken it out on my parents because I've been gone so long it's like I never really lived there, but if I showed up now . . ." In the distance, the lights of the enclave burned through the dark, and she bid silent thanks for this conversation's end. "It's my parents' home. They love it. I don't want to ruin it for them."

"You were born there. It's your home, too." Niall looked to her for some response, but before he could argue one out of her, Haárin security cut in with an ID request.

"Not anymore." Jani whispered it under her breath, so he couldn't hear. They veered north and followed the beach. Before long the first enclave outbuildings came into view. She saw Tsecha standing at the head of the dock, Dathim at his side.

Tsecha led Jani onto the glass-walled veranda of the enclave's meeting house. The building had been constructed atop an artificial hillock. The veranda itself faced the lake, and overlooked the rest of the enclave. Nighttime security lighting cast eerie shadows on the short streets that ran below, lined with smooth-walled houses, the business exchanges and other buildings that served the needs of the Chicago Haárin.

"So you travel with Shroud." He lifted his right hand waist high, then curved it in puzzlement. "There is a Neoclona hospital in Karistos for him to visit. Otherwise, what purpose does he serve?"

"Cover, inshah. If it is thought that I travel with him, no one will question closely why I travel to Elyas." Jani fielded Tsecha's bewildered posture. Despite his extensive experience with matters humanish, the ways of the heart left him lost. *Well, that makes two of us.* She waited for more questions, and when she didn't get any, looked to her teacher to find him staring out the window.

"The injured Haárin are well. They walk, and have returned to their homes. The Vynshàrau Feres is most likely dead, but Shai still confers, and Sànalàn informs me of nothing. Such, she said, is of no concern to me, as she is now Chief Propitiator, not I. Yet I knew Feres, and feel the concern I am not allowed." Tsecha started to pace. He wore a typical Haárin color-clash of purple overshirt and yellow trousers. His shirtsleeves billowed over his hands, sweeping back and forth in time to his stride. "If your John treated him, there would be no question of recovery. Feres would be made whole again. New limbs, as were given you nearly twenty of your years ago. New organs. But because he is idomeni, the extent of his injuries are seen to cast doubt upon the wholeness of his soul." He paused in mid-stride and regarded Jani, amber eyes dulled by worry to old gold. "Did you ever question the wholeness of your soul, nìa, after your treatment?"

Jani looked down at her hands, pressing them together as though in prayer. The real right and the animandroid left, outwardly identical, inwardly so different. Red blood flowed through one, dark pink carrier through the other. The same held true for her legs, fake left and true right. *My cobbled-together limbs.* Just one aspect of her cobbled-together body, which if one pushed the point, could serve as an outward manifestation of her hybrid psyche. *Watch your step, Kilian—philosophical waters run deep.* "Quite often, inshah," she admitted, because the faster she admitted to it, the sooner she could stop thinking about it.

"But you knew enough to consider such, which is something that I find most indicating an unchanged state of self." Tsecha nodded at his own response, too wrapped up in thought to notice his pupil's discomfort. "Sànalàn, of course, would deny such. Such an ungodly chief propitiator she is. To her, Feres's destroyed body indicates that his soul is no longer whole. If he has not yet died, I fear he soon will."

Jani spread her hands apart, then lowered them to her sides. "When I see you consider as a priest, I wonder if you wish you still served as ambassador. Politics is easier than religion."

"No longer, nìa. It seems to me, and truly, that Chicago is

as Rauta Shèràa was when you schooled at the Academy. The nearness to humanish would destroy us all, so they said in Temple and Council. Six documents students, and a Consulate set behind high walls. So few, to be accused of so much."

Jani stood near the center of the bare room, absorbing the Vynshàrau-level heat through every pore. Wishing she merely paid a social call, and could leave the difficult questions she needed to ask out in the cold where they belonged. "Our nearness helped destroy the Laum."

Tsecha chopped the air with his right hand, a harsh Vynshàrau Haárin negative. "The Laum destroyed themselves. They took the worst of humanish, the greed and the need to control with secrets. If they had taken the best of humanish, the ability to adapt and explore, to change, they might have survived."

Jani took a step nearer the window. "The hell you say?"

Tsecha hung his head. "You are most correct, nìa. The best of humanish is not what I am seeing now."

They stood side by side, watching the occasional Haárin, swaddled in ankle-length coat and trailing scarves, emerge from a building and dash down the street. "Even before I left Acadia to school on Shèrá, before I realized the depth of variation between worlds, I never thought of myself as a citizen of the Commonwealth. I always referred to myself as Acadienne. *Une jeune fille de les Vieux Rouges.*" Jani caught Tsecha raising a curved hand in puzzlement, and smiled. "A young girl of the Old Red. My birthplace, Ville Acadie, is built on red clay. The first colonists christened it 'Le Vieux Rouge.' That's also the name of our football team."

"Ah. The Commonwealth Cup." A little of the confusion cleared from Tsecha's face. "Acadia Central United. They lost the final match to a group from this place."

"Gruppo Helvetica." The name still stuck in Jani's throat, months after the fact. "Acadia tried too hard. They wanted it too badly. Gruppo had its weaknesses—they'd have beaten themselves if given the chance." She watched a youngish trudge up the street, kicking a stone. "Niall thinks the Haárin tried too hard to force their way in here, that I tried too hard helping you. We set Chicago back on its heels, threatened them. Gave them something to fight."

"Your scarred colonel does not like me. He believes I keep you from what you should do, whatever that is. I most doubt he could tell me, if I asked." Tsecha drummed his fingers against the window. "So little I understand of humanish pairings, even after so many years. You are not with Colonel Pierce as you are with Lucien?"

"No, inshah." Jani sighed. *Maybe if I drew a diagram . . .*

"We are friends, as you were with Hansen Wyle."

"Angevin's father. My Hansen of the godly hair. He taught me much of humanish ways." Tsecha brightened for a moment, baring his teeth wide. Then the expression faded. "Not enough, most sadly, to understand your colonel. He seemed most as upset when you said you would speak to me alone."

Before Jani could reply, the door to the meeting room opened.

"Glories of this damned cold night to you, Kièrshia!" Dathim Naré, Tsecha's secular suborn, strode in coatless and hatless, his gold-brown skin paled to dun from the cold. "Pierce has returned to his skimmer, to smoke. I remind him of the protocols forbidding open displays of eating on idomeni lands. He tells me that a nicstick is not food, and I should look the other way. He enjoys argument, that one." Two meters tall, broad-shouldered, a face of shadowed hollows and heavy bone, he seemed suited to chill and wind even though he had been born in a desert and craved heat as much as Jani. "He tried to question me of what you both would speak of. I pretended I did not understand his English." He dragged a wireframe seat from against the wall and set it by the window. "So," he said as he sat in a humanish male sprawl, "do you speak of Kièrshia's bruises, and why I shall always be able to defeat her with blades? Do you speak of Feyó? Of mines? What?"

"We speak of football, and old clay, and old times." Tsecha looked down at his suborn and shook his head in a humanish display of frustration. "Ask your questions, nìa. Dathim grows impatient."

"I played him to a draw the day before yesterday. Only the third time I fought with two blades—I think I surprised us both." Jani caught Tsecha's teeth-baring and Dathim's grimace, then turned back to the window to watch the youngish continue to kick her stone. Another young Haárin had joined her, darting back and forth in front of her in an effort to distract. "How much did Feyó tell you, inshah, about this challenge to her dominance?"

"What I have told you, nìa, is all I know," Tsecha replied. "I have no secrets."

Jani heard the youngish cries through the glass, the stone clatter against a metal post. "John received a shipment from Amsun some days ago. Inside the container he found an imager, a device that displays recorded holo images."

Tsecha sighed. "I do know of such things, nìa."

"The image contained in the device looks just like a male hybrid. Did Feyó tell you anything that might indicate that someone on Elyas engaged in that sort of research?" Jani looked to Dathim, to find him regarding her, back straight, gaze fixed. *This is the first he's heard of this.*

"Another hybrid?" Tsecha raised a hand to gesture surprise, but stopped halfway. He looked Jani in the face, eyes now clear and bright. "Feyó told me that she did not trust the security of our communications. This was why she gave so little information, and made certain she spoke in terms most vague." He made to gesture again, and stalled again. "Another hybrid." He fell silent, left hand curved and resting against his chest, a gesture of great surprise cut off in mid-flourish.

"Holo images may be easily forged, may they not?" Dathim stood and walked to Tsecha's side. He hovered over the elder male, his usually blank posture tensed and curved with worry.

Jani nodded. "Yes, ní Dathim. But if the image is indeed a forgery, it then begs more questions than it answers. Why use a hybrid image as a lure, and what, if anything, does this image have to do with Feyó's problem?" Outside, the youngish had moved on to other distractions, leaving the street empty and quiet.

Tsecha let his hand fall to his side. "Dathim fears that I will take such joy in the discovery of another hybrid that I will forget how to question." He turned away from the window and made a slow promenade of the room, his hands clasped behind his back, half hidden by his shirtcuffs. "He does not know me as well as he believes he does." His tone sharpened, his English harsh with impatience. "What do you believe, nìa?"

"I can speculate until the sun comes up." Jani turned and leaned against the glass, wondering if any of the Haárin could see the three of them from their houses. "I wish I had more facts. John and Val recognize the possibility that the image could be faked, a lure to draw them to Elyas. Add to this the chance that Eamon DeVries may be involved, and the plot gets murkier and murkier."

"*Eamon!*" Tsecha threw his head back and emitted a barking laugh. "Always the secrets, with that one. Always *money.*" Cruel humor shaved years from his face and posture. "I most envy you, nìa, for you will learn so much strange truth, and I fear you may not trust the security of our communications sufficiently to inform us of your discoveries. Thus will I live for months and months without word." His posture softened. "Do you believe it possible, nìa, that this hybrid exists?"

Jani looked about the room. Dathim had worked his tile-mastery on the surfaces, decorating them with interlocking networks of cord and chain that made it seem as though the walls were lashed together. All linked. All inseparable, one from the other. "I exist. Why not another?" She followed the path of one chain, tracking it until it lost itself in a tangle near one corner. "But I refuse to speculate. I will wait for facts."

"Ah." Tsecha clasped his hands. "I know many at Temple who would say that you do not sound much as a priest."

"It is better to wait for facts." Dathim walked to the far wall and traced one length of chain with a discerning hand, frowning at an imperfection only he could see. "We will remain here, and wait for Mako's facts about his mine. Kièrshia will go to Elyas, and search for facts of an image that vanishes when one alters a switch." He rapped the wall with his fist, then walked to the door. "Safe journey, hybrid priest. Do not cut yourself, and glories of the damned cold night to you."

Tsecha watched Dathim leave, then tilted his head and curved his shoulders in a posture of regret. "He and his suborns have spent the time since the incident scanning the enclave for more mines. I have seen in him a fear of humanish that I have never seen before." He straightened. "Do you feel prepared, nìa, for this journey?"

Jani hesitated, caught by the abrupt change in subject. "No," she said finally, "but I've never felt prepared for any journey I've taken. I learn what I can beforehand, and deal with each thing as it comes."

"You depend on your Lord Ganesha to remove all obstacles from your path, as always? Your wise elephant god who sits atop a mouse?" Tsecha offered a close-lipped, humanish smile. "Your Lord must have every room in his house filled, so many obstacles has he cleared over the years."

Jani laughed. "He complains to me that he must build more." She crossed to where Tsecha stood, and as she approached saw him as Feyó, as any of her Haárin would. Reassuring in his age, his lined face a testament to a common history, a common belief, both in their gods and the path down which they led. *When they see me, they must not see* me, *but what I am through him. Tsecha vo Kièrshia. Tsecha's toxin.* She felt a now-familiar inward quaver, and hoped her old teacher couldn't see her fear of failure. As she joined him, they uttered a prayer to Shiou, the goddess of order, and as she did with Niall, Jani concentrated on the words, not their meaning. *I go to help Feyó, and find a hybrid.* Saving souls would have to wait for another time.

"You leave a cold place behind," Tsecha said after they uttered the closing. "I understand Karistos is quite warm."

"That, I look forward to." Jani walked to the door, pausing so Tsecha could catch her up. "It's possible that I may be able to communicate with you via Neoclona—they're known for their security. But if I see any problem, I will not risk it."

"And if you see the hybrid?" Tsecha leaned close, the lack of gesture in his speech betraying his excitement. "I would so wish to know, if possible."

"I'll do my best." Jani gave his arm a tentative pat, felt old muscle like cord beneath her hand. "You will take care? Stay out of trouble?"

Tsecha looked her in the eye. Bornsect idomeni reserved such familiarity for their most intimate moments, but as a whole, their Haárin had adopted the humanish approach. "I will do as I do, nìa."

"One more thing to worry about." Jani sighed. "Glories of this strange night to you, inshah." She took her leave of him, her boots sounding a muted cadence down the empty hall.

She walked down the deserted street, conscious of being watched yet unable to tell by whom. Down one alley, then another, until she came to the bare dunes. Niall waited for her there, huddled inside the skimmer, coat collar pulled up to hide his contraband nicstick. He released the passenger-side door as she drew near; she lowered inside. Niall then banked the vehicle around and they headed back across the lake.

The other shoe. Jani rested her head against the seatback, the soft thrum of the skimmer motor providing counterpoint for her thoughts. *With all that's happened, why is he here?* She glanced at Niall, then away before he sensed her gaze. *All hell's broken loose at Sheridan, Mako's on the hot seat, and where's his right-hand man? Carting one of the root causes of all the trouble back and forth across the lake like a hired driver.* Granted, Niall did see to her security. *But that can't be foremost in his mind right now.*

She yawned. However long she'd slept, it hadn't been enough. "This reminds me of a few nights at Rauta Shèràa Base. I'd get dragged out of bed to answer questions about this or that shipment that the Laumrau claimed we hadn't cleared with them. When I showed them the signed-off paperwork, they pulled out the tweezers and looked for mistakes." She smiled humorless remembrance. "Foodstuffs, mostly, that they couldn't classify under their strict fruit-nut-meat-veg system. Prepack meals drove them crazy."

"I couldn't have handled that crap." Niall shook his head, voice heavy with the man-of-action's disdain for the clerk's side of things.

"Turned me into a stickler where the rules were concerned." Jani ignored Niall's derisive snort. "And it wasn't like a Sheridan transport dexxie's job. The Families still controlled the Service back then, so you found yourself faced with these situations where you knew no one had broken rules, but yet and all they had these cesspit aromas about them. I spent half my time digging for the rest of the story." She laughed. "Chicago at its worst had nothing on a Family member out for their due. They had a way of turning the most simple procedure into a personal mint. Billet privileges were the worst. Chapter and verse, quote, 'Any civilian craft is required to offer any and all assistance to a Service member requiring emergency transport in the course of performance of his duty,' unquote. In my day, the owner of the ship involved could bill the Service for expenses incurred. Service members who were also Family members used it as a way to billet themselves in style on one of their own ships.

Then they'd bill the Service for the cost of everything from food to fuel to crew salaries and uniforms. Abascal, the Treasury Minister—his uncle once tried to pass off the cost for a complete refit for a spaceliner. I made a lot of friends shutting that one down."

"That's changed," Niall said quietly. "The reg now states that assistance is to be provided free of any financial consideration."

Jani studied his profile in the half-light. Too sharp to ever be bland, too wary to ever count as unassuming. "Had reason to look it up recently, did you?" She tried to feel angry, but settled for a vague dissonance. The echo of that last shoe hitting the ground. "And your duty is?"

"Observe the situation in Karistos. Report same." Niall held up a hand, let it fall. "Better me than anyone else, like I said before."

"Yet you'll do your duty as you see fit."

"So will you, Jan. So will you."

It was still many hours to sunrise. The wind had picked up, driving spray over the skimmer. They'd left the lights of the enclave behind, and the glow of Chicago had not yet come into view. The only light was the moon through the clouds and the skimmer headlamps shining off the black water.

They pulled into Jani's drive to find two skimmers had beaten them there. Jani recognized Val's sportster, and assumed the nondescript brown four-door as yet another of Lucien's refugees from the vehicle pool.

"Sounds like a reunion," Niall said as they entered the house, voices raised in loud discussion reaching them from the library.

John, Lucien, and Val had staked out separate corners of the room—they rose as one when Jani entered. She tried to catch John's eye, but he had fixed on Niall, his pale skin reddening.

Niall nodded in brusque acknowledgment. "Doctor."

John didn't nod back. "You might have come to me first before sending in the Judge Advocate's rep with a writ."

Niall walked to the bar. He hefted the scotch decanter but set it aside and took a soft drink from the inset cooler instead. Duty called, after all. "I might have." He popped the cap, took a long swallow. "And you would have agreed without any argument whatsoever, wouldn't you have?"

John opened his mouth to dissent but thought better of it and turned to Jani. "Bad weather moving in." His look gentled. "Our departure's been shuffled. We leave before sunrise."

"Doesn't leave a body any time to say good-bye," Lucien said. He stood at the far side of the room, out of range of the trio of male glowers that greeted his veiled comment. "I'll keep an eye on the place."

"Thanks." Jani burned a mental image of the boyish grin she received in reply, to savor as needed. "I can sleep on the shuttle, I guess." She backed out of the room. "I'll get my gear."

She mounted the stairs and entered her bedroom, walked to her closet and opened the door. Pushed aside a rack of Lucien's clothes, revealing the shelf hidden behind. The narrow ledge contained one thing only, a small blue duffel of the sort the Service had issued twenty years before. *Jani's Noah bag*, Lucien had dubbed it. *Contains two of everything, in case of disaster.* Coveralls, underwear, bandbras, socks. Other essentials she'd added as the date of the trip grew closer. One scanpack, however. And one shooter, nestled in the scanproof depths.

She pulled the bag off the shelf and hitched it over her shoulder. Rearranged Lucien's clothing, then slid the door closed. Trotted down the stairs and back to the library. Four examining stares moved from her face to her bag, then back again, none showing the least surprise at the lightness of her load.

"OK," she said. "Let's go."

CHAPTER 6

Micah Faber keyed into his flat, waiting until the door opened completely before stepping inside. A minor point for some, but important to him. His training dictated that door panels were to be rammed aside, punched through, demolished, if necessary, that they were barriers to be breached rather than portals to be entered. His home, he had decided from the start, needed to be treated differently.

The lights came up, revealing a sitting room in disarray from the previous night's panic. Contents yanked from drawers and shelves and strewn across the floor, cushions pulled from the small couch and single armchair and tossed about like playing cards. In the far corner, the holoVee display, an indestructible one-piece panel spot-molded to the wall, flashed and fluttered in silent cacophony. A woman, weeping and gesticulating, the CapNet reporter who stood beside her nodding in professional concern, while behind them bystanders waved, made faces, or yelled as the spirit moved them.

Micah groaned. He'd seen the same story a half-dozen times since returning to the base that morning. The woman spoke for a group that had banded together to protest the proximity of the Vynshàrau Haárin enclave to the city. Only one Spacer had died as a result of this accident, but what if there were more accidents, and what if more humans died? She couldn't sleep at night for the fear. None of her friends could sleep.

Micah walked to the console and shut it off. "Spare me." If the Weeping Madonna, as he'd dubbed her, wished to protest the enclave, there were things she could do, and sobbing to a reporter wasn't one of them.

He turned away from the holoVee and stumbled over one of the chair cushions. He picked them up and rammed them back in their wrought-wire framing, then did the same with those for the couch. Rust-red polycanvas, water and stain-proof, identical to the cushions one would find in any of a dozen flats in the wing. The other dozen units lay claim to cushions in a green so moldy looking that it served as the deciding factor when Micah had gone flat-hunting that previous summer. He'd had to cough up a ten percent lease premium for a corner location, but considered the resulting cramp to his financial style an acceptable price to pay for cushions that didn't look like they'd been liberated from a damp cave.

The furniture seen to, Micah moved on, picking up the magazines, training manuals, and other things he'd emptied from the drawers of the storage cabinet. Within a few minutes he'd restored the room to its former order, and celebrated the feat by braving the mayhem of the corner kitchenette to liberate the half-liter of vodka he'd bought a few days earlier. He cracked the seal and took a long, hard pull, the alcohol heat burning down his throat and rattling his sinuses.

"Don't know why the hell I did this." He picked up a few pieces of cutlery, the first things that he'd strewn across the floor after he received Wode's call. Wode should have known better, of course. Flat-to-flat comport calls were a definite thumbs-down. Common sense dictated that Service Investigative couldn't possibly bug every enlisted housing unit at Sheridan, but Wode and Micah had been taught not to take chances. *Use public at all times* had become their mantra since they each learned of the other's existence.

Micah stepped around a scatter of plastic bowls and leaned against the counter, bottle still firmly in hand. The last thirty-six hours had ripped past in a blur—the mine site evac, the return to Sheridan, the report-filing, the interviewing. Qualified personnel had been in such short supply that Micah had set up the recording for his own debrief. He'd been tempted to leave the wafer out of the recorder, but he knew somebody would figure it out eventually, and the next time around they might not go so easy on him. As it was, no one had asked the right questions. Interrogators from the vaunted Service Investigative Bureau, and they missed every clue.

It had all been there for them to see, plain as the sun in the sky. Wode's stupid errors, the too-peaceful look on his face as he worked the biobot. Hell, it had been his idea to have the Vynshàrau witness the actual excavation—Micah had been standing near the tech truck pulling parts for the bunker console when he overheard Wode put the bug in Dubrovna's ear! *Ask the Vynshàrau to appoint a witness, ma'am.* And Micah had remained by the truck, his heart pounding until he thought his chest might burst, and kept his mouth shut for the good of them both.

Fabe?

Micah took another swig of vodka. He hated alcohol, the fact that he poisoned himself, but it was the only thing that seemed to help him sleep lately. Help him work. Get through the day.

Fabe, there's a problem.

Micah closed his eyes, and heard Wode's voice in his ear. Heard it as he had that short day and a half earlier, soft and preternaturally calm.

The mine. Someone screwed up—they found the mine. I switched tags with Ling. I'm taking the call.

That's what staggered Micah—the calm. As though Wode

talked of home, his favorite lake for fishing, the girl he thought he loved.

Can't let them find it. Can't blow the Group. I just wanted you to know. They'll probably call you in to run com-arrays and you'll know what's happening and I want you to please, please leave me be. I know what I'm doing.

Another swallow of vodka, even though his gut ached already.

You don't know me. Remember that.

No food since that morning. He knew he asked for trouble.

They'll be there. The frog-eyes. Maybe I'll take some of them with me.

But some things just needed to be washed down as quickly as possible, and this was one of those things.

I wanted you to know that I regard you as the truest of friends, that knowing you has meant the world and all to me.

Another gulp. Another.

Good-bye, Fabe.

Micah leaned against the counter, his breath coming in fits and starts, blood roaring in his ears. His stomach lurched—saliva flooded his mouth. Only a stride away, yet he barely made the sink in time. He vomited until his abdominal muscles cramped. Tried to rinse his mouth from the tap, but the touch of liquid on his tongue set him off again.

After he finished, his nose ran and his eyes teared, a mockery of grief. "That's all the break you get, Faber, *all* the break you get!" If he lived to 150, he'd always despise himself for what he did after Wode disconnected. "Worried about my own cheap ass!" Smashed the comport, then tore his flat from one end to the other, searching for any trace that Wode might have left behind during his infrequent visits, ripping and shattering from kitchenette to sitting room to bedroom and bath in a paranoid rage so fierce he knew that if anyone had come upon him then, he'd have killed them.

"Coward." He filled his hand from the tap, sluiced it over his face. Then put his head down on the cool countertop, sheltering himself with his arms as though the ceiling shook down. Breathed.

Heard the knock eventually. The entry buzzer. The voice.

"Fabe! Hey—open up!"

"Damn." Micah straightened as quickly as he dared. Wiped his face with a dispo cloth. Walked from the kitchenette through the sitting room to the entry, fought for control of his rubbery knees, checked his reflection in the mirror by the door and saw the red-rimmed eyes and blanched face of a ghoul staring back. Opened the door, because the knocking and buzzing rattled his head like artillery and he wanted it to stop. "Yo, Cash," he said, turning his back immediately on his visitor. Of all the people he didn't want to catch him in the middle of a private flameout, that meddling pain-in-the-ass Cashman had to head the list.

"Where the hell you been?" Cashman squirted inside and hurried after him, round-faced and springy of step, bobbing at his shoulder like a balloon. "I heard you leave Saturday night. Figured you got lucky, but then I saw Court at the Veedrome later and she said you switched on-calls with Howie earlier in the week and you got reeled in." He grabbed Micah by the shoulder and spun him around to face him. "You were *there*." He looked Micah in the face, and took a step back. "What happened to you?"

"I was sick." Micah patted his stomach, and almost doubled over again.

"Hey, no disgrace there, my friend, no disgrace at all." Cashman trundled to the chair and flopped down. He wore winterweights, and had already yanked out his shirttail and undone his collar. "So what happened? All we heard was the official accident report, then that garble on CapNet."

"Afraid I can't add anything." Micah sat on the couch, forcing thoughts of Wode from his mind as he struggled to construct a reply to Cash's question. Nothing too informative, just a tidbit or two sufficient to get the creep off his back and out the door. "I didn't work at the site. I was holed up in a bunker outside the cordon."

Cashman sat forward, all goggle eyes and messy shirt. "Oh, a bunker. Fabe hits the big time. Only VIPs hole up in bunkers—who'd you pull to baby-sit?"

Micah coughed, groaning as a gut muscle cramped. The idea of him, of *anybody*, having to baby-sit Colonel Pierce turned his head inside out. "Scarface, for one."

"The Pierced One?" Cashman winced in sympathy. "Bet that was a party. Who else?"

"Just two others." Micah tried to swallow the names in the hope Cashman wouldn't catch them. "Tsecha. Kilian."

"You were holed up in a bunker with Jani Kilian!" Cashman's mouth gaped. With his round eyes, he looked like a fish. "I saw her once. Last summer, when she was still in. Walking across South Central on the way to the Doc building." His mouth slowly closed, his eyes narrowing.

Micah's throat tightened. He'd seen the same reaction all too many times and it made him sick. The wondering. What she looked like. Felt like. As if any man who called himself "human" would lay a finger on her. *"And?"*

Cashman raised his head, blinking as though he came out of a daze. "Nothing. Just saw her once is all." He sniffed. "Tsecha too, huh. Saw him make a speech once." The thought of the Haárin dominant didn't make him quite as dreamy-eyed. "Aren't you hot?" he asked, pointing to Micah. "You still got your coat on."

Micah looked down, saw the belt ends of his field coat curled in his lap like dead snakes. How could he have forgotten? *Haven't been back here since that night—had to wear it—then I got here, had to clean up first—* "I had just come in when you stopped by. Didn't have a chance to take it off." He shook his shoulders, felt the coat slide down, pulled his arms out. *She wore this.* He tried not to think about it. *I'll get it cleaned.* What he wanted to do was burn it, but then he'd have to pay for a replacement, and his rent was due next week.

I promise I'll touch it as little as possible.

Micah felt the heat rise up his neck at the memory. Kilian standing over him, with her giraffe neck and frog eyes. The disdain in her voice, so matter of fact, as if she talked to everyone that way. *Hero of Knevçet Shèràa*, he'd heard someone call her last week. Another colonial, of course. Figured. They always stuck up for one another.

"Fabe?"

Micah glanced over at Cashman to find the man staring back, his chin propped on his fist.

"You need to get out, my friend. They finally got the latest installment of *Raven's Raiders* at the Veedrome, and Court thinks the gang should see it together." Cashman pointed at him. "And Court has a friend."

Micah groaned inwardly. Court was a civvie clerk at Base Admin. A frustrated general, with more friends than hairs on her head. "Really."

"Yeah, you need to get out. We all need to get out." Cashman leaned over and patted Micah's shoulder. "Nasty deal, man. I wouldn't want to be whoever put that mine there. But we're just a couple of Supreme Command comtechs, and the weight of the world is not ours to carry." He headed for the door. "I need to clean up. Be back in a half."

Micah waited until he heard the door slide closed. Then he slumped forward, his head in his hands, and tried to push all thoughts of Wode from his mind, as he'd been taught. "Some will die. Don't think of their deaths as an end. Don't even think of the sacrifice. Instead, think of what the act accomplished, of the good that resulted." One dead Vynshàrau, or as good as dead, according to CapNet.

He reached around and dragged the field coat onto his lap. Stood and walked to the kitchenette. Picked up a knife from the floor. Held the coat in front of him with one hand, punched the knife into the back seam with the other, and ripped down.

Like gutting an animal, really. Sleeves off. Collar. Separate the back from the sides.

"One little two little dead little frog-eyes." Micah cut and kept cutting, rendering the coat into smaller and smaller scraps. He could wear his duffel coat to the Veedrome, and he'd think of something to cover the rent.

He thought of Kilian standing over him, inserted the knife in a seam and yanked.

"Now if you'd been Raven, would you have trusted the Star Queen when she said she'd cure Foxy's alien virus if you turned over the plans to the Death Cruiser?" Cashman's head popped above the divider that separated his cube from Micah's. "I mean, come on, you haven't been able to believe a damned thing she says for nineteen episodes, all of a sudden you're trusting her with your girlfriend's life?"

Micah adjusted his workstation display to block as much of Cashman's face as possible. "Cash, give it a rest. You've been moaning since we got in this morning."

"I'm going to write a letter to the producer." Cashman's head vanished. A few seconds later the chiming sound that heralded the activation of his workstation rang out.

"Raven had no choice. Foxy's the only one who can activate the Death Cruiser's killcode." Hough, a new addition to the ComSys bullpen, kicked his feet back and weighed in. "The virus affected her memory—if she can't remember the code, they'll never be able to stop the Cruiser from destroying the Queen's homeworld."

Cashman's head popped up once more. "But—"

"Good morning."

Cashman fell silent. Hough's feet hit the floor.

Micah stood.

"I need to find the Lakeside One-B conference room, but the one I found has been gutted." A captain stood in the bullpen entry, decked out in dress blue-greys, his brimmed lid tucked under his arm. Tall. Blond. *Famous for all the wrong reasons*, as Lieutenant Bloch, the bullpen wrangler, once said. *They don't give medals for what he's good at.* Lucien Pascal, who sometimes rivaled Raven and Foxy as the topic of bullpen conversation.

No one answered him. They all just stared. Then Micah gave himself a mental kick.

"You need One-B Junior, sir. The interim conference room." He cut through the cubicle maze and past Pascal into the hall. "The directions are a little convoluted. If you'd follow me, please."

"Thank you, Lance Corporal." Pascal fell in behind him. "*Raven's Raiders.* Poor Foxy's virus is the hot topic everywhere, it seems."

"Yes, sir." Micah tried to keep the sharpness out of his voice. He'd bailed out of the bullpen to get away from the endless yammer. Even talking about talking about it made him want to break something.

"Gives them something else to talk about, I suppose."

Instead of the death of a good Spacer? "Yes, sir."

"You're not a fan?"

"No, sir." Micah looked back over his shoulder to find Pascal eyeing him. Pascal, who jumped everything from old ladies to guys to hybrids. *Shit.* He turned around and quickened his step. "Some friends took me to try to cheer me up, but it didn't work very well." *Shut up, shut up, shut up—he couldn't care less and it's none of his business anyway.*

"I saw the first installment. I didn't find it very coherent." Pascal's French Provincial accent broke through with his r's, that peculiar, throaty sound that every female who'd met him seemed to comment on.

Sounds like gargling. Micah rounded one corner, then another. "Just down this hall and make a left, sir. Second door on the right." He stepped to the side so Pascal could pass him.

"Thank you, Faber." He blew past Micah, a pair of majors in his sights, catching them up just as they entered the conference room.

Micah stared at Pascal's back, his heart tripping. Then he

looked down at his winterweight shirtfront. "My nameplate reads 'Faber.' He read it. That's what they're for." He flicked the gold rectangle with his finger, then double-timed it back to the bullpen.

"I heard Bloch call him 'the CMO.' Chief of Mattress Operations. He'll do anything once, and most things as often as possible." Cashman leaned forward and kept his voice low so no one at the surrounding tables could hear him.

Micah smashed a cracker inside its packet and poured the resulting crumble atop his chili. Lunch at Far North Enlisted Mess—table after table of chatter in a glass-walled cavern designed to magnify every sound. *Wode's memorial service today*. But he hadn't dared go. Couldn't even send a note to Wode's parents. Members of the Group weren't supposed to know one another. He and Wode should never have even met. It had been happenstance. Accident. Almost a year ago. Cold spring rain, much like today, and a mess filled to bursting. No place to sit but with a stranger.

So they talked, and found they had more in common than they possibly could have imagined. A hatred of the idomeni as fierce as their love for their humanity, deep as marrow, vital as blood. A determination to do whatever they could to drive the alien from their homeworld, their Earth, their Commonwealth. A disgust for the attraction Chicago seemed to feel for the idomeni ambassador, Tsecha.

And as time went on and the trust between them grew, the realization that they both belonged to an organization that until then had seemed like a figment of their imaginations, a wish not quite come true.

Micah grabbed another pack of crackers from the pile on his tray. If he kept mucking about with his food, maybe no one would notice he wasn't eating.

"Bloch's going to get his ass creamed if he doesn't keep his mouth shut." Hough stabbed the air with his soup spoon. He looked like a lecturer—too skinny, with thin hair and pinched features. Someone who loved the sound of his own voice. "Everybody knows Pascal has an in with Old Man Mako."

"Who's everybody?" Cashman singsonged. "You's everybody?" He batted his lashes until Hough chuffed in disgust and started eating again. Then he glanced sidelong at Micah. "Fabe's a somebody, is what he is. Did bunker duty with some pretty special people night before last." He paused. "Well, one of them is people, anyway."

"Who?" someone downtable asked.

"Kitty-eyes Kilian, and Tse-cha-cha-cha." Cashman rocked his shoulders in time. "And Ol' Scarface."

"Pierce is good." Hough shook his head. "Scares the hell out of me, man."

"My mother scares the hell outta you," Cashman muttered, interrupted again and ticked about it.

"Too bad she didn't scare the hell outta your dad," shot the downtable interrogator, to the amusement of some.

Micah took the sugar round from the table service and shook some into his hot tea. His mother had always given him hot tea when he felt bad, with lots of sugar and lemon. He knew it would take more than hot tea to make him feel better now, but anything was worth a try at this point.

"Pierce left this morning on a long haul," Hough said when the laughter died. "I shoved through a billet privilege chit first thing I signed on." He exhaled through his teeth. "He's tighter with Mako than Pascal is, and Pascal's bad enough." He buttered a roll, pressing it so hard that crumbs tumbled to his tray. "Everybody should just learn to shut up."

"Including you, maybe?" Cashman took a too-big bite of his sandwich. "Where were you before you came to Com-Sys?"

"Finance. Time-reporting." Another chorus of jeers greeted that admission. "Laugh all you want," Hough said, coloring. "All expense reports go through there so we can charge trip time to projects. Pascal traveled more than any looie that wasn't a courier, and all the time got buried in places where you couldn't follow up. No classes, training, meeting minutes. Just billets, meals, and miscellaneous." He looked from face to face to see who listened, but he needn't have bothered. He had everyone's attention now. "His spec's communications matrix design—how best to lay out an array to gather info—but you'd never know it from how he spends his days." He took a bite of his roll, butter shining his lips as though he licked them. "Sometimes specs got nothing to do with what you do, and sometimes rank's got nothing to do with what you are."

"He's in on the mine thing now." That from a full corporal named Chou who did scheduling. "That was the room he asked about—Junior's where they met to talk about how the full-bore Slager got confused for a trainer."

Micah's spoon hit the side of his cup, splashing tea. No one noticed, luckily. They'd all fallen into a Hough-induced funk, eating in silence, their eyes fixed on their food.

He checked the view outside. The rain still fell, needling cold. Craving the solitude, he'd walked to work that morning, and found he'd needed every bit of warmth his duffel coat provided. *Maybe it'll stay cold for the next couple of weeks.* Until he saved enough for a new field coat. After returning home from the Veedrome, he'd stayed up half the night incinerating the hacked remains of his old one in his trashzap. The unit charger had gone dead twice, and toward the end he'd had to make do with charring the scraps, then tearing them apart with this fingers until only fine black fluff remained. And thinking about Kilian as he did so, because for all he loathed the idomeni and their intrusion into his humanity, her medically induced hybridization sickened him even more. Saved her life, he'd heard someone say once. Better she'd died above the sands of Knevçet Shèràa, an honorable Spacer's death.

"So, Fabe?" Cashman gave Life of the Lunchtable one last try. "What's Jani Kilian really like?"

"Tall," Micah replied, to the biggest laugh of the day.

* * *

Micah stepped out the side door of the Supreme Command C-wing, one arm of the multilimbed sprawl that comprised Fort Sheridan's brain. The sky hung low and smoke-hued. The wind had picked up as well, stealing the ends of his muffler from the confines of his coat and whipping them about.

"It's supposed to be spring soon, damn it." But the cold rain still fell, its soft *pat-pat* against his garrison cap interspersed with the occasional icy *tick* of sleet. He broke into a trot, weaving through the end-of-shift crowd that filled the walkway. He thought for a time to catch a shuttle to his flat block, but each shelter he passed was packed with fellow Spacers who'd had the same thought. He'd have to stand and wait in the rain anyway. May as well keep moving.

The crowds thinned as he left the lakeside office buildings and reached the flat expanse of the Quad. Less shelter from the wind now—he hunched his shoulders and wiped a hand over his tearing eyes.

"Good afternoon, Lance Corporal Faber."

Micah slowed, despite the fact that every muscle and bone in his body urged him to run. Run and not stop until he'd put as much distance as possible between himself and the pounding footsteps that drew closer with every stride. "Good afternoon, Captain Pascal, sir." He drew his hand out of his pocket to salute.

"Never mind that. Hands are for pockets today." Pascal drew alongside. He looked as cold as Micah felt, his face half hidden behind the turned-up collar of his field coat. "I hear rumors that it will dry out eventually." Rain dripped from his lid brim, spattered his face like sweat.

Micah swallowed hard. "Yes, sir."

"I didn't realize." Pascal looked down at him, eyes shadowed by his lid and the angle of the walkway lighting. "You'd said this morning that your friends had taken you to the Vee-drome to cheer you. You're a comtech. You ran the bunker com-array at the enclave night before last." A flash of white teeth, framed by the dark blue collar. "You were there."

"Yes, sir."

"We went over the site roster during my meeting this morning. I saw your name." Pascal paused. "You met a friend of mine, I'm sure. Jani Kilian."

"Yes. Sir."

"Funny how things go. We all know someone who knows someone. No one ever remains unknown for long." Another flash of teeth. "*Au revoir,* Lance Corporal." Pascal broke into a lope. "That means 'until later.'"

"Good afternoon, sir." Micah slowed and watched the man dart around scattered pedestrians, turn a corner and disappear. His jaw ached from clenching, and he didn't quicken his pace until someone jostled him and told him to wake up.

CHAPTER 7

Elon stood outside the entry to nìaRauta Shai's rooms and awaited the summons that she had expected for two human-ish days. Her right hand ached, the healing of her finger and wrist bones not yet complete. Her physician-priest had offered her relief from the pain, but she had denied such. Pain focused the mind, and she had much this day on which to focus.

"Elon?"

She looked in the direction of the voice, tilting her head in regard even as she raised her left hand in question. "Ghos. You have taken leave of the journey room?"

Her suborn moved next to her against the wall, then took a half step forward so that Elon stood behind him, as was seemly. "When there is no journey to take place, it is un-seemly to remain. We pray, but to what end? We wait, but to what purpose? We know what the decision must be, yet we delay." He had finally discarded the soiled and torn outdoor uniform he had worn that night at the enclave, and now dressed as Elon had, in the garb of his skein and standing, the pale green trousers and overrobe of embassy security.

Elon contemplated the color, savoring its calming blend with the pale sand of the walls and floor, the metal tones of the ceiling lamps, the pale brown of Ghos's braided hair. "Ní Tsecha believes the decision should be as different."

"Ní Tsecha is no longer Chief Propitiator of the Vynshàrau. If he came to such a decision as Chief Propitiator, he would be made as outcast as he already is." Ghos's shoulders rounded in anger. "Why does Shai allow him here? His place is over the water."

"Shai has asked nìaRauta Sànalàn to prepare an argument and use such to debate ní Tsecha. Such is Sànalàn's first attempt to define a point of theology. As Chief Propitiator, it is something she must learn, and truly."

"The priests debate, and delay Feres's godly death." Ghos brought up his arms and crossed his wrists so that he hid his face. "Anathema."

"Perhaps." Elon flexed her injured fingers, spread them wide, and savored the throbbing spasms that resulted. A self-punishment for her belief in theology. "But there are those in Council who consider times as they once were, Tsecha as the propitiator and Sànalàn as his suborn. Tsecha is Haárin now, and Sànalàn speaks for us to the gods. Such is as it must be. Such is as they must accept. Therefore, nìaRauta Shai will ensure that they do so."

Ghos slowly lowered his arms. He stood hunched, his wrists still crossed before his chest. "Feres must die."

"Yes." Elon enclosed her right hand in her left. Her physician-priest would berate her for damaging his handiwork, but such could not be helped—she tightened her grip until her heart stuttered and her stomach felt emptied of her soul. "But first, there is theology." She heard the door open behind her, and drew up straight. She felt as though she floated upon water, the coolness of sweat trickling beneath her shirt.

"NìaRauta Elon." Shai's suborn stepped aside, and held the door for her to pass.

"Go to Feres." Elon gestured in departure to Ghos, raising her right hand and turning it palm out, so that it obscured the side of her face. "I will bring word." Shai's suborn stared at her hand, and she hid it within the folds of her overrobe before she entered the room.

NìaRauta Shai's workroom comforted the eye as none other in the embassy. Rectangular in shape, each curved display niche in one long side had been set perfectly opposite a narrow window on the other. The two short sides each contained a doorway, again in perfect opposition. Little furniture marred the fineness of the space: Shai's worktable, a semicircle of chairs in sufficient number to seat those attending, a sculpture stand in one far corner.

"You must sit, Elon. I have heard from many that you sustained injury in the explosion." Shai sat to the left of the midpoint of the semicircle, in the second lowest-level seat, as befitted her penultimate status. She glanced up in Elon's direction, then waved her hand in the vague, unreadable manner that she had adopted for use with humanish and unfortunately employed in her dealings with her own. "Sit, Elon."

"Indeed, sit, Elon." NìaRauta Sànalàn, possessing the highest standing as the guardian of the soul of every Vynshàrau, sat at the midpoint of the semicircle, in the lowest-level seat. As Shai, she wore trousers, shirt, and overrobe in palest sand. Only the red banding that adorned the cuffs of her overrobe served as disruption. Her light brown hair she still wore gathered in the tight napeknot of an unbred. That would change, though, for an overture had been made by Shai's suborn and the pairing had been deemed seemly. Soon, Sànalàn would wear her hair in the braided fringe of a breeder, as did Shai and Elon.

Elon walked to one end of the semicircle. Because of her lesser standing, her chair stood higher than Shai's or Sànalàn's—the height of her seat required her to brace her feet against a crossbar and boost up. To do so required two hands to grip the chair arms—she set her right hand atop the cold, hard metal, to use it as guide without putting weight on it.

Her pain was her own. There were those in the room with whom she did not wish to share it.

Yet they understood anyway, as was their way.

"I will not ask you to sit, Elon." Tsecha spoke Vynshàrau Haárin, his voice stripped of gesture. "It seems to pain you to do so, and truly." He sat at the end of the semicircle opposite her, in a chair at a level slightly below hers, yet higher than Shai's. Such was a compromise position, since as an Haárin, he had no right to a place of respect behind any bornsect, but as former Chief Propitiator, he had once held the dominance over every idomeni, as Sànalàn now did.

Elon eased into her chair, her hand throbbing with a sharpness that spoke of a bone rebroken. "What pain I feel, Tsecha, is made even greater by the sight of your clothes." Shirt and trousers of differing hues of purple and a headwrap of dull green, discordant as chemical fire against the sand and stone hues of the walls and floor.

"We know you despise one another." Shai sat slightly slumped in her chair, her hands pressed together at the fingertips, another conflicting display of humanish posture and gesture. "The whole of the embassy knows you fought in the circle prior to the war of Vynshàrau ascension, that you each bear scars inflicted by the other. Even nìaRauta Sànalàn, who was as youngish at that time, knows your story. Spare us further, if you would. I have sat these last days amid carping humanish, each blaming one for the existence of the other. I have no patience left." She uncurved, but only a little. "I speak here now as Suborn Oligarch. If we sat now in a meeting room in Temple in Rauta Shèràa, the chief propitiators of all the bornsects would preside over this debate and cast final judgment as to the soundness of argument. But this is damned cold Chicago—they are not here, and the issue is such that we have no time to send a transmission and await their response. Thus will I act as Temple conclave, and decide." She tugged at the edge of her overrobe, straightening a fold. "The technicians record this, Tsecha."

"Yes, Shai." Tsecha sat in a humanish posture, his elbows on the chair arms, his fingers interlaced.

"After I have cast my decision, this meeting will be transmitted to Temple. There, the chief propitiators will determine whether I decided properly."

"Yes, Shai."

"I explain this to you now, so that you have no reason to dissent later."

"I will dissent if I need to, Shai, now or later. Such is my way."

"Then you will look as a fool."

"As is my name. 'Tsecha' is as 'fool' in Sìah Haárin."

"It is as fool in every language." Shai pressed her fingertips against her forehead just above the bridge of her nose and held them there. "I will begin by saying that Admiral-General Mako has informed me that he regrets this incident with his entire heart and soul, for whatever such regret is worth. The fact that Dathim Naré and his facility suborns have uncovered no other weaponry thus far supports the Admiral-General's claim that the mine uncovered two humanish days ago was an aberration, and that his Service left no other weapons behind on the enclave property." She lowered her hand. "Is this not true, Tsecha?"

"It is indeed the case, Shai." Tsecha nodded in an annoyingly humanish manner. "It would be most helpful, of course, if you permitted us to allow Service Ordnance to screen the area with their equipment. It is their weaponry, after all. Who better to scan for it? But we do what we can."

Shai's shoulders rounded. "Such is not the reason for this meeting, Tsecha."

"No." Tsecha raised his right hand, then let it fall, another of his meaningless gestures. "The reason for this meeting is to decide upon a death."

Time passed. Shai may have believed that Tsecha wished to speak further. When he did not, she exhaled heavily and pointed to Elon. "Let us begin."

Sànalàn hesitated. Then she stood, her posture most straight in honor of the gods, and pronounced the opening prayer. An invocation to Shiou, a plea for order.

Elon glanced at Tsecha, and saw that he mouthed the prayer as Sànalàn entoned. She touched a scar on her left forearm, a ridged hack he had given her so long ago, and rejoiced in his downfall.

Sànalàn finished the prayer and lowered to her chair. Shai then gestured to Elon. "Tell us of Feres's injury."

Elon sat up most straight. She had already described the circumstances many times, yet each instance felt as the first. She labored to recall the details, yet could only call up sensation. The cold rain that numbed her. The sound of the wind through the bare trees. The low hum of equipment. "At the time the mine detonated, I stood with Ghos beside the enclave vehicles, just outside the boundary set by the humanish technician. Colonel Dubrovna, General Burkett's suborn, had advised that one of our number act as witness to the removal of the mine from the ground. 'An act of good faith' is how she referred to such. I watched Feres enter within the boundary and approach the humanish technician. The technician spoke to him, and Feres moved closer, until he stood within reach. Then I heard a shout—one of the humanish soldiers sought to halt the excavation. 'Wode,' he shouted. 'Pull up now.' Feres and the humanish technician, Wode, both turned toward the soldier." Elon drew her right hand over her soul and pressed her left hand over it.

"I saw a flash, heard the detonation. I lay on the ground. Ghos lay atop me—he bled from shrapnel that would have struck me. I fell atop my hand, and broke bones." She raised her hands before her, as though to push. "I ordered Ghos to move so I could rise. He did not understand. He could not hear. I could not hear. I pushed him from me and rose, and looked to the center of the boundary circle." All she could recall. Red upon white. The disruption. "I could not see the humanish. I saw Feres. His legs. One arm. Gone. Blood. I pulled Ghos to his feet, behind the Haárin vehicles. I sought to run to Feres, but Dathim Naré blocked my way and said he was for the priests." She lowered her hands. "That is all."

"Feres also received an injury to the forward third of his brain. A fragment of the mine." Sànalàn spoke. Her voice seemed at youngish, as wind through a pipe. "The physician-priests administered to him most quickly. In a physical mode, he lives, but great damage has been done to his processes of thought. I have consulted with them, and determined thus. If Feres recovers as he is, he will be not-Feres. If Feres becomes not-Feres, he cannot continue the journey to the Star, for Feres had no proper death, and not-Feres had no proper birth. They would each be as half-beings, without sequence to their lives, neither with a clear path to the Star. Feres must therefore be allowed to die, to complete his path in the way the gods intended."

Elon listened, each word Sànalàn spoke touching her soul. *He must die . . . his soul is as lost now, for it can no longer think and knows not the path.* She shivered as from cold, imagining its wanderings.

Tsecha still sat with his hands linked. Even during Sànalàn's invocation, he had not altered his position. "When I still dwelled within Temple, before the Vynshà ascended to rau, I knew Feres. As a youngish, he took his place in Temple school, in the classes taught to seculars." He bared his teeth. "Once, he took colored rounds of plastic and hung them from the branches of all the garden trees. When we sought to reprimand him, he climbed to the top of the tallest tree and could not be compelled to lower himself down. Aeri, my then-suborn and Sànalàn's body-father, had to request a skimmer from the warrior base that could rise as high as the treetop. Thus did we bring Feres down." He unlinked his fingers, then spread them wide, yet another unfathomable gesture. "Vynshàrau evaluation of brain function is not of sufficient depth to ensure the proper decision is reached. Many of the parameters for assessment have not altered since the time of my predecessor, Xinfa nìRau

Cèel, at a time when Pathenrau ruled and the first colonies had just been founded. John Shroud once calculated the time as over 150 humanish years. Such is stagnation!"

"You now confer with humanish physicians concerning matters of idomeni medicine, Tsecha?" Shai's hand chopped the air in an Haárin gesture of dismissal. "You have conferred also with Feyó of the Elyan Haárin, this I know and truly, one who should be made outcast from outcast if such were possible."

"If you wish to enter this debate, Shai, you must complete the exams you failed when we were both at Temple. Otherwise, it is to Sànalàn that I speak." But even as Tsecha spoke thus, he positioned himself as though he lectured at Temple and spoke to no single idomeni, for it was well-known at the embassy that he despised his former suborn as weak, and disdained any contact with her. "Feres is, possibly, not-Feres now. But if time is allowed, if he heals, he may return to that which he was. Methods of evaluation must be improved. More intensive testing must be performed. It is not enough to say 'the wound is here, therefore the damage must be thus,' for each brain is as different, and at times wounds thought grave may be strangely overcome."

Sànalàn had rounded her shoulders, comprehending her former dominant's insult. "And if Feres does not overcome his wound completely, then what? He is still not as he was, still not-Feres. What then, Tsecha? How then do we treat this incompletion?"

"I maintain that even an incomplete Feres is yet something-of-Feres, and as such still recognizes his particular Way, at least in part." Tsecha sat forward, left hand clenched in a fist. "That part must be allowed to continue Feres's journey until as much as possible has been done to recover all of what he was. Humanish act as thus, preserving as much as possible of what was, conserving, aiding the soul in adapting to the trauma of the loss. Otherwise, you allow to die one that would have lived, and affected, and labored. You mock life by surrendering too readily to death."

Sànalàn's voice deepened as her anger grew. "I have said before, humanish fear death too greatly."

"And Vynshàrau fear it not at all, which leads to waste. Which is the greater sin, Sànalàn, to labor greatly to preserve, or to turn one's back, and do nothing?" Tsecha turned on Shai so quickly that she flinched. "You are not qualified to decide the merits of our arguments, Shai, or questions of theology. I will enter my protests of this mockery to Temple as well. This is not a decision to be made quickly. The physician-priests must research. Arguments must be prepared—"

"As Feres's soul stumbles on some path not his own, on some path inconceivable to any godly idomeni." Elon knew she did not speak aloud, yet she heard her words. As did Tsecha, who looked from her, to Shai, then Sànalàn, and curved his mouth in a humanish smile.

"You reached your decision before you heard any argument, this I know and truly. No matter my reasoning, no matter if Sànalàn remained silent and declined to speak at all, your decision would be the same. Feres must die, so order may be maintained. Feres must die, so that your souls may rest as content. But of Feres himself, you do not know, you will never know, because he will never be allowed to speak." Tsecha stood and walked to the door, his shoulders so bowed it was as though he could never straighten. "Each time we meet for argument, you disgust me more."

Sànalàn rose to her feet, even as Shai sought to pull her down. "You have not been given leave to go by your propitiator, Tsecha!"

Tsecha turned. "Then let me say to you, Sànalàn, whom I reared as a youngish, whom I sought to instruct in the ways of the gods, and so failed. Let me say to you here, so that all may know—I do not recognize you as propitiator. The Chicago Haárin do not recognize you, for you condemn the innocent to death. It is you who are as anathema. You whom the gods disdain!" He strode to the entry and out before the door even swept aside completely, before Shai's suborn could attend him.

Shai took on the same posture as Tsecha's. Time passed before she spoke. "It is most as convenient, is it not, that Tsecha spoke as he did on an official transmission. Thus verification of his words has already been accomplished." She gestured to Elon. "Go, and do as the gods compel. I must confer with Sànalàn."

Elon slid off her chair. Her broken hand had swelled past the wrist, and burned to the touch. She felt as though she ran even as she moved quite as slowly. "Glories of the evening to you, nìaRauta Sànalàn," she said as she awaited benediction. But Shai and Sànalàn already conferred, and no longer saw her even as she stood before them.

Elon followed Shai's suborn to the entry, stepped into the hallway, waited as the door closed behind her. Then she saw the physician-priest's suborn standing at the hallway's end, and followed her without a word.

Elon entered the journey room, then stepped to the left side of the entry. The room held little. A bed in its center, surrounded by the instruments and machines of the physician-priests. A side table, draped with an altar cloth and set with a scroll along with the handhelds and scanning devices used to test response and level of consciousness.

Ghos stood at the foot of the bed, head high, hands raised above his head, his prayer voice a keening that resonated within the bare room.

The physician-priest stood at Feres's swaddled head, from around which the bracing framework had been removed. She held out her hands, palms down and slightly cupped, so that they covered his face as a hovering mask. Then she walked to each monitor, each instrument in turn, and deactivated them.

Elon remained near the door, even though custom required she stand behind Ghos. She feared sickness, as did every idomeni, especially those who traveled beyond the worldskein. Unprotected by a blessed environment, surrounded by tainted air and soil, any occurrence, any accident, infection, fever, could leave them as Feres was now. *Such is what happens when we leave our godly home. Such is what happens when we live in the damned cold places.*

Her thoughts stopped as Feres made a sound. Quiet, almost as nothing, a soft gasp. Ghos ceased his prayers. The priest returned to the head of the bed.

Elon waited for another sound. Any sound. She watched Feres's hand, rested atop the bed covering, still as the sculpture in Shai's room, and listened. Listened. Listened.

And heard nothing more.

The physician-priest brought together her hands so the cupped palms faced one another, still above Feres's face. Then she reached outward and opened them, sending Feres's soul to Ghos, his dominant.

Ghos lowered his hands, crossing them before his chest, capturing Feres's soul and holding it close. Then he turned to Elon, head tilting in question when she delayed drawing near.

With a stride so heavy her boots scraped the floor, Elon stepped deeper into the room, holding out her hands just as Ghos dropped his arms. Feres's soul fled to her for safekeeping, feeling as a weight within her broken hand, stopping her breath in her throat and causing her heart to pound, her own soul to ache. She walked to the side table and stood before the scroll. If she had stood on the godly soil of Rauta Shèràa, she would have walked outside and offered Feres's soul to the sky that in the end would claim them all. In its stead, however, she could only show him this construct of parchment, wood, and gilt from his birth house. Such would he inhabit until the next transport ferried him to the Shèrá homeworld, where a Temple propitiator would release his soul and send it upon its godly way.

Elon placed her hands upon the open scroll until her hand

ceased paining, and she knew that Feres's soul had left her. She then closed the cover.

The three of them stood in silence. Then the physician-priest stepped back from the head of the bed, and in doing so pronounced their vigil finished, and Feres's life officially ended.

Elon watched the priest's suborns enter with the floatbed. Muttering prayers, they removed the bed covers and lifted the remains of Feres's body onto the hovering platform. She contemplated the still face for the first time, and found it as pale and smooth as stone, strangely undamaged by the impacts that had destroyed his brain and body and forced him to the end of his journey.

Why? Because Tsecha, whom she had fought, prophesied a joining of races, and because Feres, as a member of the security skein, had pledged to protect the holders of such chaotic opinion whether he believed in such himself or not. Feres, whose soul stumbled in blind pursuit of that which all godly idomeni merited without question, an orderly death.

An orderly death. She followed Ghos from the room, and contemplated such.

CHAPTER 8

Elon sat in the veranda enclosure, cradling her bandaged right hand in her lap. Her physician-priest had berated her about the damage she had inflicted upon herself, as she had expected him to. An assault to the soul, he had said, to rebreak bones that had already been set and mended. Thus had he shielded the hand in a poly case and bound it with strips of altar cloth. Thus, as well, had she come to sit upon the veranda in the middle of the damned cold night, with a command to pray to Shiou to bestow a sense of order upon her soul.

"There is no order." Not in this place. This she now knew, and truly. Even Shai and Sànalàn, whom she trusted, had in the end shown more concern for trapping Tsecha in his admission of heresy than for the state of Feres's soul. From Shai, this might have been expected—she believed that the only way to prevail against humanish was to act as they did. Thus had she prohibited godly disputation in their presence, and altered her own posture and gestures so that even those who knew her since youngish days could no longer determine her thoughts.

But Sànalàn . . . Elon had expected more from the one who had displaced Tsecha. There had been no benediction at meeting's end, and no prayers for Feres. For one who enjoyed the special esteem of both Temple and the Oligarch, Sànalàn had shown herself most unworthy.

Elon lay back her head against the stone, blessedly warm from the heating devices set within. The veranda consisted of a series of enclosures such as the one in which she sat, walled-off spaces furnished with floor mats or low chairs and tables, where Vynshàrau could meditate in solitude or gather to engage in godly disputation. She could overhear one such debate, far off in one corner, a marvel of contention involving some point of Council law. She listened for a time, taking solace in the raised voices as she sometimes took such in the sound of the lake waves striking the shore, or the heat from a flame that reminded her of the blessed warmth of home.

"Elon?"

She flinched at the sound of her name. Such was not her habit to take to the veranda in the middle of the night. None whom she knew would think to look for her here—

"Elon?"

—except one.

"*Ghos.*" Elon strained for some sound of movement. "*I am here.*" She waited. "*Ghos!*"

A shadow fell across the enclosure entry. Then a looming figure in shirt and trousers, a boot in each hand.

"What good does it do for you to walk without sound when you shout my name and I must shout yours in return?" Elon pushed the low table to one side with her foot so that Ghos could unroll one of the mats and seat himself. "Your hearing has not yet returned from the night of the mine. You must go to your physician-priest."

"I have had enough of priests." Ghos lowered to a crouch, then fell back onto the mat, a sign that his muscles still ached from that night as well. "Hearing returns with time. This I know, and truly."

"Not at all times, and if the damage is permanent, it must be repaired or you risk injury to your soul!"

"Hearing returns with time." Ghos pulled on one boot, then the other. "Breaker of fingers."

Elon bent one leg to her chest, sheltering her bandages from Ghos's view. "Why are you here?"

"To report of the embassy, which I could not do as we attended Feres." Ghos took up the handheld that hung from a cloth wrap about his waist and activated it. "The border with Interior is active, as always. Their guards have not ceased patrol since the night Minister van Reuter faced arrest, over one of their years ago. Whatever they search for, they have not yet found it." He tapped the display with his knuckle to change the entry. He spoke Vynshàrau Haárin, his voice completely stripped of gesture, as was his way when he reported to Elon. "The border with Exterior is quiet, as always. Interior should send some of their guards to them, I most believe." Another tap. "The lake is as quiet. We detect demis in flight well north of here. Service exercises, one assumes, but we await confirmation." Another tap. "The biodefense trials have been completed. The research dominants fear, and truly, that revised pink is not yet deployable throughout the embassy as a way of protection. It attacks all humanish biodevices evaluated, but it also damaged certain types of medical implants, as the material your physician-priest used to remend your broken bones. It attacks some of our device boards, rendering them useless. The biologics dominants fear contamination. Humanish have walked these halls since this building began its function. Vynshàrau have interacted with humanish, then entered the laboratories."

Elon gestured in disagreement. Most unfortunately, the action required the use of her right hand. She could not curve her fingers properly, and felt the anger rise as Ghos bared his teeth. "The workers are trained in methods to prevent such cross-contamination, and laboratory air systems are configured to remove such as well."

"One might believe." Ghos deactivated the handheld and returned it to his belt. "It is my feeling that embassy systems have not functioned as properly since Dathim Naré's time. He understood them, how to maintain them."

"Dathim Naré now lives over the water, Ghos."

"He should return to this place, where he belongs." Ghos raised his gaze and looked Elon in the face. "It is a matter of security, as the humanish say. We would be more safe if Dathim Naré resided here. Therefore, he must reside here."

Elon regarded Ghos just as openly. "He will not do so, nor will Shai compel him. He is more outcast even than Tsecha, and thus she does not trust him."

"Within the worldskein, such would not matter. He would do as he is bid."

"We are not within the worldskein, Ghos."

"No. We are outcast, beyond all godly bound." Ghos looked away. Then he pulled the low table toward him and reached for his belt once more. "Feres's scroll has departed for the embassy dock at Luna. His remains have been burned and dispersed by Sànalàn's suborn, whose training I most doubt." He removed a small bag, untied the opening, then poured the contents atop the table. Pattern stones, which caught what light there was and reflected it in ever-changing spirals of blue, green, and yellow.

"This is no place for games, Ghos." Despite her displeasure, Elon found herself drawn to the stones, marking the patterns as they changed, watching Ghos align those that matched, then deducting the points he lost as the patterns changed before he finished.

"No. This is a place of discussion." Ghos gestured frustration as the spirals altered to lines just as he constructed the final row. "And what will we discuss, Elon? How little Shai has informed us of her discussions with the Service humanish concerning the mine? How humanish reporters speak of Feres as though his error killed the technician Wode, and not the reverse?" His fingers played over the stones, never stopping even as he spoke, aligning them as quickly as the patterns reformed—whorls, sprays, lines—yet not completing the sets in time. "How much we are hated in this city, yet we stay? How with each humanish day, we lose more of our souls as the injury that is this place wounds us, never to heal? How we are damned?"

Elon picked up one of the stones, ignoring Ghos's mutter that she interfered with his game. "We are all those. There is nothing to discuss." She turned the stone over, held it to the light. A yellow and blue whorl, tightening to a spiral, then swirling into concentric circles. "Is there a remedy? Such is what merits discussion, Ghos." She bared her teeth as Ghos looked her in the face once more. She relished his strangeness, his grey eyes against paler skin than hers, much as his body-mother, who was as Sìah. "Ghos of the stones."

Ghos did not respond to her humor. He concentrated on his patterns, as he always had when he contemplated action. "If the Oà challenge Cèel, we will be called back to Shèrá to fight. Oà must not succeed. They have never ruled as rau. They have not the experience to deal with humanish."

"Oà will not challenge without the Haárin, and the Haárin follow Vynshàrau." Elon set the stone back upon the table. "For now."

Ghos's hand stopped in mid-play. "Explain."

Elon watched the pattern of the stones change. *Ghos has completed only half the lines—he has lost too many points.* Yet she knew from his attention to her that he no longer cared of stones. "Tsecha repudiated Sànalàn when his plea to maintain Feres's life failed. He said he did not recognize her as his propitiator. Cèel will thus move against him. When the Haárin learn of this, and they will, some will remove their support from Cèel."

"For what reason?"

"Tsecha is dominant of the Chicago Haárin, and as such is considered by most Haárin as their dominant as well. Thus will they turn from Vynshàrau and support the bornsect that Tsecha supports, whether such is Oà, or Pathen, or Sìah." Elon touched her bandaged hand, which had numbed. "We will not know what may happen for some time. First Shai must tell Cèel, then Cèel must confer with Council and Temple. Then the word will spread throughout the worldskein, and all will know . . ." She listened for the sounds from the other side of the veranda and heard nothing. Did they listen to her now as she spoke of Tsecha's heresy? "It becomes most as complicated."

"Politics." Ghos mixed his stones together, then waited for the new pattern to form. "Blood is cleaner."

"—and it should be a pretty good party." Cashman dragged the beer dispenser out of the skimmer boot and lowered it onto the two-wheeler he'd appropriated from the apartment building's utilities chase. "I invited the bullpen crew, and some of the folks from SysAdmin, and Court's bringing a couple of friends."

Micah hoisted the last bag of food out of the boot and set it atop the dispenser. "The exam for Comtech One is in a few weeks. I need to hit the manuals."

"That's my Fabe. They finally give us a day off from all this inquiry crap, and you decide to celebrate by studying." Cashman slammed down the boot hood, then dragged the two-wheeler around in a wide circle and pulled it across the garage toward the lift. "This was the first day in two weeks that we didn't have to record some poor bastard's inventory screw-up or requisition miscalc or scheduling cross-over, and I for one intend to take full and complete advantage of it." Without warning, he yanked the cart into a sharp turn and headed toward the locked cage that housed the building's delivery slots, row after tightly packed row of lockers set aside for packages and other bulky personal mail. "Only take a second. I haven't checked in a few days. Last time I let it go too long, my sister sent me real ice cream. Who the hell sends anybody real ice cream? Stuff melted. Stunk up my box for a week."

"I remember." Micah waited as Cashman keyed into the cage, then followed him in. His heart tripped—he felt a warmth spread through his body that was almost embarrassing. *It's been over three weeks.* He approached his locker as if it were a girl waiting for him, his emotions warring. Eager to the point of euphoria. Terrified enough to turn and run.

"Not even a snack food sample from the exchange." Cashman slammed his locker door closed. "I need to call my folks and make them feel guilty."

Micah palmed open his locker—his hand sweated so much that he needed to press it down twice. *Please . . . please . . .* He caught sight of the familiar white mailer amid the trashzap chargers and building announcements, small and battered, bearing the mail code of an off-base holoVee store.

"Looks like some of us have friends." Cashman grabbed for the mailer, wresting it from Micah's grip. *"Whoa ho,"* he cried as he read the mail code, "I know what this is!"

Micah froze, his heart still pounding, mind racing. *This place gets too much traffic.* He glanced at the rows of lockers, the narrow aisles that separated them barely wide enough to walk down. *Couldn't hide a body here.* At least, not for very long.

Cashman gave the mailer closure a half-hearted tug, then tossed it back to Micah. *"Studying."* He grabbed the two-wheeler's handle and pulled it out of the cage. " 'Space Vixens from the Planet Clitoris'—that's what you'll be studying."

Micah gripped the mailer so tightly his fingers cramped, and still he held on. He wanted to shout *How dare you! That's what you think! You're wrong!*

But a wilier part of him interrupted. *Let him think that. Let him think whatever he wants, as long as he doesn't guess the truth.* He tucked the mailer under his arm and walked out of the cage. Closed the gate after him. Headed for the lift only to find Cashman waiting, sly grin in place.

He stepped aside so Micah could board, then let the door slide closed. "So." He watched the floor numbers creep upward. "Can I borrow it when you're done?"

Micah sighed. "Sure." That meant he'd have to waste tomorrow's lunch break on a trip to the shop to search for something appropriately smutty. *It's called cover*, the wily part of him said. He thought of Captain Pascal and his miscellaneous accounts. *This is what it feels like*. He pondered it, and found it good.

Micah keyed into his flat, pausing until the door opened completely even as his nerves screamed. Stepped inside, waited for the panel to slide closed, then activated the lock.

"Space vixens." Sometimes he despaired of his fellow Spacers, their lack of imagination. He set the mailer atop the storage cabinet. Then he hung up his coat, activated the kitchenette and bedroom lighting, all the usual first-few-minutes-at-home business that he did every day. He already wore suitable clothes, base casual pants and a heavy knit athletic pullover. To ease his grumbling stomach, he raided his cooler for a dispo of milk and a candy bar. Hunger dulled if not sated, he returned to the cabinet and picked up the mailer.

"Why did they wait so long?" Micah tore open the tough plastic envelope and removed a small white foldover the size of his palm. Opened the flap and removed an ummarked wafer. He held it by the edge, tipping it from side to side, watching the light reflect off the surface in pale curved rainbows and wondering who else had touched it. Had it been a leader of their Group? Someone like the Old Man, who monitored their scattered numbers from some all-seeing vantage point and chose or discarded for the good of humanity? Or had it been a trusted second-in-command, someone like Scarface Pierce, whose job was to take the raw material his master gave him and mold it into a defender worthy of his race?

Micah opened the bottom drawer of the cabinet and removed a headset, along with a pair of earbugs and linked gloves and socks. The usual virtual training gear, used by pilots, surgeons, mechanics, anyone who needed to learn a highly specialized skill.

"If I planned to watch *Space Vixens*, I'd need another linking connection." He frowned. He'd need to get it tomorrow when he stopped at the shop to buy his decoy holo. That way, in case his flat was ever searched, there would be no question in anyone's mind that the only thing Micah Faber was guilty of was an unfortunate predilection for interactive pornography.

"That means I should get more than one holo." If you're going to build a cover, may as well make it shooter-proof. "This is getting expensive." He walked over to his couch and sat, then bunched a couple of cushions against the armrest and lay back. Pulled on the socks. Stuck in the earbugs and donned the headset.

Micah listened to his breathing, magnified to a slow gale within the confines of the face-covering headset. Ambient sound had been blocked. Incident light. He slipped the wafer into a slot in the headset, then dragged on the gloves. Waited.

First came a series of tones. Like chimes, they sounded, first louder, then softer. Repeating. Repeating. The preparative hypnosis, designed to lower the barrier between his conscious mind and the scenario that would soon play before it like a—

—classroom. Chairs in two concentric circles, arranged around a woman dressed in a steel-grey T-shirt and baggy fatigue pants. Razored Service burr, accentuating a face too broad and bony to be feminine. Chrivet. Sergeant. Micah's god-on-earth for the duration of his training. He'd sat before her three times so far, and liked her within certain tight limits. She knew her job—therefore, she was worth listening to. Beyond that . . . he tried not to think of her beyond that.

"The V-790 exoskeletal array is the most advanced exo yet developed by the Service." Chrivet stalked the center of the circle, the focus of all attention and savoring it. "When you wear it, you will be able to run farther and faster, jump higher, and shoot better than any human being who ever lived. You will be damned nigh invincible."

Micah snatched glimpses of his classmates around Chrivet's stalking form, twenty-eight young, fresh faces each evidencing varying degrees of attention. Bevan, narrow and dark, who thought he already knew it all but deigned to listen anyway. Foley, shorter and lighter, who followed Bevan like a starved pup. Manda, pale-skinned and black-haired, who glanced back at Micah across the gulf of Chrivet's circle and smiled.

Micah smiled back. Felt the heat creep up his neck. Down. Knew that Chrivet still spoke, and couldn't have repeated a word she said if his life depended on it.

Don't do this to yourself, man—that isn't even her face. He and Wode had talked about the scenario setup many times after they stumbled upon the fact that they were both members of the Group. How the odds were that since their names had been changed, their faces most likely had as well. That only the downloaded personalities remained the same. Voices, maybe. Enough to train. Enough to bond. Enough to befriend. Not enough to identify.

Those eyes. So blue. It would have been unspeakably cruel of the scenario brain to render Manda's eyes a fiction. *So what does she see when she looks at me?* Micah saw his own face in every reflective surface, but that was because that's what he expected to see. *How different are we?* And would it matter come the day they all finally met?

Without warning, an expanse of darker blue obliterated his view of Manda. He blinked, realized he stared at Chrivet's crotch, and lifted his head as though she'd jerked him under the chin.

"Can't you hear me, Mister Tiebold!" She glared down at him, cheeks reddening. "I asked you a question."

Tiebold. He still hadn't gotten the hang of his scenario name. No one else seemed to have a problem with theirs— why did he with his?

"I didn't . . ." He took the deepest, longest breath in the world. It ended too soon. "I didn't hear you, ma'am."

Chrivet's eyes narrowed. Small, close-set, piggy eyes, dull clay without a glimmer of beauty.

Not like Manda's—Micah gave himself a mental slap. No

more Manda. Not now. Not if he wanted to remain with the Group. Learn about the V-790. Avenge Wode, and drive the idomeni from every corner of the Commonwealth.

"You didn't hear me, Mister Tiebold?" Chrivet smiled. Her teeth were square and white with no spaces between, as though they'd been carved from a single block of poly. "You're bored. Nothing here of sufficient interest to hold your attention. You know it all." Her voice, which normally skirted the edges of agitation, emerged dangerously calm. "Well, since you know everything—" She stepped to one side and pointed to a place outside the circle, beyond the double ring of chairs. "—perhaps you'd like to show us all how to suit up."

At first glance it seemed that someone had beaten Micah to it. A helmeted figure stood outside the circle, taller than he and broad-shouldered, tricked out in a tight black coverall with articulated joints. Dull-finish body armor plated across the chest, abdomen, and thighs, while metal framing ran along the outsides of the legs and undersides of the arms.

Micah took one step toward the still, silent figure, then another, conscious as ever of Bevan's sneer, Chrivet's eagerness to pounce on his anticipated screw-up. *It's just an exo, stupid—no one's inside.* He studied the smooth front of the suit, looking for fasteners, clasps, groping for some hint as to how to get into the damned thing. *Shit.* He stopped in front of it— it was taller than he by half a head. *I sat through a presentation once.* His job had been to set up and monitor the imager, but he'd stuck around at the speaker's request and got to listen to the whole thing. *There's a release near the top of the left shoulder—*He reached up, his fingers brushing what felt like a raised seam. He pressed down, and the shoulder sagged open with the sound of cracking ice.

Keep peeling down. He sensed Chrivet move in beside him, and glanced over to find her regarding him with thin-lipped disgruntlement. *Yanked away one chance for you to humiliate me.* He turned back to the exo. *Sadistic bitch.* He opened up the side seam down to the ankle. The metal frame supported the coverall as he worked his way inside, felt the slip of the material over his hands. Rubbery yet silky, nubby in places from inset connections and sensors.

"Unlike previous exos, the V-790 is designed to allow the wearer to suit-in themselves. But in the interest of time—" Chrivet started at the ankle and worked up, yanking the seams together and sealing them tight. "The suit contains a constrictor array so the wearer can tighten or loosen as needed—"

Micah drowned her out again as he adjusted his helmet, then started fiddling with the controls. The air inside the exo smelled metallic, burnt, as though the suit was brand new and still outgassing.

"A damned manual would be nice," he muttered under his breath. He heard a *ping* in his left ear, followed by a flash of light. Then, as nicely indented and numbered as you please, a series of headers scrolled across the inner surface of the faceplate. "Voice activation—good to know." He scanned the words that flowed before his eyes. Bodily Functions. Weapons. Defensive Equipment. "How about walking?" He looked past the words, through the display, and saw Chrivet and the others eyeing him expectantly. *Oh boy.* He bunched his muscles as though he prepared to leap off a ledge, and legged forward—

"Shit!" Micah went airborne, hitting the inner ring of chairs, scattering wireframe in all directions. Shouts filled his ears. A woman's scream. Another stride and he hit the opposite side of the circle, blowing chairs aside like bits of foam. Heard Chrivet yell, *"Stop!"* One more immense stride. Another. The wall came to meet him like a fist in the face—he dropped his weight on his back heel like a ped-wheel kick brake, and stopped a hairbreadth in front of the painted brick.

Four strides. His heart pounded, columns of red bobbed on the display. Five meters a stride—had to be. "I ran—" Across a huge cavern of a room in the time it took to shout one word. "Shit." He said it again, softer this time. He felt like the animal he rode had taken off beneath him and run down the face of a cliff, carrying him along for the ride. *But I stopped it*. Could he have gone through the wall? *I'd rather not find out*.

"Turn around, Mister Tiebold," Chrivet called after him, "and take it a little more slowly this time."

Micah lifted his left leg, edged it to the side, and felt it swing out. *Little movements go a long way*. He let the momentum take him, moving into the rotation like a dancer. It worked. He felt as though he drifted into position, like a leaf falling from a tree, but in the end he found himself facing Bevan and the rest, standing straight and tall.

"You certainly know how to walk across a room, Mister Tiebold." Chrivet had moved well out of Micah's direct path, and now stood against the wall to his left. "Now take one step forward. Then peel out and give someone else a turn." She looked around. "Clear the rest of these chairs out of the way."

Micah took the lesson from his turnaround, and edged his leg forward. Felt the low glide. A single step—only a meter or so this time. He raised his right hand beside his head and imagined the muzzle of a mid-range at his right shoulder. According to the presentation, the weapon would be bolted to the rear framing, all charged and ready to go. *Just pull it down and fire*.

"Peel out now, Tiebold."

Micah sighed. Lowered his hand, crossing it over to his other shoulder. Popped the seam. Exited the suit. Took a seat against the wall and watched everyone else. Imagined again and again the thrill of those few strides. Daydreamed of the power inherent in the flick of a finger. The kick of a leg. Lay his head back against the wall and—

—opened his eyes. As always, he felt as though he'd been under for hours. But when he checked his timepiece, he found that only twenty minutes had passed. Not as compressed as a dream, but not real-time, either. In between.

Micah sat up. He removed the wafer from his headset,

then pulled off all the gear piece by piece. Rose shakily, his thigh muscles aching from tension, his gut rumbling. When he walked, he felt the exo about him like a shield.

For a time he felt the urge to crash Cashman's party. He wanted to shoulder his way through a room full of people, shout to make himself heard above the din. Drink and laugh.

"Except..." He knew what he'd hear as soon as he walked in. *Hey Fabe—what happened to the holo? Hey everybody, meet my buddy, the scholar.* "I'll stay in." Heat up a prepack. Watch the 'Vee. First thing in the morning, he needed to stop by the public comport kiosk at Forrestal Block, two apartment buildings removed from his. Tuck into a booth and punch in the code that had arrived with that very first training wafer, three months before. Then stick his latest wafer into a player, jack the player into the comport, and send the entire transmission on its way to God knew where, this time supplemented by his physical data, his bioemotional scan, his responses to the training scenario. A DI's recruit report, packed into a few seconds of transmission chatter. After that, melt the wafer down in his trashzap. Then wait for the next mailer to arrive.

"How long?" Not three weeks, not if a training regimen had begun. "More often." A couple of times a week, maybe, for weeks and weeks to come.

He relived sensations. The lightness. The power. Then he shut his training gear away in its drawer and walked to the kitchenette to make his supper.

Micah decided later that he hadn't paid sufficient attention to his surroundings. He had risen early, showered and dressed, then transmitted his data in the usual fashion. Caught a shuttle to Far North Lakeside and settled into his cube early enough to catch the tail end of third shift. He took advantage of the downtime to tap into systems and dig up a schematic of the V-790, secure in the knowledge that it would be at least an hour before Cashman peered over the divider and regaled him with details of the party.

He was immersed in the Motion Control section of the manual when he heard a throat-clearing behind him—he spun his chair around, his heart in his throat.

"I didn't mean to alarm you, Lance Corporal." Pascal stood in the cube entry. He still wore his field coat; a black briefbag hung from one shoulder. "Emergency meeting in Lakeside Junior—we're having trouble with the conference calling system."

"Yes, sir." Micah reset his workstation to standby and pushed to his feet, blowing past Pascal more quickly than was mannerly. *Back down—you haven't done anything wrong.*

Pascal quickened his pace and caught him up. "You're interested in exoskeletons, Faber?"

Micah's heart skittered. He hated the fact that Pascal knew his name. "I ran the imager for a V-790 presentation a few weeks ago. It looked interesting."

"The engineers took too many shortcuts in the environmental controls, and diverted power to movement and weapons systems." Pascal's voice sounded tight. "They feel that if you can run away from it or shoot it, you don't need to protect against it. Not sound, in my opinion. But no one asked me."

"No, sir. I mean, yes, sir." Micah ducked into the conference room ahead of Pascal and headed straight for the combooth in the far corner. Flicked the switches he had to, then ran a systems check. Emerged from the booth. "Should be good to go now, sir." Made for the door, conscious as a hunted beast of the gaze that tracked him until he left the room and emerged into the safety of the hallway.

"Jerk." So no one asked the great captain's advice on the design of the V-790? Well, soon a lowly lance corporal would know more about it than he would, and wouldn't that be a great feeling? The thought made Micah smile, until the memory of those dead brown eyes eyes boring holes in his back wiped it away.

CHAPTER 9

"Because of the distance from Earth, the
Outer Circle worlds are the least traditional of
all the Commonwealth colonies . . ."

Clase, *Thalassan Histories, Book I*

"I'm a colonial, too, Jan, a point you seem all too willing to
overlook." Niall walked the edge of the exercise mat as
though it were a tightrope, heel-to-toe-to-heel, arms held out
to the sides for balance. "And when it comes to the Jewelers
Loop gross domestic product rankings, Victoria is the poor-
est of poor relations. I understand deprivation. I learned all
about having to make do with the dregs while others with
more clout got the cream." He wore summer base casuals—
grey T-shirt, dark blue shorts, and white trainers—and
seemed well-met with the ship's small gymnasium. His
arms looked hewn from wood, his legs muscular and still
faintly tanned despite five weeks spent under ship lighting.
"Just because Elyas and the other Outer Circle worlds can't
get chocolate sauce for their sponge cake is no reason for
them to allow the Haárin to take over their damned shipping
networks."

Jani sat on the far end of the mat and watched Niall totter
and turn. "The issue that brought all this to a head last fall
involved something a little more serious than chocolate
sauce. As I recall, the quality of Karistos's water was at
stake." She crossed her trousered legs at the ankle. She wore
a long-sleeve pullover as well, topped with a heavy crew

113

sweater in a jewel shade of purple, their ship name, DENALI, etched across the front in silver. "You insist on trivializing the fact that the colonies have been chronically undersupplied for decades, at times to the point of crisis."

"I don't trivialize it!" Niall halted in mid-wobble and stepped to the middle of the mat. "The Families screwed up. They didn't think past the ends of their credit balances. A few of them behaved in a remarkably stupid manner. Well guess what? They're finally waking up. The great beast is blinking and looking around and sees reason for concern."

"For its credit balance."

"For its security."

Jani worked to her feet and walked to the games rack, which had been bolted to the far wall. "If Cao and her cronies want to win back the confidence of the Outer Circle Merchants Associations, their task is simple." She took a wooden martial-arts sword from one of the slots and swung it back and forth like one of Dathim's practice blades. "Let them revamp the Commerce and Transportation ministries. They've cleared the wharf rats from a few docks—let them keep going. Let them divest themselves of the shipping companies that they own to eliminate any nasty little conflicts of interest, and let the new owners win business in the competitive arena, not take it as something they're owed." She stilled, then began to shift her weight from side to side, knees bent, guiding the blade in a slow sweep before her.

Niall tracked the end of the blade as if it were the head of a snake. "Dathim teach you that?"

"He told me that my old bones require a gradual progression of movement. In other words, I need to warm up." Jani smiled. "He's older than I am and he needs to warm up even longer, but that's different, of course. He is the teacher and I am the student, and his is a life pure and free from contradiction and pulled muscles."

Niall watched her for a time. Then he walked to a bench set against the far wall, beneath which he'd stashed his gym bag.

"I'll say this, you're getting better at changing the subject. You even managed to get the last word in the bargain." He dragged the bag atop the bench and scrabbled through it, removing a short-handled racket and a hand towel. "We've had the same discussion in different forms since we boarded this bucket at Luna. Why don't we call it a draw and be done with it? You won't change my mind, and I won't change yours."

Jani stopped in mid-arc, then drew the blade to a neutral stop against her right shoulder. "You're angry."

"Resigned, more like. Returning to the role of concerned observer with a heavy sigh." Niall began his own warm-up, rotating his wrists, then flicking the racket back and forth. "You talk a very good game. But you play it, as well, and have the scars to prove it. Proof for the doubting Thomases. You possess a hefty share of credibility." He offered a sad half smile, twisted into a smirk by his scar. "And you've got this revolutionary gloss that's difficult for we more boring souls to ignore."

Jani rolled her eyes. "I'm not a revolutionary. I'm not—"

"Jan, if you tell me you're not political, I'm going to clout you across the back of the head." Niall pivoted from side to side. Forehand. Backhand. "You're about as political as they get, whether you choose to believe it or not."

"My political options dwindled to nothing when the ministries shut me out. I'm a priest-in-training now." Jani walked back to the rack and slid the blade back into its niche. "I don't understand how you can defend the Commonwealth as you do. It certainly hasn't treated you much better than it has me."

"I believe in the ideal, if not always the execution. Then there's the colony kid in me—I hate waste. If a system is flawed, you repair it. You don't turn your back on it." Niall's back and forth slowed. "Unless you want it to continue to devolve so that you have a knee-jerk justification for doing something that you know you shouldn't be doing in the first place."

Jani waited for Niall to stop, to shoot a pointed look in her direction, but he continued his warm-up as though she wasn't in the room. *You bastard—you don't even have to check to see if you hit the target, do you?* But then, he'd hit it back in Chicago, where he'd first attached himself to her like a second shadow—it was just a case now of gathering the details. *Which I've managed to keep from him.* But they would dock at Elyas Station the next ship-day. At that point all bets were off. He'd find out about the hybrid, real or faked. About Feyó's problems with her Haárin. And he'd transmit it all back to Chicago, for Mako to take to Cao on a silver platter, the peace offering found just in time to save his Admiral-Generalcy.

"Good morning."

Jani turned toward the gym entry to find John standing there, smile fixed in place as he looked from her to Niall and back again. "I've interrupted another political argument. I can tell." He had dressed as Niall had, in shorts, T-shirt, and trainers, but any resemblance ended there. He had chosen white and pale blue for his outfit, colors that matched his skin and the veins that ran beneath. He was taller and lankier than Niall, and looked as though he might break in a stiff wind until you saw how the muscles of his forearm bunched and defined when he clenched the handle of his gym bag.

"You'd think that after five weeks cooped up together, you two would have hashed everything out." He exhaled with a rumble. "I guess not." He strode toward them, the soles of his trainers squeaking on the coated flooring. He skirted the edge of the mat and tossed his bag atop the bench next to Niall's. Then he dug out a racket and a dispo of balls, popping the container lid and shaking one out so it bounced toward Niall. "Odds or evens?"

"Odds." Niall plucked the ball out the air, then turned it so he could read the vendor mark. "Serial number ends in five. My serve."

John swung his racket in a relaxed arc. "It's a little late in the trip to say this, Jan, but I'd appreciate it if you didn't rile the colonel before our matches." He tried to sound humorous, but a warning glint hardened his blue-filmed gaze. "He tends to take it out on me in an annoyingly predictable manner."

"He means that I whip his ass." Niall jerked his chin in the direction of the door that led to the ballcourt. "After you, Doctor."

"Colonel."

Jani lagged behind the two men as they walked to the ballcourt entry, listening to their banter. It sounded good-natured enough on the surface, but she had sensed their mutual dislike bubble to the surface more than once over the course of the trip, especially when John perceived that she and Niall had argued. *John never liked him, and now he doesn't trust him.* If trust stemmed from knowing exactly what a person would do in a given situation, however, Jani trusted Niall completely. *He'll do what he perceives is his duty.* Just as she said he would back in Chicago. *And so will I.* Just as he said she would. *We know one another too well.* Trust, therefore, was absolute on both sides. *Pull the other one, Kilian, it sings "Oh, Acadia."* She settled in front of the observation window and waited for the game to begin.

After a few minutes of warm-up, the men moved into position. Niall bounced the ball off the floor and struck it, his racket hand a blur. Behind him, John lunged for the rebound as best he could, but it sailed past him, striking the window with a solid *thuck*. He took advantage of his location to glare at Jani. She shrugged an apology.

"One to the server," Niall announced, grinning. His good mood vanished, however, when John won the next exchange and claimed serve.

Go, John. Jani pumped a fist below the level of the windowsill and braced for John's serve until a movement in her periphery claimed her attention. She looked to the side and found one of the *Denali* comtechs standing there, professionally sharp in a coverall of the same rich purple as her sweater.

"Transmission for you, ma'am," the young woman said. "From Elyas."

"Thanks." Jani settled into the combooth seat, then nodded for the tech to shut her in. As the door closed, the lighting in the booth dimmed to half power. The display, meanwhile, brightened with a series of vendor logos, followed by a warning of the awful fate that would befall any unauthorized viewers of the message about to play.

"How about the authorized viewer?" Jani grew conscious of her sweaty palms, and wiped them against her trouser legs.

The display image stuttered for a few seconds as idomeni and humanish technologies collided. Then a face that had grown more and more familiar since the autumn took shape. A high-boned oval, the paler gold-tan of the Sìah, graced by dark grey eyes softened by silvery sclera.

"Glories of the day to you, ná Kièrshia." Ná Feyó Tal, dominant of the Elyan Haárin, spoke lightly accented English, and appeared as relaxed and comfortable as she usually did during transmissions. She wore her grey-streaked brown hair drawn back in her usual humanish-style horsetail. Her visible clothing was simple in cut and pale in color, an open-necked crossover shirt in the light green shade she favored. "We anticipate your visit. I look forward and truly to news of ní Tsecha." She had angled her face so she would look Jani in the eye if they sat in the same room, an attention to detail that many Haárin overlooked and bornsect eschewed on principle. "I trust your journey proved most pleasant, and that you anticipate our reunion as much as I."

"Glories of the day to you as well, ná Feyó." Jani sat back, folding her arms so she could tuck her hands up the sleeves of her sweater. "Ní Tsecha sends his regards as well, and wishes he could have made this journey himself."

Feyó's lips curved in a vague almost-smile, which on a human female would have been considered enigmatic. "I most wish he could have as well." She lowered her gaze for a time. When she raised it again, the clear-eyed reserve had returned. "Tomorrow, ná Kièrshia. It would be most appropriate, I believe and truly, if one of my shuttles docked with the *Denali*, and if we took you off thusly and I escorted you to Karistos myself. If you could consult with your ship's engineer and tell me if docking arrangements are possible? I may transmit to you all the information needed for this determination."

Jani studied Feyó's image for any sign of tension. The transmission was taking place in real-time, with minimal smoothing of any delays. Was it an instrument hiccup that made for the tightening around the Haárin female's mouth, the furrow between her eyes? Or had the worry that she'd so far managed to hide finally broken the surface? "What's wrong with meeting at Elyas Station?"

"The station is most crowded, the humanish docks especially. Transfer to the Haárin side of the station is not always smooth." Feyó waved a hand in a meaningless gesture. "We would have more of a chance to talk. Of ní Tsecha, and the damned cold winter of which he complains."

Chatter like a couple of old, dear friends? Catch up on old times? Jani waited for Feyó to give her some hint, and knew she could sit there all day. *She wants me under her control as quickly as possible.* "I will get the engineer, ná Feyó." She pressed the alarm touchpad and summoned the comtech.

The next half hour passed in a flurry of discussion and data transmission. Feyó called in one of her technical dominants to speak to the Haárin side of the docking equation. Jani wedged into a corner of the booth and watched the universal language of headshakes, mutters, and mathematics, but in the end the conclusion was what she expected. The designs of the ships were too different, and the time too short. A straightforward junction wasn't possible, and a retrofit inside twenty-four hours out of the question.

"Ná Feyó." Jani returned to her seat after the engineer departed. "What is going on?"

Feyó raised her right hand, palm facing out, and rested it against her left cheek. That fallback to a High Sìah expression of confusion told more about her state of mind than any words could. "I know little. I suspect much."

"You believe someone will try to get to me before you do. At Elyas Station, or on the ground in Karistos."

"We have heard rumors. We have learned over the months of the need to listen to such."

"Ní Tsecha believes that your dominance has been challenged. Is your challenger the one who wants to get hold of me?"

Feyó's hand dropped, the sound of her sharp intake of breath gasping through the speaker system. Then the tension left her like a drawn-out sigh. "When we spoke in Chicago, ní Tsecha told me how necessary it became for him to learn to read between humanish lines. He explained to me how such is to be done." Again, the High Sìah gesture of confusion. "It seems, and truly, that he has learned to read between my lines as well, for I told him nothing of any challenge."

Jani waited for Feyó to continue, but the female remained silent, the back of her hand still pressed against her cheek. "It seems to me," she said finally, "that the Elyan Haárin have taken to subterfuge with a vengeance. Unfortunately, you're still not clear as to which side you're supposed to hold back information *from*." She tapped the display with her fingernail until Feyó looked up. "I'm the one who's the focus of untoward interest. You can talk to *me*."

Feyó nodded, then drew in a deep breath. If she'd been humanish, one could say that she was screwing up her courage. "The one who would challenge me wishes to state her case to you in person, to persuade you to intercede for her with ní Tsecha. She believes that with his support, she will face acceptance."

"You are the acknowledged dominant of the Elyan enclave." A twinge of paranoia compelled Jani to check the seal on the combooth door, and make sure no one standing outside could overhear. "You enjoy the support of the Outer Circle Haárin, and the confidence of humanish as well. Anyone who would challenge you would have a difficult time arguing their case. And if they tried to kidnap me, or harm me in any way, they would lose any chance of gaining Tsecha's support."

"This one does not understand such. She is arrogant, and believes that she has only to speak to you to convince you of her position."

"What is her name?" Jani asked. "What is her standing?"

Feyó hesitated. "Her name is Gisa. She is an agronomist, as I am. Her beliefs are most as extreme. She attracts the impatient, those who do not understand how an enclave must function if it is to survive alongside humanish!" Feyó's eyes gleamed with anger. "My security will protect you, ná Kièrshia, of that you have my pledge. Gisa will not find hold of you."

Jani experienced a a sickeningly familiar turn of stomach. *It's like I never left Chicago.* The same undercurrents. The same power struggles.

She thought of the single bright spot, the only thing that offered her any sort of reprieve. "Among the rumors you've learned to listen to, ná Feyó, have you heard anything concerning another hybrid? A young male, to be precise?"

"No, ná Kièrshia." Feyó shook her head. "No rumors of young hybrid males." She looked Jani straight in the eye, her gaze unwavering.

Jani reached the gym entrance just as John and Niall emerged, sweaty and silent. John offered a rueful smile. Niall, on the other hand, eyed her with a wariness he normally reserved for strangers.

"Ná Feyó contacted me. She thinks someone may try to kidnap me at Elyas Station." She tried to maneuver to John's side but found her way blocked by Niall's strategically placed foot.

"Kidnap?" He toweled his face, then stuffed the cloth in his bag. "Why?"

Jani backed off, then wandered a semicircle in the middle of the corridor. *"Kidnap" is so strong a word. Should she have said "accost"? "Delay"?* Besides, all Feyó had to go on was rumor and guesswork, and she didn't possess the experience in handling either to make the most reliable of sources. "It isn't definite. But a rival named Gisa has challenged Feyó for the dominance of the Elyan Haárin. Feyó believes Gisa wishes to convince me of the rightness of her cause. She'll try to talk me into supporting her, and ask me to intercede for her with Tsecha."

"We'll be disembarking on the human side of the station." John set his bag down at his feet. He held a towel, too, but instead of wiping his face, he worked it in his hands, first bundling it, then shaking it flat, then bundling it again. "Any Haárin who tried to infiltrate the dock area would stand out."

"Those docks have enough twists and turns for someone to hide in, assuming they decide to try infiltration rather than assault." Niall's grim expression lightened as he focused on their new problem. The wolf on the scent. "What did Feyó tell you?"

"Pretty much what I told you. She couldn't provide specifics. All she has is a feeling."

"A *feeling*?" Niall still held his racket. He tightened his hold on the grip, working the head up and down as though he shook someone's hand. "What's that worth?"

"I don't know." Lacking a racket or a towel to worry, Jani shoved her hands in her pockets and paced. "All I can say is that I've never seen her this angry."

The three of them pondered, expending varying levels of nervous energy as they did.

Niall finally ended the silence by flicking his racket in a sharp backhand, then stuffing it in his bag. "I can start with station security. Fort Karistos should be able to spare me some bodies." He turned to John. "What about Neoclona, Doctor?"

"Whoever you need." John started down the corridor toward the comdeck. "We can light a fire under them right now."

Niall fell in behind, lagging until Jani caught him up. "Did Feyó give you any other information? Anything at all?"

Jani shook her head. "She's promised me her security. If there's anything else to know, they should know it."

Niall kept his attention fixed on John's back. "This political issue—is this what you didn't want to tell me?" He clenched his hand into a fist and pounded his thigh. *"Damn it, Jani."*

Jani thought of a bright smile and badly filmed eyes, and said nothing.

The comdeck get-together lasted well into the ship-afternoon. John bailed first, after tempers flared and it became obvious that there could only be one Chief of Operations and Niall was it. Jani remained behind to act as Haárin translator, but as it turned out, both Feyó's suborns and the Haárin who worked station security all spoke passable English. Not only that, but they seemed to thrive under Niall's blunt direction, which in turn rendered Jani's fears of diplomatic incident moot. When she finally slipped out the door, no one noticed that she left.

She meant to return to her own cabin, but she didn't feel like being alone, and that meant there was only one other place for her to go. *I've done it often enough this trip.* And never stayed longer than a few minutes. *I respect John's privacy, just like he respects mine.* And all in all, they had both done an excellent job of avoiding anything even approaching a delicate situation.

More fool me. She pushed the thought from her mind as she turned down a short, dead-end corridor, stopped before the lone set of doors, and hit the buzzer.

"Come in," sounded the so-familiar bass.

Jani hesitated. Even in the middle of a brightly lit hallway, John's voice inspired thoughts of the dark. She wiped her hand along her trouser leg, then touched the doorpad. The panel slid aside—she crossed the threshold and walked down a short entry that opened into the white and yellow sitting room. "Every time I come in here, I think the same thing." She took in the woodweave chairs and couches, the brightly patterned cushions, and as usual felt as though she'd walked onto the veranda at a sunny resort. "No Neoclona purple? No Persian carpets? No ebony hardwood?"

"Very funny." John rose from his lounge chair, the latest issue of the Karistos *Partisan* in hand. His hair was still wet from the shower, and he'd changed into a more familiar long-sleeve pullover and trousers in shades of tan. "The colonel still whipsawing my security?" He rolled the newssheet into a tight baton and slapped it against his hand. "I don't know how I managed to stay out of harm's way for the last twenty years without having him around to bark at me."

"John, it's his job. He's good at it."

"I've only been shot at *once* that entire time. Guess who I can thank for that?"

Jani held up her hands and backed away. Then she walked to the wall-spanning display case and pretended interest in an aquarium. She heard nothing for a time, then a slow tread of footsteps from behind that set her heart pounding.

John moved in beside her, a relatively safe arm's length away. "Are you frightened?"

Of what? The unknown danger awaiting at Elyas Station, or the more immediate peril standing beside her now? *Take my pick.* Jani wanted to move closer to John and take his hand in hers. Instead, she leaned close to the aquarium and tapped her finger against the glass. One of the fish, a blue and orange swordfin, floated up toward the sound and shadow, bumping the glass with its nose as it tried to draw near. "According to Feyó, Gisa just wants to talk. It doesn't follow that she'd try to hurt me. She'd squander any chance she had to influence Tsecha." She raised her finger higher.

The fish followed. "I'm concerned about what this challenge could mean. To the Elyan Haárin. To Outer Circle stability."

"I'm afraid my concerns are more immediate." John pulled open one of the case drawers and removed the same S-40 he'd shown her in her Chicago kitchen over a month before. "Do you still have your shooter?"

"Yes. Stowed safely in the bottom of my bag." Jani reached out and took the weapon from his hand. "You planning a shootout in the middle of the VIP dock area?" She checked the powerpack and was relieved to find it disengaged. *Glad to see Doctor Marya your shooting instructor actually taught you something about shooting.* "Speaking of weapons, how did the match go?" she asked as she handed back the S-40.

John took back the weapon and slipped it back in the drawer. "I played him close the first game. Lost it eight-ten. Then it got ugly. He swept me—four straight." He tapped his finger against the glass to draw the swordfin's attention, but it ignored him, intent upon Jani. "Whatever happened between you two, he needed to take it out on somebody. Lucky me."

Jani pressed her face to the glass and looked more deeply into the aquarium. Toward the rear of the tank a miniature shark swam a lazy circuit, occasionally grazing the bottom and kicking up silt. "He knows I'm hiding something from him. He's known since we left Chicago. For now, he thinks I held back information about Feyó, but once he finds out about the suspected hybrid . . ." She rapped the side of the aquarium with her knuckles, sending fish darting in all directions but for the steadfast swordfin. "John, he's my friend."

"I know." John folded his arms and leaned against the case. "You and Niall are halves of the same whole. Moody. Introspective. Hard on others, but even harder on yourselves. A couple of damaged idealists on a never-ending quest to find something to believe in. He thought he found that thing in you. Now you're moving away from him, and he's angry."

The room was too bright for him. Like a moon or a star, darkness defined John Shroud best.

Jani looked up into tired eyes, filmed a pale amber that reminded her of Tsecha's. "You've been thinking about this a lot."

"Val does most of that sort of thinking. I listen and take notes." John smiled, then walked over to a free-standing terrarium and smoothed a hand over a broad green leaf. "I confirmed for the umpteenth time that Eamon DeVries has had no more than a paper relationship with Neoclona-Karistos for the past six months of the Common calendar. His labs are closed. His office is dark."

"Do you believe them?"

"Eamon was never the type to command loyalty. I see no reason for senior staff to lie on his behalf, especially if they know that any illegal action on his part could lead to criminal charges against them all." John walked back to the aquarium and grinned at the swordfin. "Looks like you made a friend."

Jani gave the glass a final tap, sending the fish wriggling in a series of tight circles. "I didn't do anything special. I just tapped the glass and it followed."

"I know how it feels." John sniffed, then turned quickly away. "It was a pleasant trip, overall, considering." He looked back at Jani, his expression expectant but guarded, withholding his reaction until he could gauge her response, then temper his accordingly.

"Too bad it couldn't have been under different circumstances." Jani turned away from him just as he moved toward her. "I wish you'd have given a thought to yourself, though. You're a powerful man, and if you throw that power behind me, my enemies will become yours, and potent enemies they are. You're not untouchable."

"I started you down this path. I swore a long time ago that I'd see you through to the end."

"I don't know where the end is."

John stuffed his hands in his pockets and scuffed his shoe

against the carpet. "Probably a good idea to have some company along the way, then, isn't it?"

"Probably." Jani headed for the door before John could answer. The hallway was colder, darker. She kidded herself that she knew where she was going and why.

CHAPTER 10

"Fort Karistos has sent up a welcoming party to meet us at the dock. There's a major named Hamil, with whom I've dealt in the past, and a colonel named Brondt, whom Hamil says is sound." Niall set down his coffee cup. "After we disembark, we'll take a scoot ride over to the shuttle slips in the next concourse. We'll be watched all along the way—the usual precautions. Hour or so later, we'll be on the ground at the fort." He took a long pull on his nicstick. "We've cut Feyó and crew out of the picture completely," he continued through a stream of smoke. "And with them, the mysterious Gisa."

Jani tore flakes of crust from a roll, then dropped them onto her plate. "Feyó must have been upset when you told her I wouldn't ride down to Karistos with her."

"She must understand that she left you no choice." John hefted a carafe and refilled Jani's coffee cup, followed by his own and finally, grudgingly, Niall's. "She told you that you were at risk, but couldn't define what that risk was. You had to deal with the information as you saw fit."

The three of them sat in the passenger dining room, the remains of their final *Denali* lunch spread about them. Jani took in the stark blondwood tables and slat chairs, the ceiling coated to display blue sky complete with scudding clouds, the panel walls that exhibited a continuously shifting array of terrestrial nature scenes. *Picnic's over*. She sensed Niall's sidelong examination, John's more direct scrutiny. "I need to pull my gear together." She stood, waving both men back in their seats as they made to rise with her. "Meet you at the ramp after the docking klaxon sounds the all-clear." She sensed their surprise at her leave-taking, and hurried out the door before one of them could ask her why the rush.

"Plague of conscience." Jani wove down the narrow, bright corridors for the next-to-last time, marking the turns and exits, the alarms and dead ends as she had for every ship she'd ever traveled on. "Nerves." Fear at what might await at the dock despite Niall's efforts at incident aversion, and what she knew awaited her on the Elyan surface.

She passed one of the crew members, nodded a greeting, fielded the polite, professional response. *John's people, and he's trained them well*. Not once during the voyage had she noted even the slightest glimmer of reaction to her green-on-green eyes, her dietary requirements, her extended forays in the gym or the library as she worked with the practice swords or hunted for some obscure tract on bornsect history. "I wonder if John ordered them to baby me, or if they made that decision on their own?" She turned down the short corridor that led to her cabin, keyed her way in, and passed through the green and copper sitting room into the bedroom.

She got down on her knees and reached beneath the bed, dragged her duffel into the light, and pulled out underwear and socks. Tossed everything atop a chair and boosted to her feet, savoring as she often did the smooth workings of her changed body. "No more aches. No more pains. Only rebel Haárin who want to kidnap me. Lord Ganesh giveth, and Lord Ganesh taketh away. Remove this obstacle from my path, oh Lord, I pray." She opened her closet and removed the sole item hanging within, a cream white wrapshirt and trousers she bought during their layover at Padishah, simple and flowing enough to pass even Vynshàrau muster. She tossed it atop the bed. Then she undressed and adjourned to the bathroom to shower.

The first warning klaxon had sounded by the time she emerged, giving notice that Elyas Station had confirmed the *Denali*'s ID and docking privileges and that approach could commence. She dressed with more than usual care, making sure that she tied the wrapshirt sash neatly and gave her brown boots a brisk wipedown.

"Where's Lucien when I need him?" she muttered as she retied the sash. He'd performed cabin steward duties for her during her first trip to Earth, and embedded a sense of doubt concerning her clothes sense that had stayed with her ever since. "No makeup," she added as she dug once more through her duffel. The Haárin didn't paint their faces, and the gold undertones in her brown skin tended to overwhelm any other color she added.

She pulled a small net bag from a side pocket and removed the single object it contained. "Time to show you to company," she said as she held the ring up to the light. The gold band glittered, the clear red stone darkened to burgundy by the chemical illumination. "My ring of office." A long-ago gift from Tsecha that she had only been able to wear in the last year, fashioned as it was not for the human she had been, but for the hybrid she'd become. She slipped it on the third finger of her right hand, then reached back in the bag for her outfit's finishing touch.

"You are going to piss off some folk, I think," she said as she shook out the off-white overrobe. One of Tsecha's long-discarded robes of office, its rough cloth pulled as she drew it on, bunching the sleeves of her wrapshirt and dragging across her shoulders.

It was most as difficult to wear, nìa, and truly. When Sà-nalàn helped me don it, she was forced to yank it as though she dressed a squirming youngish.

"That's because you are a squirming youngish, inshah," Jani said with a smile. She shot the red-slashed cuffs, then regarded herself in the full-length mirror set into the opposite wall.

She didn't recognize herself at first. The pale color of the clothing threw her black hair and dark skin into sharp relief, making her face and hands seem like holes in the air.

Then, slowly, she slipped into focus, this half-woman she had become, clothed in the vestments of an alien religion she had yet to claim as her own. Her jaw and chin, too long for humanish, too narrow and rounded for an adult Vynshàrau. Taller than most humanish females, yet shorter than most Vynshàrau by half a head or more. In-between neck. In-between eyes. Not quite idomeni, yet no longer human enough.

You believe in order, nìa. Therefore you are of Shiou whether you honor her or not. One of Tsecha's lessons wended through her head. *You are my toxin, my Kièrshia, bringer of pain and change. Therefore you are also of Caith, whether you honor her or not as well. When you act for me, you are of me, as much as though I myself attended.*

Jani studied herself for a moment, then turned back to the chair and hefted her duffel. Looked around the bedroom for the last time, a delicate place in bronze and shades of blue that despite its richness still felt as transitory as every billet she'd ever traded her documents services or language skills for. In the background, the final docking klaxons sounded, first softly, then louder and more strident as the *Denali* drew into its slip and ended its five and a half week journey with a single, barely detectable shudder.

She set the duffel back on the bed, dug into the scanproof pocket, and removed her shooter. She held it up to the light as she had her ring, and examined the casing. Scuffed blue, the metal nicked and gouged. "And now I am of Jani Kilian as well." She drove the powerpack into the grip with the heel of her hand, felt the weapon purr to life. "This I know, and truly." She slipped the shooter into her trouser pocket, shouldered her duffel, and left.

John and Niall waited for her in the ramp enclosure. They had returned to their usual formality, John in a daysuit of light blue, Niall in dress blue-greys. They both started when they saw her walk toward them, their gazes riveted as though they'd never seen her before. John smiled eventually. Niall didn't.

Jani rounded her shoulders as she drew near, and slipped into a croaky, crabbed mutter. "When shall we three meet again, in thunder, lightning, or in rain?"

John's eyes widened. Then he threw back his head, his dark laugh filling the enclosed space.

Niall's reaction proved more subdued, the corner of his mouth turning up slightly as he cleared his throat. "When the hurly-burly's done, when the battle's lost and won." He finally grinned, then shook his head. "Figures you'd read that one."

"The Scottish play—yes, I liked it." Jani slipped in between the two men. "Dathim read it, too. But then, he's drawn to anything with knives in it." She heard a thump from the other side of the door as the first set of seals opened, and her breath caught.

John squared his shoulders. "I buy the first round after we touch down at Fort Karistos."

Niall faced the door and nodded once. "You're on."

Elyas Station's singular decor had been counted among the legends of spaceport architecture from the day rumors of the plans first reached beyond the Outer Circle. The designer, for reasons no one ever fathomed, had ignored the eastern Mediterranean culture that flavored the Elyan colony, instead choosing to indulge her personal fascination with things Gothic, as in stained glass, stone vaults, and the odd gargoyle or two.

"Damned place always reminded me of my worst hangover." Niall led Jani and John into the arched and transepted Service concourse, the clash of voices and background music battering them like artillery. "If I'd been the Elyans, I'd have blown the damned thing to bits before it opened."

"Well, they always did have an odd sense of humor, as I recall." John turned to Jani. "I was last here five years ago, when we opened the Karistos facility. They had dubbed this place 'Our Lady of the White Elephant.' I've forgotten the Elyan Greek translation."

"Should've been 'Our Lady of the Hangover,' " Niall grumbled as he eyed the gargoyle that glared down from atop a nearby shop awning.

"Colonel Pierce, sir. A pleasure to see you again." A mainline major in summerweights broke away from the edge of the concourse bustle and started toward them, followed by a sideline colonel in similar kit. "Major Hamil, Diplomatic Annex." He smiled at Jani, then stepped back to allow the colonel to come to the fore. "This is Colonel Brondt, Office of the Station Liaison."

Niall nodded to Hamil and shook hands with Brondt. "I thought you'd have met us right at the gate, Colonel, considering the gravity of the situation."

"You haven't been out of sight since you disembarked, Colonel." Brondt had the relaxed air of a man who handled at least one major crisis per station-week. He was the same height as Niall, with the stocky build and broad-boned face that betrayed the Hortensian German origins his schooled accent managed to hide, and an indoor pallor that spoke to a career spent in stations like this. "Your shuttle is a five-minute walk down the first starboard transept." He shook John's hand, then turned to Jani. "Ná Kièrshia. *A tún a vrest dinau.*" He tilted his head to the left and brought up his curved left hand, palm up, in a single easy motion, a sound gesture of respect.

"A glorious afternoon to you as well, Colonel." Jani's gesture mirrored his, even though she stuck to English. "My compliments on your Sìah Haárin."

"You learn fast on this job, ná Kièrshia, or you don't have

it for long." Brondt stood back and gestured for them all to walk ahead of him. "Now, let's get you out of here."

Niall and John walked ahead, followed by Hamil, who seemed adept at stepping aside and staying out of the way. Jani fell in behind, soaking in the Station ambience for the first time in years. *Ah, the insanity.* She passed a carving of a long-unseated Prime Minister done up with the doun face and robes of a medieval saint, and put her hand over her mouth to hide her smile. No telling the political leanings of her Service hosts, and she didn't want to risk ticking off the very folks charged with seeing her safely out of the station.

"How was your trip?"

Jani glanced to the side to find Brondt walking beside her. "Not bad. Pretty uneventful, really. I worked. Studied. Caught up on my sleep. The usual long-haul pastimes."

"So you're ready to just dive in here and get to the matter at hand?" Brondt's face brightened, the emotion casting an unnatural sheen over his skin. "Whatever that happens to be," he added, the flush rising. "None of my business, of course."

You're absolutely right about that, Colonel. Jani quickened her step as the distance between her and John and Niall grew. "Yes. The matter at hand." Either several troop transports had disgorged at once or all the shops held sales at the same time—Spacers clogged the concourse, veering in front of them, cutting around them, their shouts and laughter bouncing off the hard, nonabsorbing station surfaces.

Jani pressed her hands to her temples to ease the throbbing in her head.

"You could have brought us in to a less busy area of the station, Colonel!" Niall shouted over his shoulder.

"I'm a great believer in hiding in plain sight, Colonel." Brondt smiled at Jani, his manner as unperturbed as if the concourse had been deserted. "Alone's not the same as hidden." He quickened his step so he walked slightly ahead of Jani, bumping her shoulder just as she was about to pass a pair of giggling SFCs and veering her off course.

"Colonel, I was trying to—" Jani turned to Brondt as they

passed beneath a round of stained glass—the gold and pink lighting shone on his face, coloring his skin and defining his features. His forehead, so broad and high. His jaw, a shade too full and long for his round face. His eyes, a brown so dark as to be black. Flat. Dead. As blank as those of the young male in the image. As empty as her own eyes had been when she used to film them, when their green-on-green had become so dark that only the most opaque covering would do. When their hybrid nature—

Hybrid—

Hybrid—

Brondt met her gaze, and she knew. He sensed her surmise—his expression brightened for the barest instant, making him look quite young.

Then Jani heard sounds of argument, and looked ahead to find Niall barking at Hamil and pointing at her, John craning to sight her in the crowd. Felt a hand on her arm, and looked down to find Brondt's fingers closed around her wrist.

"There are currently three shooters trained on them." He spoke Sìah Haárin, stripped of gesture and barely audible above the noise. "If you try to get away, we will force the situation. But I don't want that to happen. Please." He shook his head. "The ones helping me—they're rather excitable. They don't understand half measures, and we were told to do whatever was necessary to bring you in." He pointed down a narrow chase that ran between two storefronts. "This way."

Jani rebalanced her weight so he couldn't pull her forward. "Call off your dogs and I'll go with you."

"Not until we have you secured."

"Call them off."

"*I. Can't.*" Brondt pulled her toward the chase. "Your friends are trying to force their way back here—we have five seconds, probably less—please, Kièrshia, *now!*"

Jani looked ahead. Saw Niall shoulder Hamil aside and push back through the crowd toward her. Saw John reach into his pocket, where he'd no doubt stashed his S-40. *No,*

John—they'll think you know what you're doing! "I'm going. I'm going."

"Hurry." Brondt pulled her after him through the gap.

Jani felt her head clear as the noise damped to nothing, the only sounds her boots and Brondt's tietops striking the bare flooring. She tried to loosen his hold on her wrist, but he just gripped tighter, glancing back at her as though he sensed her trying to make her move. "I'll remember this."

"We—" Brondt lifted his free hand in pleading. "We have our reasons."

"You don't have any that are good enough." Jani tried to drag back as sounds reached her from behind. Shouts. Running.

Then Brondt pushed against what looked like bare wall. A panel slid open, and he yanked Jani after him into the dark. "Cooperation is the best move now, really." He let her momentum carry her ahead of him, stripping her duffel from her shoulder and tossing it aside, grabbing her free wrist from behind so he trapped them both. Then he moved in close, shoving one of his feet between hers and kicking them wider apart so she couldn't gain the leverage to kick back or pull forward. Then he raised her hand to her own mouth and clapped it over so she couldn't cry out, and held her for the few vital seconds it took for the footsteps pounding down the chase to reach the panel then pass it by.

Jani took in the tight, dusty space lined with array boxes and exposed conduit, inset safety lighting barely sufficient to cut through the gloom.

"The woman who designed this place, bless her, loved her cubbyholes. The shopkeepers here lost merchandise like water until we mapped them all out." Brondt pulled Jani's hand from her mouth. "I'm going to step back and release you. Now."

As soon as Jani felt Brondt's grip loosen, she turned, swinging out her arm and kicking her leg out and around. Unfortunately, she struck empty air—Brondt had leaped clear and stood against the far wall, breathing heavily.

"Your reputation precedes you, Kièrshia. I will admit to feeling concern when ná Gisa told me that I needed to subdue you by myself." He ran a hand over his rumpled shirtfront, then pushed away from the wall. "Now, if you would follow me, please."

Jani freed her shooter from her pocket. "One thing you can say for Service docks—they never scan for weapons because most everyone is armed." She aimed at Brondt and sighted down. "We're going back out to the concourse. Unfasten the top two closures of your shirt and turn around, arms at your sides."

"Ná Kièrshia, *please*." Brondt sighed heavily, then did as she asked. "You don't understand the situation."

"In my experience, no one who took me hostage ever had my best interests at heart. That's the only aspect of the situation I've ever needed to understand." Jani edged close enough to Brondt to grab his shirt by the collar and yank down, dragging it around his elbows and effectively pinning his arms to his sides. "You walk out ahead of me," she said as she patted him down. "Try to strike me, I'll shoot you. Try to run, I'll shoot you."

"I'm not armed," Brondt said.

"You should've been. Kidnapping isn't a gentleman's game." Jani backed off and waved him ahead of her. "We'll wait in the concourse for John and Niall. Then we'll return to your office and have a nice long talk."

"Aren't you even going to ask?" Brondt moved toward the panel while trying to look at her over his shoulder. "I must be the first hybrid you've ever met. I must be. Don't you care?"

"No, she doesn't, boyo," a familiar voice rasped through the murk. "She's too busy thinking about how best to drop you if you try to run." A wet chuckle sounded. "I know where Johnny and the colonel are. They're still under our guns, so to speak. Drop your weapon."

"Doctor DeVries." Jani let her shooter hand fall. "It hasn't been long enough."

"Tell me, Kilian, tell me." Footsteps crunched. A figure

cut through the dimness, as short and stocky as Brondt, but bent, with the plod of the terminally desk-bound. "With rings on her fingers and blood on her clothes, she shall sow chaos wherever she goes." Eamon DeVries moved beneath one of the inset lights, which cast a sickly green light across a slack face, a wattled neck. "I take it back. No blood. Only because I got here in time." He raised a shooter, a sister to John's S-40. "As you can see, I'm no gentleman. But we've both always known that, haven't we? Brondt, you damned fool, button yourself up and take her shooter." He jerked his head toward the rear of the space. "There's an opening back there that leads to the shuttle docks. Let's go."

CHAPTER 11

The rear opening of the cubbyhole led to a series of short corridors, the drift in design of doors, the rise in temperature, and the language on identity plates indicating the transition to the Haárin wing of the station. Humanish seldom did business there in person—both Brondt in his Service uniform and Eamon in his Elyan-style overshirt and loose trousers drew attention from the passengers and crew members who walked the concourse. Jani, however, managed to trump them both by virtue of her propitiator's overrobe. The clash between the traditional bornsect garb and her distinctly humanish hairstyle attracted puzzled postures, and more.

"We're being followed." Eamon glanced over his shoulder at the scattered groups that shadowed them. "You should have stripped that damned shirt off her first thing, boyo."

"I couldn't do that," Brondt muttered under his breath. "She's ní Tsecha's suborn. She's Kièrshia."

"She's a gutter-bred git named Jani Moragh Kilian, and she'd have shot you without a second thought." Eamon glared at her sidelong. "You knew this would happen, didn't you?"

"Didn't occur to me, no. Just a happy accident." Jani made a show of sniffing the air. "That's one thing you always notice on the Haárin side of a station—no food odors. Scents as fresh as recycled air can be."

"Belt it." Eamon steered her down a half-lit walkway. "Thank bloody God," he said as they approached a shuttle boarding ramp.

"You're sure it's the right one?" Jani looked around in mock anxiety. "You're sure you didn't pick the wrong ramp in a panic?"

Eamon grabbed her arm above the elbow and yanked her to a stop, then shoved his shooter in her face. *"I should just shoot you now!"*

Jani looked down at him over the barrel—she stood a full head taller, and could tell from the way his glare flickered that it bothered him. "John would kill you," she said softly, "and I would save you a seat in hell."

Eamon's eyes narrowed at the mention of John, his finger twitching above the shooter charge-through.

"We have to go." Brondt pushed Jani aside until he stood in the shooter's path. *"Now,* Doctor. This is not the place." He stared Eamon down until the man turned away with a huff. Then he prodded them both down the ramp toward the shuttle entry as a crowd of curious Haárin watched from the concourse.

The shuttle appeared half filled by the time they entered the main cabin. "They saved you the throne of honor in the back of the craft." Eamon pointed to an empty seat in the middle of the rearmost row, located at the end of the aisle. "Go there and sit tight and shut up."

Jani headed down the aisle toward her seat, mindful of the rapt gazes that followed her. She tried to study them without seeming to, curiosity warring with anger at her predicament. *One . . . ten . . . seventeen . . .* Seventeen faces, hybrid all, yet . . . *Some of them look humanish. Some look Haárin. And some . . . I can't tell.* Humanish who looked much as Haárin, who wore flowing trousers and overrobes and had arranged their hair in braided fringes and napeknots. Haárin who wore trousers and tunics, shirts with neckpieces, long skirts and wrapdresses, their hair worn long and loose or trimmed close to their heads. *Dathim would howl.* His sheared head, which he thought so daring, wouldn't have earned him a guest pass into this club.

She reached her seat and lowered into it, gripping the arms for support as her knees went wobbly. As one, the hybrids turned back to watch her, their expressions ranging from expectant to eager to, in a few cases, fearful. One of those belonged to the helpful Major Hamil, who sat by a window and seemed intent on ducking behind his seatback whenever Jani looked in his direction.

"Let's get going!" Eamon called out from his seat in the middle of the cabin. "Half the Haárin in the station saw us. Someone must have reported us by now."

"We can't." Brondt paced the aisle and checked his timepiece. "Torin's not—"

A commotion in the front of the shuttle claimed everyone's attention. At first Jani thought that John and Niall had tracked her down, but the disturbance turned out to be a late arrival, a young hybrid who shot through the cabin door as though someone tossed him. He careened off the wall opposite the opening, then staggered down the aisle as he tried to regain his balance.

"Sorry! Sorry!" He righted himself, all elbows and long legs, and leaned against Brondt for support. "The stationmaster just closed down the connections between the humanish and Haárin sections. If we don't break away in the next five minutes, we'll get caught in a sweep. They've already called out—" His eyes met Jani's and he fell silent.

The face from the image, the hair a little lighter than she recalled, the skin a little darker. *It's summertime in Karistos.* She tried to calibrate her knowledge of the place's seasons against the Commonwealth calendar. *Late summer, edging into autumn.* He must have spent a great deal of time outside. *Torin.*

"They've already called out station security." Torin started toward the rear of the cabin again, his step slower and steadier, eyes still on Jani. "The Haárin are always slow to respond to any alarms from the humanish side. If we're in the breakaway queue, they should let us leave."

"We'll be in the queue as soon as you sit yourself down and strap in." Eamon reached out and pushed Torin toward an empty aisle seat. "Now get to it!"

Jani saw Torin make a sour face at Brondt as he fell into the seat and secured himself, saw Brondt clench his fist close to his body, out of sight of Eamon, and pump it once in encouragement. *The two of them are allies—they sent Torin's image to John.* She adjusted her own safety straps as she pondered what she sensed so far. *Torin and Brondt don't like Eamon, and I'm guessing Eamon doesn't like them either. This would mean that Eamon doesn't know about the image. Assuming he's working closely with Gisa, that means she doesn't know, either.* The cabin lights fluttered, and she felt the telltale vibration of the shuttle engines rattle up through the bottom of her seat. *Threats, kidnappings, hurried exits, and dissension in the ranks.* She sat back. "Chicago, it's as if I never left you."

"Did you say something, ná Kièrshia?"

Jani looked up to find Brondt standing over her, her duffel in his hand. "I prayed, Colonel. Spacecraft make me nervous."

"I can't see much of anything making you nervous." Brondt lowered Jani's bag to the floor at her feet, then bent low to grapple it to the seat support. "I've returned everything but your shooter," he said as he straightened back up.

"Trusting of you." Jani drew in her legs so he could maneuver into the open seat in the row in front of her.

"Personally, I think I could have returned it to you. If you were going to try something, you'd have done so by now. Your history is one of a woman who doesn't hesitate." Brondt sat down and strapped in just as the shuttle accelerated, pushing them both back against their seatbacks. "You're angry, yes, but I also think that you're as struck by us as we are by you. If I'd released you at any time during our gauntlet run here, I'd have bet a year's paychit you wouldn't have made a move to flee. And I'd have won."

"You're sure about that?" Jani stared at the back of Brondt's head, but he didn't turn around or respond, and deep down she knew it was just as well.

Jani eased out of her seat and scooted down to the observation port at the end of her empty row as soon as the shuttle had punched through the Elyan stratosphere. She knew the other hybrids watched her and that they would probably report her interest to Gisa. *I just want to see where I'm going*, she told herself, and almost believed it.

"Have you been to Elyas before, ná Kièrshia?"

Jani turned from the port to find Torin at her elbow. Like Brondt, he'd settled upon a humanish look, filming his eyes the same dead green he wore in the image and dressing in trousers and a short-sleeve pullover in shades of brown. Up close, the gold tone of his skin was more easily defined, the slight elongation of his facial bones more readily discerned. He had a mobile, expressive face and restless hands, the corners of his mouth twitching as he plucked at the seatback in front of him.

"Only the station. Not the surface." Jani looked out the port again as the shuttle banked over a midnight-blue sea, then coursed along a line of steep cliffs.

"The largest settlements are built around the Bay of Siros." Torin pushed an empty seat forward and wedged into the row beside her. "Karistos is on the opposite side. So's the fort. We're on this side."

"The hybrid enclave." Jani repeated the phrase to herself once, then again, wondering at its sound, its meaning. Reminded herself that she had come here for a purpose, and that she was being held against her will. That John and Niall searched for her. That she was a hostage among captors, one of whom would cheerfully shoot her if she gave him any reason at all.

"We've called it Thalassa," Torin said, his eyes fixed on the view outside the port. "We're coming up on it . . . *now*."

The shuttle rounded a cliff bend, and Thalassa appeared. Narrow streets crawled along the cliff edges and partway down the slopes, lined with boxy white and cream structures, single and multistoried, some topped with colored domes of pale blue or yellow, others with flat roofs patched with small gardens. In the center of it all loomed a larger building, four stories of white and cream stone, edges rounded and polished, which seemed to emerge from the layered rock like the nose of a star liner that had crashed into the far side of the mountain and tunneled through to rest near the cliff's edge.

"That's the main house." Brondt had worked his way into the gap behind Torin. "Doctor DeVries lives there, and our dominants. Our meeting rooms are there, and the library, and the clinic." He glanced at Jani, gauging her reaction. "It's quite a settlement."

Paid for with Neoclona money, in direct violation of a Neoclona contract. Jani felt a tingle between her shoulder blades, and turned to find Eamon staring at the three of them. *As soon as John reaches Fort Karistos, he's going to track you down.* She turned back to the port. *And when he sees all this . . .*

"We have to strap in," Brondt said. "We'll be landing soon."

After another bank and turn, the shuttle touched down on a well-maintained runway about 250 meters from the settlement. Everyone stood as the door opened and the exit ramp lowered, except for Brondt, who remained in his seat in front of Jani.

"You'll leave last, of course." He held back as the others streamed out, row after row. "What do you think so far?"

"I think I've seen performances at the Lyric Opera that

were less rehearsed." Jani reached down to unstrap her duffel so she wouldn't have to witness the way the color flooded Brondt's face. "I'm not here by choice, but by threat. I'm your prisoner. I'd advise you to not forget that fact, Colonel, because I certainly won't."

"I understand your anger." Brondt smoothed a hand over the arm of his seat, a back and forth action that seemed to calm him. "All we ask is that you watch, and listen, and keep an open mind."

Jani rose. "You're asking a lot."

"I don't think so." He offered a half-smile, then rose and started down the aisle.

Jani waited until he had gone halfway down the aisle before she shouldered her bag and followed. When she reached the ramp, she stood at the top of the stair for a time and let the Elyan sun beat through her clothes and pummel her bones, and watched the other hybrids hurry up the path. Some were met by those who had stayed behind, while some remained alone. Torin, she noticed, hooked up with an older female and another young male and disappeared down one of the winding lanes that led to the smaller houses.

What sort of place is this? Jani stepped down the ramp stair, mindful of the salt-scented breeze that whipped her trouser cuffs around her ankles and floated her overrobe behind her like a cape. *Thalassa was a goddess, a personification of the sea.* She raked through the scant remains of her classical education for anything else concerning sea deities or legends. *I remember lots of monsters, and drownings.* Her boots crunched on the runway. *Ships dashed upon the rocks.* From her vantage point she could see only the top of a few of the domes, the main house jutting above it all like the prow of an ancient watercraft.

It was a stark, desolate landscape. What trees there were grew gnarled and stunted, with silvery-green leaves and thorns as long and thick as fingers. A scattering of knee-high tufts of reddish grass formed the only ground cover; Jani caught sight of tiny rodents darting from beneath them to the more reliable shelter of the rocks as she walked up the path that led to the settlement.

Brondt waited for her at the point where the path graded up toward the house. He had appointed himself her escort—that much was obvious—but whether he did so in his name or Gisa's had yet to be determined. "We had some rain last night," he said, holding up his hand as though waiting for more drops to strike. "That floods the smaller animals out of their holes. Insects come out at dusk that burrow under your skin to lay their eggs. If you have any cuts or sores, better bandage them. You saw some of the rodents. They like to get into the closets and build nests in your shoes—the scent repellents don't seem to work. And you'll hear howling. Those are the feral dogs. Walking alone in the dark isn't advised—the sound fences don't seem to work very well to keep them away. No one's ever been attacked, but a pair of them did follow Torin right up to the entry of the main house once." He'd switched out his tietops for hiking boots on the shuttle, and handled the rocky path as easily as if he walked on pavement. "That remark you made about the opera, and performances." He sighed. "You have a reputation for seeing things as they are. All I'm asking is that you reserve judgment until you see the rest of the play."

"That's the second time you've mentioned my background." Jani quickened her pace to catch Brondt up, only to have him hurry that much faster, to stay one respectful stride ahead of her. "My reputation. My history. My past is not the issue here."

"Your past dictates our present. Our future." Brondt looked back at her. "Don't you understand? You were the *first*." Before he could say more, the front door of the house opened. Two figures stepped out into the shaded entry, but only one of them continued into the sun. A female in her middle years, dressed in humanish-style trousers and a short-sleeve shirt in the same yellow and blue as the domed roofs.

"Glories of the day to you, Kièrshiarauta!" she called in

lightly accented English. She wore her brown hair in a braid that draped over one shoulder, and a series of gold hoops along the edge of one ear. "It is a great and godly thing that you are here. All of Thalassa rejoices, and I, Gisa Pilon, rejoice the most!"

As Jani drew closer, more details of the female's appearance came into focus—her forearms, which bore the scars of multiple challenges, and her Sìah grey eyes, which contained a coolness missing from her voice and her manner. "Ná Gisa." Jani raised her right hand in a simple humanish greeting, a gesture calculated to reveal nothing of her dismay.

Feyó looked me in the face and denied knowing anything about Torin. But how could she acknowledge Gisa as her rival without knowing about Thalassa, and who lived here? *She couldn't.* That meant she lied, as blatantly as any humanish. *But why? What the hell have I walked into?* She blanked her expression as best she could. The time had come to count the cards and play them close to the vest. "Godliness, I most fear, had very little to do with my attendance here."

Gisa's step hitched as she walked down the path. She glanced at Brondt, then quickly away. "All that is fated is godly," she said after a moment, "and your presence here was foretold by ní Tsecha himself."

"Ní Tsecha. Yes." Jani brushed past Gisa and continued up the path. "We must soon speak of ní Tsecha, and truly," she added as she passed into the shadowed entryway.

"Glories of the day to you, ná Kièrshia," Gisa's companion called out in English, sibilant and monotonal.

"Glories of the day—to you." Jani stopped, and hoped the darkness hid her expression.

Gisa's companion was apparently female, judging from the higher pitch of its voice and the narrowness of its shoulders beneath its thin green coverall. "Indeed was your presence foretold, and we have waited for so long." A figure from a dark place, skin a mottle of pale yellow patched with tan and brown, eyes milky blue like dirty snow, dull brown hair close-cropped, the discolored scalp visible beneath.

Jani nodded once in acknowledgment, and hoped that the shock she felt didn't show. She had spent years subsisting in the less traveled reaches of the Commonwealth, and knew that medical conditions that would never have existed in the Jewelers Loop or the Channel Worlds sometimes cropped up in such places. But this female appeared more Haárin than humanish, and even the most radical outcasts kept their illnesses private, for they believed such exposed weakness threatened the welfare of the soul. "What is your name?"

The female bared her teeth, red-brown as the darkest patches of her skin. "I am Bon." She took a step back, then beckoned in humanish invitation with a bandage-swaddled hand. "You must enter, ná Kièrshia, and see the place we have prepared for you!" She keyed the door open and stepped inside the house, waving for Brondt and Gisa to enter before Jani, in keeping with protocol.

Jani waited for the pair to precede her, then stepped inside. She sensed that she was being watched, but she couldn't tell by whom, or where they had hidden themselves.

What she finally saw comforted the eye with its simplicity. The bottom floor of the house formed a graceful U-shaped flow of half-open rooms separated by waist-high barriers and flower-filled planters. In the center was a partially roofed courtyard decorated with fountains and fruit trees, walled at the open end of the U by the mountain and around the curve by walkways that trimmed the three upper floors. The pale earth tones of the stone predominated, accented by the jewel colors of the foliage. Only in Rauta Sheràa had Jani seen houses so well-met with their surroundings.

"Stunned unto silence, she is. A miracle." Eamon walked out of the gloom to join them, a frosted glass in hand. "The last time I saw you this quiet, Johnny and I had just pulled you out of the regen tank. Had to siphon out your mouth with a hose. I told Johnny that was a mistake." He raised his drink in a toast, then tossed it back as though he stood at a Karistos bar, not in the presence of two Haárin.

Jani checked Gisa and Bon for their reactions, and found

them regarding her calmly. *They planned this. It's all part of the show*. She looked around, and found that she was indeed being watched—heads poked up over the backs of chairs and around the ends of couches, and took note of her every move.

"You hide your surprise well, ná Kièrshia." Gisa looked toward the assembled hybrids, a glow of pride informing her sharp features with a lightness seldom seen on an idomeni face. "Whatever you believe, ní Tsecha would be most as pleased. This is his blended world. This is what he prophesied so long ago. It is the future as we all know it shall be. Why then must we continue to suborn ourselves to old ways, and those who promote them?"

Jani looked toward the representatives of the blended world, and felt a roomload of bright-eyed expectancy enclose her like a noose. "By 'old ways,' you mean ná Feyó. You would challenge her for dominance of the Elyan Haárin."

"Such is my right, as dominant of the Thalassans."

"Is this place recognized by the Outer Circle Haárin as an enclave? Have members of the Trade Association visited to pay their respects?"

"Such is only a matter of time."

"When that time comes, if it comes, will be the moment to offer challenge, not before." Jani kept her voice low, speaking rapid, ungestured English she hoped most of the hybrids couldn't understand. "You will have to do better than that if you wish to dominate Haárin, and you will have to do better than that if you wish ní Tsecha's support."

Gisa offered an arrogant smile. "That, ná Kièrshia, is why you are here."

"I think I'll take a walk outside." Jani brushed back her overrobe and shoved her hands in her trouser pockets to stop their shaking. "By myself, if I'm allowed."

"But ná Kièrshia," Bon called after her. "We wish to show—"

"A walk. Alone." Jani's boot heels struck the bare tile, the sharp clip echoing throughout the space. The door opened as she approached, and she shouldered through before it opened completely, the whine of the mechanism following her like a siren wail.

CHAPTER 12

Jani walked around to the bay side of the house, veering off the path and through the red-green scrub toward the cliff. The sun pressed down like a physical force, while the breeze brought with it the smell of the sea, but little coolness.

"John, did you get away? Niall?" She toed the cliff edge, kicking a stone over the side and watching it plummet to the waves below. "Are you still at the station? At Fort Karistos? Did you contact ná Feyó?" She squinted out over the water and watched white seabirds with black-tipped wings swoop and drift, answering her questions with screeches. Then she scanned past them toward the cliffs on the opposite side of the bay, straining to catch sight of Karistos, or the fort, searching the skies for the telltale glint of a shuttle coming in for a landing.

"They're trying to sandbag me. Everywhere I turn, I see eyes like mine. Faces. They want me to feel at home, to forget that they brought me here by force, that they threatened my friends." The noise of the seabirds faded into the background as her thoughts turned inward and her perceptions narrowed. Now she saw a rodent skitter across the rocks, heard the rustling hum of insects emerge from the dried grass. Sensed movement behind her even though she couldn't see it, and reached into her duffel for the shooter that wasn't there.

"We mean you no harm, ná Kièrshia."

Jani turned to find Brondt standing behind her, off to one side. He still wore summerweights, but had removed his eye-films—his irises proved a strange yellow-green that reminded Jani of a cat. *And he moves like one, for all his heft. Now you see him, now you don't.* "Colonel." She nodded. "You'll have to forgive me. Imprisonment makes me jumpy."

Brondt stepped forward as far as he could, so he stood a half a pace or so in front of her. While the position may have been more respectful, it was also dangerous—the tips of his boots extended beyond the cliff edge, and pebbles tumbled and bounced down the steep incline each time he shifted his weight. "You're not imprisoned, ná Kièrshia."

"I'm not?" Jani let her arms hang at her sides, swung them forward so her hands met with a soft clap, then back again. "You mean that if I happened upon one of the enclave skimmers and made to drive out of here, you'd let me go?"

"Yes."

Jani fanned her face with her hand. For the first time since the Chicago summer, she felt sweat trickle down her back. She let her duffel slip to the ground, removed her overrobe, and tied the thin garment around her waist. "You sent Torin's image to John Shroud. Why?"

Brondt stared out over the bay. "I don't know what you're talking about."

Still human enough to lie. Jani picked up her duffel and slung it across her back, a position that left her arms free and allowed her to reach the strap disconnect if she needed to drop the bag in a hurry. "Neither you nor Torin like Eamon DeVries—that's obvious. Do you feel his medical skills have proven inadequate to the task of caring for the hybrids? Do you think he needs help? Don't tell me that he wanted John to come out here—he'll lose his place as Neoclona's third leg when John confirms that he's been engaging in research his contract bars him from performing." She stepped back from the edge, picked up a stone, and flung it into the bay. "Eamon seems fairly well allied with Gisa. Does your disaffection with him extend to her as well?"

Brondt stared back at her, eyes wide, sclera glinting yellow in the bright sun. "Disaffection is too strong a word," he said softly. "Concern, perhaps. Uneasiness."

"Gisa has brought the Outer Circle to the edge of disorder."

"Perhaps she had help."

Jani walked the cliff edge. Then she started down a narrow path that widened as it angled toward a row of houses that had been built on a road cut into the cliff face. "Tell me about Thalassa, Colonel Brondt."

Brondt hesitated, then started after her. "My name's Dieter," he said as he edged past Jani on the path and reasserted his suborn position in front of her. "We've lived here for six months of the Common calendar. Construction is still going on, but we've all the primary structures in, courtesy of Doctor DeVries. Houses. Storage. Community buildings, garages and such." He led her past the first of the houses, a two-floor white structure with rounded corners, its windows shuttered with yellow slating. Like the other houses on the cliff side of the street, it had been built flush against the cliff face, so that the rock served as one of its walls. The houses on the bay side, however, were freestanding, the sun lighting them into brilliant boxes of coated stone.

"Six months?" Jani followed Brondt down the street. "Is that how long you've been hybrids?"

"No—some of us have been receiving treatment for quite some time." Brondt glanced back at Jani and smiled. "You should see the look on your face. So surprised. You've been one of many for several years now."

Jani heard the sounds of opening doors—before long, a small crowd of hybrids lined both sides of the street. Some waved at her, while others bared their teeth. She recognized a few from the shuttle, but other faces were new. The youngest were teenage like Torin, with spindle limbs and faces that brought back memories of the bazaars of Rauta Shèràa, when the sharp scent of *vrel* blossom permeated the air and the rise and fall of a score of idomeni tongues had filled her ears. "Why did you do it?"

"Some of us had no choice." Brondt stopped to pick a dead leaf from a potted shrub set in front of one of the houses. "You've heard the hypothesis that there are environmentally induced diseases that can only be cured by hybridization?" He waited for Jani to nod. "We had a few here. Bone and metabolic disorders. Horrible to suffer, to see. Neoclona Karistos could do nothing. Then Doctor DeVries let it be known that other things could be done." His face lit. "What an incredible experience to bear witness to the healing. Within weeks, in some cases, after the treatments began."

Jani wandered farther down the street. Past the last of the houses a building that was little more than a door was set into the cliff face. "And the rest of you?"

"We believe in change, and the need for a better world." Brondt's quiet, clipped voice infused the words with a sincerity that a more passionate pronouncement would have overshot. "In blending, there is strength."

"You're a Service officer."

"Yes. Hamil and I both."

Jani thought of Niall, tracking Brondt through Fort Karistos systems, closing in. The wolf on the scent. "You're finished."

"We expected to be finished about the time our next physicals rolled around, anyway." Brondt reached up and touched the leaf that studded the corner of one collar tip. "They were good posts while they lasted. We had access to a great deal of intelligence. We knew all about Colonel Pierce's assignment, for example. That allowed us plenty of time to cover tracks and rearrange the furniture." He smiled, this time more coolly. "The man is, in many ways, almost comically obvious in his methods."

Jani felt the blood rise. "He's just as obvious in his temper, his influence, and his dedication."

"And he's your friend." Brondt's smile faded. "Considering the circumstances, I wonder how that can be possible."

Jani paced the street, beating down an idomeni temper that struggled to surge to the surface. "Any significance to the domes?" she asked, because the color drew her fevered eye and she fixed on it for want of anything more calming.

Brondt fell back into his role as tour guide. "In Karistos proper the domes signify places of worship, or the homes of priests or rabbis. Here . . ." He shrugged. "The Haárin picked them, for the most part. They like the color." He pointed to the door in the cliff face. "You should be warned—we do experience some heady storms, as well as the occasional land tremor. Each house has its own emergency gear. We also have stations like this set up throughout the enclave." He led Jani down the incline to the hole in the wall and palmed inside.

The interior lit up as soon as they crossed the threshold, to reveal a single, rock-walled room, the walls lined with carton-stacked shelves. The shelving had been bonded to the floor and ceiling to prevent collapse, with nothing stored above shoulder height.

"This is one of the storm shelters. We have flares, food kettles and water generators, blankets and spare clothing and such." Brondt patted the shelving framework, then walked deeper into the room. "In case of tremor, get off the cliff. Go above to the land around the main house, what we call 'the flat.' We've bolstered the houses with shock-dissipating poly infusions, but I'm an old-fashioned boy in that regard. The land always wins."

As Brondt talked, Jani wandered from shelf to shelf, lifting carton lids and checking the contents. When she came upon the flare pistols, she checked her escort to see if he watched. Then she slipped a pistol into her trouser pocket, adjusting her overrobe so it obscured the bulge. She followed up with a couple of charge cartridges, and set the carton lid back into place just as Brondt rejoined her.

"We should get back to the main house." He walked to the

door, then waited for her to join him. "It's almost time for mid-afternoon sacrament."

"Cocktails at fifteen-up?" Either she'd kept her voice low enough that Brondt had not heard, or he decided that ignoring her was the better course. She stepped back out into the glare of the day, and found the hybrids gathered at the end of the street. Several others had joined them from other parts of the enclave. Those in the back rows had leaped atop planters for a better view, while some looked down from verandas or second-floor windows.

"Tell us of ní Tsecha, ná Kièrshia!"

"When will he come here?"

"Does he know of us? What will you tell him?"

Jani walked across the street to a shoulder-high boulder that had been left in place like a free-form monument to the rugged terrain. She set her hands and clambered to the top, then edged forward until she stood at the very tip. *Don't look down.* She did anyway, and watched the waves crash against the rocks a hundred meters below.

Then she reached beneath the overrobe into her pocket and pulled out the flare pistol, keeping her back to the other hybrids so they couldn't see what she did. She shoved the charge cartridge into its slot, raised the pistol above her head and squeezed it off. One—two—three—

The flares lofted upward, contrailing blue smoke. The charges blew one after the other, splaying streaks of yellow-white that fanned over the bay like fronds of starlight, brilliant even against the daylight sky. Visible from Karistos, surely. Visible from the Fort.

"Ná Kièrshia!" Brondt tried to climb up the rock after her, but cat-quick though he was, he didn't hoist and scramble well.

—four—five. Jani pressed the charge-through again, heard nothing but a hollow click. "Defective cartridge. That's the problem with flare pistols—you can never be sure what the damned thing will do." She reversed the chamber and ejected the clip, then turned to the hybrids, who muttered among themselves and watched her in puzzlement.

"If you wished to notify Doctor Shroud and Colonel Pierce of your presence, ná Kièrshia, you could use one of our comports. It is more direct, and does not smoke and flame."

Jani turned, and saw Gisa standing in the middle of the road, eyeing her in bemusement.

"You are not a prisoner here. There is no reason for you to resort to such actions—you may contact your companions and leave at any time." Gisa cocked her head, her look turning thoughtful. "We all have read of your life." She pointed to Torin, who watched from the upper level of one of the houses. "Torin Clase has drawn together all the records, as is his way and his duty as our historian." She let her hand fall to her side, and took a few steps closer to the rock. "I most understand why you would fear entrapment. Your history is that of one who has been chased. Imprisoned. But much as we despised to do what we did, such was the only way we knew we could talk to you as ourselves. If you had gone with Feyó, she would have never brought you here. You would only have known us through her words, her fears."

Jani felt the tug of Gisa's own words. Her voice. *Feyó dominates by simple authority. This one tries to be your friend.* She wasn't sure which method she distrusted more. "You despised to do such, yet you did it. You threatened my friends."

Gisa shook her head. "We would not have harmed them."

"I was led to believe differently." Jani glanced at Brondt, who declined to meet her eye. "The Elyan enclave is well-established, while Thalassa is a young place. Why should Feyó fear you?"

"*Because we are not of the old ways!*" The shout came from one of the houses, and was soon echoed up and down the street.

Gisa remained quiet until the last murmur died away. "Because we are not of the old ways," she repeated softly, showing an actor's gift for timing. "We treat food in the humanish manner, as is sane. We study all aspects of all our many gods. Yet in order to maintain her place among the conservatives, Feyó would compel us to behave fully as Haárin. To take our meals as solitary once more. To take our rules from her." She drew close enough that Jani could see the hard shine in her eyes. "That is the issue, ná Kièrshia. Are we of ourselves or are we of the Elyan Haárin? Who will represent our wishes in the meeting rooms of the Outer Circle? Feyó, who has never visited this place for fear of contamination by our new ways, or I, who have taken the first steps down the road of ní Tsecha's prediction?"

"Feyó is esteemed by ní Tsecha." Jani stood on the edge of the rock, the flare pistol dangling from her hand. "To humanish and Haárin outside this place, she represents the solidarity of the Outer Circle. If her power is seen to weaken, others will see it as a chance to attack, and Karistos will be as it was only a short time ago. A lawless place, controlled by those who could not give a damn for Haárin, and even less for Thalassa." She tucked the pistol into her waistband and leaped down from the rock. "You must know this if you know anything. Yet you battle Feyó, and Feyó battles you. What neither of you realize is that by your actions, you have put me in the middle. If you know my history as you claim to, you know this is not a sound thing for either of your strategies." She walked past Gisa and the other hybrids, and trudged up the road toward the main house.

After a few moments, she heard footsteps behind her. She picked up her pace, thinking it might be Gisa trying to catch her, but when she heard the muttered curse in Hortensian German, she slowed. "You lied about the threat to my friends, Colonel."

"No, I didn't." Brondt drew alongside her. "Feyó hasn't endeared herself with her heavy-handedness; there were rumors that she had sent her security to wrest you away from Colonel Pierce and escort you back to the Elyan enclave. Some of our more militant denizens took that rumor to heart." His step slowed as his breathing grew labored—the slope was steep and the heat relentless. "They tend to overreact, and Gisa does us no favors by looking the other way. She believes the occasional skirmish will cause everyone to respect us. She does not understand the fear that such behavior could raise, that hybrids are violent, unstable." He stopped to wipe his sleeve across his brow. "At times I feel as though I'm juggling grenades." Jan paused at the cliff's edge and looked to the other side of the bay, where the white buildings of Karistos shone like snow against the red-brown of the rocks. "Could Feyó see those flares? Are they enough to let her know that I'm here?"

"She knows." Brondt spoke so quietly, one might have thought he hadn't spoken at all.

Jani turned back to him, where he stood amid the rocks and stared down at his hands, a weighty figure with a deceptive ability to maneuver. "I work with a captain back in Chicago who has a lot in common with you." Yes, the pieces fit. Yes, they made the usual sort of messy political sense. "You're a spy for Feyó. You're the one who let her know that Gisa planned to kidnap me, then you turned around and did the deed yourself to keep Gisa's trust."

"Ná Feyó knows you're here. She contacted Doctor Shroud and Colonel Pierce immediately after we left the station. She charged me with keeping you safe." Brondt shot Jani a look of Niall-grade frustration. "As I said, you don't make it easy." He took a deep breath, and started up the incline.

Jani waited for him to draw even with her, then continued toward the main house. Other hybrids passed them now, singly or in groups, their looks filled with confusion, anger, or a warring combination of both. "Why didn't you tell me?"

"How would that knowledge have made you feel toward me, better or worse than you do now?" Brondt eyed Jani sidelong, then looked away as though he guessed the answer. "You must understand, I am not against ná Gisa. I just . . ." He sighed. "I want Thalassa to thrive, to prosper. But ná Gisa is too bold and ná Feyó is too timid. There must be a place that is as we are. Somewhere in between."

As she and Brondt turned onto the walkway that led to the house, Jani caught sight of ná Gisa walking up the road behind them, regarding her with a mixture of expectancy and annoyance. A phalanx of hybrids preceded her, muscular males who had once been humanish, rough-edged and callused. *Behold the more militant denizens of Thalassa.* Unpleasant images coursed before her mind's eye of their reaction if they discovered a double agent in their midst. "You're walking a thin line, Colonel."

"Indeed." Brondt drew ahead of her as they approached the entry, and wrestled his expression into one of bland formality. "Remember, ná Kièrshia," he said as he preceded her through the door, "my future is now in your hands."

They entered the house to find the demirooms lit by inset lighting and floor lamps, the chairs and couches occupied by hybrids, many of whom held glasses or cups. *I'll be damned—it really is the cocktail hour.* Jani veered away from the scattered groups toward the courtyard, where a series of long tables had been assembled into a U-shape. Some of the younger hybrids, Torin among them, finished laying out dishes and cutlery, then set out candle bowls at measured intervals, shallow dishes filled with oil atop which floated sparkling fuel cells.

They all eat together. In one room. At the same time. Even though the incident with Eamon's drink had prepared Jani for the fact, the realization still shook her. *Tsecha still follows the old protocols.* As did Dathim, despite his daring in other areas. *How would they react to this?* She settled into the role of observer, so she could describe the scene to them when she returned to Chicago, and so she could set her feelings aside, to deal with later.

"Ná Kièrshia?" Gisa joined Jani at the opening to the courtyard, her composure regained. "You wish something to drink?"

"Water, please." *Followed by a shower, please.* Jani tugged at the overrobe, which remained twisted around her waist, the flare pistol still hidden beneath. Sweat beaded her face, while grime streaked her trouser suit from her scramble up the rocks. "Alcohol isn't worth the bother anymore, and I'm picky when it comes to coffee."

"Been drinking a lot of Johnny's brew of late, have you?" Eamon wandered over, a lime-garnished glass well in hand. "A proper little couple you've become, so I've heard."

"We see one another once in a while." Jani took a glass from a tray carried by an agitated Torin. He'd removed his films since their arrival—as she expected, his eyes proved the same deep green that she saw each time she looked in the mirror. "It isn't very complicated." She watched as he cut across the courtyard, looks passing between him and Brondt as well as the older female that Jani had seen him with after their arrival. Shorter and rounder than any idomeni, her red-dish hair in a scalp-hugging clip, she wore a simple shirt and long skirt, and a worried frown.

"I still do not understand humanish pairings." Gisa stepped aside so that Bon could join them. "Here at Thalassa, I see so much I do not understand—fighting and weeping and sad-ness—all over something so simple. With the blending comes peace to the soul, this I know and truly. The fighting ends, and pairing is approached with reason." She crossed her right arm on her chest, palm inward, in a gesture of humility, then de-parted for the opposite leg of the U, Bon preceding her.

She doesn't want to talk to me. Jani tasted the water and winced over its bland processed purity. *I've upset her plans to sweep me off my feet.*

"Lost in the surreality of it all, are you, Kilian?" In the few minutes that had passed, the sweat had soaked through the front of Eamon's white overshirt. "You've got that look about you. Dead-faced and still as stone, just like you were the day Johnny explained all the things he'd done to you when you were too comatose to object."

Jani looked across the room as Bon turned toward Gisa and tilted her head in acknowledgment of something her dominant had said. The afternoon sun shone upon the open courtyard and played across her sheared hair, through which showed patches of scalp as mottled and scarred as her face. "What's wrong with Bon?"

Eamon sniffed, then took a healthy swallow of his drink. "Analogue of Günther's disease. One of the autosomal recessive porphyrias. A cutaneous variety, not the neurologic version that you had. She was already heterozygous for it; I had tried to tweak her heme pathway, and damned if I didn't nail just the right mutation to make her homozygous. A one in a million chance, that, but every so often you hit those." He shrugged. "Anyway, a month or so after her last treatment, we moved here. The day was sunny, like they all are, and we whiled away the hours going in and out, ferrying personal belongings and furniture and such." Bon looked toward them, and he lowered his voice. "The porphyrins accumulate in the tissue, the skin. When sunlight hits them, they give off singlet oxygen. Wreaks hell on things organic. The blistering started almost immediately she walked outside. She looked as though she'd been torched by the time we got her downstairs to the clinic."

Jani looked down at her hands, the real and the fake, imagined the ravaging wrought by the heat of the transport explosion, and wondered what it felt like to watch the destruction unfold. "So why haven't you cured her?"

"Do you think I'm a bloody incompetent then?" Eamon curled his lip. "I repaired the mutation that day, but she wouldn't let me mend the scars. They were *à lérine*, she said. A challenge by the sun, which represented any who would prevent her from hybridizing, from becoming as she was meant to be." He held up his open hand in front of Jani's face, then slowly curled his fingers. "Her hands—they're like claws, twisted with scar tissue. She could lose fingers if she doesn't get treatment, but she doesn't care. Her hands for her enclave. Her life, if needed, for her enclave. Fair trade, she calls it." He leaned close, bringing the soupy stink of humanish sweat with him. "They're all like that. This is a religious experience to them—they're the chosen of the gods. You're going to have your hands full managing this herd, my little tin divinity, and it couldn't happen to a more deserving soul." He straightened. "Any other questions?"

"Just one." Jani gave the tasteless water one more chance, then set the glass on the edge of a planter. "Why?"

Eamon's dissolute face set in cruel lines, his weak mouth firming. He'd always been odd man out among the Neoclona Three. He lacked John's elegance, Val's wit and good looks. But he shared their scientific arrogance, and it emerged now, like a mask of youth. "Because they wanted it. Needed it, some of them, to survive." He smiled. "And because I could. Because old Johnny thought he'd nicked my tendons but good, and I proved him wrong."

"I thought you had a contract." Jani grew conscious of movement around her, and stepped closer to the planter to allow hybrids bearing serving dishes room to walk around her to the table. "John and Val stayed out of gadgets, you stayed out of genetics."

"Contracts were made to be broken." Eamon shook his drained glass so the ice rattled. "We'll see how eager Johnny is to rack me after he gets here and we've had a chance to talk. He gets a chance to see what his castoff has done." He headed for the table, then paused and turned back to Jani. "I did it better than he did, you know, the bonny Bon notwithstanding. None of the problems you had with food, with bone and muscle disorders. And I worked over fifty-seven of them. Johnny only worked you." He took a seat near the top of the U and poured another drink from the bottle one of the hybrids had left beside his plate.

Jani waited, knowing that everyone would seat themselves according to rank and that soon only she and Gisa would be left standing. She sniffed the air, expecting the harsh tang of Sìah herbs and spices, and stilled as a more familiar aroma rattled her sinuses. *Curry?* She sniffed again. *And hot plum sauce?* She looked across the room toward Gisa, who had taken her low seat near the top of the U and now gestured to her and pointed to the chair next to hers, the seat of honor, the lowest seat at the table.

"Anything in a blue-rimmed dish is mine," Eamon said as Jani took her place, his burr hatcheting through the softer voices around him. "I made them work out a code after I damned near lost the lining of my mouth to a veg stew."

Jani examined the server that Gisa handed her, which contained a green bean and potato *toran*. "What does a gold rim mean?"

Eamon raised a hand and rocked it up and down in a so-so gesture. "Medium. Anything in the paisley is about your speed. Death to mucus membranes."

Jani lifted the lid of one of the paisley tureens and inhaled. *"Dahi machi."* She ladled some onto her plate. "Fish curry," she added for the benefit of a bewildered-looking Brondt, who sat several seats uptable and poked through the servers as if they could poke back.

"That was our surprise for you, ná Kièrshia. Your fellow Acadians thought to prepare you a proper welcoming meal." Gisa gestured downtable toward two of the younger hybrids, a male and female who nodded toward Jani, pride battling dismay on their faces and not quite winning the battle.

"It's very good." Jani took a large bite for the benefit of one and all.

"Good, yes." Gisa speared more delicately with a twin-pronged Sìah fork. "And yet you question us. Stand upon rocks and shoot pistols into the air. We who cook so as to honor you, who take so much pride in welcoming you here."

Jani sensed the stillness in the air, the charge of expectation. *You're undercutting my authority.* Hungry as she was, she set her fork aside. *Putting me on the spot in front of your suborns.* "Your interpretation of hospitality is most odd, and truly. You did not behave as seemly, yet you expect me to respond as though nothing untoward has occurred."

"We were so happy—"

"Happiness does not preclude diplomacy, or for that matter, common sense." Jani detected Ambassador Shai's tartness in her speech, and wondered how low she had fallen that she considered the Vynshàrau bornsect a model for anything. "We face a political crisis here of your making, Gisa. If you wish to discuss such over fish and fruit, by all means let us do so. But if you suppose that hunger, fatigue, and the stunned awe I feel at this place will affect my judgment or predispose me in your favor simply because you are as you are, you are most an idiot!" She picked up her fork and resumed eating, conscious of the brittle silence that had fallen, broken only by the sound of Eamon's snuffling gurgle as he laughed into his drink.

"Do you always set the room on its ear like that?" Brondt led Jani up the stairs to her quarters. "I mean, I've listened to idomeni in-your-face for years, but *Christ*."

"She asked for it."

"She has a point."

"But wielding it like a club doesn't help." Jani glanced over the railing, where the clean-up crew cleared dishes and linen and disassembled the table. "I'm sorry, but I have to weigh fifty-seven hurt faces against the stability of the Outer Circle. If you were in my place, what would you pick?" She waited for Brondt to reply, but he kept his thoughts to himself as he led her to a set of double doors at the end of the hallway.

He palmed open one panel and it swept aside, revealing a huge curve of a bedroom, the far wall floor-to-ceiling glass facing the bay. Decorated in blues and greens shot with coral, it included its own sitting room and, upon further examination, a bathroom larger than some flats in which Jani had lived.

"Nice." She tossed her duffel atop the bed, walked to the dresser and noted, with a stab of discomfort, that she looked as worn and battered as she felt. "More than nice. Lovely. Really."

Brondt positioned himself just inside the doorway. "I should have told you everything. I'm sorry. I thought seeing the hybrids, this place, would slow you down for at least a couple of hours. I was wrong." He pressed a hand to the side of his face. "Boy, was I wrong."

"You think I'm not affected?" Jani perched on the edge of

the bed. "I'm . . . stunned doesn't begin to cover it. But a situation has developed that needs to be headed off quickly—I don't have time to sit back and marvel at it all."

"Is that the sort of life you lead back in Chicago? Never a chance to breathe?" Brondt jerked his chin toward the view out the window. "It's different here."

"No, it's not. Put two or more bodies in the same room, you get what you've got here now. Same race. Different race. Different species. It doesn't matter."

"Isn't there anything here you like?"

"I'm not cold anymore." Jani dragged her duffel onto her lap. "And the view across the bay is very pretty."

Brondt eyed her with something that struck her as perilously close to pity. "Glories of the evening to you, ná Kièrshia. If you wish to leave in the morning, all you have to do is say so." He reached into his trouser pockets, removing Jani's shooter from one and the disconnected charge packet from the other. He walked to the dresser, set them down, then left.

Jani sat on the bed for a time, staring at nothing. Her anger had receded, leaving edginess and a certain heaviness of limb behind, mood and sensation that reminded her of post-augie letdown.

She finally stood, duffel still in hand. Walked to the dresser and retrieved her shooter. Adjourned to the bathroom, undressed, and showered off the grime and sweat. Dragged on an ancient Service T-shirt and a slightly newer pair of base casual shorts to serve as sleepwear. Returned to the bedroom and lay her trouser suit on a chair atop her duffel. "No need to unpack." She wouldn't be staying.

She opened the window, and felt the warm breeze off the water, touched with the scent of storm. "Rain tonight." She adjusted the pane to close in case water came in, then doused the lights. Tucked her shooter beneath her pillow, then lay atop the bed. If she listened closely enough, she could hear the waves and the occasional cry of a seabird.

CHAPTER 13

"Ná Kièrshia! Ná Kièrshia!"

Jani's eyes snapped open, her heart thudding as the bang of a fist against a door panel shook the air.

"Ná Kièrshia!"

She sat up. Pushed her legs over the side of the bed. Grabbed her shooter from under her pillow and stood.

"Ná Kièrshia!"

She stilled. Felt cool tile beneath her bare feet. Heard the patter of rain outside the window. Her head cleared. "Kièrshia. That's me." She sat back down, one hand over her mouth, and waited for her heart to slow.

"Ná Kièr—!"

Jani dropped her hand. *"Wait a minute!"* She stood once more, tucking her shooter into the waistband of her shorts as she walked to the door.

The panel slid aside to reveal Brondt standing bleary-eyed in the hallway. "Enclave security detected a skimmer headed this way. Two males. Humanish." He wore civvies, a long-sleeve pullover, and baggy trousers, topped off by a shoulder holster complete with shooter. "I thought you'd want to meet them personally."

* * *

167

"I instructed the guards to hold them at the property boundary, and to inform them that you were on your way." Brondt guided the four-seater down the path, then turned onto a wider road paved with crushed stone. "They won't try anything heroic, will they?"

"Depends how convincing your guards are." Jani watched the road by the light of the skimmer headlamps. "Are they hybrid from the human side, or from the Haárin?"

"Both." Brondt accelerated, sending rain droplets skittering across the coated windscreen. "But one of them is former Service. She should be able to keep the lid on things."

They coursed through the dark, the enclave receding into the distance, its brightness supplanted by the inset illumins in the road itself. It lay before them, like a ribbon of pale gold, the rain changed to silver needles by its light.

Jani hugged her duffel close. She'd dragged on a coverall over her shorts and T-shirt, plunged her bare feet into her boots, and followed Brondt to the skimmer in a daze of movement. Now she battled a lingering sense that the hounds closed in from behind. *That's just memory.* Remembrance of other late night escapes, hangover from her time on the run. *No one's after me anymore.* That didn't hold true, however, for the other occupant of the vehicle. "Speaking of Service," she looked at Brondt, who kept his eyes on the road, "you might have been looking at a medical discharge before you decided to give me a guided tour of the Haárin side of Elyas Station. But at this point I'm thinking desertion of post as well as whatever other minor charges the Judge Advocate can dig out of his desk drawer."

Brondt glanced at her. "Not kidnapping?" When Jani didn't reply, a change came over him, a subtle shift as though some tension left him. Then he twitched one shoulder in a not-quite-shrug. "I did what I had to. When the time comes, I'll pay the price."

"You and Hamil both." Jani squinted through the rain, on the lookout for shapes in the distance. "Are you the only active-duty hybrids?"

"It's just the two of us. For now." Brondt decelerated as the outlines of a checkpoint dome shimmered in the distance. "Pierce and Shroud—will you be going with them?"

"I think it may be best." Jani sat up straighter as several figures resolved in the misty half-light. *Everyone seems to be talking calmly. No bodies laid out by the roadside.* She searched for a telltale white head—her breath caught when she saw John look toward their approaching skimmer.

"I wish it had worked out differently." Brondt halted the vehicle in the middle of the road, then slowly rotated it so it faced back toward the enclave. "Pardon me if I don't get out. Pierce won't react kindly to seeing me, and I don't want to give myself over to the JA just yet." He fingered the steering mech. "Don't cast us aside too quickly. Please."

"I'm not unmoved. No one could see the things I have and remain so." Jani popped her gullwing and pushed it upward. "But ná Gisa has helped put both you and the Elyan Haárin in a difficult position, and she doesn't strike me as someone inclined to back down." She slid out of the skimmer—the warm rain brushed her face and spattered her coverall. "I'll talk to Feyó. That's all I can promise."

"I'll carry that promise to those who think as I do." Brondt lifted one hand from the mech. "Glories of the early morning to you, ná Kièrshia." He accelerated as soon as Jani slammed down the gullwing, and sped back toward the enclave.

Jani waited until the skimmer had dwindled to a slice of shadow against the light of the road. Then she hefted her duffel and headed for the checkpoint dome. *When shall we three meet again?* She looked to the sky. *No thunder. No lightning.* Only the rain.

"We had just left Fort Karistos Command when we saw the flares play out over the bay." Niall broke away from the small group and walked toward her, impeccable in tan desert-weights. "I knew it had to be you."

"Are you all right?" John followed close behind. "We tried to contact the enclave using codes Feyó gave us, but no one responded." He looked less natty than usual, in drab grey trousers and short-sleeve shirt, the shine of his hair quenched by the wet.

"I'm fine." Jani gestured a quick *Be quiet* out of sight of the enclave guards, who watched her with the same perplexed agitation as had their brethren back at the house. Either they had witnessed her fits of idomeni temper, or good news traveled fast. "Let's go." She headed for the skimmer, a white four-door with the bland lines of the vehicle pool, popped the gullwing and piled into the rear seat.

Niall slipped in behind the steering mech and yanked his door closed. "Was that Brondt who drove you here?" He twisted around to look back at Jani, the overhead light defining his bloodshot eyes. "He and that bastard Hamil are mine."

Jani held her tongue until John got in and closed his door, then bent over her duffel to hide her face from the guards as Niall kicked the skimmer out of standby and circled around onto the road. Odds were that the hybrids didn't possess a directed pickup or any other sort of long distance monitoring device, but her on-the-run paranoia still rode her shoulder and she couldn't make herself take the chance. "Brondt is Feyó's mole," she said after they moved some distance down the road. "He's the one who told her about Gisa's plan to kidnap me. He also let Feyó know that I had made it to the enclave safe and sound."

"His last year's physical raised some eyebrows at the Service medical facility." John grabbed a dispo cloth from an in-dash compartment and used it to towel his wet hair. "Some of the test results could have been attributed to various metabolic disorders, but to have them all show up in one person at one time captured attention." He lowered the passenger mirror and watched Jani as he checked his eyefilms. "At the time, no one suspected hybridization. They all thought that big white house across the bay was simply home to some Haárin-human experimental living arrangement, and being Elyan, they shrugged and looked the other way. Lately they've been putting two and two together and not liking the answers." He let loose a grumbling sigh. "Needless to say, they think I'm involved. One reason it took us so long to hook up with you is because I've spent most of the evening sitting in a room packed with lawyers and Service investigators."

Jani sat quiet, aware of the stiff way Niall held himself, the stillness of his hands on the steering mech.

"I had to tell him, Jan." John's voice guttered in resignation. "You disappeared, and we had no idea where Brondt had taken you. The dockmaster shut down the human side of the station to keep shuttles from leaving, but she has no authority over the Haárin section, and they ignore her unless she insists with intent. Niall threw the threat of Service intervention into the mix, but by the time we convinced the Haárin to cooperate, your shuttle had already broken away."

Jani slowly raised her gaze until it met Niall's in the rearview.

"I knew you were hiding something from me." His voice came soft, his Victorian twang barely noticeable. "A colony of hybrids, courtesy of Eamon DeVries. Imagine."

"Until—" Jani's face burned. Her throat tightened. "Until I met Brondt, I thought there was only one hybrid."

"Ah well. Only one." Niall shrugged. "That makes all the difference, doesn't it?" He reached into his front shirt pocket and removed his nicstick case. "That would be the young man with the flat green eyes whose image Doctor Shroud was kind enough to finally show me an hour or so ago." He shook out a 'stick and crunched the tip.

"His name's Torin." Jani sat back and rested her head against the seat.

"How many are there?" John's voice held a tension that indicated he didn't really want to hear the answer.

"Fifty-seven." Jani monitored John's reflection in his mirror, watched his eyes close, his mouth set in a thin line. "Eamon's living with them. He built the big white house across the bay. The outbuildings. He's quite pleased with himself."

"Is he?" John folded his arms and slumped in his seat, the darkness of his thoughts reflected in his shadowed face.

"You have a busy day ahead," Niall said, this time ignoring Jani's reflection in the rearview. "First, Feyó wants to see you. Then some members of the Service Investigative Bureau are hoping you can spare them a few minutes of your valuable time." He chewed his 'stick, working it from one side of his mouth to the other, his usual agitated tic.

"You don't need to talk to them." John glanced over his shoulder at her. "The head of Neoclona Legal referred me to a good firm—we can stop by their offices after you speak with Feyó."

Jani felt her gut roil as her temper flared. She tried to fight it down, then wondered why she bothered. Such was as she was now. The hell with pretending otherwise. "I haven't done anything wrong, I don't require legal assistance, and I'll thank you to stop trying to think of new and better ways to lock me down!" She cut off John's protest with a two-fingered Sìah gesture that looked scatologically humanish enough to draw a double take from Niall.

They fell silent, each prey to their own grievances. After a time, they turned off the main road, the vehicle shuddering as it left skimtrack control. They shot across the scrub, the road receding into the distance behind them, thinning to a thread of gold. Ahead, the beam of the skimmer headlamps sliced the darkness, bringing a narrow arc of the scrubland to day-life.

Then Niall banked the vehicle through a short maze of rocks and down a long, winding decline. Shimmering reflection filled their sightline as they neared the bay. The skimmer shook once more as they broke out over the water, and they fast-floated toward the distant lights of Karistos.

Thalassa had taken its architectural lead from its big sister across the water—that struck Jani as soon as she caught sight of the first bright domes of Karistos, backlit by security lighting and dotting the cliff like a scatter of party balloons.

Linking them were the same steep, winding streets, only more numerous. Serving as contrast were the same blocky white and tan commercial buildings and houses, only taller and more complex, and separated by parks and plazas instead of rock and scrub.

And Karistos has different trees. Jani leaned forward so she could see them out the window as Niall steered up a steep incline. They were stuck like clusters of onlookers near the intersections of roads, tall and spindly, with stiff, swordlike leaves of the same red-green hue as the Thalassan scrub. They reminded her of the palm trees she'd seen in holoVees, and she watched them drift past until Niall's mutterings broke the silence that had claimed them since she'd snapped at John.

"The streets in this city"— Niall tapped the vehicle directional array with one finger—"would make a plate of spaghetti look organized."

"It's all the one-way streets." John craned his neck as they passed yet another park. "I think I recognize that fountain. Neoclona should be just on the other side. More or less. I say forget the signs and directionals and just turn where you have to. It's still dark. There's no traffic. I'll take the hit if we're stopped."

Minor traffic violations proved the order of the early day. Scant minutes later the three of them trudged across the Neoclona garage, boarded the lift, and floated up ten floors to the penthouse flat.

"Coffee," John said as the door slid aside, revealing a sitting room in cream and blue that complimented Karistos's bayside ambience. "Then a war council." He shouldered into the kitchen, Jani and Niall in close pursuit, and assembled the brewer with a speed born of practice. "But first, I really, really need a shower." He left just as the heady aroma of too much caffeine infused the air, and seemed surprised to find Jani at his heels when he cut down a hallway and stopped before a double-wide door panel.

"I don't want to be alone with Niall just yet." Jani pushed

past him into the room, slowing as she took in the large bed that dominated the decor. "Just give me a few minutes." She steered to the opposite side and dropped her duffel atop the dresser. "You wouldn't happen to have a cleaner, would you?" She dragged her grimy trouser suit out of her bag. "I think I should dress for my meeting with Feyó."

"No more 'coverall for every occasion'?" John grinned weakly as he walked to a seemingly blank section of wall and touched it—a panel swung outward, revealing tiered racks of hangered suits and filled shoe racks. "Can't help you with the cleaner, I'm afraid, but you're welcome to root around in here."

Jani peered into the closet, feeling as inadequate to the task as she usually did when it came to the right clothes. "You keep all this stuff here in case you happen to drop by?"

"That's the point of having pieds-à-terre at all our facilities." John stepped inside the closet and jerked his chin toward the racks mounted on the right-hand wall. "Anyway, these aren't all mine—everything on that side is Val's." He cast an assessing eye toward Jani. "You may have more luck with his suits—you're about the same height now. His back is broader than yours, of course, but droopy shoulders are easier to cover up than trousers and jackets that are too long." He took a step back and waved her inside with a broad sweep of his arm. "Have at it."

The suits were arranged by color. Jani bypassed the dark hues that filled the front racks and headed for the cooler pastels and ashy shades in the back. "I feel like I just dropped inside the ultimate lost lambs' bin."

John folded his arms and leaned against a shoe rack. "I doubt you ever found anything like what's in here."

"You'd be surprised at some of the things I managed to snag over the years." Jani pushed past tans and greys to lighter greens and pale blues. "Coats. Boots. Empty diplomatic pouches, which I admit I found rather alarming. Different sorts of devices—those could be hocked or stripped for parts." She took a jacket the color of a new leaf from its hanger and slipped it on. "I always took a pass on the underwear."

"Glad to hear it." John covered his eyes with one hand and shook his head. Then he stilled, seemingly deep in thought. His hand moved lower, to the point of his chin, finally coming to rest on the neck of his pullover. "What would it take for you to get past that mind-set?" He tugged at the already bagged cloth. "The knowledge that it would never happen again? A few years of stability?"

Jani rejected the jacket for length, stripped it off and returned it to its rack. "I don't think I'll ever lose it completely. I'm too much of a fatalist." She gave herself a mental kick as John's shoulders sagged. "It's not your fault. You're not responsible for each and every aspect of my character."

"I know that. I just wonder sometimes whether—" John loosed his grip on his clothing, then filled the fidget void by plucking a shoe from the rack behind him. "Whether all the things you've experienced over the years, including those that I am responsible for"—he turned the polished slip-on over and over as though he'd never seen one before—"if they eliminated whatever chance you had to be happy."

"I'm happy now." Jani held up another jacket, this one a mossy jade piped with brown. "Free clothes." She smiled, stopping just short of an idomeni tooth-baring, then sobered as John responded with a look just short of stricken. "This really isn't the time to worry about the personal." She yanked open the jacket's fasteners, then dragged it on. "I don't know why you've decided that it is."

"Don't you?" John shoved the shoe back in its niche. "Mines. Kidnappings. Cross-species political crises." He stepped away from the rack and paced. "I just want to sweep you away—"

"That's where you get it wrong."

"I know that." John stopped, then kicked at the thick carpet. "I've done a fair job of keeping my nose out of it, in case you haven't noticed. The offer of the lawyers was a lapse. It won't happen again."

Jani checked the fit of the jacket in the mirror that hung on the end wall. "I think this one's an option." She hunted down the trousers and pulled them off the hanger, then unfolded them and checked the waist against hers. "These are going to bag every which way, but the jacket's long enough to cover." She tossed the trousers atop the rack, doffed the jacket, then started peeling back the coverall until she remembered where she was and with whom. "It's not that I don't need anyone's help. *Your* help. But the answer isn't to keep me from doing what needs to be done, it's to help me do it." She ran a finger over the jacket's lasered seaming. "I need clothes more than lawyers. Access to secure communications. Someone to stop the bleeding, if it comes to that. But . . ." She touched the rich cloth once more, then pulled her hand away. "I've said it before. I'll say it again now. Someone is keeping track of every thing you do for me, and it will all come back to haunt you."

John stood with hands in his pockets, gaze fixed on the floor at his feet. "A man doesn't always get to choose his ghosts. That makes me one of the lucky ones." He walked to the rack and pulled out a tunic in an icy shade of melon. "I always thought this color would look good on you. If you need something else in addition to the green." He laid the jacket across the top of the rack. "I'll be outside."

Jani waited until the door closed. Then she hung up the green daysuit and hunted for the trousers that matched the melon tunic. The cut of the suit was severe enough to pass Feyó's conservative clothing muster, and the trousers fit better than she'd hoped. She considered the fact that as far as she could recall, this was the first time she had donned clothing for no other reason than because John liked it. Then she pushed the thought from her mind, slipped on her boots, raked a hand through her hair, and reentered the bedroom proper to find John sitting on the bed, sorting socks.

Head bent to his task, he looked as he had in the Rauta Shèràa basement. Focused. Serious. *Until* . . . Until the touch of her hand or the brush of her lips over his gave rise to a different brand of concentration.

He looked up when he heard her—a stillness took hold of him when he realized what she wore. "That is your color." He tried to smile, but the attempt died, leaving him wide-eyed and rapt. "It warms you." He looked down at the jumble in his lap, and cleared his throat. "I'll—meet—"

"Outside." Jani grabbed her duffel from the dresser and hurried out of the bedroom, fighting the all-too-familiar heat that set her heart pounding and rattled her nerves.

She entered the sitting room to find Niall perusing the contents of an inset display case, a mug of coffee in hand. He barely glanced at her. Instead, he opened the door of the case and removed a small book bound in burgundy leather leafed with gold.

"There's a certain type of collector who gets under my skin." Niall lifted the cover with his thumb and examined the flyleaf. "Acquiring for the sake of acquiring. Locking beautiful things away, like a miser his money." He closed the book and returned it to its shelf. "Shroud at least reads these, from what I can tell."

"Answered all your test questions correctly, did he?" Jani fell into a chair, sagging more deeply into it as the last of her sexual shakes abated.

Niall walked to a set of glass doors that opened onto a balcony. Outside, the sky had lightened to dawn, streaks of pink and lilac backlit with gold. "So what's the new objective?" He paused to take a swig of coffee. "When we left Chicago, you were to deliver a gift and I was tagging along to fact-find. Shroud was the man with a fast ship, a generous heart, and nothing better to do with his valuable time than cart you all over hell and gone." He rocked back on his heels, then forward, then back again. "Now that's changed. Shroud's partner in all things medical has gone into the hybridization business. Shroud denies all knowledge, but no one believes him. You're trying to figure out how to deal with a hybrid

Haárin who wants to bump the acknowledged dominant off her perch, and I'm dealing with security breaches at Elyas Station and Fort Karistos." He finally looked at her, the cool appraisal in his eyes the only outward sign of his anger. "Is there anything you would like to add?"

Jani drummed her fingers against her chair arm. "Off the record?"

"Forget it." Niall moved away from the window and sat in a lounge chair on the side of the room opposite her. "I will now sit back and finish my coffee while you sieve your response through whatever filter you think necessary at this particular moment."

"I can't think of anything to add to your sterling assessment." Jani unfastened the bottom closure of her tunic, then refastened it.

"Is Tsecha involved with the hybrids? Did he know about them?"

Jani started to answer, then stopped. *He would have told me if he knew.* She unhooked the closure again. *If he did know . . .* It took three tries before she refastened it. *Please Lord, let him stay out of trouble long enough so that I can throttle him.* "You may well speculate in that direction. I prefer not to."

Niall set his mug atop his chairside table with a bang. "*Listen, damn it—*"

"No, *you* listen, damn it." Jani pushed to her feet. "Even better, open your eyes and look at me. Look at me, and see me for what I am."

"I have." Niall's voice held a deadness that struck harder than any slap. "Thank you."

"The lines of communication have opened, I see." John swept in, looking vampirical in Neoclona purple. "Like floodgates." He handed Jani a mug of coffee, then hied to the balcony doors. "Neither of you mean what you said, of course. Just injured feelings on the Service side and delayed reaction to the shock of discovery on the civilian. Well, we can't afford either right now. The complications are drop-

ping litters all over the place and we three need to stick together, however little the prospect pleases." He looked from
Jani to Niall, new to the role of peacemaker and clearly uncomfortable with it. "In a few months' time we'll be talking
of this over dinner, wondering what the fuss was about."

Jani held the mug to her nose and breathed in the steam.
"When the hurly-burly's done."

"My gel." Niall shook his head. "It hasn't even started."

CHAPTER 14

" 'Morning, scholar."

Micah looked up from his workstation to find Cashman's moonface looming above the cube divider, then closed his eyes as the rapid movement made his head pound. He'd just signed in—he needed time to get his bearings. He'd awakened with a headache, the trailing ends of a dream playing past his mind's eye. *No, not a dream.* More his other reality, a replay of his twenty minutes a day of Chrivet-driven hell.

We're walkin' in Jesus' footsteps, boys and girls!

At the sound of her imagined voice, he felt his limbs lift, as though he had donned his exo and even now ran through the Sheridan training field, the Wabash tunnels, across Lake Michigan to the enclave, then back again to the embassy, his mechanical stride chewing the kilometers like candy. *I need to stop this now.* With resolution born of a month's practice, he willed his arms and legs heavy, willed them seated, dragged himself back to the present. "What's your problem now, Cash?"

"I've got no problem. It's you with the problem. They want you on Five. The latest in the series of never-ending mine meetings—they need you to run the recorders." Cashman draped himself over the curve of the divider and batted his eyelashes. "You jumped over a few looies to get that gig. What's your secret? Your winning smile? You supplying fun holos for them, too? What?"

Micah locked down his workstation and gathered his gearbag. "If you ever stopped talking, would you turn blue and fall over?"

Cashman puffed out his cheeks. "Regular cupbearer to the gods, this makes you. You know what the gods did to their cupbearers, don't you?"

"Kiss my ass."

"Close, scholar. Very close. You must have moved on to the history section. I'm looking forward to watching that one when you're finished with it." Cashman gestured appropriate accompaniment. "One word of advice before you go."

"Only one?"

Cashman pointed to the mirror by the door. "You better brighten up. You look like hell."

Micah turned and studied his reflection. He'd shaved close. His hair was freshly trimmed. Springweights brand new from the package.

Then he looked at his eyes and saw what Cashman saw. Too much white. Stare too fixed. "I had a rough night."

"What was her name?"

"Shut up."

"Come in, Lance Corporal."

Micah stood in the conference room doorway, a chill cramp working through his gut. "I was told I needed to run the recorders for a meeting."

Pascal sat at the head of the table, hands clasped before him, and smiled. "I must not have made myself clear to Lance Corporal Cashman. My apologies." He gestured toward the man sitting next to him. "Come in. Captain Veles and I just want to ask you a few questions."

Micah stepped into the room. His legs felt as they did after a session with the sims. Weightless, yet stiff. Toned and fit, yet aching. "About what, sir?"

"Just have a seat. We need to clarify a few things related to your initial debriefing." Pascal smiled again. As before, the expression began and ended at his mouth. "You recall, surely. The one that took place after the mine explosion."

"Yes, sir." Micah took a seat several places removed from Pascal. Even if the man stood and threw himself across the table, he wouldn't be able to reach him. "That was over a month ago." He glanced at Veles. A stringy man, dark with hooded eyes—he also bore the gold capital *I* on his dress blue-grey tunic collar that marked him as Intelligence. *Intelligence isn't investigating the mine. The SIB is.* For all the good it did them. Meetings from mornings to late at night, work schedules turned on their ears, and damn-all to show for it. It had become comical, really. Unfortunately, he couldn't openly express his appreciation of the joke.

"How well did you know Lance Corporal Rikki Wode?" Pascal asked.

Micah snapped back to the present, raking his memory for any recall of that long-ago interrogation. *But it wasn't an interrogation, just questions.* Informal. Easygoing. No one had suspected him of anything, and had treated him accordingly. "He was the tech who died."

"Did you know him *personally*, Lance Corporal?" This from Veles, in a voice like fine abrasive.

"No, sir." His first lie. He knew that because no one had asked him before if he knew Wode. *I have to remember the lies.* Otherwise, he'd risk giving the wrong answer if they asked him the same question again. *I wish I could take notes.* Maybe he should ask if he could. *Maybe I should just cut my throat now.* That settled it. No notes.

Pascal sat forward and placed several objects on the table. A headset. Earbuds. Gloves and socks. "We found these among Wode's personal effects. Do you know what they are?"

Micah nodded, stopping as his head rocked. "It's a virtual training rig, sir. Pilots use them. Surgeons."

"Other people use them, too." Veles again. "Infantry. Mechanics. Anyone who likes interactives."

Micah tried not to wince at the grate of the man's voice. Why didn't he do something about it, training or something? Better yet, why didn't he keep his mouth shut? "Yes, sir."

"You're called the 'scholar' by several of the other techs." Pascal's voice, on the other hand, sounded too cultured by half. "Why is that?"

Micah gripped the edge of the table. "I'm studying for the Comtech One exam, sir. I've begged off a few parties over the last several weeks as a result." He pulled his hands away, saw the damp prints left by his sweat, and sat forward, crossing his arms over the wet spots. "Just good-natured teasing, sir."

"Is there any other kind?" Pascal smiled again, then looked down at the table in front of him as though consulting something, even though he lacked even a handheld for taking notes. "You weren't originally scheduled for duty the night the mine exploded. You switched on-calls with a Corporal Howard three days earlier."

"Yes, sir." Micah exhaled, heard the shake in his throat and caught his breath.

Pascal's brow arched as the silence lengthened. "Why did you switch?"

Micah swallowed, then coughed as saliva trickled down his airway. Damn it, the switch had nothing to do with anything, and it looked the worst of all the things he'd done. "I did it for a future consideration, sir. Nothing in particular. I work a weekend night for her, maybe sometime in the future, she'll do the same for me. The techs do it all the time."

"They do." Veles frowned. "Plays merry hell with the schedule after a while."

Pascal nodded. "Well, that certainly clears up that issue. I will admit that we wondered about it, and it wasn't covered in your initial debriefing." He appeared as relaxed as Micah had ever seen him, as though he felt the questioning a waste of time but needed to see it through anyway.

Then he ran his index finger over the headset faceplate, and pushed it a little closer to Micah. "Just out of curiosity, do you have one of these?"

Shit. Micah started to chew his lip, then stopped. He'd recorded enough interrogations to know that lip-chewing was bad. It meant you needed time to think about how to phrase your answer, that the simple truth wouldn't serve. That you had something to hide. *He knows why they really call me the "scholar."* Hell with it. "Yes, sir. I do."

Veles glanced at Pascal, but the Chief of Mattress Operations had eyes only for him. "What do you use it for?"

Micah counted to five. His face burned until he felt sure he'd combust. "Interactives, sir."

"Oh." Veles had the sort of thin-lipped smile that begged for a fist.

Pascal barely managed to conceal his own grin. "I imagine you have a . . . library of holos."

Burn . . . burn . . . burn to ash. Even though it was better this way. Even though this was necessary camouflage. "Yes, sir."

Pascal nodded. "See. This is where they've gotten it wrong." He spoke to Veles as though Micah had already been dismissed. "Wode had nothing in his flat. No wafers, either legit, pirate, or homemade. Just the headset and the rest. No one I know just keeps the gear and nothing to play on it. That doesn't make sense." He looked off in the middle distance for a few moments. Then he turned to Micah, blinking as though he'd forgotten he was there. "When is your exam?"

Micah bit back a curse. Every time he thought he knew which direction Pascal would take the questioning, the captain would jerk the steering mech. "Next week, sir."

"Well, good luck to you." Pascal leaned forward to say something to Veles, stopping when he realized Micah still sat there. "Thank you, Lance Corporal. You can go."

"Yes, sir." Micah stood. "Thank you, sir." He brushed his hand as unobtrusively as possible over the sweat spots he had left on the table. Then he walked to the door, all the while expecting to hear that damned voice, that damned accent. *Just one more thing, Lance Corporal* . . . He palmed aside the panel and stepped into the hall, his expression as relaxed as he could manage, ready to turn as soon as Pascal called him back. He kept walking, and waited, kept walking, and waited, and had boarded the lift by the time he realized that the call wouldn't come.

They suspect Wode of something. Micah slipped back into the bullpen, walking on tiptoe to avoid betraying his return to Cashman. *What the hell do they think?* What's more, did it matter? The investigation had yet to turn up anything other than the obvious—a misplaced mine, and an inexperienced tech. *That's all they have.* He sat at his desk and reactivated his workstation. *That's all they'll ever have as long as I keep my mouth shut.*

He sorted through messages for a time. Then the gnawing in his gut got the better of him, and he opened the latest revision of the Service Code. "Rights of the accused." He mouthed his words, determined to avoid Cashman's irritating attention yet too aggravated by the bullpen silence to keep from trying to fill it. He needed to walk off his mood, but who knew who he'd encounter in the halls, or outside? He hadn't seen Pascal for weeks until today, not since the conference call array bung-up. But that didn't mean the man wouldn't turn up in a corridor, or a vend alcove. Appearing out of nowhere seemed a talent of his.

Micah focused on the code. "If they try to talk to me again, I'm going to ask for an advocate." The idea of thwarting Pascal with the request appealed to him. For about a minute. "No one who's innocent asks for an advocate." Besides, they'd just wanted to find out about the duty switch, which even he had to admit appeared suspicious. "And about Wode and his headset." That bothered him. What did they think they knew about Wode?

"Excuse me, Lance Corporal."

Micah straightened as though someone shoved a knee in his back. He knew he did, damned himself for it, and couldn't help himself. Knew who he'd see when he turned around, yet couldn't help for that, either.

"Looking up a point of law, I see," Pascal said as he squinted toward the display. "I hope our little session didn't alarm you."

"No, sir." Micah dug his fingernails into his chair arms. He'd rather have been anyplace on Earth instead of his cube at this moment, and there wasn't a damned thing he could do about that, either. *This is part of the game, too.* To pretend it didn't matter. He wondered if you needed to be someone like Pascal in order to play. If you needed to be someone like Pascal to even take the field.

"We need some help upstairs with one of the imagers." Pascal stepped back to allow Micah room to get by. "I've been advised that it's better to come down personally to request assistance. You folks have been so inundated over the past month and a half that you've turned off your handcoms."

"That's not true, sir." Micah reached into his gear holster and held up his own activated handcom for inspection. "It's the 'how do you turn this thing on' aspect that's getting to us. You'd think that some people had never seen a touchpad before." He pressed a hand to his forehead, then lowered it fast. "Apologies, sir. It's my job." He stood and gathered up his gearbag yet again.

"The joys of Technical Support." Pascal followed him out the bullpen door, then drew alongside as they headed back down the hall toward the lift bank. "I remember it well from my on-call days. You wonder if some people's mothers know they're here." They boarded a car. The doors closed.

"You're from this area, Faber?" Pascal stood to the rear of the car.

Micah nodded. "Yes, sir." He took his place near the front, facing forward so he didn't have to look Pascal in the face. "Small town north of here—Fort Jefferson."

"You must have some opinion about all this trouble with the idomeni."

Micah watched the figures on the floor indicator display increase, and willed them faster. *I thought you were finished with me, Pascal? What are you trying to do?* He thought over his activities, six weeks pondered in a few seconds. *What did I do to attract his attention? Why does he think me suspicious?* "They're odd, sir." Every hate-filled slogan he'd learned from Chrivet scrolled through his head, bubbled to the base of his throat, tickled his tongue like soda. One by one he choked them back down. "I suppose they're all right."

"You suppose they're all right." Pascal snorted. "That has got to be the most tepid assessment I've ever heard." The doors opened and he brushed past Micah into the hall. "We've moved to another conference room." He glanced back over his shoulder. "One of your penmates has been trying to help us set up, but he's not having much luck. Lance Corporal Cashman?"

Oh, hell. "Yes, sir." Micah followed Pascal into one of the larger rooms and found Cashman standing over the pieces of a room-rated imager, fiddling with the mirror array.

"Hey, sch—" Cashman caught himself, eyeing Veles as though he expected the man to pummel him for the infraction. "Hey, Fabe. I've been over every millimeter of this thing and I can't find what's wrong."

Micah took the array from him and examined it. "What's the problem?"

"The thing won't display. Switches work. Signaling checks out. I thought the mirrors were misaligned, but they check out, too." Cashman scratched his head.

"Powerpack charged and loaded?" Micah thought he'd spoken under his breath, but Cashman's dropped jaw and Veles's sharp look indicated that he hadn't. "All right, let's pull apart the image sync."

While he and Cashman worked, Micah sensed the movement around him as Pascal continued to set up for the meeting, removing materials from a coffinlike carrier set against the near wall. The wafer folders containing graphs and figures were expected enough, but the last display piece captured even the dour Veles's attention.

"Excuse me." Pascal set a mid-range shooter the size of a tall man's leg in the middle of the table as though arranging such things atop conference tables was something he did every day. "Show and tell," he said by way of explanation as he pointed the muzzle in the direction opposite the occupants of the room, then returned to the carrier.

We use those. Micah imagined the heft of the weapon in hands, hid a smile as he recalled the excited look on Manda's face when she blasted her first target to dust.

"What the hell?" Cashman backed a half step away from the table. "Keep that thing away from me."

"It's a dummy." Micah tried to keep his attention fixed on the imager, but something about the mid-range bothered him. The loadlight just fore of the grip fluttered like a beating heart, and that meant only one thing with this particular model. *Damned thing's loaded*. His grip on the image sync tightened so that Cashman muttered, and he handed the thing off. *Damned thing's for real*. Powerpack in place and ready to fly, as Chrivet loved to howl at the top of her lungs.

Micah waited for Pascal or Veles to notice, but they had adjourned to the far side of the room to discuss some aspect of the upcoming meeting, conversing in low tones as they checked a handheld display. *Shit*. Meanwhile, the loadlight continued to pulsate, promising all sorts of wall-blowing mayhem to whomever bumped or prodded the thing hard enough to engage the charge through.

Oh hell. Micah reached across the table and hoisted the weapon, taking care to keep it pointed away from everyone. *As if it matters*. As if the damned thing wouldn't blow out two adjoining walls if it let loose. *Damned fools*. He squeezed the grip and jammed back a nearly undetectable lever, discharging the powerpack with a loud click.

"Is there a problem, Lance Corporal?" Pascal gave the handheld to Veles and walked to the table.

"This thing was in firing mode, sir." Micah set the mid-range back on the table, then handed the pack to Pascal. "The power supply was engaged."

"That's the optics light, not the loadlight," Veles muttered.

"Captain Veles is correct." Pascal took the pack from Micah, then lifted the mid-range as though it were a feather and rammed it back into place. "There's a prototype still under development that has the indicators reversed, but the old hands charged with testing the thing are complaining because they're used to reading the loadlight through the sight. That's what this meeting is about." He set the weapon back in its place, shaking his head. "It is a dummy, by the way. This isn't the Haárin enclave." He shot Micah an annoyed glare, then returned to his conversation with Veles.

"How the hell did you know about the prototype?" Cashman removed the first in a series of alignment cartridges from the image sync and held them up to light.

Micah stared at Pascal's back, willing him to turn around, yet fearing what he'd see if he did. *He caught me . . . he caught me . . .* "I saw . . . a presentation."

"That must have been one hell of a presentation." Cashman's face brightened. "Hey, success!" He held up the sync, which now glimmered in activation. "Poles reversed on the left aspect." His brow knit. "I wonder how the hell that happened. No one had any problems with it yesterday."

"I'll bet." Micah waited for Pascal to turn around, to look at him, to drive home with a superior smile the fact that he had won this round. But the man still seemed too involved with the upcoming presentation to care. He didn't even bother to dismiss them, but let them leave without a word.

The day continued free of incident, which meant that Micah didn't see Pascal anymore. He hunted the meeting files for any information concerning mid-range prototypes, any presentation or article that he could point to and say *I learned this here.* But he couldn't find a single reference, including one to the meeting that Pascal claimed to be chairing. *He made it all up. Jazzed the imager and switched weapons, just to trick me.* He wondered what Pascal's next move would be, and if he stood a chance in hell of seeing it coming.

He pondered his situation during his walk home. As he cooked his solitary dinner. As he changed into his casuals, grabbed his sim gear from its drawer, then donned it and lay back on his couch.

The tones sounded. Micah struggled to concentrate on them, and waited. Waited. Waited—

"We're walkin' in Jesus' footsteps, boys and girls! Across the water, one, two, three!"

Micah spotted the back of Chrivet's helmet through the lakespray, and imagined clobbering her with his mid-range. *This is no time for blasphemy, Sergeant.* A swell chopped his ankle, and he barely caught his stumble in time. *If this is the embassy, then we need all the help we can get.*

He tried to imagine what they looked like as they bore down on the shore, larger-than-life figures in full exoskeletal kit, running atop the lake surface as though they splashed through puddles. Superhumans. Metal-framed giants. The first wave in the nightmare war.

Sitting ducks. Micah swallowed, and tasted acid from his overworked stomach. *A fully loaded idomeni lakeskimmer can pick us off from three kees away.* Five, if the exo's emission scramblers malfunctioned, as they had been wont to do lately.

He flicked off his infrared viewer and looked to his right. Bevan ran next to him—he knew that from the position grid on his helmet display—but he couldn't see him. The refractors on the suit surface reflected the color of the water, the nearby shore, the cloud-filled night sky, leaving only the appearance of *something* that might be a shadow of a cloud across the moon, or a breaking wave, or a swooping gull.

But the idomeni will see something. Or they'd believe their instruments instead of their eyes, and shoot.

"Tiebold, where's your infrared!"

"Ma'am!" Micah turned it back on, and watched the dark

horizon bloom with shape and color. They passed the last outbuildings of the Exterior Ministry, hazy dull white from trapped heat. *Thermabrick*. He fixed on the view and calibrated. The outlines sharpened.

"Target at eleven, distance zero point two four two kilometers."

Micah looked just off to his left, Chrivet's tinny voice ringing in his ear. *One and a half minutes to landfall*. The first outbuildings of the idomeni embassy came into view, lakeskimmer dry docks and maintenance sheds, cool grey from inactivity.

Or damping. Micah cranked the gain on his comdetect. "Idomeni in the maintenance shed. Three, maybe four."

"O'Shae. Foley." Chrivet gestured toward the shed. "Go!"

The two peeled off and skirted atop the swells, exoclad legs churning. They hit the skimmer ramp at speed, barely missing stride as O'Shae shot a concussion grenade into the shed and Foley ran ahead and sprayed the grounds with deadhead to wreck the biosense.

Micah watched his helmet displays burst into multicolor as the grenade blasted his sound dampers and the deadhead clouds chilled through the air in a purple tumble. *Filters*. He checked the status of his inlets, and breathed a shaky sigh. Deadhead had been manufactured to counter idomeni-made biosensors, but shit happened at the damnedest times and he didn't want to test the limits of his suit systems at this particular moment.

He hit the ramp two strides behind Bevan—any misstep meant collision meant disaster. The grounds swept past, deadhead swirling around them. Twenty meters ahead, Foley bulled through the gardens, spraying brickwork, and hit the entry full-force with his ram. The door blew inward, fileting any idomeni standing within ten meters.

"Lakeskimmers in one minute!"

Micah looked to his right just before he shot through the opening and saw the idomeni vessels ride up over the rocks, mid-range shooters at the ready. One of them fired, then another. A charge cracked over Micah's head, sending his displays into seizure.

Three peeled off to take care of the idomeni. Bevan. Two others. *Too easy, glory boy—the real shit's on the inside.*

Through the hole. Inside the embassy living quarters. No lights. Purple clouds everywhere—Foley, pumping out deadhead, blowing more systems. Micah stayed with O'Shae while the others peeled off down the maze of halls. O'Shae blew the doors, while Micah followed up with blasts into every open room. More concussion grenades. Plaster powdered from the walls and ceiling. A chandelier crashed down.

"Enemy at six five oh!" Manda, one wing over. *"Contact imminent!"*

Six five oh. The main hall. *Through those doors.* Micah dogged O'Shae's heel, advancing another grenade clip just as the displays in his sightline went mad.

"Contact—" A crackle. Nothing.

Manda! Micah checked his display. Blitz of colors. Overload. Through the doors behind O'Shae—purple smoke everywhere. Shouts. Screams. Idomeni, otherworldly giants in exos, fighting hand-to-hand, typed weapons useless, blitzed by deadhead.

Untyped weapons—just fine.

An impact in his right side. A shower of red from below, spraying across his faceplate.

A scream. His.

Micah removed his headset, taking care to wipe away the sweat. He sat up, surprised as always by how drained he felt. Well, maybe not so surprised anymore.

He rose from the couch and checked the clock. *Forty-two minutes.* The actual training exercise still took only fifteen to twenty. *Means the hypno took longer to lull me.* Five minutes more than the last time, and fifteen minutes more overall. *You can build up resistance over time.* What effect that could have on his training, he had no idea.

Micah walked to the kitchenette, working his arms and shoulders along the way. His upper back felt like a board, his legs as stiff as if he'd hiked the Devil's Trail at Fort Aqaba. He filled a cup with cold water and drank it. Refilled, and drank that, too. Then he stood at the sink, cup dangling from his hand, and tried to think about what had happened.

"I should have ramped down my gain before entering the embassy. That's why my displays kept blitzing—settings too sensitive." Micah lifted the cup, regarded the inside, and poured the few drops of water remaining into the sink. "I shouldn't have burst in after O'Shae. What happened to Manda should have alerted me. Instead of storming the main hall with the rest, I should have searched the halls for more living quarters to blitz." He'd have looked for hostages as well. So far it didn't seem they were being encouraged to take hostages, but if a highly placed Deputy Whatever meant the difference between blood across his faceplate and escaping with his life, it didn't seem such a difficult choice.

"You have the wrong attitude, Lance Corporal." He was supposed to be willing to die for the Cause. "And I have. Fourteen times, so far." Bevan, on the other hand, always seemed to survive, at least longer than he did. That pissed him off. "Why do I keep dying?" What the hell had hit him hard enough to kill him—the exo liners had been built to take grenade-level impacts, and no metal blade in existence could hack through them.

He opened a drawer, removed a flask, and uncapped it. "To the Group. To the Cause." He raised the flask to his lips and threw back his head. Took a pull of whatever the hell it was—gin, vodka? Swallowed fast. Recapped the flask and tossed it back in the drawer, which he kicked closed on his way to the bathroom. "I don't think we should come in off the water." He stepped into the shower, activating it. The spray hit him in the face, jolting him. "Damned Bevan." He muttered over the man's apparent luck. It kept his mind off Manda, and the memory of his own blood coating his faceplate.

CHAPTER 15

Micah expected to find MPs waiting beside his desk when he arrived for work the next morning. Instead he found Cashman, standing vigil with a doughnut and a dispo of vend alcove coffee.

"I have a favor to ask." He followed Micah into his cube and set the office breakfast down on his desk. "It will only take an hour of your time."

Micah stared down at the coffee. He wondered what it would taste like with vodka in it, and if anyone would notice if he hid a flask in his desk. He'd dreamed again the night before. Relived the lake assault from a different angle. Saw what happened to Manda.

"You see, we've got this skimcart that has to be returned to the main receiving dock." Cashman leaned against Micah's desk and dropped his voice to a whisper. "We borrowed it, sort of. I mean, we meant to take it back right after we finished—we used it to help Kirit in SysAdmin move last week and—"

"You stole a cart, and you want me to take it back because someone in Central Receiving knows you took it and they're laying for you." Micah broke off a piece of the doughnut and bit into it. It proved to be coconut, which he hated. But he'd thrown up his breakfast earlier that morning, and his stomach ached from emptiness. "Where is it?"

"In the west stairwell alcove." Cashman patted his shoulder. "And if you ever need anything, anything at all—"

"I'll add it to the list." Micah refastened his coat, then polished off the doughnut, alternating with gulps of coffee. "If anyone stops by for me, tell them whatever you want." He crumpled the cup and tossed it in the trash, then counted his steps as he walked out of his cube to the door, something he hadn't done in years. It was a habit that had taken him through rough times in his youth, one that allowed him to concentrate on the immediate and ignore whatever waited around the corner, forget about whatever he had left behind. . . . *five . . . six . . .*

"Fabe?"

Micah stopped. *Step number seven.* He turned to find Cashman staring after him. "What?"

"You OK?" Cashman shifted from one foot to the other. "You look like somebody died."

Micah smiled, wondering if the expression looked as fake as it felt. Then he faced the door again and resumed his walk. *Eight . . . nine . . . ten . . .*

He found himself watching the faces that passed him on the way to Receiving, on the alert for anyone who looked like he felt. If he did find someone, he decided, he'd swing the cart in front of them, pretend it was an accident, then engage them in conversation. Ask them why they felt the way they did, and if their replies sounded at all likely, whether they belonged to the Group, too.

He needed a friend like Wode again. He needed someone to talk to. His constant dying had gotten under his skin over the weeks, but last night had been the worst of all. He still felt the impact in his side. Saw his blood spatter across every blank surface.

The sun shone warm, but he couldn't feel it. The sky filled his eyes, clear and blue, but he didn't care.

Receiving dominated the Far North region of the base, a five-story whitestone mass set in the middle of a skimway hub jammed with trucks and vans. Micah dragged the cart onto the main platform, told the civilian foreman that he'd found it under a tree in the South Central region of the base, then departed before anyone could ask him any questions. He wasn't in the mood for questions. Answers, yes, he could do with a few of those, but not questions. He trudged back along the main walkway, still watching faces, and counting his steps.

"Good morning, Lance Corporal."

Micah felt the doughnut and coffee meld together into a leaden mass. "Captain Pascal, sir. Good morning."

"Funny seeing you in this area of the base," Pascal said as he drew even. He wore civvies, a blue shirt and darker trousers, a short coat. "Someone who lives in the enlisted housing blocks would come in from the south."

"I needed to drop off a cart in Receiving, as you no doubt saw." Micah gave up on commiserating faces and quickened his step, wondering whether he could lose Pascal in the day shift crowds and knowing just as surely that it would take a bomb to shake the son of a bitch off his tail. "I've already been in the office. But I'm guessing you know that, too."

Pascal watched Micah for a few strides, his face deceptive in its kindness. Then he nudged him toward a snack kiosk, first maneuvering him to a table, then watching him while he purchased two coffees and a couple of breakfast rolls. "If you're ready to talk," he said as he set two dispo trays down on the table, "I'm ready to listen." He sat in the chair opposite Micah and unwrapped his roll, a meat-and-cheese-filled turnover glistening with fat glaze.

Micah watched Pascal bite into the sandwich, the meat juice drip and the cheese string, and quickly looked away. "I'm afraid I don't know what you mean, sir."

Pascal nodded. "All right. Let's back up." He set down his

sandwich, wiped his fingers on a napkin, took a swallow of coffee, and sat back. "It's been noted by people you work with that your mood has undergone a gradual but definite change over the past weeks. This change, to the best anyone can determine, first became noticeable shortly after the mine incident at the Haárin enclave." He leaned forward again. The cheap plastic chair creaked under his weight. "Are the two events necessarily related? No, of course not. You may be upset over a family matter, or another personal issue. If this is the case, just say so, and I'll leave you be. But if it's not . . ." He spread his hands wide, then picked up his sandwich and took another bite.

Micah sat, his arms folded across his chest, and tried to concentrate on the people walking past. Uniforms, gym clothes, civvies, all shapes and sizes.

Then a lithe, dark-haired girl caught his eye. She cut through the crowds like a fish around rocks, briefbag jogging against her hip, young face lined with concentration born of stress. *Manda?* He almost boosted to his feet to chase after her, but Pascal's steady stare weighted him down.

"Someone you know?" He finished his sandwich and tossed the tray into a nearby trash receptacle.

"No, sir." Micah sagged back, then picked up the coffee cup and held it for the warmth. "I thought I recognized the eyes."

Pascal watched him, as though waiting for him to say more. Then he set his elbows on the chair arms and linked his hands, legs stretched out before him as though trying to catch every available ray of sun. "You never showed an aptitude for infantry training while you were in Basic, or an interest, for that matter. All your test scores highlighted your technical abilities." His gaze moved over the passing crowd, then back to Micah. "We all change over time, of course, for varying reasons." He smiled. "Some do so because such is their way. They are always altering, adapting, trying new things. They could no more remain static than I could breathe underwater. For them, change is life." He picked up his napkin, tearing off bits and rolling them between his fingers. "But there are others who change only because they feel they have no choice. They look about them, and see a world they no longer understand. A world they fear. They change because it is the only way they believe they can return things to what they consider normal. They force themselves into situations for which they're ill-suited, ill-trained, in the hope that if they act emphatically enough, their world will revert to the way it was." After he had built a pile of rolled bits of napkin, he started picking them up one at a time and flicking them into his coffee cup.

Micah watched as one piece after another arced into the cup, and prayed for Pascal to miss while knowing as surely as he breathed that his prayer would go unanswered. He broke off a piece of his sandwich, which proved to be the same meat–cheese mishmash as Pascal's, and chewed slowly to keep from getting sick. The morning crowd had thinned, allowing him a clear view of the grounds, the rolling lawns and flowering trees, the bright white buildings beyond. *He's been reading my ServRec.* He swallowed, the food going down like hot cement. *Well, so what? There's nothing there.* Only things that he knew. Nothing he *felt*. Nothing he believed.

"Take the late Lance Corporal Wode." Pascal had stopped flicking napkin nibs, and now tore a long strip and wrapped it around his finger like a ring. "His psych evals revealed a man who felt very strongly that tradition should be maintained, even at the expense of growth, of knowledge. Quite the hidebound individual. You could group him with those people you see on CapNet, the ones who shake their fists at the holocam and shout 'idomeni, go home.'"

Micah set down his cup, then brushed away the coffee droplets that dotted his fieldcoat. He'd flinched at the word "group," but he didn't think Pascal noticed. Hoped he didn't, anyway. *You freak-fucking bastard—you're not fit to speak Rik's name.* He almost blurted his opinion out loud, and barely stopped himself in time. *That's what you want, isn't it? For me to blow up, give myself away. Well, forget it.*

"Some of my superiors feel that Wode took his interest in interactives one step too far, that he obtained the means to engage in some sort of simulated combat training, with an eye toward someday fighting idomeni." Pascal worked the napkin ring from his finger, then started twisting it into a tighter band. "The problem with that was the fact that he skipped the bioemotional pre-conditioning. I've gone a few rounds with the sims over the years, on both sides of the headset. I've seen what it does to people. The hands never get bloody, but the brain can't tell the difference. You kill one too many, or die once too often, and your judgment goes over the side. You lose the ability to think clearly. You hear about conditions like sim synesthesia, sim psychosis, and wonder if they could happen to you." He worked the paper ring from one finger to the next. "At times like that, you need someone who'll listen. Who'll understand."

Micah pressed a hand to his right side, to the ache beneath his ribs that grew sharper and deeper the more Pascal talked. "There's someone in our department who knows all about you. You had an emotional augmentation when you were a teenager, courtesy of Exterior Minister Ulanova. It damps down your emotions, keeps you from feeling." For a mad moment, he wondered if Pascal somehow knew the girl who was Manda. Whether she had fallen for the face and the accent as so many had. Whether Pascal had taken her. "Empathy's only a word to you, so don't even try," he said, rage choking him. "In fact, why don't you just shove it up your ass!"

"I don't understand why you're taking this attitude." Pascal twisted the ring into a figure eight and tossed it into his cup. "I only want to help."

"Yeah, right." Micah forced another bite of the roll. "You know, it's not really the done thing for you and me to be seen together like this. I suggest that given your reputation, a charge of fraternization or even sexual misconduct would give somebody the excuse they needed to bust you right out of here." He stood, brushed the crumbs from the front of his coat. "Thank you for breakfast. Now I really must be going."

"If you believe you have legal recourse, by all means, give it a try. I look forward to answering questions about my interest in you." Pascal stood and performed table-clearing duties, tossing their mess into the trash receptacle. "I'll be watching you, Faber."

Micah started down the walkway. The place between his shoulders burned—he knew Pascal watched him, but would sooner have dropped dead than turn around to confirm. Instead he kept his eyes fixed straight ahead, shoved his hands in his coat pockets to warm them, and counted his steps.

Elon adjusted her headset, struggling to discern anything useful from the burst of voices that battered her ears. Godly though the argument of Vynshàrau might have been, this was not the time.

"I see them, nìaRauta." Ghos steered the skimmer past trees and over logs and rocks, gesturing in anger as branches scraped against the sides of the vehicle with a sound as the claws of demons. "They are . . . *there*!"

In the near distance, the skimmer they pursued became visible, skirting around a stand of evergreens and slicing low-hanging fronds as a blade. A battered thing, its blue color faded from sun and chemical damage. *Humanish*. Elon's shoulders rounded. Only they would allow a vehicle to degrade so.

"They move too quickly for this place!" Ghos slipped into Vynshàrau Haárin, his words as clipped and his voice devoid of gesture. "They will collide with a tree, and the humanish newssheets will say that Vynshàrau are to blame for forcing such." He sped up as well, gaze fixed on the path ahead, hands moving over the controls.

"Humanish blamed us for the mine. For the death of our own. Such would be a change, to blame us for a thing we actually did." Elon removed her shooter from her belt holster and activated it. "This is the fourth such incursion since the mine, Ghos. I tire of such. It must cease."

Ghos slowed as he maneuvered through the forest maze, speaking more than he had since Elon knew him as he declaimed over the madness of the humanish driving. Trees closed in from all sides. A branch thudded against the skimmer roof, sending a frantic fur-tailed animal sliding down the windscreen and off onto the ground.

Ghos half rose from his seat as they careened into a clearing. "We have them, nìaRauta!"

The tree-ringed circle appeared as an animal pit. Four embassy skimmers surrounded the battered two-seater and slowly closed in, backing it toward the trees. Then they moved more closely together, so that they faced it in a line and could fire upon their quarry at Elon's order. As a captured thing, the blue vehicle flitted about the shrinking space, probed for an opening, then stilled as it found none.

Elon activated the skimmer audio array, then paused to beg the gods for calm. She spoke English only when necessary, and as such, did not speak it well—with the prospect of combat, the ability to do such threatened to leave her completely. "You have trespassed upon idomeni land, deeded as such by your dominants." Her words cut through the air as a weapon. "You will throw your weapons from your vehicle to the ground, and disembark." She deactivated the array and gestured to Ghos. "What do you see?"

"Three occupants—two male and a female." Ghos monitored the scan display set in the middle of the control array. "They are all armed—expect four shooters, including a mid-range."

"To activate a mid-range in such a small vehicle—would they be so stupid?" Elon evaluated the distance to the humanish skimmer. "The recoil would send them backward into the trees, and the newssheets would blame us for such as well."

Ghos unholstered his weapon and activated it. "I could leave our vehicle and approach them, compel them to shoot at me, and force them to do such."

"*Ghos!*" Elon slipped into Vynshàrau Haárin, such was

her anger. "Feres's soul has just been released—I will not officiate at another Vynshàrau death in this damned cold place!" She gripped her right hand within her left and squeezed. The rebroken bone had long since healed, but if she compressed enough, she could induce some pain, and employ it to focus her mind. "I repeat to you," she said, reactivating the audio array, "throw away your weapons and disembark your vehicle!"

The humanish two-seater hovered low to the ground. Then, as though it awakened from sleep, it elevated slightly, rotating until it faced Elon head-on, until she could discern the vague shapes seated behind the tinted windscreen.

"They are to charge." Ghos reached for his door lever. "They are to—"

Before Ghos could disembark, the humanish skimmer launched toward them, advancing in the beat of a heart, elevating at the last instant, leaping above them so that Elon could see the waves of iridescence the magnetic drives had induced in the metal of the lift array.

Then the audio array screeched, the sound filling her head as a white-hot thing. She screamed and tore the headset away, as around her scan displays blanked, then flooded with light and gibbered signals.

"Their shielding is damaged—they attacked us with such!" Ghos tried to steer the skimmer around, but the magnetic battering had rendered it crippled. The engines whined. The displays showed only fragments of words and histograms.

The other embassy skimmers streamed past them in pursuit of the humanish. Ghos muttered in Vynshàrau Haárin and tried to reset all systems at one time, while Elon aided him, half deafened, her ears ringing.

At last they reactivated. At last they turned and gave chase. Ghos followed the scan, the trail of broken branches, as Elon contacted her suborns. "They have attacked!" She barely heard her words. *"Take them!"*

They entered another circle of trees, this one nearer the

road that led to the humanish skimways. They found four skimmers in a line, facing a wall of brush and stone, and eight Vynshàrau milling in the grass.

Elon disembarked and walked across the circle to her suborns, slowing to allow Ghos time to overtake her and precede her, the cries of birds piercing her deafness.

"They have escaped, nìaRauta." NìaRauta Laur gestured toward the wall. "I witnessed them leap over the barrier as an animal, yet none of our scans detected the disruption of the security array."

"Humanish skimmers do not *leap*." Ghos holstered his shooter and walked to the wall. He climbed to the top, using the brush as handholds, and kicked at loose stones that lay scattered on the surface.

"Scan the grounds," Elon said to Laur. "If these humanish were able to arrive and depart without detection, they most likely spent much time here. It is therefore even more likely, and truly, that they left something behind. Contact the humanish Service and ask them of their mines. Ask them if they ever used this land as a training ground as well." She watched Ghos and another suborn pull at the stones and gesture displeasure. "And contact ní Tsecha. Wherever he is, whatever he does, bring him to me."

Elon returned to the embassy and retired directly to her rooms. Her cook-priest berated her for missing the time of her mid-morning sacrament, then led her to the altar room and stood over her as she begged forgiveness of the gods.

She prayed as she ate, her still-damaged hearing making her voice sound as something far away. Then she removed her grimed coverall, laved, and donned the pale green trousers and shirt, the off-white overrobe more appropriate to hallways and meeting rooms. Sat at her worktable and studied the layout of the embassy, and tried to determine how the humanish gained access to the grounds. Felt the rage build within her as a living thing as she pondered how she had come to be sent to this damned cold place, to watch her suborns die, chase down decrepit skimmers, and remove that which they left behind as a keeper of beasts removed their waste.

Her door chime sounded, though such was its pitch that it took some time before she realized it did so. She rose from her table and walked to her door, forming a fist with her right hand and striking the entryway arch as she passed beneath.

"NìaRauta." Ghos still wore his coverall, and had tucked a documents case under his arm. "You are as deaf."

"Yes, Ghos."

"When the mine deafened me, you compelled me to go to my physician-priest. I will do the same now to you."

"After I speak with Tsecha." Elon cradled her hand, which throbbed and stung when she sought to straighten her fingers. "What is your report?"

"Laur is leading the scanning of the land." Ghos walked inside. He had bound his braided fringe into a single rope of hair to keep it away from his face, which had been scratched in several places by brush and had bled accordingly. "They have already found small amounts of humanish food in storage sheds, in greenhouses and security bunkers."

"No explosives?" Elon waited until Ghos gestured in the negative. "I have read of such things. They wish us to know that they have breached our defenses, that they may do so again as they will. And to do this, they taunt us with their food, for they know that no greater insult to our way exists."

Ghos set the documents case atop Elon's worktable. "I have brought the readouts from the stations confirming no sign of incursion." He removed a sheaf of wafers and set them beside her workstation. "They have overridden our defenses, Elon. What is there to do?"

"Implant our structures with sensors that are not integrated into our systems. Fit those sensors to loud alarms." Elon rubbed one ear. "Drive them as deaf if they invade again." She drew alongside Ghos, tilting her head in puzzlement as she comprehended the condition of his hair. "Ghos, you wear twigs." She reached up and plucked a thin branch from one of his braids. Half a finger in length, brown and grey, a hard bud at one end.

Ghos unbound his braids and shook them out with his hands—three more twigs fell onto the table, along with a strip of leaf. He picked them up, one by one, then handed them to Elon. "Burn them. Smear the ash on pieces of scroll and burn them again."

"Such will not serve as enough. Such as this place can never be purified." Elon rubbed the objects between her hands as though to grind them to dust, but the wood was too hard and the leaf too new, and thus did not powder but remained intact. "Yet you would have left our skimmer and walked before the humanish, drawn their fire and most surely been injured. Or died."

"You will say that it would be better to die within the worldskein than here. I maintain that it would not." Ghos rebound his braids, tying them as tightly as though he prepared for *à lérine*. "I maintain that we are already damned, all of us damned, so what difference? Tsecha denies Sànalàn, and should thus face the wrath of the gods. But time has passed, and what is the decision of Temple? Of Council? Have you read a decision, nìaRauta, for most assuredly I have not. Have you seen him confined, returned to the worldskein, executed, as he most assuredly should be?" He paced. "*Politics*. Cèel ponders if he may risk Haárin wrath by doing as he must to Tsecha, by treating him in the way the gods demand. Thus do I pronounce him damned, and with him, each of us, for he is as our Oligarch, and he has failed in his duties, and thus have the gods rejected us all." He stopped before her, took her damaged hand in his own and opened it. Took one of the twigs and held it before her face, looking her in the eye as he did so, as had become more and more his way. "Each of us to be burned, and the ashes smeared upon scroll, to be burned again, and even then we will not be clean."

"*Ghos.*" Elon felt the horror of disputation carried too far. "You blaspheme."

"Do I, Elon?" Ghos tossed the twig upon her worktable, then released her hand as though it were a thing of glass. "Yet even so, this place must burn." He took a step back from her, his eyes still meeting hers. His pale eyes, so bright against his pallid face, against which the blood shone like jewel.

Elon looked down at her hand, still felt the departed pressure. Then she crossed her arm over her chest and tilted her head in confusion, and even as the entry chime rang out, she did not hear it until Ghos gestured toward the door.

"NìaRauta?" Laur entered, looked from Elon to Ghos, and stood most straight. "Ní Tsecha attends."

Elon gestured in affirmation, aware of Ghos's anger as a living thing between them. "I will speak with him."

"*Politics.*" Ghos swept a hand across the worktable, sending the twigs and leaf to the floor, and strode to the door, forcing Laur to step aside to allow him to pass.

CHAPTER 16

Elon entered the primary meeting room to find Tsecha standing before one of the low tables that lined the far wall of the sparsely furnished space, contemplating an arrangement of stones. He dressed most as Haárin, as was his habit since his outcast, in a blue that pained the eyes and an orange so near to red as to be ungodly. He looked to the door as she entered, regarding her as he used to at Temple when she argued with him over his blending heresies, his gaze fixed on the floor at her feet, hands clasped behind his back.

"So, Elon. Humanish food in your buildings, and skimmers that leap about as beasts and evade capture." He turned his attention to the stones once more, this time picking one up and stacking it atop another, then removing it and doing the same again. "A grenade of pink could have halted your invader."

"No, Tsecha." Elon's shoulders rounded. Now, as when he served as ambassador, Tsecha felt he knew her duties better than she. "We would have damaged ourselves just as we damaged them. The new pink is not yet ready."

"It was not ready when I served in this place. It takes its time readying itself, and truly." Tsecha picked up another stone, but instead of adding it to his pile, he passed it from hand to hand. "What has Shai said of all this?"

"NìaRauta Shai attends a conclave with Prime Minister Cao. They discuss expansion of GateWay rights, I most believe. As always, Samvasta serves as issue due to its nearness to Shèrá. The humanish wish it so very much, and Cèel has ordered Shai to withhold." Elon stepped across the room to a window that looked out over the gardens. The sky pained the eyes as did Tsecha's shirt, yet such did she esteem, for it lit the hybrid grasses and shrubs to a brilliance that took her to Rauta Shèràa. The time just before first planting, when the leaves greened and the sun burned low in the sky.

Tsecha set down the stone. "You have not told her of this latest incident?"

"No." Elon remained at the window. "I most prefer to examine such matters most completely before I inform nìaRauta Shai. I prefer to understand reasons, and determine that which must be changed." She pressed her hand to the windowpane, imagined heat, but felt only cold. "Humanish did not attack us in this way until the enclave came to be. They did not despise us so until you went out among them. They once enjoyed you, for they believed you only a visitor here. Now they fear you, for they know you mean to stay and force your blending prophecies upon them." She paused, laboring to think of words to describe that which to this point had only been vague impression, the unformed sensation of the soldier who recognized menace she could not define. "Therefore, I would ask you to leave this place, and return to Rauta Shèràa. Today. Tomorrow. As soon as you may."

Tsecha moved down the table, away from the stones and toward a bowl fountain. "And the other Haárin? Dathim and the rest?" He placed his fingers beneath the water stream, and the gurgling softened to a quiet patter.

"They should return with you." Elon stepped back from the window, but remained some distance from Tsecha and his table contemplations. She had never entertained a wish to draw close to him, and now, more than at any time, she wished to remain well away. "I have thought of this a great deal since the time of the mine explosion. Since the time I conveyed Feres's soul to his final place. It is with you that all this began, Tsecha. It is with you that it all will end. It is with you that it all must end."

Tsecha raised his hand from the fountain stream, watched the water drip from his fingers to the tiered bowls beneath. "As always, Elon, your reasoning is flawed. Even at Temple school was it so. When you were required to think as a soldier, you pondered as a student, and when you were required to ponder as a student, you thought of nothing but advance or retreat." He shook the last drops from his hand, then wiped it over the front of his shirt. "My leaving this place will not end these attacks. They would have occurred if I had never lived, for they speak to the weakness of both humanish and idomeni. Humanish, who only know advance and retreat, as the soldier, and idomeni, who withdraw to ponder and suppose, as students until death."

Elon drew back from the window, away from the light that pained her eyes and the color that struck at her soul. Yet she did not want to leave the view, and the need to do so angered her. "We are warriors as well, Tsecha."

Tsecha took a step closer to her, nearer the sun that entered through the window. The brightness accented the water stains of his shirt, the almost-red darkened to blood. "We attack one another within the bounds of our classroom. We argue points of law with blades. But we do not advance. We have built ships of space for as long as have humanish. Yet we have only ten poor colony worlds to show for our labors. They have near to fifty, and bother us as starving youngish for our share." He once more clasped his hands behind his back, and studied a flaw in the ceiling that only he could see. "But as starving youngish, they think only of their own hungers and how to assuage them—if a slap gives them what they wish, they will continue to slap until their target sickens of being struck and slaps back. If I departed, they would most believe, and with reason, that they drove me away. My remaining, all our remaining, serves as a return slap. It is necessary, Elon. It is as it must be. Therefore will I stay."

Elon rubbed her hands together, imagined the twigs between them, the twigs that even now remained scattered across the floor of her rooms. "Allow the humanish to think as they will, but do that which is godly. That which is best for Haárin."

"Such a day it is, Elon, when you think at all of Haárin." Tsecha bared his teeth at the ceiling, then lowered his gaze once more to the place at her feet. "No. Such is my answer. No, and no again." He walked to the other side of the space, toward a cloth-draped pedestal. "I see that Shai maintains sculpture in the meeting rooms." He removed the cloth and poked at the half-formed mound beneath. "During my time at Temple, I never saw her but with a lump of clay in her hand. She required it, so she said, to quell her anger. When she first arrived here, she did not use such. Now I see that she has taken it up again." He studied the sculpture for a time, then shook out its cloth and covered it once more. "Is this why you summoned me here? To beg my return to Shèrá?"

Elon walked to the middle of the room and circled a ring of chairs. Her body ached as it always did after the discord of a pursuit, yet she could not sit. Instead she paced, and pondered what to reply. *As a student.* She gripped the back of a chair, squeezing until her knuckles paled to white. "That is why, Tsecha. Yes."

"Shai will not appreciate this fact. She prefers to know when I am about this place." Tsecha walked to the door, his stride relaxed, as though he had not sentenced a race to despair with his decision. "If you are not occupied with more impossible requests, I would ask and truly that you come with me. Someone is here with whom you as security dominant should speak."

Elon followed Tsecha down the wide corridor that led to the verandas. "I must meet with my suborns most soon to talk of this attack." She had fixed her eyes on her former dominant's narrow shoulders, which had seemed as old when she schooled at Temple and now seemed as those of a youngish, clothed as they were in Haárin blue.

"Then you will want to discuss such here first, I most believe." Tsecha pushed open a hinged door and stepped out onto the walled veranda reserved for humanish.

Elon followed Tsecha out onto the veranda. By the far wall, near a pedestal fountain, stood Pascal, the Service captain, dressed in the clothes of the street. Pale stone colors, she noted, that did not offend the eye, however much their wearer did. Such strangeness. His stunted body, too broad and bulky. His hair, so pale as to be Oà, sheared as close to the skull as Tsecha's and Dathim's, his narrow face and weak jaw. *Ugly beings, are humanish.* How she wished, and truly, that she would never see one again. Next to him stood Dathim, clothed in green and brown, such subdued tones that Elon wondered if he sought mercy from the gods for Tsecha, who dressed as one who could not see that which he wore.

"NìaRauta." Pascal stood as a carving, his back most straight, gaze fixed at a point above Elon's head as a show of respect. "Ní Tsecha has told me of the attacks against the embassy," he continued in adequate High Vynshàrau. "I am most interested, and truly, as to the details, for this is the first I have heard of such."

Elon heard the movement of the door behind her, and turned to find Ghos standing in the entry. He now wore the clothing of the embassy, green and off-white, as she did, and had unbound his braids so they fell freely past his shoulders.

"We have not told humanish of these assaults." He spoke High Vynshàrau. Yet his voice and posture still held his earlier anger, and his intonations came as chopped and truncated as his harshest Vynshàrau Haárin. "What purpose would be served? Feres's soul has already arrived within the worldskein, so long ago did he die, yet humanish know nothing of the source of the mine that killed him. What good, then, to consult with you of this? More time spent, more worthless meetings, more politics, and less knowledge gained for all of that. You are as nothing, and truly."

"Ghos, silence." Elon sensed Pascal's surprise at Ghos's anger, Dathim's and Tsecha's irritation, and took what pleasure she could from the discord. "Even now, nìaRauta Sànalàn labors to purify those places." She stood aside so Ghos could move half a pace ahead of her, as was seemly. "So many are there that she will labor far into the night."

Pascal looked to Tsecha, then away. He drew his hand to his mouth, then recalled where he stood and let it fall. "My High Vynshàrau is adequate to most of my embassy dealings, but it may not prove so if the speech becomes too technical, or too heated. In such instances, I will speak English, and ní Tsecha or ní Dathim will translate. Is such acceptable?" He waited until they all gestured in the affirmative. "Any vehicle that managed to evade your security systems would have to have been specially equipped. Did you obtain any images of this one you saw today? Any scans or other identification?"

"Why should we discuss such with you?" Ghos looked to Pascal. "Strange humanish who befriends Haárin. Suborn of ná Kièrshia, who is anathema to all that is godly. What are you?"

"Ghos!" Elon looked to her suborn, who seemed most as determined to forget her existence, then to Pascal, who gestured again in question. "Yet such is something we would want to know, Pascal. You possess some standing in the humanish Service. Your loyalty is to them. Why, then, would you assist us?"

"Such is a most fair question." Pascal's right hand drew up in hesitation. "I fear the subtleties I must express to explain myself are beyond my grasp of High Vynshàrau, but I will try." His hand lowered. "As nìRau Ghos said, I am indeed suborn to ná Kièrshia. While she is absent from Chicago, I work for her, serving as her eyes and ears."

"But you wear the clothes of the Service, when you remember to." Ghos stepped closer, his hands clenching as his back bowed. "You act as the most ungodly Haárin—all know this who know anything. You serve any and all. You do not comprehend the meaning of order, or loyalty!"

"Ghos! Such is enough." Tsecha's back bowed. "You wish to know more of the humanish who have invaded. I have one with me who can determine such."

"He is disorder!"

"He is between the lines, as he has always been! Such is no surprise to me!" Tsecha pushed up one sleeve. Silvered *à lérine* scars reflected the light, a warning to Ghos.

"He serves only the Kièrshia." Dathim stepped forward, his hands low before him, his weight balanced as a warrior who expected attack. "If you accept nothing else, you must accept that, and if you accept that, you must accept all that follows." He tilted his head, his shaved scalp a glinting mockery of the old ways. "Even a bornsect must comprehend such."

Ghos ignored him, his gaze fixed on Pascal. "Why are you here, humanish? To spy for your anathema, or your Service?"

Pascal raised his left hand chest high, palm out and fingers curved, a gesture of pleading. "I only wish to help. You are being attacked. I wish to find out more of these attacks— I believe I can assist you in preventing them."

"And I should believe you why?" Ghos moved to the side as a fighter trying to find his feet, while Dathim moved with him in an effort to stay between him and Pascal. He moved again, and again Dathim moved with him.

The movements of à lérine. Elon felt her own body sway in response as her fingers closed around the ghost of a blade.

"Elon." Tsecha drew close to her, his voice lowered in a damned humanish whisper. "Ghos is yours—order him to still."

"Why, ní Tsecha?"

"Because my Lucien does not understand what occurs."

"Yet you compel us to understand him? To trust him? Unfair, ní Tsecha. If your humanish does not understand us, then it is time he learned."

"You damn this place with each breath and beg the gods to deliver you, yet when you sense blood, you act as the animals you condemn?" Tsecha stepped around Elon toward Dathim and Ghos, who still moved in strange unison. "*Ghos*. Stand back. My Lucien does not comprehend."

Ghos took a step toward Tsecha. "You brought him here. You, who damned our souls by your outcast."

"You damn your own soul now, Ghos." Tsecha pushed up his other sleeve, revealing another lifetime of scars. "You have not listened. You have not thought. You only attack."

"I attack. Such should be no surprise to you." Ghos punched the air, his fist finding a space past Dathim's shoulder, a handsbreadth from the dodging Pascal.

The action shook Elon from her violent reverie. She stepped forward. "Ghos. Do not waste your honor on such as that. His blood offers nothing but chaos."

Ghos kept moving, foot crossing sideways over foot, a half step ahead of Dathim. "Then I will offer his blood to Caith, and beg her blessing." He dodged in, out, then in again, leaving Dathim still a half step behind. Then his fist shot out. The strike of a beast.

Pascal raised his open palm and met the blow. The crack of flesh and bone against flesh and bone sounded. Another strike. Another defense. Pascal darted away from Dathim so that he could move freely, took his place in the center of the floor. Ghos followed, and the two of them continued to punch one another, landing blows on torsos, shoulders, and arms. The godly moves of the circle of challenge, the only thing missing the blades.

"*Ghos!*" Tsecha closed in on the male from behind, and barely dodged an elbow in the pit of his soul. "Lucien! Stand behind Dathim. Do so now. End this!"

"There is no end to such as this without blood," Ghos said as he struck Pascal's chest and pushed him back.

Dathim closed in, back bowed. "Do you declare, then?"

He closed his hand around Ghos's wrist, stopping him in mid-strike. "Do you declare!" He shook him as a youngish, back and forth, as though he scolded him, his *à lérine* scars flashing pale in the light.

"Dathim! Silence!" Tsecha pushed himself between Ghos and his suborn and grabbed their hands, struggled to pry his suborn's hand from Ghos's wrist. "You have let your anger take you before, and this is not the time for such! Challenge for yourself, if you must, not for Lucien!"

Pascal breathed heavily, sweat coating his face. He straightened slowly, his fists still raised, ready to block Ghos if he struck again. "Dathim, back down."

Dathim turned on him, shoulders rounding. "Ghos has declared against you in every way but the last. You cannot walk away!"

Pascal lowered his fists. "Yes, I can."

"Then." Dathim released Ghos's wrist and backed away. "*Humanish*, who only pretends to learn."

"Ghos." Elon struggled to control her shaking voice. Old scars ached in memory. She longed for the finality of the circle, wished every humanish could leave their blood within its confines, felt her heart pound in response. "Not his blood." *Yes, his blood*, her soul told her, and she closed her mind to its pleas. "It is not godly."

"How godly are the damned?" Ghos flexed his hands, massaged his knuckles, looked toward Tsecha, then away. "I declare."

Pascal looked to Dathim; after a time, Dathim looked to him as well.

In the eye. Elon watched them, uncomprehending. *Most strange*.

Pascal pulled his sweat-darkened shirt from his body. "What do I say?" he asked in English

Dathim responded in English as well. "You say, I accept challenge."

Pascal nodded once. "I accept . . . challenge."

Tsecha pressed a hand to his forehead, a humanish gesture that at times denoted pain. *"Dathim."* He looked to Pascal, then away.

"I don't believe we have a procedure in place for this back at Sheridan." Pascal's voice emerged as dead. "Who contacts who?"

"You are the challenged. Therefore your dominant must contact Ambassador Shai." Tsecha spoke in his English, broad, flat sounds that did not seem to emanate from an idomeni mouth.

"There are—" Pascal paced a tight circle. "There are Service rules prohibiting duels. They're old, and haven't been enforced for a long time, but—" He emitted a harsh sound. "I can think of a few people who might want to try and dust them off."

Tsecha raised a hand, then dropped it, a gesture that for humanish may have meant something but for Vynshàrau meant nothing. "So, it is done." He ran a finger over one of his many scars, then pushed down his sleeves. "My Jani once fought as you will, Lucien, against nìaRauta Hantìa. I will contact General Burkett, who served as her dominant—he may offer advice to yours. He will be most surprised by this, I am sure." His posture altered to one of dismay. "My Jani will be, as well. Is she to be told now, or when she returns?"

"She'll read it in the newssheets, I'm guessing." Pascal looked to Dathim. "I have right of a second."

"I have acted as such before." Dathim nodded once, in an aggravating humanish manner. "I will train you as I trained ná Kièrshia."

"Thus and so." Tsecha pointed toward the entry, then stood most still as Pascal and Dathim walked ahead of him. "Inform Shai, Elon, that if she wishes to berate me, I will not listen." He took his place behind his strange suborn pair and followed them out of the veranda, his step most heavy.

Elon walked to a stone bench set in the veranda wall and sat. "Why, Ghos?"

"Because Pascal is anathema, and he who was Avrèl nìRau Nema brought him here to help us." Ghos seemed most as relaxed now, his shoulders straight, his hands un-clenched. "Because it is most fitting for a humanish to bleed here, in this soulless place. Because a cleansing rage is required to burn the cold dead from this place."

"Your hatred is indeed so strong?"

"Yes, nìaRauta. Did you doubt such?"

Elon crossed her right arm over her chest, gripping her left shoulder as hard as she could with her right hand. "I asked ní Tsecha to return to Shèrá, to take the Haárin back into the worldskein with him. To end his damned prophecy."

"Did you truly expect him to agree to such?" Ghos walked to the bench and sat beside her. "Such would be as Dathim rejecting challenge. An inconceivable thing, and truly." He reached for the pouch of pattern stones that always hung from his belt and removed it.

Elon watched him shake the colored ovals onto the bench between them. "Will you kill Pascal, Ghos of the Stones?"

"If I am able," Ghos replied as he worked the lines.

CHAPTER 17

"... for she is the bringer of pain and
change ..."

Clase, *Thalassan Histories, Book I*

John steered the skimmer up the narrow two-lane skimway,
slowing briefly as one of the momentary pockets of conges-
tion that passed for the Karistos morning rush closed in
around them. "Nervous?"

Jani finished smoothing her overrobe, then folded it in her
lap and sat back to play passenger for the last few minutes of
the drive. "Yes and no. I know Feyó. I like her. I think she
likes me." She looked out the window and watched the copper dome of the Haárin Trade Board loom ever larger, its
polished roundness at odds with the multistory white and
sand blocks that surrounded it. "It's all those nasty un-
knowns that have me jumpy. How much does she really fear
Gisa? How do the Elyan Haárin consider the hybrids? As a
curiosity? A threat? Will my presence as a substitute Tsecha
help or harm matters?" She stretched a section of overrobe
sleeve across her hand and tried to rub out yet another grimy
souvenir of her Thalassan rock-climbing exhibition. "I'm
not sure nervous is the right word."

"Terrified?" John grinned, his expression made riveting
by the black sunshades he'd donned to shield his eyes from
the morning dazzle. With the purple daysuit and his
blanched skin and white hair, the overall effect was less that

of a vampire than Death-takes-a-spin-around-town. "Do you want us to wait?"

Jani shook her head. "You don't have to."

"We'll wait," Niall announced from the rear seat. "I have nothing planned for this morning except to make sure you get to Fort Karistos after we finish here. You, Shroud?"

John's smile wavered. "I wanted to return to the hospital. Drop in on a few folks. See if a personal appearance could jog anyone's memory concerning Eamon." He raised his sunshades, regarding Jani with eyes filmed the same too-dark purple as his suit. "Hence the ensemble. Something about me looking funereal inspires truth-telling in the more impressionable."

"I'll keep that in mind." Jani batted her lashes at him, and they fought a skirmish of weird-eyed stares until a proximity alarm blared, forcing John to steer the skimmer back in their lane and focus on his driving.

Jani sneaked a look at Niall, who occupied the rear seat as if it was a couch, his feet up, Karistos *Partisan* in one hand and a smoking nicstick in the other.

"I can stay behind, then," he said. "Sit vigil in one of these parks." He set down the sheet and took in the view out his window. "Attractive town. Quite classical." He grimaced. "Hotter than hell, though."

John maneuvered the skimmer up to the curb in front of the Trade Board. "I must say, the location of this place surprises me." He leaned forward to catch a better look at the dome through the windscreen. "It's smack in the middle of town. There are outdoor restaurants right down the street."

"Look at the front." Jani pointed to the flat white facade. "No windows. No doors. I'm guessing that the air-handling system filters out all odors, and that any verandas are well sheltered from unseemly views. No Haárin has to tolerate anything they don't feel comfortable with, and the human-ish don't have to travel to the enclave for face-to-face meetings." She gathered her duffel and cracked open her gullwing. "Thank Feyó. She opened up the Board to humanish members, making it easier for them to deal with Haárin, which in turn demystified both sides. Some didn't like it, but most saw the advantages. So far, it's working." She pushed out the door, then swung her legs out of the cabin. "Well, wish me luck." She started to boost to her feet, then stopped when she felt the warm press of a hand on her shoulder.

"Luck." John squeezed lightly, then pulled away as though she burned. "When you're finished—"

"I'll be watching for her. I'll call you when she's done." Niall folded the newssheet and tucked it under his arm, then popped his gullwing and got out.

"Thank you, Colonel," John muttered under his breath. "If you lure him in front of the skimmer," he added, leaning close to Jani, "I should be able to at least graze him."

"I don't know—he's pretty fast." Jani straightened the straps of her duffel, conscious to the point of fixation of the memory of John's touch. "I don't blame him for being angry. He'll cool off eventually, I hope. The problem is that in the meantime, he's not going to let me out of his sight." She took a deep, bracing breath—the aroma of grilling meat mingled with the heavy sweetness of flowers and the tangy undercurrent of skimmer battery hyperacid. "Ah well. Onward." She got out, closed the door, and joined Niall, who paced the sidewalk.

"So how do you get in?" He took the half-spent 'stick from his mouth and used it as a pointer. "There's a walkway there." He indicated a pavered path that ran from the sidewalk around the right side of the building.

"That's probably it." Jani dropped her duffel between her feet and pulled on her overrobe. "You could come with me if you wish. Feyó knows you now. I'm sure she wouldn't mind." She glanced back at the traffic in time to see John's skimmer fade around the corner. "You'd have to lose the 'stick, though."

"It's all right. You'd just slip into Sìah Haárin, and leave me behind for lost." Niall looked across the street. "There's a park." He waved his newssheet toward a flower-packed square of green set with benches and tables. "If I get too hot, I'll dive into one of the shops."

"Your choice." Jani hoisted her duffel and headed for the walkway. "See you later."

"Luck."

Jani stopped, then looked back to find Niall regarding her, eyes narrowed by the sun's glare.

"I didn't specify good or bad, mind. We'll let fate decide that." He'd only stood outside for a few minutes, yet the sweat already dotted the front of his desertweight shirt. "I'll be on the lookout for you." The subtle threat of his words hung between them until he broke away, dodging a sudden flurry of skimmers in his dash across the street.

The Trade Board didn't have a lobby, per se. No reception area, no nests of chairs and tables set aside for shooting the breeze. Just a vast open space with a bare tiled floor and plain walls in shades of stone and sand that curved upward to form an arched ceiling, the only decoration a Sìah-style chandelier that resembled a jumble of blades. At the far end, a triple-width door of hammered copper marked the entry to the meeting rooms.

Jani set out toward the doors, her boots sounding muffled echoes. As she drew close, one copper panel swept open. Four Haárin emerged—Feyó, another female, and two males—all attired in shirts, trousers, and overrobes, their hair arranged in the breeder's braided fringe. Jani noted the jewel colors of Pathen on the males, while Feyó and the other female wore the more somber earth shades of Sìah. Feyó stood rearmost, which was to be expected since she possessed the greatest status and wielded the most power.

"Glories of the day to you, ná Kièrshia." Feyó spoke Vynshàrau Haárin in deference to Jani, and through her to Tsecha.

"To you as well, ná Feyó." Jani took in the grey gaze, sharp yet fatigued, that seemed drawn to the red-slashed sleeves of her overrobe.

"Your arrival at Elyas Station was, according to your Colonel Pierce, most as an incident. My apologies."

"You would have been unable to prevent it, I most fear. Some of the hybrids worked at the station. It was what we call in Chicago 'an inside job.'"

"Ah." Feyó cocked her head. "So you have borne witness to Thalassa, ná Kièrshia. You have seen those who live there, who call you 'the first.' You will inform ní Tsecha, of that I am most sure. His dream realized." She raised her cupped right hand in a gesture just short of supplication. "What say you?"

Jani remained silent as the realization of exactly what Feyó feared struck her. *She's afraid of Tsecha. She's afraid of me.* She glanced at the other Haárin, whose expressions and postures held more obvious discomfort. *They all are. They think I'll support Gisa because she's a hybrid, that Tsecha will do the same.* She struggled to quench the anger that flared like flame. Did they think her so simple that she would disregard the stability of an entire network of worlds for such a reason? Did they believe Tsecha, who had survived war, house arrests, and life on the bleeding edge of his stratified culture, would do the same? She stood in place, her face averted, and inhaled deeply and slowly of air that smelled as nothing at all. "It was only by luck that I learned of the existence of a hybrid before I departed Chicago, and even that was not a definite thing. It would have proved most helpful to have been apprised of Thalassa, the fact of which you have known for a very long time."

Feyó drew up straight. "Ní Tsecha will be displeased," she said, her voice pitched high in entreaty.

"He esteems you and values your advice. First with the

synthetic foods, then with this, you have led him wrong."
Jani struggled with an ire made more profound by the fact
that she liked Feyó, and thought she knew her. "Do you
comprehend in any way the risks to which you expose him
when you do so?"

Feyó's shoulders rounded as anger threatened to supplant
any sense of remorse. "I comprehend much that you do not,
nà Kièrshia."

She turned and walked through the copper door, and gestured for Jani to follow.

"Ná Gisa had served as suborn to me since her outcast. She
had once functioned as a Temple acolyte in the Síah dominant city of Ràlun, and was made Haárin for defending ní
Tsecha's prophecies. This was soon after the war of Vynshàrau ascension. Not a wise time to speak of blending."
Feyó led Jani to a pair of chairs situated near a window.
"From the beginning, she behaved most as difficult, but such
is the way of Haárin. And she served the enclave well. She
was trained as an agronomist, as was I. Much of our work in
synthetic foodstuffs may be credited to her, and truly." She
sat, then arranged the drape of the cuffs and hem of her off-
white overrobe. "But when ní Tsecha became ambassador,
she grew even more as difficult. The time had come, she told
me. Soon the blended race would dominate both Commonwealth and worldskein. This is when, I believe, she sought
out Doctor DeVries. It took most of a Commonwealth year
to build the Thalassan compound. Most of a Commonwealth
year until I noticed her change."

Jani sat in the chair next to Feyó's, then sought to settle
her nerves by contemplating the room. The sand-toned walls
had been painted with representations of grasses and flowers
in the corners and where walls and ceiling met, decorations
of pale green and light blue accented with the occasional
startling purple or pink. Flowering trees, both carved and
real, had been placed in copper planters and set throughout
the space, adding to the sense of lightness.

Wish it lightened my mood. Jani lowered her duffel to the floor, then nudged it beneath her chair with her heel. "What form has Gisa's challenge taken? Does she wish to meet you within the circle?"

"She sent communications to the dominants of the other Outer Circle enclaves, announcing that she declared my leadership unsound, that she is chosen of Tsecha to lead the Elyan Haárin." Feyó contemplated the view outside the window, a walled garden of native trees and tufts of scrub grass, interspersed with *sanna*, a green and purple striped plant native to the region around Rauta Shèràa. "When one says 'chosen of Tsecha' to Outer Circle Haárin, it can mean more than a single thing. To the more conservative, it means free trader who wishes to expand business. To the more liberal, it means a free thinker who wishes closer dealing with the humanish, as we have in this place. It has not yet come to mean hybrid to either faction, and that is where it all becomes most as confusing."

Jani shifted in her seat. The mantle of negotiator had never fit her well, and she could feel its imaginary collar tighten about her throat. "Have you and ná Gisa ever spoken together? Have you sought to discuss your conflict openly?"

"She is not sound."

"Have you tried?"

"Yes, ná Kièrshia. She will not comprehend sense."

Jani removed her ring and tilted it back and forth. The red stone caught the light and flashed a crimson needle on the wall opposite her chair—the flicker reminded her of a warning signal. "The other Board members will not put Gisa in your place. With or without ní Tsecha's sanction, the simple fact is that she lacks the standing to replace one such as you. Therefore I believe that we may discard that notion right off the bat." She ignored Feyó's look of confusion. Maybe the occasional dose of humanish slang would serve to fix the Haárin's attention on her visitor's words instead of her own arguments. "The underlying issue, from what I could gather, is the status of Thalassa in relation to the enclaves. Could you please clarify your position?"

Feyó remained silent for a time. Then she stood and walked across the room to one of the planters and fussed with an inset illumin attached to the end of a branch. "I offer Thalassa a chance at community, as is necessary for it to function, and to gain esteem from the other Haárin."

"Ná Gisa stated that you sought to treat it as part of the Elyan enclave, that you demanded allegiance to the dietary laws and acceptance of you as dominant."

"Gisa exaggerates."

"Then explain to me what you meant."

Feyó removed a flickering illumin from its holder and examined it. "An idomeni must belong, to a sect, to a skein. We must know how we stand among all others, at all times. Even we the outcast form our enclaves. Rare is the Haárin who survives as one alone, as you have." She glanced back at Jani, catching her eye for a bare instant before turning her attention back to the tree. "But just as important as how we see ourselves is how others see us. The Board members are, as you would say, conservative in their attitudes. Some will perceive Thalassa as disordered no matter what I do. But some will be persuaded that it has a place within the skein, and their opinions must be nurtured if we are to prevent the fracturing of Outer Circle alliances that Gisa's actions invite." She returned the illumin to its holder. It shone more steadily now, the flicker replaced by a faint pulse. "Some Haárin, I most fear, accept ní Tsecha's teachings in the abstract only."

Jani stared down at the ring in her hand, given her a seeming lifetime ago. Not for the first time she wondered if Tsecha realized what he had sucked her into. "You called me 'Haárin' even though I am not truly so and never will be. I am part humanish, as are all the Thalassans. Not only that, but some of us were born humanish. We will therefore always be different. Even as we come to resemble you physically, our minds will never work as yours. What you would perceive as a godly request from a dominant, we might see as an aggression, an untoward domination." She replayed Gisa's walk up the slope toward the main house, the set looks on the faces of her followers. "That is, I most believe, what you see in Thalassa now, the fear that you use the issue with the Board as an excuse to claim Thalassa as part of your enclave."

"It cannot remain alone as it is. The other dominants will not understand."

"Yet it must be allowed something of itself. The other Haárin must understand from the outset that it is as different, so that they do not expect its inhabitants to act in ways of which they are not capable."

Feyó left the planter and walked to a nearby cabinet set in the wall. "The Thalassans must change."

So must you, I think. Jani executed a slow ten-count. "Maybe they must, but not completely. They are a blending of two peoples. Such is the definition of hybrid." She looked down at her ring once more, this time so that she could hide the anger she felt take hold. *Yes, Gisa is out of line.* But Feyó was proving no better, merely less obvious. *Small thanks for little favors.*

"Ná Kièrshia?"

Jani looked up to see Feyó slide aside one of the cabinet doors and remove a hard-sided documents case.

"Three seasons ago, you aided us and the Karistosians in a matter of water supply." Feyó set the case on a table and opened it, removing a wafer folder and a portable display. "Much has occurred since then. If you attend," she indicated the place by her side, "I will show you."

Jani stared at the display as the last chart faded to nothing. Before her on the table lay stacks of documents, arranged according to language and source, function and content. Dock statistics, transit schedules, metric tonnage moved.

What was shipped and who shipped it, to every world in the Outer Circle.

"I had invited Colonel Pierce to participate in our talk." Jani powered down her scanpack. "I am very glad he turned me down." She tucked it back in its case, then returned the case to her duffel. It hadn't been mistrust that had caused her to pull out her dependable device and scan the paper that Feyó had shown her as much as the need to do something—with nerves came the need for motion. "He's concerned that the Haárin control too large a proportion of Outer Circle shipping." She lifted her chin toward the dead display. "He'd send the Service to lock down Elyas Station if he ever saw those numbers."

"We did not behave against humanish law, ná Kièrshia." Feyó gathered a handful of documents folders and tucked them back into the case. "The routes were there. The docks. Humanish had needs that their own did not see to. That being the case, at whom should Colonel Pierce be angry? At Haárin, for doing as they would in a legal manner? Or his own, for neglecting that which they might have taken as their own?"

"Both. He likes to spread it around." Jani lifted the cover of one of the folders and peeked at the topmost document. "Seventy-two point three percent of the transport traffic. Sixty-four point one percent of the shuttle traffic. The total percentage of slips controlled is on the light side—only 58.2—but that's only because whoever ran the tally included private and spaceliner docks. Subtract those, the number jumps to 73.8." She let the cover fall closed. "I'm amazed the Families didn't notice what was happening."

"Haárin suffered lost shipments. Disabled ships. But not so many, and the colonial humanish always seemed most interested in aiding us to recover that which was ours, and capturing those who injured us." Feyó put the last of the folders into the case, then collapsed the display and set it on top.

"They preferred us to their own, so it seemed. A strange concept for Haárin, but we adapted, as is our way."

"Apparently." Jani dragged her bag off the table and tossed it atop her chair. "You've heard of the attacks against the Chicago Haárin? You've heard of the mine explosion, and the death of the bornsect security suborn?"

"Yes—ní Tsecha informed me of such." Feyó shut the case back in its recess, her hand lingering upon the door. "Such will not happen here in the Circle. Our enclaves are old and well-established, and humanish have grown used to us."

"That's true for now." Jani walked to the window. The Trade Board building sat atop a hill, and thus commanded a formidable view of Karistos. Roofs of buildings, both flat and brilliantly domed, the palmlike trees popping up in between like strange dandelions. In the background, the blue sweep of the bay, shot through with ripples like liquid silver, backed by the coppery cliffs. *This place . . .* She turned away from the scene, because she wanted nothing more than to contemplate it for the rest of the day. "According to Colonel Pierce, humanish are just learning that those who lived at Thalassa are hybrid. Their . . . esteem for you may change now that they've learned of them. They may blame you for their existence, even though you bear no responsibility."

"We will announce such."

"They may not believe you."

Feyó gestured understanding. "Humanish do so seem to ignore that which is. Ní Tsecha told me of such during our talks in Chicago." When she uttered Tsecha's name, her voice rose in pitch, her back straightening in a posture of respect. "Many of my Haárin have taken to wearing their hair and clothing as humanish, especially since ní Tsecha's outcast. And humanish sometimes wear their hair in a way most as a napeknot. Those who were treated lived in their own places until Doctor DeVries completed the building of Thalassa, and took great care with their appearance so that they could continue to labor in Karistos. But they perhaps need not have done so, for the line, as you might say, had blurred even before DeVries began his work. Such may aid the humanish here to accept that which is."

"Hair and clothing are one thing, blood and bone another." Jani held out her hands, then pressed them together, palm to palm. "And the Thalassans didn't aid their cause by kidnapping me. Even humanish who don't like me—and they are legion—will seize upon that as proof that the hybrids are outlaws, and that animus will transfer to Haárin."

Feyó leaned against the table and crossed her arms in the humanish manner. "And then there is Gisa, who would lead the Haárin in my place."

Yes, Feyó, and if you continue to push her, this situation may get even more interesting. Jani remained with her hands pressed together, still conscious of the peaceful scene that called to her from behind. "All possible must be done to insure that some sort of concordance is reached, just in case we ever reach the point where it all hits the fan." She paused when Feyó gestured puzzlement. "I mean if humanish–idomeni relations deteriorated past the point of no return."

"You mean war." Feyó pushed away from the table and paced, her braided fringe swinging gently in time to her step. "We do at times speak of such. It is part of our business scheme—who would remain, who would depart, who would control. Would we transport bornsect goods? Humanish? Both?" She stopped and turned to Jani, her head held high, and crossed her right arm over her chest. "I would fight for this place, beside whoever would also fight for this place, Haárin, hybrid, or humanish. I would do so because the worldskein cast me out, and so lost all claim to my loyalty. I would do so because this place is my home."

Jani sensed the weight of Feyó's words, the feeling that she spoke from the same place as Gisa. *Feyó abandoned the Shèrá worldskein when she made this place her home, and Gisa took the rejection one step further.* Now it seemed as though they both sought to reclaim traditions they had left

behind. *That must be why they're making such a muddle of
it—they're out of practice.* Before she could reply, a series of
tones echoed through the room. One of the copper panels
slid aside, and one of Feyó's male suborns entered.

"Ná Feyó, there is a transmission from Shèrá." He
glanced at Jani, his respectful posture at odds with his obvious desire to speak to his dominant privately. "It arrived by
courier. Ná Voln has taken it to the communications room
for decode."

"Then I will join ná Voln." Feyó waited for the male to
precede her, then started after him toward the door. "And
will you join me, ná Kièrshia?" She looked back over her
shoulder at Jani. "This transmission, I most sense, will concern you as it does me."

The Haárin communications room, in order to allow for the
recording of posture and gesture so necessary to idomeni ar-
ticulation, was larger than any humanish combooth Jani had
ever used. This was offset, however, by the fact that Feyó
and her suborn trio apparently made a habit of listening to
transmissions together. Jani stood against the back wall of
the space, boosting on tiptoe to look around and over the
four Haárin to the display at the front.

"I say it is of Temple," one of the males said as the other
inserted the wafer into the unit reader. "They have not
scolded us for some time now—it is our turn." Before he
could say more, the display lightened, which in turn cued
the room illumins to lower.

Jani watched the Haárin darken to fluid shapes. The warm
air of the booth had grown even warmer in the few minutes
since they'd entered. She inhaled the soapy odor of Sìah per-
spiration, listened to the rustle of cloth and the creak of
leather boots.

The display lightened further, and a dour figure, an elder-
ly female in a red-cuffed overrobe, appeared.

"Temple." The talkative male gestured toward the display.
"So I said. *Hah.*"

The female began to speak, her High Vynshàrau jam-packed with nuance and loaded phrases. Jani listened. Watched. *A meeting . . . with Shai and Sànalàn . . . over the fate of the bornsect killed at the mine site.* Except the born-sect hadn't died, and Tsecha had argued for his life, repudi-ating both his propitiator and generations of religious doctrine in the process.

Oh. Damn. Damn. Damn. Jani saw Feyó's growing dis-may in the rounding of her shoulders, and felt her own curve in response.

"Ní Tsecha Egri had lived his life in conflict with all that is godly. All that is orderly. He is the first Chief Propitiator to be made outcast, the first to give over his place to his suc-cessor while he lived." The female paused, her back bent in anger. "In denying Sànalàn her right as Chief Propitiator, he has displayed once more his disdain for his people, for our gods. We therefore command him to return to Shèrá, so that he may face the discipline of Temple, which should have been his so long ago, yet which he eluded as a beast eludes a trap."

"They will execute him," Feyó said.

"They cannot!" The female suborn turned to her. "They must not!"

"They'll try." Jani leaned against the wall for support. "Cèel has been after him since the end of the war of Vyn-shàrau ascension. Now he believes he has him. He won't let this opportunity pass." She pushed past Feyó to the door, disregarding the female acolyte's salutation, for the first time since she arrived hoping for cool air to ease the buzzing in her head. She pushed the entry panel aside, leaning against the wall, then crouching low, her head touching her knees.

"You are . . . ill, ná Kièrshia?

Jani looked up to find Feyó standing over her, worry tens-ing her face like pain. "It occurs to me, ná Feyó, that if you had informed ní Tsecha of the hybrids when you first knew of them, he would have sheltered that knowledge, and behaved accordingly. I'm not claiming that this episode would not have happened, but it might not have." She slowly straightened, her thigh muscles trembling. She recalled her last meeting with Tsecha before her departure, the expression on his face as he told her of Feres, the pain of loss she had never before associated with idomeni. *He's changed.* A hybrid in his way, as she was in hers, and damn the consequences. "We need to stop him."

Feyó cocked her head in puzzlement. "Ní Tsecha?"

"Cèel." Jani started down the hall. "We need to cut him off at the knees." She stopped and turned on her heel, and barely avoided a collision with Feyó. "Do you still stand with ní Tsecha, despite what you learned here today?"

Feyó drew up, raising her chin to appear taller, then looked down at Jani. "What I have learned does not change my thought."

Jani raised her own chin, acknowledging Feyó's response and her own humility. "Will the other Haárin follow you?"

Feyó hesitated. "Most, I do believe."

"Can you make sure?" Jani waited, her heart tripping, until Feyó offered a slow humanish nod. "The other Outer Circle dominants have probably heard the message by now. You need to gauge their reaction, assure them that you're still dominant, persuade the ones who aren't sure. Meanwhile, I need to talk to Gisa." She fell silent as an Haárin female approached. The female wore the battered coverall of an outdoor worker, a brightly patterned scarf wrapped around her head.

"Ná Kièrshia?" Her voice emerged as a high-pitched keening, so great was her regard. "There is a humanish searching for you in the gardens. His name is Pierce. He said something of—" She grabbed her right shoulder with her left hand in a fit of confusion. "—hur-ly bur-ly?"

Jani exited the board building to find Niall pacing the pavered walkway.

"Your boyfriend left the hospital over an hour ago. 'Shot

out of here like a bat out of hell' is the term the desk used."
He kept patting his shirt pockets, a sure sign that he needed
a nicstick. "Three guesses where he went. First two don't
count."

CHAPTER 18

"I messaged the fort from a public comport. Told them we might be a little late." Niall steered the borrowed Trade Board skimmer with a light hand, as though he expected it to bolt from under him at any moment. "So? How did it go?"

"Same as usual." Jani's knees banged against the dashboard as they shot down the steep cliff road that led to the Karistos shoreline. "More problems."

"Oh, that's news." Niall glared at the Sìah instrument array, tapping gauges and grumbling. "How the hell do you read these things?"

"I'll tell you if anything goes south." Jani braced for the shudder as the skimmer left the road and took off over the water. "Can you raise Thalassa on the com-array?"

"I can't even tell where the damned com-array is."

"It's here." Jani touched the nearest of the flat-faced indicators, then followed with repeated hail codes in English and Sìah Haárin. "Nobody's responding." She set the com-array to standby, then checked her timepiece. "Either they're all at mid-morning sacrament, or they've made it a practice to ignore contact attempts by Feyó's fleet."

"And I thought Supreme Command infighting was bad." Niall reached into the shirt pocket that held his nicstick case.

"Wait a minute." He lowered his hand. "I can't smoke in here, can I?"

"It would be better if you didn't, no." Jani lay her head against the seatback. "If we could, I'd probably ask you for one."

"That good, huh?" Niall pointed the skimmer toward the distant white specks that marked Thalassa. "Did Shroud tell you that he planned to confront Eamon DeVries?"

"No." Jani bit back further commentary. Niall's anger had eased to background noise, and she had no desire to set him off again. "Why would he?"

Despite the fact that he couldn't ignite it, Niall had inserted a nicstick in his mouth anyway. "You're kidding, right?" He worked the cold cylinder from one corner of his mouth to the other. "I figured he told you everything."

"Well, you figured wrong." Jani looked out her window, concentrating on the roll of the water and the occasional swooping seabird, ignoring Niall's pointed looks and the heat that flooded her face.

"He loves you." Niall fiddled with the bank of touchpads and switches until he found the one that controlled the windows. "Much as it pains me to say. I mean, you've apparently narrowed your choices to him and Pretty Boy Pascal, which to me defines rock and hard place. But I stopped trying to figure out women's criteria years ago." He lowered both his and Jani's windows, and the salty green smell of the sea filled the cabin. "But at least Shroud has some feeling beyond his own immediate gratification. He's a man of substance, to say the least. You seem to enjoy one another's company. Judging from that sheep-eyed look you get on your face whenever he comes in a room, I'd guess that you're as over the side about him as he is about you. Then there's all that shared history." He exhaled with a rumble. "I've seen people start out with a lot less and make a go of it."

"I never thought I'd hear you defend him." They were close enough to Thalassa now that Jani could pick out the details of the main house. The windows and balconies. The shadowed overhang of the main entry. *John, what are you doing now?* Arguing his way past Gisa's suborns? Holding Eamon's head under a faucet? "I thought you didn't like him."

"I don't." Niall sensed the tension of the approach as well. His hand hovered for a moment over his holstered shooter. Then he pulled the nicstick from his mouth and shoved it in his pocket. "I just watched you two tiptoe around one another for the last five and a half weeks. It proved quite an education in how far two people will go to avoid the obvious." He backed off the accelerator as they drew near the shore, increasing the vehicle's elevation to avoid the spray of the waves. "Are you worried about this?"

"A little." Jani dug into her duffel, removing her shooter and tucking it into the waistband of her trousers. "Gisa has some overly enthusiastic followers."

"How overly enthusiastic?"

"They had shooters trained on you and John at Elyas Station. Brondt warned me that they'd overreact if I put up a fight."

"Brondt's playing both sides against the middle, and you're a damned fool if you trust a word he says."

"He's all I have."

"Then we're in trouble." Niall reached for his holster again. This time he unfastened the top. "Damn Shroud. Why couldn't he have waited?" He coasted along the beach, weaving to avoid rocks and moorings, until he came to a steep grade. "Is there anyplace on this planet that isn't either straight up or straight down?" He turned up the road, which led to the first of the houses. "Goddamn roller-coastering everywhere you go—" He slowed as a group of hybrids stepped into the road fifty or so meters ahead. Males, humanish and Haárin both. They all wore holsters, though none had drawn their weapons. Yet. *"Oh, give me an excuse."* His foot brushed the accelerator as his hands closed around the steering mech.

"Don't." Jani twisted in her seat so her back abutted the door. "That's all we need is you running hybrids over the edge of the cliff." She grabbed the framing and boosted through the open window so she sat on the ledge. *"I've come to see John Shroud! Is he here?"*

The hybrids looked at one another, their attitudes altering in a blink from threatening to confused. "Yes, he is here. He is with Doctor DeVries." A heavyset male, the apparent ringleader, moved to the front of the group. His comrades helped him along by backing off a stride or three, leaving him standing on his own. He must have felt the sudden breeze at his back, for he held out his hands, palms facing out, to show that he wasn't armed. "Of course, ná Kièrshia, you are welcome, both you and Colonel Pierce."

"Glad to hear it." Jani pulled herself out of the skimmer, then reached through the window for her duffel. "Stay close," she said to Niall.

"Harkens back to the days of me misspent youth, this does." Niall unholstered his shooter and activated it, steering the skimmer with his inside hand. "Ah, the memories."

Jani patted the side of the skimmer, then started up the road. "You expected someone from the enclave," she said to the ringleader. "You typed the signal when I tried to call, and you staked out the road and waited."

The male shifted from one foot to the other, but stood his ground. "Ná Feyó is no friend of ours. She would swallow us into her enclave and subject us to the old ways."

What do you know of the old ways? Jani took in the male's lined face—he had hybridized too late to lose the telltale humanish softness completely. Then she made note of his fighter's build. *Fighter, not athlete—this one has the look of the docks about him.* What had driven him to hybridize, to turn his back on all he had known and give himself over to Eamon's medical ministrations? "What's your name?"

The male started. Then he stood at attention, as though making a report. "Adam Down, ná Kièrshia."

"Well, ní Down, I am not of the old ways either. I spoke

with ná Feyó this morning, met with her at the Trade Board, and I am still not of the old ways. They're not contagious. Besides, you're hybridized humanish, as I am—we couldn't follow the old ways with tracking sensors and holospheres—we're the wrong race. Neither of us would ever be allowed to live in the Elyan enclave, not even if we had a note from ní Tsecha himself. That being the case, listen to me now and spread the word, because I'm only going to say it once. No violence against any of Feyó's, or against Feyó herself. No intimidation. To do so against her or one of hers is to do so against me, and I do not take kindly." When he opened his mouth to protest, Jani raised her hand to silence him. "Do you understand?" She waited for his grudging nod. Then she pointed to his followers and gestured for all of them to start walking.

"Old ways." Jani spoke to Down's back as he trudged ahead of her up the road, as she felt her heart beat, slow and strong. "It's all new ways here—we're making it up as we go. And we had better make damned sure that we think very carefully before we start waving our little tin dickies in the air because we're a spit away from an enclave in which there resides very tall folk with genetically short tempers, and we're a spit and a shout away from a fort filled with shorter folk who have more weaponry than either of us have ever dreamed of. Therefore, we are going to try something new here at Thalassa. We're going to try thinking for a change, or so help me Caith I'm going to start kicking butts into the bay, is *that* clear!" She sensed movement out of the corner of her eye, and turned to find Torin pacing her as he entered notes into a handheld.

"I recorded your speech." His eyes shone clear green in the bright sun. "I've entered all your speeches so far into the secret archives. Many of us have already listened to them multiple times."

"I don't give speeches." Jani ignored the laughter that emanated from the shadowing skimmer. "What's it like here?"

"Tense." Torin shrugged. "Gisa announced at mid-morning

sacrament that you had left to go to ná Feyó and that you wouldn't be coming back. Now, here you are." He drew in closer, his step still relaxed, a smile on his face. A born actor. "Doctor Shroud arrived about an hour ago. Doctor DeVries was in his room—he lives in the basement clinic, says it's cooler. Bon escorted Doctor Shroud there, then left them. We heard shouting at first, but it died down after a while."

"What's Gisa doing now?"

"Deciding upon the fall planting. But when Doctor Shroud arrived, she said something of preparing for you."

A few of the hybrids waited for them at the top of the road. One female broke away and hurried to Down's side, casting anxious glances at Jani as she did.

"It's the look on your face that's got them jumpy, in case you're wondering," Niall called from behind.

"Thank you."

"I had a Drill like you once."

"Shut up."

"I have just filed your speech," Torin said as he fingered his handheld's touchpad. "I wish I could do so with conversation, but when I asked Doctor Shroud if I could do so as he spoke with Doctor DeVries, his face grew most red." He eyed Jani sheepishly. "I left quietly."

"A nice change of pace on your part." Jani circled to the main house entry, and wasn't overly surprised to find Bon already standing in the open entry.

Niall had parked the skimmer in the pavered circle, and broke into a trot to catch Jani up. "Good God." He stopped when he caught sight of Bon's ravaged face. "Did DeVries do that?"

"Yes and no." Jani grabbed him by the sleeve and maneuvered him ahead of her. "How are you doing on your observing?"

Niall looked back at Down and the other hybrids, who still watched Jani with a blend of trepidation and awe. "They're all like you."

"Down and the male behind him—they were humanish

once. The others began as Haárin." Jani looked to Down's . . .
Girlfriend? Female? She tilted her head to her left in acknowledgment of Jani's examination. *I wonder what Cèel would
have to say about you?* Or even Tsecha, come to that. Jani often wondered if he had ever considered all the ramifications
of his blending prophecy.

"Good God." Niall turned back to the house and the myriad faces that watched from the doorway.

"Welcome to Thalassa, Colonel Pierce." Bon bared her
mahogany teeth. "Please, enter."

"Doctor Shroud and Doctor DeVries are downstairs in the
clinic, which you have not yet seen, ná Kièrshia." Bon gestured like a tour guide toward the lift that led down to the
lower level. "We shall take the stairs, one flight only, to the library, wherein ná Gisa awaits."

Niall glanced back at Jani. "Place is a bloody palace." He
paused on the landing that overlooked the skylit courtyard,
and leaned over the stone railing to take in the whole of the
gardens. "Incredible."

"All hybrids come here to study," Bon said, a shine of
pride softening her features. "They come to take sacrament,
to discuss points of our history and our future."

"Really." Jani waited for Bon to mount the stairs. "I have
some things to discuss with Gisa," she said to Niall. "We
may slip into Sìah Haárin."

"I daresay I'll understand the gist." Niall couldn't take his
eyes from the garden view. "Something to do with how the
hybrids fit into the Haárin scheme of things, I'll be bound."

"You might say that, yes." Jani followed Bon to an entry
that she saw, was located two floors beneath her own room.
Not my room—I don't live here. The door moved aside, revealing floor-to-ceiling shelving filled with wafer folders,
display cases, a polystone floor with a glasslike finish, and a
windowed wall overlooking the bay.

"Oh." Niall stopped and stared. The scholar in him eyed
the reading and viewing materials like a starving man poring

over a banquet. Then he moved to the view, his rapt gaze marking it as the work of art that it was. He took one slow step inside, then another, as though he entered a church.

"Ná Kièrshia." Gisa sat at a desk at the far end of the room, near the window. "I am most surprised, and truly, that you have returned." She wore the same sort of humanish outfit as the first time Jani met her, this one in shades of yellow and green. "I have been preparing farm plans. We have greenhouses and processed tracts that you have not seen. I hope to show them to you today." She seemed as relaxed and confident as always, so sure of every move she made. "I walked the land and found myself wondering, and truly, what ní Tsecha will say of this place when he finally comes. So many times he fought in the circle to defend the idea of the blending. So many times he bled. The blood of the priest, binding humanish and Haárin. I am filled with awe when I think of it. The blood of the priest that binds."

"We need to talk first," Jani said in Sìah Haárin. "I spoke with ná Feyó earlier this morning."

"I know you did." Gisa answered in English, her eye on Niall, who wandered along the shelves. "You must know then, and truly, that her time is past, and that we who are blended must take charge of Haárin and show them the Way to a new Star." She sat back, her hands folded in her lap, maddening in her calm. "You understand such, this I know. What life have you with humanish now, Kièrshia? They do not think as you do. They do not feel as you do. Their concerns are not yours, for if they were you would not be here. But what life have you with Haárin, who would not even allow you inside their godly houses? Hah!" She raised a hand, gesturing about the library. "This is your place now, among your own. Sit here with me, and take it."

Witch. One who persuaded with feeling, as Feyó did with facts. "During my visit to ná Feyó, she received a message from Rauta Shèràa Temple. Tsecha had denied Sànalàn's authority as Chief Propitiator. Temple decreed that he be called back into the worldskein."

"Hah!" Gisa clasped her hands over her head and shook them. "He is hybrid in all ways but the body!"

"This is not good news." Jani dragged out a chair and sat so she could lean closer to Gisa and lower her voice. Niall might not have been able to understand her words, but he'd be able to understand the music quite well. "Your announcement as to your fitness to take the Elyan Haárin from Feyó has confused the other Outer Circle Haárin. You have said you are Tsecha's choice, but I am here to tell you once and for all that Tsecha supports Feyó—"

"If he knew of this place, if he saw—"

"He would still realize that Feyó is the better choice to lead the Outer Circle Haárin through this crisis, even though he created it himself." Jani rested her hands on the table, spreading her red-trimmed cuffs in the process. "You must back down. You have not the experience to head both hybrid and Haárin. You have put Feyó in the position where she must fight for her survival at a time when the Outer Circle Haárin must project a united front. If Cèel sees you are as one, he may stay his hand regarding Tsecha."

Gisa struck the table with her fist. "We must have a place!"

"This is not the way. This is not the time!"

Gisa wavered. Uncertainty curved her hands further, and softened the hardness of her face. "Then we are as nothing here."

Jani looked into grey eyes gone cold. "That will change. But not this way, and not at this time." She waited for some sign of Gisa's agreement. When none proved forthcoming, she bit back further argument—she had some idea how the female reacted to being cornered, and she didn't want to risk applying too much pressure. "We will speak more of this later."

She pushed back her chair and stood, then turned to find Niall regarding her narrow-eyed over the top of a freestanding display case. Ignoring him, she headed for the door, boots clipping on the glassy floor. She opened the door and stepped out into the walkway, heard the panel slide closed behind her.

Then she heard it open again, followed hard by the crunch of tietops on the tiled walkway.

"I didn't understand a damned word you said back there." Niall quickened his step and fell in beside her. "I did hear Tsecha's name a few times. What trouble is that old bird in now?"

Jani stopped, turning into Niall and halting him with a bump of her shoulder. "If you really want to know, I'll tell you. Communications Ministry techs are bound to plumb it out of the spaceways soon anyway." She waited for his slow nod. "He denounced Sànalàn. The Rauta Shèràa Temple has ordered him back to Shèrá to face disciplinary action. The translation Feyó and I both took from that is that they'll kill him." She waited for him to close his mouth. "We might stand a chance of saving him if a union of Outer Circle Haárin demand he be spared—Cèel's power base is shaky and he needs Haárin support to keep his Oligarchy. But ná Gisa has challenged ná Feyó for the dominance of the Outer Circle Haárin, and if they're hung up with this little episode, they'll be too splintered to compel Cèel to spare Tsecha." She locked her hands behind her back and bent forward at the waist like an instructor teaching a class. "Is that clear?"

"As mud." Niall paced a tight circle, then turned to face her. "I know how you feel about him—"

"Thank you."

"—but how does this affect the Commonwealth? That's my concern. What does an Haárin union that's powerful enough to push around a bornsect Oligarch mean to Chicago?" Niall's beautiful eyes hardened, became one at last with his predator's face. "You see my dilemma? I watched you out there, spouting off like a Drill, ordering everyone around, terrifying them yet drawing them in at the same time. They follow every move you make, as if you were a knife blade catching the sun." He looked off into the middle distance. "Charisma, yes. Mystique. Legend. And as

I watch this . . . history unfold before me, I constantly need to remind myself that I'm on the other side. There was a time that I'd have followed you into the maw of hell, Jan, but I can't anymore."

Jani nodded. "I know. I'm not asking you to."

"But you're asking me to stand aside and watch, and I can't do that, either." A shadow found Niall's scar, deepening it to a cruel gash. "I need to inform my superiors of a brewing issue with the Haárin. They'll inform Cabinet Row, who will have to decide what outcome best suits them and push accordingly, and you know as well as I do that a weakened Cèel isn't the worst news for the Commonwealth." He waited for Jani to respond, but had the sense to drop the point when she didn't. "I have to take that skimmer back to the Board. Then I need to check in at Fort Karistos." He stepped around her and headed toward the stairs. "They still want to talk to you."

Jani folded her arms, hunched her shoulders. Idomeni anger, combined with an ache like a punch in the pit of her stomach. "They can go to hell."

"Is that your answer as a Commonwealth citizen?" Niall looked back at her. Raised a pleading hand to her, then let it fall. "Glories of the morning to you, ná Kièrshia. I believe that's the proper phrase." His step sounded once more. "The proper name."

He took the stairs two at a time. Jani looked over the railing and watched him stride across the courtyard to the door, back straight and head held high, like the soldier he was.

CHAPTER 19

Jani wandered the lower level of the house for the first time. It did feel cooler than the upper levels, the white walls and high ceilings allowing a sense of space and light that she had never associated with a basement. Maybe it was the lack of windows that caused her closed-in feeling, the knowledge that the fresh, hot wind never blew through this place. Or maybe it was the memory of Niall walking across the courtyard, on his way to perform his soldier's duty in the way that he saw fit.

She grew conscious of the faces eventually, watching her from the examining room doorways, from around corners, like mice waiting for the feral dog to pass so they could go about their business. She turned to a female who stood in the entry to a laboratory, a hybridized Haárin outfitted in the same medwhite shirt and trousers that had been John's uniform for years, and tried baring her teeth in the interest of good will. When the female backed off a step, however, she realized that at this particular moment, simple questions were probably the better course to take. "Is John Shroud still down here? He came to speak with Eamon DeVries."

"Yes. Ná Kièrshia." The female first pointed down the hall, then stepped out of the room. "The directions . . . too complicated, and truly." She led Jani down one corridor, then another, glancing back at her every few steps as though afraid she might pounce.

Damn it, I'm not a brute. Jani took her shooter from her waistband and tucked it into her duffel to reinforce the opinion, then tried to straighten her back and uncurve her shoulders—the posture of anger came so easily now that she wasn't even aware when it took hold. They came to a stop in front of a plain white door identical to all the others. Only a small plate set off to the side, etched in both humanish and Sìah numbers, marked its identity.

"Thank you." Jani nodded to the female, who bolted as if freed from a prison. *I have got to work on my social skills.* She waited until the corridor was free of traffic, then knocked. "John? It's Jani."

Silence followed for a long beat. Then came the click of a lock being disengaged, the hollow slide of a mechanism. The panel slid open, revealing John, his face set, his suit jacket and sunshades discarded, the sleeves of his white shirt rolled to the elbow. A softening came to his eyes when he looked at her, but he didn't smile. "I wondered when you'd show."

He stood aside, opening Jani's view to the rest of the room. It was an office, air chilled by a space cooler, redolent with the goaty odor of male shut-in and an undercurrent of prepack meals past. A desk filled the middle of the room, surrounded by shelves, file bins, and a worktable set with two workstations. Holos hung from every spare centimeter of wall space—Eamon DeVries with ministers past and present, actors and actresses, sports stars.

The man himself sat on a couch set against the far wall, beshirted and trousered but barefoot still, surrounded by the pillows and rumpled blankets that marked the furniture as his bed. The arrogance that he carried at the station and the bizarre cocktail party had given way to sullenness, his slack face and bagged eyes reflecting the days spent operating on nerve, liquor, and too little sleep.

"Well well." Eamon looked at her, then lay back his head and frowned at the ceiling. "If it isn't the second team."

Jani entered, waiting for John to close the door and find his seat before deciding where to perch. "I doubt I have anything to say to you that John hasn't already covered, and better than I could." She tested the strength of a waist-high bookcase, set her duffel on top, then hoisted aboard, legs dangling.

"He did tell me that you asked him why he did it." John sat at Eamon's desk. "We've spent the last few hours discussing those reasons in greater detail."

"As if they weren't good enough." Eamon jerked his chin toward Jani. "As if they weren't better than the ones you used with *that*. At least Gisa and her crew came to me. At least I had permission!" He yanked his blanket onto his lap and started matching edges and corners. "You're a bloody hypocrite, John—you always have been. Free to do as you will, but God forbid anyone else should presume." He started to fold the mass of cloth, but it overwhelmed him, and he tossed it to the floor in a hail of cursing. "And as for your bloody contract, a decent attorney could hack it to bits. Assuming, of course, that you're looking forward to having Neoclona's laundry basket dumped in full view of the Commonwealth population." He worked to his feet, then knelt on the floor. "Think of all that bad publicity. Just might be the boost that Service Medical and some of those new independent med services are looking for—twenty years of John Joseph Shroud's chicanery, laid open for the public to paw over." He lay flat on his stomach and reached beneath the couch, grunting and muttering imprecations before finally emerging, shoes in hand.

"The problem with taking on Neoclona, Eamon, is that your worth is as tied up in its perceived value as is mine and Val's." John exuded calm edging into boredom. "You could indeed rake us over the public coalpit, but in the end you might find yourself stuck with a portfolio of battered valuations and attorneys' fees based on what you were worth before you opened your mouth." He locked his hands behind his head and hoisted his feet atop the desk. "Then there's the Commonwealth to deal with. I made one"—he cocked his head toward Jani—"you made fifty-seven. The former's a curiosity. The latter's a complication in every future human-idomeni negotiation, and don't think that won't be noted and appreciated by Li Cao and all the highly placed others who will have to grapple with the fallout for years to come."

Eamon remained kneeling, shoes dangling in his grip, eyes fixed on John with a hatred intensified by the smell and clutter and the wall-hung testimony to a life gone by. "You won't win this one, John. You and your deep pockets and your conceit and your Halloween suit." He struggled back atop the couch, then tossed his shoes to the floor and shoved his bare feet inside. "I put as much into this company as you and Val. More, come to that, so don't suppose for a minute that I'll go quietly with a pittance and a scolding as my payment." He tottered to his feet with an unsteadiness that spoke of a hangover as well as overwhelming rage. "I won't be set aside twice." He walked to the door, slowly at first, then faster as he found his balance. "I have rounds now." He grabbed a medcoat from a wall hook next to the door. "Then I'll have my work to do, and I'd prefer it if you were both *out* by the time I return." He pounded the doorframe with his fist until the panel slid aside, then forced through the gap and into the hall.

"That didn't go well." John cocked his head as though listening to the fading pound of Eamon's footsteps, the closing of the door. "I didn't mean to refer to you as a curiosity. Such is the language of negotiation." He lowered his feet to the floor and sat forward, picking through the piles on Eamon's desk like a technician isolating a particularly vile sample. "He'll push. I'll push. In the end we'll work something out, but it won't be pretty. No image for posterity. No handshakes all around." He liberated a wafer folder from the middle of a stack of files, glanced at the cover, then tucked it back in its place, his face reddening. "I see Eamon's taste in entertainment hasn't changed." He leaned on his elbows and cradled his chin in one hand. "And how was your morning?"

"Even better than yours." Jani filled John in on the news from Shèrá, Gisa's and Niall's reactions. "I've asked Feyó to contact the other Outer Circle dominants and rally support. My job was to try to convince Gisa to see sense. I'm giving her time to think before going back for round two."

"For all you know, Tsecha might already be on his way to Shèrá." John poked through the stacks again, freeing a cookie packet and digging out a broken half. "We do it all the time at Neoclona—fix the problem, then announce that we had one." He popped the piece into his mouth and chewed reflectively. "Getting in touch with the home team is, I believe, the order of the day."

Jani drew up her legs and crossed them. The ache in her gut had subsided to a grumble, and she debated asking John if there was any more food to be unearthed from the depths of Eamon's desk. "I don't trust the communications here. There's the Elyan enclave, but I'm not sure that the embassy doesn't tap into enclave-to-enclave communications when it suits them, and they'd be interested in this. Service is the most secure of all, and they are most definitely out."

"There's always Neoclona." John concentrated on smoothing the creases from the cookie packet. "Due to the sensitive nature of some of our data, we've systems in place that would give Niall pause."

Jani thought back to Niall's chill expression, his voice wrung dry of any attempt to argue because he had finally realized it would do neither of them any good. *I'm on the other side.* A malleable phrase, adjustable to fit both of them. "We're edging into a delicate area. The messages Val would be receiving would contain intelligence that could be considered important to the Commonwealth for both strategic and security reasons. It would concern Outer Circle dock ownership. Holding companies. Copies of communications with Rauta Shèràa Temple and Council." She looked across the room at John, met his steady, too-dark eye. "You realize what I'm asking?"

"Yes."

"Someone with a broad definition of treason might even think it applies to you."

"Let me worry about that."

"Easier said than done."

"Be that as it may." John clasped his hands together, then tapped his chin with his doubled fist. "Who would act on the receiving end?"

"Lucien."

"Are you sure?"

"He won't play fast and loose with this. He'd realize that if I found out, the Commonwealth wouldn't be big enough for him to hide in." Jani pulled her overrobe around her in an effort to fight the cold. "I'd like to keep Val out of it."

"I can tell him to have Lucien there at a particular time. The message never has to pass through his hands. I can tell him that they're classified Service communications, word it in such a way that he knows to keep his hands off." He grinned without a trace of humor. "We're being so careful. It's as though we're already preparing the story for the lawyers." He stood and gathered his jacket from the back of Eamon's chair. "Where do we start?"

"I need to dig my report-writing skills out of my duffel and put together a preliminary something." Jani pushed off the bookcase, then dragged her bag onto her shoulder. "Wait for Feyó's update. Bug her for it, if I can get a message to her."

"I can do that before I go to Neoclona." John rolled down his sleeves, then dragged on his jacket.

"Then I get to work on Gisa again." The duffel slid from Jani's shoulder. She caught it just before it hit the floor. "I never thought this trip would turn out like this. I'm sorry." A weight pressed down on her from above, bowing her back.

Her heart pounded. Panic and anger, unabated by an augie that couldn't stop it anymore. "Damn it!" She raised her duffel over her head and slammed it down on the worktable, scattering data wafers and documents, sending an old coffee dispo skittering across the floor. *"Damn it!"* She raised it once more and brought it down. Again. Again.

"Jani?" John rounded the desk and closed in. "Stop it. *Stop it.*" He wrestled the bag from her hand and let it fall to the floor, then grabbed her wrists and struggled to force her still. "Stop this. I said, *stop it!*"

Jani battled the instinct to strike. John stood too close, his stance too open. So many ways to hit him. So many ways to bring him down—

Her mind's eye filled with the visions that poured from her memory, of battles fought and battles feared, past and future joined. She slowed, then stilled, as the humanish that remained in her fought the idomeni and slowly gained the upper hand, at least for now. Who'd have thought she'd find such mercy there? She sagged against John, shaking free from his grasp as she pressed her face against his chest, felt his heart beat through his thin shirt. Wrapped her arms around his waist and pulled him closer and felt it beat stronger still. Faster.

He touched her hair first, a tentative fingering, as though he'd never seen such stuff as that before. Then his hands moved down, over the back of her head, coming to rest on her shoulders.

Jani waited. She could sense his thoughts as though he spoke aloud, knew he wanted to push her away yet couldn't summon the will to do so.

"You're not yourself." His bass rumbled as though it came up through the floor. *The voice of the machine*, Eamon had once called it.

Not a machine. Oh, didn't she know. She raised her head and looked into eyes filmed to intimidate, set in a face blanked by the determination not to care. "Every day, I change a little more. That means that at this moment I'm as close to myself as I will ever be again." With that, she reached up and worked her hands through white hair like shredded silk and pulled him down. His lips hovered near hers, the barest breath apart, allowing them both one last chance to end it. Then they met, closing a gap of millimeters, of twenty years' worth of other lives and other lovers and the ever-present knowledge that all they'd done was mark the time.

Jani savored taste and sense and scent long-lost and long-imagined. Touched a scar on the back of John's neck, the result of shatterbox shrapnel from the first wave of Rauta Shèràa bombings. Ran a hand under the neck of his shirt and over his shoulder, and felt the bump on his collarbone from a youthful fall from a tree. *I know his body better than mine.* She felt her heat rise, overwhelming the chill of the room. She held John closer, ground against him and heard the groan rise in his throat, then felt him pull back.

"Now what?" His breathing came rough and his lips had swelled and reddened—his eyes held triumph and lust and joy and love and just the slightest shadow of fear.

"I don't know. The usual, I suppose." Jani looked over John's shoulder to Eamon's rumpled couch. "Just not here, please." She took his hand, held it up to her face, pressed it against her cheek, then kissed it. "I have a room upstairs. I think it's still mine." She felt fully humanish now, suffused and distracted and aching for release. "It'll be a little hot for you, though."

John ran a finger along the line of her jaw. "Somehow, I don't think I'll notice."

Jani picked up her duffel and headed for the door. Her knees had gone to rubber, while her skin had turned into an instrument that sang as the cold air danced over it. The hybrids who stood in the corridors watched her pass but said nothing. She wondered if those who had been humanish noticed the dreamy look she knew must have inhabited her face, saw John walking a discreet distance behind, and added one plus one.

She heard voices behind her and turned. One of the medwhite-clad hybrids had stopped John, asking him a question about some testing protocol. John stared after her as she kept walking. Into the lift, then up to the fourth floor. She strolled along the railing, her eyes on the courtyard, feeling the stares of the hybrids who stood and talked, sat in the adjoining rooms and read. *How can I think about sex at a time like this?* Then she saw John dash out of the basement stairwell and across the courtyard, jacket tails flying, searching for her like the hero in a melodrama.

Then he stilled. Looked up. Saw her, and walked more slowly to the lift. She waited for him in front of the bedroom entry, standing with her back to the door, waiting as he disembarked and headed for her with the determined stride that a long-range shooter couldn't have repelled.

Jani keyed open the door and looked around the bedroom. "Hello?" She walked in, saw the bed still rumpled from her visit a day ago. "All clear."

John walked in after her, taking in the room, the view. Then he turned to her and froze, fixed by the sight of her. "For months I've been playing the 'What if?' game. Would it happen? Where? I thought of the Neoclona flat in Chicago, a clear moonlit night overlooking the lake." He looked around again, then shook his head. "Wrong time of day. Wrong body of water. Wrong . . . circumstances."

"When was it ever easy with us?" Jani tossed her duffel aside, wondering at the condition of the devices it contained, then driving the thought from her mind. "You reach a point when you decide to take things as they are." She laughed, from nerves and fatigue and the call of a love so long denied.

John reached out and pulled her to him. "Are you all right?"

"I will be." Jani could feel the thin layer of sweat that coated his hands. *Good—that makes two of us.* She kicked off her low boots as John swept off her overrobe and jacket. Her back arched as he pushed down her bandbra and cupped her breasts. Then he picked her up as though she weighed nothing, carried her to the bed and lay her down, pulled her trousers down and off, then followed with her underwear, his movements as rapid and ragged as his breathing.

"Day's looking better and better." He pulled off his jacket, then his shirt, revealing wire-frame shoulders and skin like old marble. "At least from where I'm standing." He undid his trousers and let them fall, then fell to his knees beside the bed and leaned over Jani, planting a few quick kisses on her stomach before coming up for air. "Are you going to say anything?"

Jani reached out and pressed her hand against his chest, fixed as she had been years before by the contrast between their skins. Her brown, now tinged with gold. His too-white, blue veins threading beneath. "I love you." She laced her hand through his hair and pulled him close, rising half up to meet him, kissing him as he boosted atop the bed. His hands explored everywhere, every place he'd regrown, rebuilt, reassembled. When she tried to move against him, he held her still and toyed with her, until she thought the build of sensation would make her scream. The clumsy probings of a novice had been replaced by the skilled exploration of a master—her world narrowed to the maze of fire he'd traced over her body, the one place where it burned the hottest. "You bad boy." Her voice emerged drugged. "You've been practicing."

"I had a lot of room for improvement," John said as he pressed atop her. Their breaths caught and they lay, still as death, as between them the wall of two decades of loss and hate and inexorable change faded to nothing.

"I love you," John said as he stirred, and they began to move as one.

Jani caught the play of chemical light across his white hair, flashes of silvery gold that for a discordant moment compelled thoughts of Lucien.

Then John called out her name, and she didn't think of Lucien anymore.

CHAPTER 20

Jani sat at the bedroom window, examining her scanpack under a glaring combination of Karistosian sunlight and the more focused beam of one of the floorlamps. "I think you're OK." She ran a hand over the black poly case, scratched and nicked from years of use. "Didn't mean to shake you up, but I wasn't feeling quite up to speed." She smiled. "I'm feeling a little tired now, but that's OK, too. Not that you care, I'm sure."

"Do you always talk to your scanpack?"

Jani turned in her chair to find John standing in the bathroom entry. "Only when I've been really rough on it. I'm not sure it means anything. There was a paper published about the time I graduated the Academy that posited that since scanpacks did contain brain tissue, they could evidence emotion, feel stress, and respond to sensory stimuli."

John fastened his shirt, frowning every so often and stopping to tug at his cuffs. "Did you believe it?"

"When it's oh-two in the morning and you've got idomeni on one side and Rauta Shèràa Base Command on the other waiting for you to confirm the dating on a handwritten, lubricant-soaked cover page that's all that remains of a fourteen page manifest, you'll believe anything." Jani's smile faded as she watched John continue to fuss with his shirt. "What's wrong?"

"I hate putting clothes back on after I've worn them." He vanished into the bathroom for a moment, then emerged into the bedroom, jacket in hand. "Someone must have a cleaner in this place, but I'm reluctant to go knocking from door to door."

"I have a spare coverall you can borrow." Jani followed his every move as he walked, bent, straightened. He moved with weighty fluidity, like a man formed of mercury, and she could have watched him until the sun flamed. "Might be a little short in the arms and legs."

"I'll manage." John walked to the table where Jani sat and picked up her shooter. "You had this in your duffel when you were banging it around?"

Jani nodded. "I always disengage the powerpack when I stash it, but still." She took the weapon from him and held it next to her scanpack. "Everything looks all right. Tried all the scanning equipment—everything checks out. I checked the room in the process—we seem to be insect-free."

John paused in his examination of her assorted antimonitoring hardware. "Were you concerned?"

"I'm always concerned." Jani picked up a still-activated monitor and turned it off. "So, no damage to anything but my pride."

"You've no reason to feel that way." John laid a hand on her shoulder and squeezed lightly. "You're still adjusting." He made as if to say more, but stopped, turning abruptly and walking to the bed. "Have you given any thought to coming with me back to Karistos?" he asked after a time.

"I need to stay here." Jani returned her scanpack to her duffel, followed by various other gadgets, then finally by her shooter. "I need to lobby. Seek out like minds. Rally them 'round the banner. Be political, something I'm not necessarily good at." She turned off the lamp, pushed her chair away from the table, and stood. "Call me the minority whip."

"I've wondered once or twice what you'd look like in leather." John's brow arched, as though he managed to surprise himself. "I haven't made a habit of it." He sat on the edge of the bed and started pulling on his socks, then stopped. "I realize how important Tsecha is to you. I know that every move we make now, or don't make, will affect humans and idomeni for years to come." He gave one sock a hard yank. "Pardon my selfishness, but I really don't want to leave now."

"Pardon my selfishness, but I don't want you to go." Jani meant to head across the room to the armoire to store her duffel, but she detoured to the bed and sat next to John. "You must be uncomfortable in this heat."

"The view makes up for it," he replied, giving her the same bewildered look that he had a hundred times in the Rauta Shèràa clinic basement. Then he reached for her.

Jani felt immersed in a sensual wash of soap scent, freshly shaved skin, and a rustle of expensive cloth. *I don't have time for this.* She felt his weight shift as he eased her back, pressed her lips to the place above the pulse in his throat, then held her breath as she felt him still, then loosen his arms around her.

"I hate rushing." John sat up, adjusting his clothes along the way. "I feel like a starving man who has to make do with whatever he can grab from someone else's table." He looked down at her, swallowed hard, then looked away. "Do you think a face-to-face meeting between Feyó and Gisa would do any good?"

Jani worked into a sitting position. "They tried that already. The idomeni aren't much for working past disagreements." The writing implements that she had dug out of various drawers and cupboards beckoned from the desk. "I still need to write that report for transmittal."

"I have some things to wrap up here." John stood and slipped on his shoes, then headed for door. "I'll try to talk to Eamon one more time, now that he's had the chance to ponder his options." He doubled back around and bent to Jani, kissing her hard. "Keep that in mind." This time he walked to the door and didn't stop.

Jani stared at the closed door, then turned back to the brightness of the view with a sigh. Sat on the bed for a time, tapping her boot heels together as she tried to rough out an introduction to her report, and drifted instead to thoughts of love and how she had lived without it for so long.

"Ah, well." She stood up, and carried the sensation of John's embraces with her as she sat at the desk and settled down to work.

Jani left her room, waiting until she heard the lock mech slide into place before continuing down the walkway. Cooking aromas rose from the courtyard and enveloped her, grilled meat and myriad spices and herbs—she peered over the railing, to where the hybrids had gathered to eat, then checked her timepiece.

"Mid-afternoon sacrament." Her stomach grumbled, complaining more loudly the harder she pressed her hand against it to quiet it. She shunned the lift for the stairs and galloped down, inhaling the air in gulps, her mouth watering. "Maybe if they don't let me eat with them, I can strain enough food out of the air." Like John's coffee, the Thalassan cuisine packed a wallop.

Jani reached the bottom of the stairs to find John hovering near the courtyard entry, pacing the short stretch like a tiger in a cage. "It's the smell." His nostrils flared. "I'm so hungry I think I could eat the dishes."

"Eamon said that blue-trimmed dishes hold the mildly spiced foods." Jani squinted toward the table, then ducked down when a couple of the hybrids looked her way. "They've set a few out. No idea what they are, though."

"I don't care." John stilled. "Shall we risk the slings and arrows?" He turned to her and held out his arm.

Jani took it, pulling him close. "All they can do is toss us."

"If they throw food, we'll grab plates and catch what we can." John leaned toward her and spoke out of the side of his mouth. "You head for the door—I'll cover you with one of the lamps." His joking ceased when the hybrids turned toward them as one and watched them enter the courtyard. He sombered and straightened.

"Ná Kièrshia." Gisa raised a glass in a humanish toast. "We are most honored." She took a sip of her drink, then gestured to the empty seat of honor beside her. "Please."

Jani walked around the table to her chair, counting the filled places as she went. *Twenty-five.* Not even a simple majority.

"Looks like most of them work in Karistos during the day." John held Jani's chair, then took the empty place next to her.

"Yes, Doctor Shroud, this is most the case." Gisa offered her hostess smile. "Most work in smaller businesses. Some own their own. The government, not so much, nor the Service. Such places demand a loyalty that we reserve for Thalassa." Her manner was light and practiced, as though all was right between her and Jani, and their argument had never occurred.

Jani scanned the table and caught sight of a familiar face at one end. *Make that two familiar faces.* Torin and Brondt, their chairs angled in such a way that they could see her.

I'm guessing neither you nor Major Hamil can leave the compound, Colonel Brondt. Jani detected a shifting back and forth of Brondt's water glass that she knew counted as his greeting, a whisper compared to Torin's wave of his fork. *I have no idea what Niall has planned for you.* She accepted one of the paisley tureens from Bon and ladled a fish stew potent enough for the rising steam to burn her eyes. *All I can say is that I doubt you'll like it.*

John dished out sliced kettle meat and gravy from one of the blue safety servers. "So far, so good."

Jani took a piece of crisp flatbread from a basket. "They

think I've come around to their side." She snapped the bread in two with a decisive turn of wrist. "Which has its advantages."

John glanced at her, his eyes widening. "Oh, I know that look." He seemed about to say more, but before he could, an unfortunately familiar figure took a seat nearby.

"John." Eamon placed a half-empty vodka bottle beside his plate. "I'm amazed that you've managed to stay away from your dear, dear offices this long." He looked from him to Jani, and an instinct honed years before brought a flush of color to his already raddled cheeks. "Oh, Johnny, you let her do it to you again. I remember that sick look on your face, oh how I remember. What was the term I coined? Ah, yes. The overeducated social maladjust wallowing in afterglow."

John stiffened as the decades-old insult hit home. "You haven't changed since Rauta Shèràa, Eamon. Still confusing coarseness with honesty."

"A little coarseness would do you a universe of good, old man. A little of the rough to cut through that gauzy filter you've wrapped 'round your memories."

"Can it, Eamon."

"Damned fool."

"I said, can it."

Eamon fell silent, glaring daggers at Jani between bites of food and gulps of vodka.

Jani took advantage of the silence to monitor Torin and Brondt. They declined to acknowledge her presence further after their first wordless greetings, finishing their meals quickly, then taking their leave a few minutes apart. She noticed others of the group leave abruptly as well—the older female she'd seen with Torin her first day, other solemn faces whose names she had yet to learn.

Jani ate enough to quell the worst of her pangs. Then she reached into the pocket of her coverall and removed the note and message wafer, palming them as she placed her hand on John's thigh. She let them slip onto the seat between his legs, heard the catch of his breath, the flicker of his eye as he tried to glance at her without seeming to.

"I'm off to take a walk—I haven't even seen the beach yet." Jani pushed back from the table, muscles twitching as though gearing up for a run. "Glories of the afternoon to one and all." She stood, acknowledging Gisa's surprised response, the murmurs of the remaining diners, then wandering to the door as though she had nothing but time and a world in which to spend it.

Jani walked down the same road she had climbed in a rage earlier that morning, picking up the details now that she missed before. The nameplates on the houses, fashioned from colored tiles. The occasional glimpse of clutter through an open door, which showed that actual beings lived there, who made actual messes and never quite managed to contain them, like beings everywhere.

The glare of the sun off the water could have served as a weapon. By the time she reached the beach, she wished she'd had the sense to pack sunshades. "The Chicago sun never bothers me." She picked her way through the rocks that poked up through the sand like the shattered teeth of some ancient beast. "But the Elyan sun is brighter, and we're nearer the equator here." She rolled up the sleeves of her coverall to above her elbows, then undid the neck as she felt the sweat bead. Walked past the rocks to where the sand lay wet and smooth, and listened to the slow crash of the waves and the distant screech of seabirds.

"Have you noticed the water?"

Jani turned to find Brondt standing behind her amid the rocks, Torin at his side gripping his ever-present handheld. "I haven't had time."

"Then you should find the time." He walked out to join her. He wore a long-sleeve shirt despite the heat, along with trousers and boots shiny with waterproofing. "If you really look at it, you'll see a purplish tint. Sometimes if there's enough cloud cover and the wind has been blowing in from the islands for a few days, the water looks like molten amethyst, if there is such a thing. Amazing to see. It's an algae, of course. Toxic to humanish—if it touches your skin, you might develop a nasty rash."

Jani took a step back just as the lick of a wave broke over the sand. She'd only brought the one pair of boots, which weren't as well-protected as Brondt's. The last thing she needed was a bout of contact dermatitis. "What about the sea life?"

"The usual fishlike things, some small and brilliantly colored, some dull silver and big as skimmers." Brondt eased into the role of native guide, clasping his hands behind him and rocking back and forth. "A few types are edible, if you sauce them up, but many of us have shown varying degrees of sensitivity. The native life here is just different enough to bother both idomeni and humanish."

"What about—" Jani gasped and slapped at her hand as a pain like an acid spatter stung the skin on the back.

"And then there are the flies. Different from the burrowers I told you about when we first arrived. These just sting like needles pricking." Brondt *tsked*, then fell silent for a time. "You saw ná Feyó." He toed the sand, prodding a shell from its mooring.

Jani looked back at Torin, who straightened as though someone had grabbed the back of his trousers and yanked up. "Don't record this."

"I know. I'm not completely without sense." Torin's air of deference vanished, replaced by the universal sense of injury peculiar to the teenager of any species. "I'll write it down later, when it's over. I have a very good memory."

"He does, you know. Scary, sometimes." Brondt jerked his chin toward a wide, flat rock that sat like a roughed-out table in the middle of the beach. "A few of the hybrid Haárin still maintain contact with the enclave." He sat on a low outcropping that stuck out from the rock's side. "They learned of ní Tsecha's recall. They think Oligarch Cèel will kill him."

"So do I." Jani took a cross-legged seat on the rock's edge. "Gisa needs to step aside. The Outer Circle Haárin need to convince Cèel that they're united, that any action he takes against ní Tsecha could cripple him in event of a challenge from another bornsect." She watched Torin chase a tiny scuttling creature about the sand, touching his toe to it to send it hopping. "Feyó's rounding up her supporters among the other enclaves. I tried to convince Gisa to cease her bid for dominance. Don't know if I made any headway or not."

"So now you're seeking to erode her support from within?" Brondt pulled in his boot just as Torin's creature leaped past, thumb-sized and twin-clawed, with stalked eyes and an iridescent carapace. "That could take some time. Do you think you have it to spend?"

"Probably not." Jani gave a silent cheer as the creature vanished into a gap between some rocks. As always, she felt a kinship with anything that was being chased. "First, I need to find out if ní Tsecha is still in Chicago. Whether or not he still is will dictate my next move. Until then, I'll see to matters here, and . . ."

Brondt nodded. "We shut down quite a few smuggling operations during my time at the station. We always reached a point where we had to sit and wait for something. Information. Confirmation. A noose to tighten. I always found it the most difficult time." He made a show of studying his hands. "Don't look now, but you're about to get your first shot at consensus-building."

Jani looked up the steep enclave road just as the first in a series of scattered groups reached the flat stretch of sand. She recognized most of the hybrids as those who had departed sacrament early, including Torin's older female, who joined him at the place where the hopping crustacean disappeared and probed with him through the rocks.

The others spread out, taking seats on nearby boulders. Then those perches filled, and still they came, some with blankets that they spread over the dry rocky sand, a few with folding chairs. Jani watched as they settled in, expressions guarded yet expectant. Niall's words returned to her . . . *charisma . . . mystique . . . legend . . .* and still she couldn't accept that they had come here to see her. *I'm Tsecha's representative.* Yes, that was it. A substitute for something else. That, she could understand.

"Ná Kièrshia?" A younger male with the solemn mien of a university student raised his hand. "Are you staying, you and Doctor Shroud?"

"I saw him go to your room." A young female, no more than a teenager, peered at Jani over the young male's shoulder. "And. Not. Come. Out." Her face split in a tooth-baring grin. Then clapped her hand over her mouth and doubled over, stricken by a case of the giggles.

Jani felt her cheeks flame as the humanish hybrids hid their smiles and the Haárin hybrids bared their teeth more openly. "Thank you for noticing."

"But it is just as it was before." Torin's friend had taken a seat atop a rock, while Torin sat on the ground at her feet. "He and you, creator and created. It is fitting."

Jani swallowed. *They know everything about my life. I'm an object of study.* A galling thought for someone who used to pack up and go if she encountered the same face on a street one time too many. "Are you an historian as well?"

"I am Lisse." The female looked more humanish than any of the other hybrids, most likely because she had begun the process so late in life. "I am Torin's home-mother, and an historian as well." She sat forward, eyes like crystal shining with interest. "May I ask—do you mind—your treatments? What do you recall of them?"

"Of the actual insertions?" Jani shook her head. "Nothing. I remember the time just before the explosion. Someone shouted something to the pilot. Half a sentence. 'Hey—' "
She felt the pressure of being the center of attention, of mul-

tiple pairs of eyes fixed upon her, heard the water and the birds and the nonsound of bated breath. "Month and a half later, I woke up to find John Shroud sitting in a chair beside my bed." Would she ever forget his solemn white face, or his first words to her? *Hello, creation. My name is John Shroud. Unfortunate name for a physician, don't you think?*

"Did you look as you do now?" That from a humanish-appearing female who shared a blanket with an Haárin male.

Jani held out her arm and rubbed it with her other hand. "They had just taken me out of the immersion tank the day before. My skin was shiny, and very pink." She fingered one of her curls. "I had some sparse black stuff growing out of my head that in theory was hair. My eyebrows were little tufty things. Eyes, a little lighter than they are now. Definitely not humanish-looking." The memories returned, bringing with them the long-forgotten smells of conductive gel and warm plastic. "John and Val Parini prodded me out of bed the next day, made me walk a few steps. After that came therapy—muscle stimulation, mental exercises. Amazing the things you forget when you're in an induced coma for six weeks."

Torin raised his hand. "What do you like most about being a hybrid?"

"Like?" Jani grew as still as the rock on which she sat. Her mind blanked, and she knew the sick feeling she'd had to battle whenever an interrogation had gone too long and cut too close. When the only answer that occurred was the absolute truth, and the absolute truth was the last thing she knew she should say. "I never thought about like or dislike before." She sensed the disappointment in some expressions, and pushed on anyway. If she lied, she might be able to win them for a short time, but the truth always came out, and when it did, she'd lose them forever. "As I changed more and more, as I grew sicker and sicker, I—" She licked her lips and looked everywhere but at the faces around her. "You chose this. I didn't. There will always be a difference in our feelings for that reason. Some of you chose for health reasons, others, because you believe in the blending, but you still made the choice yourselves."

"Isn't there anything about it that you enjoy?" Lisse asked.

"That I can offer my loyalty and regard or withhold them, as I see fit." Jani inhaled shakily—thank Ganesh for the shield of abstractions. "No individual, no system, merits my esteem solely because as a humanish I am bound to follow." She grinned weakly, then shrugged. "That sounds so arrogant. But I've been accused more than once of having a stiff neck." She thought of a few joking replies, but withheld them. These questions deserved serious answers, whether or not she felt comfortable giving them. Whether or not they were the ones her audience wanted to hear.

"My parents are Acadian. They returned there recently, after trying to live in Chicago." Jani imagined the scent of her mother's hair, and closed her eyes for a moment. "Acadia is their home. It calls to them. They carry something of it with them when they leave, and when they return, they bring it back with them, and they have the whole again." Did she make sense? Who would appear more bewildered to a wandering outsider, she or her audience? "I have never been in a place where I felt whole, where when I left, I took something of it with me. Humanish or hybrid, I've never felt that . . . contentment? Is that the word?" She pressed her hand to the rock, felt its warmth, but at the same time, its hardness. "That's how I'd answer you. That the enjoyment you speak of is contentment, and that I've never known it."

Lisse watched her. Did she seem so wise because of her age? Because her gaze never wavered? "I am most sorry."

"I am not," the somber student piped. "Those who are content never strive. Those who are content cannot lead. She is the Kièrshia—she will not be content until all is as it must be!"

The words echoed off the rocks, the cliff face. Jani felt the gazes once more, some pitying, others rapt with an awe that terrified her. *I'm only here because there's no other place for*

*me, because when there are things to be done, I do them—
don't look at me like that!*

"We should walk, I think." Brondt stood abruptly. "Show
ná Kièrshia this place we call home." He kept his back
turned to her as the hybrids gathered their gear. "Meet here
in five minutes." He waited until they'd begun their trudge to
their houses to turn to Jani.

"Was I that obvious?" She slid down from the rock and
bent low, stretching her back.

"I did detect a trapped look, yes." Brondt crossed his arm
over his chest in a gesture of uncertainty. "Uneasy lies the
head that wears a crown."

"Henry the Fourth, Part Two." Jani fielded his look of surprise. "Too bad you and Niall Pierce started off on the wrong
foot. You have a lot in common. A love of the classics." She
sniffed. "And an eye that's too sharp by half."

Brondt cast her a sideways glance, then looked out toward
the water. "They say that those who wish leadership the least
are the ones who merit it the most."

"Are you my conscience, Dieter?"

"Do you need one?" Brondt turned back to face the
houses, and watched the hybrids make their empty-handed
way back down the road. "No, I don't think you do. A little
peace, perhaps, but the two don't seem to go together, do
they?"

Jani stared at the man's back, willed him to face her, and
knew he wouldn't. Then she looked over the heads of the approaching hybrids and saw John standing on the overhang
looking down at her, the sun brilliant off his shirt, his hair.
She raised a hand in a small wave—he responded with a
barely detectable movement of his fingers. She could feel
his eyes on her as she turned and started down the beach.
Then the hybrids closed in around her, distracting her, and
by the time she turned again, he had gone.

CHAPTER 21

"Haven't seen Pascal around Far North Lakeside as much since the Vynshàrau challenged him to that duel." Cashman stopped in front of a store window and ogled the hologram models that danced through the air in skimpy spring clothes. "I heard he's laying low, hoping it will all blow over."

Micah closed his eyes. He hadn't wanted to join the gang for their weekly day trip into Chicago, but they'd begun remarking about his absences more and more and he'd run out of excuses. *So what happens—we're not off the train five minutes and someone brings up the goddamn—*"It's not a *duel.*" He heard his voice tight with anger, and tried to stop himself. But he'd been bottling things up for weeks now. He had to allow the occasional vent or he'd go nuts. "They explained it on *Blue 'n' Grey Today*. It's been in all the 'sheets. It's a *challenge*. They're declaring their mutual animosity to the world. A few cuts on one another's arms, a little blood, and it's all over. It's not like a real fight. Nobody dies." He tried to focus on the dancing models, lose himself in the vision of female breasts and thighs and flouncing hair. But one of them looked too much like Manda, whom he'd seen die three times in the past week alone. He turned away from the window and fixed on the midday traffic instead.

"Jeez, bust me to Spacer First Class. Take my stripes away." Cashman glared at him, then rolled his eyes.

They continued to move en masse down State Street. Micah counted Cashman and Hough, Court and her usual gaggle of hangers-on, a couple of new additions from SysAdmin, all out to enjoy the bright sun and warm breeze, the first hints of summer. Or in his case, to get them all off his back.

But who knows . . . ? Micah took in the buildings and crowds and noise. The vivid colors. The sense of a place as far removed from exos and mid-ranges and Sergeant Chrivet as it was possible to be and still remain on this planet. Maybe, if he was lucky, he'd find one thread of sanity amid the tangle of the past weeks. Maybe he'd forget for a little while, catch his breath, and decompress.

"Fabe's right." Hough shot a questioning look at Micah and cleared his throat, the resident expert determined to reassert himself. "Look at the forearms of any of the idomeni—they're all hacked up. The more scars you bear, the more declared enemies you have, the more honor. Winning isn't the point. Death sure as hell isn't." He paused, his thin little gash of a mouth barely visible. "Pascal's probably spending time training. These fights are very ceremonial, very ritualized. If he gets it wrong, he makes us look bad."

Bullshit. Micah walked to the outside of the group, near the curb, and watched the skimmers course past. *He made us look bad when he accepted the damned fight in the first place.* When he let himself get into the situation where Ghos, the Vynshàrau security officer, challenged him. When he opened up the Service to reporters and Cabinet inquiries and embarrassing questions, and sullied it with alien traditions.

"If it's not a duel, why has the Judge Advocate petitioned Diplo to intervene and get the idomeni to retract the challenge?" Court stood before another store window and watched the clothes flit by. "I mean, they've been digging out laws from the 1800s trying to find an excuse." After a few seconds, the floating images flickered and changed, so that a dozen versions of Court's blond curviness filled the space, each wearing a different outfit. "I don't think it's going to happen, myself."

"Once a challenge has been accepted, neither side can back out." Hough glanced back at Micah, his voice growing louder and more assured when he realized he had no competition for this one. "If Pascal gets hit by a skimtruck, he'll get a postponement. That's the best he can hope for at this point."

"I still don't think it will happen. Too much publicity already, and everyone's locking down. No more statements issued without Mako's OK. Public Affairs is hiring contractors just to man the comports and say 'No comment' to whoever calls for a statement. It's a nightmare." Court stepped away from the window and headed for a set of double doors that led into the store.

"No!" Cashman bolted after her. "No shopping—we made a deal!"

"I just want to see *one* thing." Court pointed in the vague direction of the dancing images, making it impossible to determine exactly which thing she had in mind. "It will only take a minute."

"Famous last words." Hough hung back to walk with Micah. "I could do with something to drink. You?"

They cut through the store to a noisy arcade, bought frozen sodas at an autokiosk, and found a table amid the press of shoppers catching their breath and store staff taking a break. A minute or so of increasingly edgy silence passed—Micah had been relieved enough to get away from the rest of the gang, but as had become more and more the case lately, he found that he had nothing to say to any of his fellow bullpen denizens. He'd monitored their behavior for some sign that one of them could have belonged to the Group, and once he realized that none of them did, he lost interest. They spent their spare time cruising the Veedrome, rattling on about girlfriends and promotions and upcoming leave. He spent his time killing Vynshàrau in a hundred different ways, then dying himself in a hundred and one. That tended to limit possible topics of conversation.

"Congrats on nailing the Tech One," Hough finally offered, poking the icy slush in his dispo cup with a straw. "They'll probably bump you up to corporal before you know it."

"Thanks." Micah used up a few seconds pulling in a mouthful of strawberry slurry. "They're offering it again next month—thinking of going for it?"

"Thinking about it. Yeah."

"Good luck."

Hough nodded, narrowed eyes fixed on a trio of girls who giggled past. "Guess you must feel pretty relieved about this challenge, huh? Got Pascal out of your hair."

Micah slowly set down his drink. He blanked his mind before any unwelcome ideas invaded, those months-ago thoughts of killing Cashman and hiding him in the delivery cage having taught him a lesson. It bothered him at times, knowing what he could do if he had to. "What do you mean?"

"I saw him a few times, catching you up in the hallways. Making conversation." Hough sucked his teeth. "I never heard anything about him and enlisteds—he's always been pretty careful to toe the regulation line. But there's a first time for everything, I guess."

Micah stared into his drink. Too pink for blood, but if he thought hard enough . . .

"He asked for you a couple of times, on days when you weren't in the pen. Seemed disappointed that you weren't around to handle problems with his . . . equipment." Hough capped his slur with another lick of the teeth.

That's the story going around? Fine. Micah felt his face heat. *Faber supplies porn to anyone who asks. Faber's got the infamous Captain Pascal aching to wipe his stripe.*

"He picked a Haárin second." Hough raised a hand to beckon to Cashman, who had wandered into the arcade looking irritated. "Dathim Naré, Tsecha Egri's suborn. Now he spends most of his time at the Haárin enclave training while Diplo and the JA try to figure out how to fit this challenge into Service protocols."

"They shouldn't have to." Micah braced for the onslaught as the rest of the group departed the store and approached the table.

Hough shrugged. "It was bound to happen sooner or later. Hell, his girlfriend, Kilian, fought a challenge last summer. Not that anyone would call her real Service." He stood, all good manners as a package-laden Court and her friends drew near. "We work with the idomeni. Trade with them. Better we figure out how to handle stuff like this once and for all."

"Once and for all, yeah. By making sure it never happens again." Micah's reply was drowned out by Cashman's loud complaints, Court's rejoinders. *By making sure*— He remained seated as the girls joined them, drawing sharp looks from Hough and Cashman. *By making sure it never—happens*. He swallowed fast as the oversweet slush bubbled up to the back of his throat.

"Let's get going," Cashman muttered. "Before something else catches her eye."

They left the arcade and walked back outside, the bickering over who would help Court carry her bags providing counterpoint to the more usual city noises, the blare of skimmer proximity alarms and the clamor of conversations in a multitude of languages. Micah hung back, anxious to avoid Hough and his innuendoes. Needing to think.

We're going to attack the embassy. Each word rang in his head like a knell. He had no proof, no clue, only the buzz in his head and the ache in his gut, and the mental hangover of a hundred sim sessions. The sure certainty he felt at times that something would happen.

"I say it's time for lunch!" Court announced. Others shouted the names of restaurants—the Interior Ministry public park was chosen, and off they headed. Micah followed well behind, leg muscles tingling with each strike of his shoes upon the walkway, as they turned off State and headed for one of the pedestrian overpasses that led to the lakeside of the Boul Mich.

Micah mounted the overpass steps, stopping when he reached the summit and looking past the sprawling Interior Ministry grounds to the line of trees beyond that marked the southern border of the idomeni embassy compound. *I know that layout better than I know Far North Lakeside's.* Every corridor, utility chase, private chamber and meeting room etched into his brain by the screams of the wounded, the combined stenches of burned flesh, blood, and shit. The shoulder-pounding kicks of his mid-range, so strong that not even his exo's force dissipaters could dampen them completely. The pound of his heart, and the rasp of his breathing as it echoed inside his helmet.

I know that layout. But then, he'd learned many layouts over the course of his training. Shèráin sites like the Temple at Rauta Shèràa. The monument-lined corridor that connected the Academy campus to the Council buildings. Colonial sites like idomeni consulates and Haárin enclaves. And the terrestrial sites, such as the facility in Death Valley, the enclave of the Chicago Haárin, and the embassy.

Combat training for the Cause. He wondered how he could have ever believed it was that simple. *But we always come back to the embassy.* Had anyone else figured it out? Manda? Bevan the Brain? Did Chrivet know, or was she as uninformed as the rest of them, a tool for whoever had chosen them, designed their training, and planned their fate?

"Jeez, scholar, will you move or something?"

Micah turned to find Cashman at his shoulder, one of Court's shopping sacks in each hand. "Just taking in the view."

"You're getting weirder by the day, you know that?" Cashman trudged past him to the opposite end of the overpass, where Hough and the rest waited. "Let's go."

He made it home eventually, sick from a lunch he hadn't wanted to eat, idiot talk he hadn't wanted to listen to. Hough had left him alone, small thanks for little favors, after a few veiled comments about Pascal failed to find their mark.

He'd stopped by the delivery cage, and felt no surprise whatsoever to find the white mailer in his locker. Headed upstairs with sweat-slick hands. Counted his steps down the hall to his flat, and remained in the hallway for some time after his front door had opened completely.

He talked himself into going inside—really, what choice did he have? Locked the door. Went directly to his bathroom and shoved a finger down his throat, eliminating the nasty, not to mention life-threatening, possibility that he'd vomit during the sim and choke in his headset. Cleaned up. Changed clothes. Collected his gear and lay on his couch, ripping open the mailer and inserting the wafer into the slot. Prayed, even though he knew it would do no good. He wanted to be wrong, and he knew he wasn't.

The tones sounded in his ears, over and over and over, until he thought they'd never en—

—Chrivet paced in front of them, an image of the Commonwealth Field of Stars showing on a wall-mounted display behind her. She wore her serious expression, a morose draw-down of the corners of her mouth that took the rest of her face with it. She was lecturing them again, about their fitness as Spacers and the rightness of their cause, something Micah had taken to calling Philosophy 101.

Get on with it. He sat in the rearmost row of seats, alone. Bevan and Foley sat in the front, of course. Manda, her hair gathered in a ponytail that made her look like a prep schooler, sat near the middle and traded whispers with another woman named Patel.

Get on with it. He stared down at his hands. As always, the thoughts that occurred to him when he was conscious intruded now that he'd entered the scenario. He'd stopped wondering whether or not that was normal, and knew he didn't dare ask Chrivet or anyone else about it at this stage of the game. Instead he kept his mouth shut and pondered the same problems that he had when he'd walked the

Chicago streets a few hours earlier. Would they attack the embassy? If so, when?

"Mister Tiebold?"

Micah closed his eyes, then opened them and raised his head. "Yes, ma'am."

Chrivet remained silent and watched him, something she did more and more as of late. It was as if she found something lacking in even his simplest responses. Something lacking in him. "Am I boring you again?"

Micah sat up straighter as everyone turned to look at him. Bevan, he noted, had one eye slightly higher than the other, so that he always looked skeptical. Foley pouted, like the brat he was. Manda, it pained him to note, fixed him with the same puzzled gaze as did most everyone else. Nothing special. Nothing special at all.

Micah's chest tightened as a surge of anger burst through him like a blown grenade. *I'm not bored, ma'am—just wondering how I'm going to die this time is all.* He breathed deep, when all he wanted to do was shout. Tried to sit on every self-destructive impulse he had as well as a few he didn't realize he nursed until now, and then decided the hell with it. *We who are about to die were wondering—* "When are we going to hit the embassy, ma'am? That's what we're working for, isn't it? That's our target." He heard gasps, sensed the tension of breaths held, and watched Chrivet's hands tighten into fists as yet again he jumped the starter gun and offended her sense of Spacer fitness. "I want to hit 'em, ma'am. The idomeni." He entoned the party line, in part because he believed it with all his heart, but mostly because he sensed that if he didn't, he'd be in even more trouble than he already was. "I want to bring them down."

Chrivet's expression shifted, from angry to a pinched annoyance that made her look a prig. "So you want to bring the idomeni down, Mister Tiebold?" She paused for effect. "Well, you're going to get your chance." She reached behind her and touched a pad fixed to the wall beside the display. The Field of Stars vanished.

Micah bit back a curse as images of Pascal bloomed before him, larger than life shots of the man walking around the base, sitting at his desk, making a presentation. *Damn it, can't I get away from him anywhere!*

Then came the shots from the *Tribune-Times*, the cheap gossip sheets. Pascal with the Exterior Minister and other assorted escorts, male and female both, their common thread the fact that they were all older than he, and much, much richer.

Then came the images with Jani Kilian. The social, at a concert, a football game. The professional, as they departed the idomeni embassy, one of the ministries, stood talking to PM Cao.

Micah compared the Kilian he had seen in the bunker with the one he saw here. The same eerie eyes. The same skinny long-boniness, as though she'd shake apart in a high wind. *It doesn't even look human anymore, and he fucks it every chance he gets.*

"I tell you, ladies and gentlemen." Chrivet tapped the display with her finger. "I would like nothing better than to drive a knife through Kilian's mutant eyes for the filth she's inflicted upon this Earth."

"Why is he allowed to remain in the Service?" That from Bevan, his voice thick with revulsion.

"A good question, Mister Bevan, one that many like minds have asked for some time now." Chrivet linked her hands behind her back. She wore a T-shirt, and her arm muscles bunched and flexed with the movement. " 'Friends in high places' is the best excuse any of us could come up with, and where has that laxity led us? To the point where this stain on our collective honor is allowed to go where he will and do what he wishes, and thus drags the Service down to his low level. To the point where he will be taking direction in a circus ring from a bunch of frog-eyed mush-mouths while our oh-so-potent diplomatic officers stand to one side and kneel to traditions that are not ours, that we don't hold with, that are alien to us in every way, shape, and form." She swallowed hard, and shook her head. "Can we tolerate this in a human Service?"

"No! Ma'am!"

"So what are we gonna do!"

"Take 'em down!"

"Take 'em down." Chrivet smiled. "On the day in question, ladies and gentlemen, you have been chosen to show certain interested parties just what true Spacers think of this insult to our great traditions, to our way of life. You have friends in high places, too—they have overseen your training, and granted you the honor of showing this Commonwealth what real Spacers are made of." For the first time, she regarded them not with hard-eyed disdain, but with a kindness, a pride, that she hadn't seemed capable of before. "It is indeed the embassy, ladies and gentlemen. You will receive the details soon. Until then, we will do as we have been—we will work through it, and work through it, and work through it again, until each and every one of you could take that place out in your sleep." She straightened up and clapped her hands once. "OK, folks. Let's move!"

They set up a jump point in the thin strip of Exterior wilderness that bordered the embassy. They'd be in trouble if an actual Exterior security patrol showed up, but the ministry ran a skeleton staff when the minister traveled off-planet, as she did now. They didn't expect discovery.

Typical early spring morning, damp and colder for it. A hard wind blew in off the lake. Micah sat in the mud beneath a bare-limbed tree and fiddled with a receiver, trying to pick up any transmissions that emerged from the scattered embassy outbuildings. Even though his suit liner protected him from the cold and wet, he still knew that he sat in *mud*, heard the damp squelch every time he moved. He adjusted the receiver earsert and upped the gain, straining for any organized sound amid the hum and hiss. The beat of code. The organized gibberish of scrambled voices. Waste of time on his part—the autoreceiver scanned the signals better than he could. But he couldn't convince himself to hand control of his fate over to the mechanicals. Not just yet.

He felt a touch on his shoulder, and looked up to find Manda standing over him, helmet in hand. She'd already donned her balaclava, from which a few stray curls escaped to frame her heart-shaped face.

"It's almost time." Her voice, never sturdy, sounded ready to crack. "I just wanted to say that however this ends—I just wanted to say—" Her lovely eyes filled. One tear spilled over. She locked her hands behind his head and bent down to him, pulling him close, kissing him. She tasted of the rank coffee they had all drunk, but her lips felt silken and she smelled like flowers and those were the sensations Micah took to heart.

Then she was gone, and the jump came to life like a waking beast, donning gear, checking weapons.

Micah rose and stared across the border to the quiet beyond.

A sun obscured by cloud. The lake turned into choppy swell by the wind. Harder to stay upright, and keep from plowing into the person in front of you. Yet still they pounded onward, following the shore, toward their target.

"Let's hit 'em in the gut, boys and girls. Let's kick 'em where they live." Chrivet picked up the pace. "Air all clear, Tiebold? No marble-eyes watching us?"

Micah checked his readouts. "All clear, ma'am."

They burst onto the beach, as they had before. Up the ramp, blowing sheds as they went. Across the gardens and through the walls. Micah applied his lessons learned from past scenarios, holding back when necessary, pushing on when every nerve in his body yelled *No!* Following behind O'Shae, taking out Vynshàrau with every blast of his midrange, pounding, pounding.

Thorough the doors to the main hall. O'Shae killing the deadhead, then switching to grenades. Joining up with Foley, blasting down every hallway. Smoke. Sparks from blown arrays. Sputtering illumins. Vynshàrau in exos, fighting like demons.

Some fell and rose again. Some fell and remained still. As the meeting room cleared, Micah slipped behind O'Shae again. More halls. Rooms. Bodies. Growing quiet.

"Six five oh, clear."

"Four eight seven, clear."

"Oh nine one—"

Quieter.

"Three four—"

"Eight one—"

"All sectors secure."

Quietest.

O'Shae stopped and turned to him, then raised her faceplate. "Whaddya say, Tieb?"

Micah looked down at his mid-range. For the first time since he'd started the training, he powered it down.

We won.

Micah still sat on his couch, his headgear cradled in his lap. "We cleared the place out. Secured it." Everyone hit their marks, pressed their charge-throughs, came across. He'd even seen Manda at the end of it, hair matted from her helmet, exo streaked with someone else's blood. Something else's blood. Not hers.

He got up. Paced the room, and felt his bones sing with every move. Pulled the wafer from the headset and gathered up his player, then pulled on a jacket and headed for the drop point in Forrestal Block to unload his data. *We did it.* He barely stifled the urge to punch the air. *We did it!*

The air smelled cleaner than Micah had ever known it, as remarkable as if he'd never inhaled it before. He walked as though drunk, barely sensing his feet on the walkway. He tucked the wafer into the inside pocket of his jacket and stopped to mime a baseball pitch. *Strike three—Vynshàrau out!* He set up, went into his windup, and followed through, powering forward into the rough grip of a civvie-clad older man who'd just emerged from the Forrestal One lobby.

"Sorry! Sorry!" Micah straightened the man's rumpled jacket. Then he backed away, giddy and sheepish, and felt the first whisper of doubt as the man stared at him, dark eyes in a dark face, familiar yet out of place.

"Desk jockey has no idea what he's in for." A voice like salt on a wound. "Desk jockey gonna die." Then he hunched his shoulders and strode away, moving a little faster than normal, the way some small men did.

Micah turned and watched the man. *I've seen him before . . . I've seen—* His heart stuttered when the name came back to him. Veles, who'd assisted Pascal during the interrogation-that-wasn't, as well as with the sucker punch with the prototype shooter.

I'll be watching you, Faber. Morning, noon, and night.

Micah wiped a hand over the back of his mouth. He watched Veles until the man disappeared over a rise, then continued on his way with a heavier step. Into the lobby, the comport booth. Sit down. Activate the unit. Breathe. *We won.*

Micah felt his jacket pocket for the wafer. Felt again. Dug deep and rooted around, pulling out a few flecks of thread and nothing else.

He took off after Veles, across the lobby and out the door, dodging pedestrians who seemed to have come out of nowhere. Over the rise, then flat out. Running. Running. Heart in his throat. On the lookout for the small dark man and knowing exactly what he'd do when he found him.

He could run when he had to, but he was no runner. His legs gave out first, oxygen starvation stopping him like a blow. He pulled in great sobs of air, doubled over, then dropped to his knees. Searched for any sign, and found nothing.

CHAPTER 22

"I still maintain that the challenge must be delayed." Tsecha, discordant in green and gold, tore a chunk of clay from the sculpture set against the meeting room wall and worked it between his palms, squeezing it as though it contained something he needed. "There is too much occurring now. Trespassers who leave food about the embassy compound. The mine investigation, which still goes on."

"An Haárin dominant who denies his propitiator and now seeks to avoid the enmity and discipline of Temple." Shai turned from the window opposite Tsecha and his sculpting and bared her teeth. "How many of the acolytes' scars do you bear on your arms, Tsecha? How many of them did you fight in the circle in the time before the war?"

"And now it is their time—is that what you tell me, Shai?" Tsecha pushed the clay chunk back into place, then punched it with his fist. "I did as I most had to, then and now."

"As did Temple, then and now. So you wish to delay matters here in order that your return to Shèrá is set back as well. I have known you too long to suppose otherwise, for I do not recall, and truly, that you were ever overwhelmed by events." Shai pressed a hand to her forehead in a vague, humanish gesture. "This is perhaps, I most think, because you were responsible for those events yourself." She let her hand fall and walked to the center of the oblong space, her sand-colored overrobe a comforting contrast to her diplomatic brown tunic and trousers. "Elon, step farther into this room, please, and prevent this Haárin and I from coming to blows."

Elon moved away from the entry and approached Shai, her posture as straight as she could manage in Tsecha's presence. *Anathema.* How could she have ever regarded such as he with any sort of respect, even that of an esteemed enemy? "I am here, nìaRauta."

"You have not brought Ghos with you?" Shai looked to the entry, her shoulders rounding.

"No, nìaRauta. He works in the practice circle now." As she had when she watched Ghos batter Pascal on the veranda, she felt herself move, a slow drift from side to side, as she imagined her suborn strike and parry with the practice blades. "I advised him to do such, since humanish do not understand the ways of *à lérine* and thus may attack improperly."

"It is good that he is elsewhere. I have no wish to see him now, for he is another with whom I would most happily come to blows." Shai walked to the last in a row of wire-frame chairs and sat, drawing her overrobe around her as though the air chilled. "It pains me as sickness to say this, Elon, but the Haárin who stands in this room now is as correct in his opinion of this damned challenge as the gods and circumstance allow him to be."

"The Haárin who stands in this room now rejoices in your esteem, Shai, and truly." Tsecha drove his thumb into the clay and worked a series of grooves across the surface. Two lines down, then two across them, so that together they formed a grid of nine squares. "If he could rejoice in a decision cancelling this damned challenge, he would feel even more as blessed by the gods." He etched a figure in each of the diagonal squares, dragged a forefinger across the entire pattern, then dipped his hand in a nearby container of water and rubbed the clay smooth once more. "My Lucien is not

my Jani. He does not understand the circle, and when he
does not understand, he strikes as a serpent." He picked up
the damp cloth that had served as the sculpture covering and
spread it over the clay. "If Ghos had asked Caith's aide in
choosing the worst humanish for him to challenge, she
would have led him to no other human but to my Lucien."

Shai squinted toward Tsecha's labors, then shook her
head and gestured to Elon. "Such was not the time for Ghos
to challenge the humanish, Elon. Especially a Service humanish, for it causes Mako and his suborns to wonder if revenge for Feres was his thought."

"It was not, nìaRauta." Elon walked across the room to
the table containing the stone formations. "This I know and
truly." She stood before one of the arrangements, taking as
much strength as she could in their order and beauty as her
heart pounded and hers and Ghos's words sounded in her
head. *Will you kill Pascal, Ghos of the Stones? If I am able.*
But not for revenge, no—Pascal's blood was as that of an
animal, and could not serve as fair exchange for that of
Feres. *It is enough that he should die for that which he is.*
For the disorder he represented, the godlessness that he was.

Elon took up one of the stones, clenching it as she fought
the desire to fling it into the rest, to scatter them across the
floor. When she sensed motion from the corner of her eye,
she half turned, her hand raised, the rounded point of the
stone facing out as the edge of a blade—

—and met Tsecha's gaze, ancient gold and arrogant,
mocking her as it had in Rauta Shèràa Temple.

"NìRau Ghos, it most seems, wonders at my Lucien's loy-
alties. He believes him a spy, although for whom he cannot
say." Tsecha took the stone from Elon's grasp and tossed it
up in the air, then caught it.

"Pascal *is* a spy, Tsecha." Shai gripped the chair next to
hers and pushed it back and forth until it aligned with the
rest of the row. "Each time he visits here with you and
Dathim, I anticipate my dealings with Service Diplomatic,

and all the new varieties of requests from General Burkett and his staff, for I know as I know my robes that Pascal goes to them as soon as he finishes here."

"He could do much worse, Shai. This I know and truly, as do you." Tsecha again tossed the stone in the air, and caught it. "But for every thing he takes, he gives something back, and now he gives us what I tell you now, what I have tried to tell you this entire day. He believes, with reason, that these vehicles that have invaded the embassy grounds are of the Service. He believes, for reasons he has yet to make clear, that there are those in the Service who would attack us here and at the enclave, and see us driven from this city."

"We always knew this, Tsecha," Shai replied. "Even without your Pascal's clarity. The mine they have yet to explain is, I most fear, an illustration of this. It was no accident—this I know and truly. It was meant to be. It was meant to kill Haárin, and took Feres instead, but we will wait unto death for the humanish to admit such."

Tsecha tossed and caught the stone one last time, then held it out to Elon, remaining silent until she took it from his hand. "My Lucien fears something greater, Shai. Greater than a mine, or food in your outbuildings. He fears an assault, against this place or the enclave. An attack by those trained to do such, outfitted with equipment and weaponry as one sees on the battlefield."

Elon placed the stone Tsecha had handed her back within its arrangement, taking care to avoid touching it where he had. "When would this attack occur?" She picked up another stone, this time cradling it between her palms so he could not take it.

"That, my Lucien cannot say." Tsecha watched her as though they stood within the circle, his gaze fixed on her hands as his shoulders rounded in mirror of her posture. "All that he may tell us now is that we must prepare, and keep watch."

Shai stood. "After the explosion of a single mine and the death of Feres, Prime Minister Li Cao and General Burkett and Admiral-General Mako became as my constant companions. I believed and truly that they would never leave my side. I would expect even greater visitation in the case of a supposed assault, Tsecha. Roomfuls of humanish who would remain with me as my shadow from early morning sacrament until the middle of the night." She paced the bare floor, her soft boots sounding against the tile as though she walked through grass. "I do not see them."

Tsecha leaned against the table in a most unseemly way, crossing his arms over his chest and his legs at the ankle, a cramped humanish posture. "My Lucien currently gathers proof. Evidence. When he possesses sufficient, he will go to his dominants, and they will come to you."

"And you must remain here as he gathers this proof, for he will work with you and you only." Shai raised her hands above her head, a plea to the gods. "I understand you, Tsecha, as no one else does. You have constructed a reason to remain here when Temple has ordered you back to the worldskein." She stopped in place and lowered her arms to her sides. "It has therefore fallen to me to enact the wishes of Temple as best I can, and to do this as I determine how much of your story is truth and how much the invention of your spying humanish."

Elon moved into the shaft of sunlight that streamed through the window, closing her eyes for a moment as she took what she could of its sickly warmth. "I most fear, nìa-Rauta, that very little of what Pascal says may be invented. The humanish who have trespassed on these grounds know our systems. Given the ways in which we protect such information, they could only have learned such through the spying methods the Service uses to monitor that which we do."

Shai turned and looked her near enough in the eye as to be as unseemly. "You agree with Tsecha, Elon?" She folded her arms and tucked her hands within the sleeves of her over-robe. "I struggle to recall when last such occurred." She stood most still. "What state our defenses, then?"

Elon pressed her hands around the stone, drawing the last

edges of pain from bones long healed, wondering how much pressure she would need to apply to break them once more. "We may increase lake patrols. We may increase our guards. We may also employ robotic devices as free-float monitors, setting them at our borders. In whatever instance, I most fear, the humanish will know that we have increased our surveillance, and while the lake patrols and guards are allowed by treaty, the devices are not, for humanish fear we would use them to observe that which they do." She relaxed her grip on the stone. "Shall I do as I am allowed, nìaRauta?" she asked Shai. "Or shall I do as I must?"

"Increased patrols may draw fire. We want no more dead." Tsecha still stood against the table, his only movement to straighten his legs, then recross them. "Pink grenades disable weaponry and systems even as they leave the humanish unharmed. Even if the variety we have here now is not fully safe for idomeni systems, such is better than live fire, for such is one thing we cannot take back."

Shai walked to the sculpture that Tsecha had lately attended. "The pink, Tsecha, is even less allowed by treaty than robotic patrols." She raised the damp drapery that covered it, then set it aside and began to work the clay that Tsecha had recently smoothed. "I do not, I most believe, need to tell you of the protests we would hear if such drifted beyond the boundaries of the embassy. Any object containing a bioarray would be disabled, any system touched would be disrupted or destroyed. Li Cao would, as humanish say, never let me forget." Unlike Tsecha, she seemed to savor the feel of the clay—her shoulders slowly uncurved as she worked her hands into the mass. "That being understood, I say to you, Elon, that we should enable the pink systems, for as much as I disdain agreement with the Haárin who leans against the table in an unseemly humanish manner, I cannot help but agree that dead humanish would do us great harm."

"Yes, níaRauta." Elon returned to the table and replaced the stone, taking care to avoid Tsecha's gaze, to avoid drawing too close. "I will begin such today."

"And the challenge, Shai?" Tsecha stood away from the table and let his arms fall to his sides. More humanish deadness.

"That must continue." Shai turned to him, her hands coated to the wrists in drying clay. "Pascal spends much time at your enclave, Tsecha. He comes here most often as well, and watches us as though he wishes to learn. Thus and so—we both know and truly that one cannot learn completely of idomeni until one learns challenge, and has fought in the circle. Let Pascal learn such then. I am most sure that Dathim will teach him."

"Shai." Tsecha's shoulders rounded so that he had to tilt his head to his shoulder to look at her. "You do not know what you do."

"I know exactly." Shai turned from him back to her sculpture. "You see to your enclave, Tsecha. You are indeed needed here, I most fear—though Temple may not wait forever to deal with you as they would, I may convince them to wait a short time." She gestured to Elon. "You, Elon—see to this place. In any way you deem fit, and truly." She plunged her hands back into the clay, and worked it so the muscles of her forearms tensed, accenting her *à lérine* scars. "I most relish the upset this challenge has inflicted upon the Service. Each day we receive messages from Diplomatic, the Judge Advocate. Even their Medical dominants wonder over how an emotional augment such as Pascal may behave in the circle." She nodded in an annoyingly humanish manner. "Disruption is a great thing, and truly."

Tsecha strode to the door, his back still bowed. "You grow disordered, Shai."

"I grow tired of trespass and sacrilege. In exchange, I request only a little humanish blood." Shai bared her teeth. "See to the arming of the pink, Elon."

"Yes, nìaRauta." Elon followed Tsecha to the door, pausing at the entry to allow him time to depart. She did not wish to encounter him alone in any hallway. He watched her as he had at Temple when he suspected her anger, and knew that a further irritation on his part would spur her to an eruption. "No, Tsecha," she uttered aloud as she walked the corridors to her rooms. She could not betray her thoughts to him now—such would wait until a time that he did not suspect. Only then would he know, when it would be too late for him to react. Then she would rejoice in his pain.

Elon took mid-afternoon sacrament, her mind as jumbled as the half-leafed branches she had driven through when she and Ghos had chased the humanish skimmer. Afterward she sought to rest. But her thoughts still raced. Her skin tingled as though stung by thorns.

She rose, laved, then donned the rougher clothes she wore to labor in the damned cold outside, a brown coverall and boots. She departed the embassy and stalked the outbuildings, moving from utility dome to greenhouse to guard bunker, receiving status reports and giving orders, as all the while her limbs moved as leaden and she ached to the pit of her soul.

She found Ghos eventually, monitoring instrumentation in one of the guard bunkers located at regular intervals along the embassy access road. He worked alongside nìaRauta Laur, but as soon as he realized Elon's presence, he ordered Laur to a task outside.

Elon waited until the suborn female departed before joining Ghos at the console, standing a half stride behind him, as was seemly. At that angle, she could see the dried mud that streaked the back of his coverall, the fragments of twig and leaf that once more sullied his braids, which he had again bound together with a length of cord. "I have met with nìaRauta Shai." She leaned forward and plucked a leaf from his collar. "We are to load the pink into the defense array despite its imperfections. Shai would rather have disabled systems than dead humanish."

"Then she is damned." Ghos turned and looked Elon in the eye, as he had so often of late. "But we know this."

"Yes." Elon reached out again, this time to brush away

dirt that shadowed beneath Ghos's eye. When he took her hand and held it, she thought to pull back, but his fingers closed as a vise and she could not have freed herself if she wished to. Her skin burned where his touched, as the sense of weight returned to her limbs. The tension, as though as she had been filled past her ability to contain.

"I have fathered four," Ghos said, first loosening then tightening his hold. "From the first, mothered by Sor nìa-Rauta Hesai, who maintained security for the hospital shrine at Nen Shèràa, to the fourth, mothered by Ailà nìaRauta Qar, who served as suborn to the Council security dominant."

Elon gestured acceptance of the information with her free hand, even though Ghos's gradual ascension within the security skein was known before she accepted his petition to serve her. If she had approached a male of greater standing, as one of Cèel's security dominants, or one of those who guarded the inner rooms at Temple, she would have spoken of the three she had mothered, each fathered by a male of increasing status over the one before. "I take comfort in your declaration of order, Ghos. So much a haven is it from the chaos of Haárin, the contamination of human joinings."

"This is not a time to think of such." Ghos tilted his head to one side, as though he surprised even himself, for he seldom restrained his thought in deference to the proprieties. "I must complete these settings." He released her abruptly and turned back to the console, examining systems readouts and recalibrating sensors.

Elon drew close behind, until she could sense Ghos's blessed warmth through the chill of the air. "Tsecha sought to petition nìaRauta Shai to forbid your challenge of Pascal." She watched his hands move over the console, every flex and curve of his fingers. "Shai denied such. She wishes humanish blood to be shed within the circle."

"Then she shall most certainly have it, and truly." Ghos's voice emerged as gentle as ever it had. "As much as her satisfaction demands, and more besides."

"We will not load the pink."

"No, nìaRauta. Nor will we increase the patrols or release the robot monitors."

"If the humanish invaders come, let them."

"Yes."

"If humanish blood is wanted, let it be shed."

"And ours with it."

"We are most in agreement, Ghos."

"I have always known such, Elon, and truly."

"Yes, as have I." Elon reached out and placed a hand upon Ghos's shoulder, then pulled back when she sensed movement behind her. She turned to find Laur in the entry—the suborn held a disassembled monitor, her posture indicating that she had no sense of how to repair it. Elon left Ghos to aid her. Then she waited outside in the weak humanish sun until he rejoined her, and they returned to the embassy together.

They retired to Elon's rooms, since as dominant the right of place fell to her. First came release, rapid joinings that dispelled the tension that had grown between them as a solid thing. Once, then rest, then again, a meld of unclothed limbs that served to express the oneness of their thoughts, their beliefs. Their fears, and their hatreds. The Way that they planned together. Their mutual Path to their Star.

They lay afterward for some time, savoring the quiet of each other's presence, the serenity that came from two minds that thought as an ordered one. Ghos held Elon by the wrist with one hand as he stroked her arm with the other, from forearm to shoulder, then down, again and again, the rhythm of the motion taking them both to a state approaching trance.

"Ghos of the stones." Elon reached to him and fingered his hair, then gestured in weak dismay as she came away with yet another piece of twig. "Ghos of the forests, who lives in the trees." She took him by the hand and led him to her laving room. There, amid tiled scenes of Rauta Shèràa that one of Dathim Naré's suborns had applied two seasons before, she unbraided his hair and laved it with soap that smelled of the sand and sun, then comb-dried it, running the nubs over and over Ghos's scalp until he bared his teeth in the pleasure of it. Finally, she rebraided the fine brown lengths, binding them at the ends with jewel-green ties that caught the light as night insects when Ghos shook his head, and clattered like beads.

"So quiet." Ghos stood, his skin as gold beneath the inset illumination, an ordered contrast to the brown of his hair. "I have not known such for so long."

"We have much to do." Elon touched his shoulder one last time, and savored the warmth, the sense of flesh and bone beneath. "But we do not know how much time we have, which means we must act quickly."

They dressed in silence born of shared purpose, then visited Elon's physician-priest, who took the sperm Ghos had deposited and preserved it for blending with one of the eggs that Elon had reserved for such interactions. The embryo would be blended there, then returned to Shèrá for growth and placement with a home-mother.

And in three seasons, a youngish. Elon bared her teeth. A declaration of hers and Ghos's likeness of mind. Another step farther down their Way to the Star, one that would be taken no matter what happened to them.

"I must see to Laur," Ghos said as they departed the physician-priest's workroom. "When she is left alone for too long, she begins to delve too deeply into that which is not her concern." He left Elon without another look or touch, as was the way it was. Their declaration had been made, Ghos' ascension assured. Now came their task, which would serve to bind them as well as any joining, any birth.

Elon walked the corridors that led back to her rooms. The way also led past Shai's rooms—when the panel slid aside and Shai emerged into the passage, Elon wondered if it had been coincidence, or if she had awaited her.

"Elon!" Shai proceeded a half stride behind her. "I have

received word from your physician-priest, and rejoice with you. A most ordered pairing, you and Ghos. Such will assure the security of this place, of that I am most sure."

"Yes, nìaRauta." Elon turned and watched Shai return to her rooms, the hallway illuminations casting shadows across her back like spreading stains of blood.

CHAPTER 23

"... a period of such change as shakes one
to the depths of their soul ..."

Clase, *Thalassan Histories, Book I*

"The second worst thing about waiting, besides the actual waiting itself, of course, is that you eventually reach a point where you feel the need to do something." Brondt dragged a chair away from the table and spun it around, then sat astraddle. "This is the point that separates your run-of-the-mill poker player from your true gambler. The ability to sit out the lulls when you realize there's nothing you can do. No play to be made."

Jani looked up from the document she and Torin had been examining. She had adjourned to the library after the walk down the beach with the rest of what Brondt called the "like minds," and had spent the last hour or so showing Torin the workings of her scanpack and not—repeat, not—thinking about John, Tsecha, Feyó, Gisa, or Niall. "Dieter." She regarded him as he did her, elbows on the table and chin cradled in hand. "Has anyone ever told you that you're a pain in the ass?"

Torin gasped, then doubled over, his high-pitched laugh bouncing off the walls. Brondt only smiled.

"It's just that I know a coiled spring when I see one." He picked up the empty scanpack case and tipped it upside down, shaking out its nonexistent contents. "I don't think

I've ever seen anyone work harder at remaining nonchalant."

Stop reading me. Jani held up the old copy of the *Partisan* that she had used to demonstrate the differences between static and mutable inks, and rolled it into a tight tube. "John should be at Neoclona by now. Assuming Gisa didn't intercept him."

"She wouldn't do that. She's still very idomeni in that regard—her conflict is with Feyó, not you, and not your lover." Brondt continued to toy with the case, closing the fasteners, then opening them. Then he sighed, the shakiness of his breathing implying that his nerve had limits after all. "If the stories I've heard of ní Tsecha's resolve are true, he's digging himself in back in Chicago. I don't see him giving in without a battle, and you and Feyó are already rallying the strongest bloc of Haárin support that exists. An interesting time will be had by all, but I do believe that in the end, you will save ní Tsecha, and prevail."

"Strong-arm diplomacy over ideology. That's a humanish argument." Jani tossed the newssheet aside, then stood and walked to the window, drawn to the view of the bay, as she had been numerous times over the course of the day. "If Cèel caves in to it, he risks weakening himself in the eyes of his more traditionalist rivals, as we've said a hundred times. If he refrains, he risks losing the Haárin, as we've said a hundred and one. I don't think I'd like to be in his shoes right now, and it's a token flip as to which way he'll finally go." Dusk neared, shading the sky in coral and indigo. Clouds grew, offering the possibility of evening rain. "It's the suicide option that bothers me, the sense that if it all gets too much, he'll just open his shirt and wait for someone to strike him. Who would come after him is anyone's guess. My fear is that they wouldn't wait for Tsecha to decide to return to the worldskein—they'd just send warriors to collect him."

"That's never happened," Torin piped as he made entries into his handheld. "I've read the histories—if Tsecha refuses to return, that alone could tie up the Council in knots. The ideologues don't think on their feet very well—he could stall them just by saying no."

"I've said it before." Jani folded her arms and leaned against the window framing. "No one's gone this way before. We're all making it up as we go, including Cèel. And he was a warrior himself, if you recall. Bornsect battles never experienced the flip-flops that humanish have, but he still needed to possess some flexibility." She looked to Brondt. "Aren't there any comlines here that you trust?"

Brondt shook his head. "No."

"Who can I count on here?"

"To do what, take over the courtyard? Mount an attack on the basement clinic?" Brondt stood and swung a leg over his backward seat, then turned the chair around and shoved it under the table. "You can't do anything worthwhile until you hear from John or Feyó. Until then you'd just be standing on the roof flapping your arms. Might make you feel better, but you're not accomplishing much, are you?" He joined her by the window, his yellow-green eyes reflecting the light like fluorescence. "Rain tonight. We're nearing autumn, which means the storms will become more and more severe." He glanced at her sidelong. "There's nothing you can do without more information, and you've sent out the runners to get it. So, you wait."

"I'm not the most patient of people."

"I'd never have guessed."

The sound of the door opening silenced them. Jani noted that Brondt, for all his talk of calm, flinched at the noise. His hand moved to his trouser pocket as well, which saved her from asking whether he still carried his shooter.

"Ná Kièrshia." Gisa stood in the doorway, less elegant than usual in the coverall and boots she wore when she plied her agronomist trade in the greenhouses and fields. "The time for early evening sacrament approaches and no one sits downstairs. Would you be willing, I wonder, to dine with me?"

Brondt looked to the wall clock. "Midweek in Karistos. End of summer. Outdoor concerts and such . . ." His voice trailed when his eyes met Gisa's, stares locking for a beat beyond casual. "Torin," he said after a moment, "let's batten the hatches—I don't like the looks of those clouds." He glanced at Jani, eyebrow cocked, then walked to the door, pausing at the desk to collect Torin, then departing without any further regard for his dominant.

"Brondt is strange," Gisa said while the subject of her critique was still well within earshot. "Eamon says he looks for a leader as a bee looks for nectar, moving from flower to flower." She bared her teeth, then gestured toward the hall. "Sacrament grows cold. Please."

Jani patted her grumbling stomach, which as usual betrayed her when faced with the prospect of a good meal. "One moment." She walked to the table and collected her scanpack, straightened the newssheets and pushed in the chairs. *So, I wait.* She shouldered her duffel and followed Gisa from the room.

Gisa hadn't been completely truthful concerning her lack of mealtime company. Jani arrived to find that both Bon and Eamon were already eating. Bon nodded to her with the mix of regard and uncertainty to which Jani had grown accustomed, while Eamon grunted in her general direction in between gulps of vodka.

"Another Acadian dish, Kièrshia." Gisa handed Jani a casserole of chickpeas and corn. "Our cooks still seek to please you."

"They must be tearing their hair out over the light turnout." Jani looked around the empty dining area, taking in the neat place settings and filled tureens from which fragrant steam escaped. "How do you plan menus when you never know how many will show up?"

"We begin to adjust." Bon shrugged. "Group meals were planned in the beginning to foster togetherness, and to allow some of those more shaken by change to feel not so displaced." The dimmer evening lighting softened her appearance, shadowing the worst ravages of her skin. "As time goes on, Thalassa will meet as a whole for holidays only. Special occasions."

"Fine with me," Eamon muttered into his glass. "Feel like I'm at bloody day camp half the time." He shoved a forkful of sauced kettle beef into his mouth, his bleary gaze sharpening as it fixed on Jani. "John's in town?"

"Yes." Jani felt Bon's veiled stare, Gisa's more direct examination. "He needed to stop by the facility."

"Better do it while he can." Eamon glared down at his plate for a moment, then shook his head. "Damned fool—" He squinted toward the demirooms, then shielded his eyes with his hand. "Is that you, Niri? What is it?"

Jani turned to see one of the clinic staff hovering at the edge of the courtyard. A young female decked out in med-whites, face set, hands clenched.

"There is a call, sir. From the outbuildings. There has been an accident on the coast road from Karistos—you are needed."

"Accident?" Jani pushed her chair back from the table, the screech of polywood against stone echoing throughout the space. "What sort? Equipment? Skimmer? Did the guards shoot someone? What?"

"Ná Kièrshia?" Bon's voice emerged calm. "We have accidents all the time at this place. The building that goes on. The work."

"In the middle of the evening?" Jani strode toward Niri, holding up her hands in a gesture of surrender and slowing when she realized the young female had backed away and stepped behind a planter. "What happened? *Please.*"

Niri swallowed. "A skimmer—"

"*Shit.*" Jani struggled to lower her voice when every cell in her body begged to scream. "Who was hurt. *Who?*"

"Doesn't matter who—I still need to get out there." Eamon raised his glass, then swore under his breath and set it down with a clatter. "Ah hell." He stood and stepped around the table. "Get Maren and Caris," he said, pointing to Niri. "Tell them to grab the ready bags and meet me in the garage."

"I'm going with you." Jani fell in beside him.

"You don't belong. You'll just get in the way."

"I'm going."

Eamon stopped and turned to her. They had moved under better lighting now—the brightness highlighted the damage that drink and exhaustion had inscribed on his face. "You've done more than enough already." He stood with his hands clenched, his weight balanced, as though he'd strike her given any more provocation.

Then he took a step back, emitting a sigh like a moan of pain. "Fine. Let's see how much worse you can make it." He started for the door, thumping his fist against every piece of furniture he encountered along the way.

Jani followed, pausing as she reached the door. She looked back to the courtyard to find Gisa still seated, Bon standing behind her like a hound guarding its mistress.

"Damn and blast it, stay on the road!" Eamon pounded the dashboard with the flat of his hand. "I should have know better than to let you drive."

Jani steered down the banked path leading from the garage, backing off the accelerator until the up-and-down whine of a straining propulsion array softened to a high-pitched hum. "The shortest distance between two points." She reentered the winding roadway until another scenic curve presented itself, then braced for the shudder as she again steered off-road and out of range of the skimtrack. "It's a straight line—remember?" She punched the accelerator again as a rock formation loomed ahead, coaxing the vehicle up and over as Eamon howled and curled into crash position, his head between his knees, hands locked behind.

"We're clear of the landscaping—you can look up now." Jani sped up as they emerged onto the flat, the road uncurling before them. "It's a straight shot all the way around the horn."

"Damn you to hell." Eamon worked upright, wiping the back of his hand across his mouth. "In a thousand different ways." He looked back over his shoulder just as a rapidly receding flare of red emergency lighting broke through the gloom, blooding his face. The ambulance, bringing up the rear. "I should have ridden with them."

The rain had begun, fat drops that splattered across the windscreen with a hard pellet sound. Jani followed the lighted ribbon of pavement, eyes locked on the darkening distance, on the lookout for flames, flares, safety lighting, or any of a hundred accident signs. "I see something." She banked off the road and veered wide, angling her approach to the distant glow in order to avoid anything that might still lie on the road.

Or anyone. She deflected power to the skimmer headlamps, lighting the landscape for half a kilometer or more. Her heart skipped as the damage revealed itself—three skimmers, two with shattered windscreens. Bodies laid out beside them, sheltered from the rain by plastic sheeting, while humanish and idomeni both ran between them or looked on from a distance.

Then she saw a slender form rise from beside one of the bodies and turn into the glare, hair agleam like molten silver, and muttered choked thanks to her Lord Ganesh.

John loped over to the skimmer as soon as Jani slowed. "There was some kind of explosion, just off the roadway." Jacketless in the rain, blood streaking his white shirt and the side of his face, he gave her the briefest glance before rounding the vehicle to Eamon's side. "Three hurt, all Haárin. Feyó—"

"*Feyó!*" Before Jani could say more, John held up his hand.

"—has a mild concussion, according to the Glasgow Scan. Some disorientation, but she's conscious and can obey commands. One of her suborns has a dislocated shoulder and a broken collarbone, if my human hand scanner can read them properly. The driver's the worst off. The steering array impacted her abdomen . . ." He moved off toward the accident scene, Eamon following close behind, the two of them fixed on what needed to be done.

Jani followed until she came to the nearest prone form. Feyó lay with her eyes closed, head elevated, her body covered by plastic sheeting. John had rigged a barrier against the rain for her, a seat-of-the-pants assembly utilizing a strip of the same sheeting stretched between a tree branch and the skimmer door.

Jani crouched by her side. "Ná Feyó?"

Feyó opened her eyes and looked at her. "Ná Kièrshia." An angry bruise had already bloomed above her right eye, centered by an egglike swelling. "You look as you did at the embassy, on the day we met. So angry, as though you could strike the gods themselves." She tried to sit up, wincing as she shifted her weight to her elbows.

"Please don't move." Jani placed a hand on Feyó's shoulder and eased her back as the surfaces around them altered to flashing red, signaling the arrival of the ambulance. "Forgive the ungodly color of the alarm."

Feyó smiled, but the expression faded quickly. "Others followed me, Kièrshia. Representatives of the dominants from Amsun and Hortensia." She raised a hand and pointed.

Jani followed the line of her hand, and saw a trio of Haárin, two males and a female, dressed in traditional garb, now dirt-smeared and rain-soaked, standing near the other battered skimmer.

"They came to provide support for me." Feyó's voice came faster. "The time had come to confront Gisa—I brought them to Thalassa to see you—"

"That's it—conversation's over." Eamon emerged through the rain and set about dismantling the sheeting. "Go wreak havoc somewhere else," he said to Jani as he helped one of his aides raise Feyó onto a skimgurney.

Jani waited as first Feyó, then her two suborns were loaded into the vehicle. Then she turned to the three visitors, gauging their postures as she approached. *The female's shoulders are rounding—oh, good*. Then one of the males deflected the female's attention and gestured roughly toward Jani, his voice a harsh tumble of Pathen Haárin. The female gave Jani another, more studied look, and slowly straightened.

Make that very slowly. Jani brushed off the knees of her old brown coverall, and wished she'd had the presence of mind to don her overrobe. Unfortunately, it had needed cleaning, and currently hung in drip-dry mode above her bathroom sink. "Can you tell me what happened?" she asked in Sìah Haárin, cutting straight to the chase. Somehow, a more traditional "glories of the evening" greeting didn't seem appropriate, given the circumstances.

"Tripbeam, most likely, and truly." The female raised her arm in gesture, the sleeve of her overrobe sliding back to reveal a hash of *à lérine* scars. "The pale humanish—his skimmer led us. It passed unimpeded. Then followed Feyó. Then came the explosion."

"Tripbeam." Jani looked over the first damaged skimmer. "Keyed to the com frequencies of Feyó's vehicles?" She fell silent—speculations coursed through her brain like comet trails, and she didn't want the Haárin to hear any of them. "Are any of you hurt?" She gestured to the Pathen male, who was attempting to cradle his right arm without seeming to. "You should be seen to, as is seemly."

The appeal to the formalities reawakened something in the two males—taken aback as they seemed by the red flashing lights of the ambulance, they headed for it, their steps quickening as one of the hybrid Haárin walked out to meet them.

The female, however, hung back. She looked Jani in the eye, her brown-gold face a study in emotion barely contained.

"You are the Kièrshia." Her shoulders curved as Jani nodded. "You ask us to enter the place that struck at us? You ask us to take treatment from those who sought to injure us by surprise?" She possessed what the idomeni called "demon eyes," dark brown irises and sclera that in the gloom looked like empty sockets.

"I know who arranged this." Jani shoved her hands in her pockets to keep from gesturing—she didn't know Pathen Haárin very well, and the last thing she needed now was a miscommunication. "I will see to them."

"Hah! Indeed? What remedy?" The female leaned closer. *"Priest. What remedy?"* She glared at Jani as though she expected an answer at that moment. When she didn't receive one, she gestured in angry dismay and resumed her trudge to the ambulance.

Jani watched the female shake off the Haárin aide's offered arm and enter the ambulance on her own. Watched Eamon and one of his assistants secure the vehicle gullwings, then climb inside. Watched the ambulance float away, red light still pulsing through the growing dark. Felt movement behind her, and turned to find John standing there.

"I'm afraid to ask what that was about." He held out his hand—when Jani took it, he reeled her in.

Jani wrapped her arms around his waist and squeezed until she felt him tense under the pressure. "When word came to the house of an accident, all I could think of was you."

"I'm not your problem, from the look of things. Hearing's a little wonky from the shockwave, but beyond that I'm fine." John brushed away raindrops that had beaded on the front of Jani's coverall. "Feel free to hang onto me as long as you wish, though. I'm sure I'm more badly hurt than I can imagine."

Jani leaned back so she could look John in the face. "I think you're right." The rain had washed the blood from his cheek, exposing the raw edges of a jagged gash. "That's deep—it will scar if you don't get it treated quickly."

"I'm not the most important thing going on right now." John gripped her hand and held it away from his face. "I don't think Gisa tried to kill Feyó. The blast wasn't strong enough."

"A warning shot across her bow? I'm afraid I'm not concerned about degree at the moment."

"What are you going to do?"

Jani worked out of John's embrace as the first red flares of idomeni temper stained the outer edges of her vision. "I told them." She paced, her boot soles clogging with the claylike mud. "*I told them.* No violence against any of Feyó's, or against Feyó herself. To do so against her or one of hers is to do so against me, and I do not take kindly." She could have been standing under glass for all she felt the rain. The Pathen female's words echoed inside her head. *Priest, what remedy?*

"Jan . . . ?" John walked to her side and placed a tentative hand on her shoulder.

Jani felt his touch like a growing weight—she shook off his hold, then set off toward his skimmer. "Wait." She stopped. In the distance a low rumble of thunder sounded. "You better drive."

CHAPTER 24

The ground floor was quiet enough that Jani could hear her boots echo on the tile. The demirooms were darkened—no one sat on the chairs and couches and listened to music or watched programs on the 'Vee. No one spoke.

Yet they were there, all the Thalassans. Jani could see them through the interior gloom, standing around the courtyard. Silent. Waiting. They turned at the click of the closing entry, and what sounded like a sigh emerged from them. A collective release.

Jani took a step forward, then paused when she detected movement off to one side, and watched the two familiar forms approach. Torin, her self-appointed historian, gripping his handheld, eyes wide, jaw tight. And Brondt, her self-appointed chamberlain, as outwardly calm as his nature and position demanded.

"Torin and I had just returned from the outbuildings when the ambulance arrived." Only a tightening around his jaw betrayed his unease. "They'd already begun gathering." He looked from Jani to the crowd, then back to her. "What are you going to do?"

"I know what I want to do." Jani held out her hands, then turned them over—they were steady, the palms dry, the fingers curved as though readying to grip the hilt of a blade.

"Jani? What's going on?"

Jani turned to find John standing in the entry, his face shiny with rain but for the dull, dark gash in his cheek. "Have Eamon bring Feyó and the Pathen Haárin up here."

John hesitated, then shook his head. "Feyó is in no condition—"

"She needs to be here." Jani sensed John's uncertainty, his fear. For her. For what he knew she wanted to do. "Tell Eamon. Bring them here yourself if he refuses to help." She waited, her nerves stretching in impatience as he looked her up and down. A doctor's examination, an evaluation of all the things about her that he no longer understood. "John, *please.*"

John pushed a hand through his wet hair, then fixed on Brondt until the other man shuffled his feet and looked away. "I'll do . . . what I can." He stepped around Jani, reached for her as he drew near, and brushed his fingers against hers. "Take care, in every way, for all the good my saying it will do," he said as he skirted the edge of the courtyard and vanished into the shadow.

Jani's shoulders rounded as she headed toward the crowd, the back row parting for her, then closing in behind her as the row in front of them parted. She passed through the innermost circle of the hybrids to find the courtyard stripped of tables and chairs, the planters pushed to the side. Someone had inscribed a circle on the tile with red chalk—Gisa stalked its center, scarred arms bared in her sleeveless shirt, which had been bleached palest dull white to allow the greatest contrast with the blood.

When she saw Jani, she stilled. "This is not your challenge, Kièrshia," she said in English, the beat of the rain against the skylight a backdrop for her words. "I fight Feyó for the protection of this place."

"Feyó cannot fight now." Jani walked the outer edge of the circle as she fingered the shoulder of her coverall, probing the seam for any gaps in the seal. "Your perimeter defenses saw to that."

"She knew she was not welcome here. Yet she came, so whose fault?" Gisa cut the air with an invisible blade. "I told her that if she came here, she would face challenge. She treats us as hers, and we are not. She acts as dominant, and she is not." Her voice rang out. "She has no place here. No right. This is Thalassa! The place of the hybrid! We live in the new way here!"

Before Jani could reply, a rising murmur drew her attention. She turned to the sound and saw John's white head move through the crowd, the darker braided fringe of the Pathen Haárin representatives following close behind.

Then John emerged and the voices ramped, for he pushed a skimchair in which sat a hunched figure. Feyó, one eye swelled shut, dressed in medwhites. Her shoulders rounded further when she caught sight of Gisa, tensing as though she would push to her feet and enter the circle despite her injuries.

Jani waited until John stilled the chair. Then she walked to it and stood before Feyó. "I am most sorry to ask you to expose yourself in your weakness. But all must see that you cannot fight." She bent low, so that only Feyó could hear. "Gisa told you that you would not be allowed into Thalassa, and that you would face sanction if you sought entry. Yet you came."

Feyó tilted her head to look up at Jani, a posture dictated more by her position than any regard. "To discuss—"

"To discuss what?" Jani backed off a step, so she could look Feyó in the eye, a move that drew some grumbling from the Pathen female. "No, I don't sense an attempt at dialogue gone awry here. What I sense is an attempt at sandbagging that didn't quite work the way you hoped."

"Gisa is chaotic!"

"Gisa is half humanish, and you insist upon treating her as Haárin. She is not fully suborn to you, and you cannot expect her to be so, yet you insist."

"We must have order here."

"Your order, as you see it." Jani glanced around, gauging

distances and modulating her voice accordingly. She spoke Síah Haárin, clipped and rapid and devoid of gesture, because the hybrid humanish stood the closest, and with any luck they wouldn't be able to follow what she said. "Gisa insists upon the new ways, you insist upon the old, and neither of you will give a millimeter."

Feyó tried to shake her head. But the motion must have dizzied her—her hands tightened on her chair arms and she sagged forward as though she might go under. "The Elyan Haárin must show unity."

"Your unity, as you see it—Gisa capitulating, and the Elyan enclave swallowing Thalassa." Jani glanced around at hybrid faces suddenly bent on avoiding her eye. "Look around you. How would you expect such as these to blend with your Haárin? I don't agree with Gisa's methods, Feyó, but damn it, you asked for it." *And I'm stuck dealing with it.*

"Are you finding remedy, priest?" The Pathen female leaned close, demon eyes glittering, and jabbed a finger at Jani. "Will you make order from the chaos of this damned odd place?"

"This damned odd place," Jani bit out. "This is *my* place." She pushed the female's finger aside with the flat of her hand. "You forced Feyó to come here, did you not? You make demands as to how things must be, and you do not even know what is here!"

"Ná Wola is a godly Haárin," Feyó said.

"Ná Wola is of Hortensia, and her concerns are not at issue here and now." Jani held Wola's glare until the Haárin gestured impatience and turned away. Then she slowly straightened, her mind a muddle.

And beneath it all, the overriding concern that Tsecha's future depended upon what happened here in the next few minutes.

Damn it. Human nerves warred with idomeni rage in Jani's heart and mind and soul, neither holding the upper hand for long. The wrong move would fracture the Outer Circle Haárin, alienate the Thalassans forever.

She looked at John, who leaned on Feyó's skimchair as though he needed the support. He still hadn't bandaged his cut cheek—at first glance he reminded her of a battered angel shepherding the survivors of some divine battle to safety.

"I remember a priest in an overrobe striding down the corridor of my ship." John's voice came so low it seemed to rumble up through the ground. "She was all I could see—I couldn't look away." His look grew pointed and a little stunned. "They can't look away either." His voice grew softer, until it barely emerged. "Just do, and it will be right."

Jani shook her head. "No—"

"*Yes.*" He looked away for a beat, then back again, shaking his head. "Trust me—the Pied Piper lives." He jerked his chin toward the circle, where Gisa waited. "Play your tune."

Jani glanced at the nearby faces, and saw expressions ranging from confusion to trepidation, depending, she guessed, on the degree of familiarity with the story John alluded to.

Then she turned back to Gisa. "You claim to honor me because I am the first." She took one step, then another, until she broke the invisible barrier and entered the circle itself. "This you call honor," she said as the mutter of voices around her ramped to a babble, "attacking one esteemed by ní Tsecha, throwing this place into discord?"

Gisa stood her ground. Her chin came up in the humanish manner, her hands clenching as though she already held her blades. "I have said already—my fight is not with you."

"So you have said. Many times." Jani heard Dathim's cadences in her voice, and wondered what he'd say if he saw her now. "Even as you brought me here by force and threat, set a network of five planets on its ear, jeopardized the life of ní Tsecha, whom you claim to esteem above all others, you have yet said repeatedly that your fight is not with me." She felt idomeni anger warm her, and imagined the strength of Thalassa rising up through her from the stones. Sensed John's dark gaze drill her back, and took strength from that as well. "You call me 'the first,' but you do not realize what that means." She caught the reflective flicker on faces as lightning shone through the skylight, saw the fear, and savored it. "I have been a hybrid longer than any of you. As such, I was alone a long time." She flexed her shoulders as the weight of twenty years' wandering bore down upon her. "It is no way to live." She closed her eyes, and saw the colored domes of Karistos, the palms pushing up in between, the slope of the city to the bay. Felt the sun warm her bones, even though it had set hours ago. "I am home now, and it is my home that I defend." She opened her eyes and looked across the circle to Gisa. "I fight for Thalassa. Give me a weapon."

As the voices rose among the crowd, Gisa raised her hand and tilted her head to one side. The posture served as a signal to Bon, who drew to the edge of the circle, a large, flat box balanced in her bandaged hands. Bracing the box against her body, she lifted the lid, revealing two stark curves of Sìah metal. She moved along the circle's edge to Jani and held out the box for her inspection.

Jani lifted one of the blades from its inset, then balanced it on the edge of her hand at the place where the blade itself met the hilt. "Quite fine. Yes." She lifted the blade and pressed the point to the left shoulder seam of her coverall. Her focus tunneled, blinding her to the bodies that pressed as close to the edge of the circle as protocol allowed, narrowing her awareness to the slow pound of her heart and the being who stood opposite her. "Remove this obstacle as you have all others, Lord Ganesh, I plead." With that, she drove the blade through the cloth, slitting the seam. "Allow me the wisdom to understand what must be done." She grabbed the sleeve and yanked down—the material gave with a harsh rip. "Allow me also the courage to do it." She changed hands and drove the blade into the right shoulder seam, slitting it as she had the other, tearing that sleeve away as well, exposing her bare arms to the light.

"Ná Kièrshia?" Gisa paced her side of the circle, blade in hand, her voice lilting in puzzlement. "You have challenged me? You have not said the words."

Jani tossed the sleeves outside the boundary of the circle. "Do you recall our conversation in the library?" Her humanish half took over now—her jaw and throat felt tight as she spoke, and her shoulder muscles ached from tension. "You spoke of your admiration for ní Tsecha. You spoke of the sacrifices he made, his outcast, his many challenges as he defended his teachings. 'The blood of the priest that binds.' Those are your words, Gisa."

The humanish part of Gisa must have sensed the undercurrent that ran through Jani's speech. She backed as far to the edge of the circle as she could, until she teetered so close to breaking the plane that Bon moved in behind her and pushed her back in.

And there Jani waited. She closed in, her blade at the ready, grabbed Gisa by the hair and yanked her face to within a handsbreadth of hers.

"Well, I speak for Tsecha, and I tell you this!" She shook Gisa until she heard her teeth clatter. "You brought me to this warm place, and you showed me these people, *my* people, and then you expected me to stand aside while you and Feyó screwed it up!" She pushed the female away. "It ends here. It ends now. With the blood of the priest." With that, she pressed the point of her blade to her own right wrist and slit her arm to the elbow. The strange warmth came, beginning as heat just under the skin and pouring down. Like water, so thin. The flow, so fast.

"You gave the wanderer a home, Gisa. Then you risked it, and thought she'd stand back and let you do as you would. You need to learn my history better." Jani switched her blade to her right hand, held her left hand to the welling gash until her blood coated it. Then she pressed her bloody hand to Gisa's forehead and swept down, painting half her face.

Gisa raised a hand and touched her blooded cheek, then looked at Jani, eyes wide and glistening. She opened her mouth to speak, but before she could say anything, Jani gripped her by the wrist and dragged her. Across the circle, then outside, toward Feyó and the other Haárin.

Shouts rose in protest, but Jani silenced them with a sweep of her blade. She came to a stop before an alarmed Feyó, Gisa fighting her grasp like a youngish—the strain clenched her arm muscles, forcing even more blood to flow.

"The blood of the priest that binds!" Jani shouted loud enough for the words to echo throughout the courtyard. Then she tossed her blade aside. Still holding Gisa fast, she wiped her left hand over her self-inflicted injury again, then pressed it to the side of Feyó's face.

"You work together, through me." She paused to breathe—her chest felt strangely hollow, her knees as weak. "That which is of Thalassa—" She squeezed Gisa's wrist hard enough for the female to flinch. "—will remain *here*, and that which is of Elyas will remain *here*." She grabbed Feyó's hand and squeezed until the Haárin gasped. "Thalassa will be with Elyas—not *of* Elyas, but *with*. Note the difference." She released both females and stood back. The room rocked as she raised her head; she saw John release Feyó's chair and beckon to one of Eamon's Haárin techs. "There are details, of course. There are always details. The main points are these—Thalassa governs itself regarding internal matters, and defers to Elyas regarding Board matters. Everything else is negotiable."

"This place!" Wola pushed forward, again jabbing her finger at Jani. "I have heard of this place." She gestured about. "I have seen. It is anathema!"

Jani slapped the Haárin's hand away. "*It is not your concern! Ní* Tsecha favors this place." *Well—he will once he knows about it.* "I represent him and I pronounce it sound. It acknowledges ná Feyó as dominant in matters of business, and matters of business are your only concern." She stopped again to breathe. Inhaling required more effort than it should have. She looked down at her arm to find the bleeding had slowed to seepage. A puddle of red dried at her feet.

"We can finish this later. So says the attending physician." John maneuvered behind Jani and steered her through the courtyard toward one of the demirooms, holding her elbow with one hand and the back of her coverall with the other as he steered her through the press of the crowd.

When they had cleared the last of the hybrids, he leaned forward. "Pied Piper," he whispered in her ear.

"Toot toot," Jani muttered, just as her knees gave way completely.

Breathe . . . breathe . . .

Jani lay on the couch and concentrated on respiration. John had bundled cushions under her legs to elevate them, and applied a coldpack to the back of her neck. The hollow feeling in her chest remained, though it had lessened. Her right arm felt pressured. She tipped up her head and saw that someone had clamped a transfuser around her elbow—the weight of the thing pulled the wound on her arm, which someone had wrapped with loose gauze. The transfuser display array fluttered, red and blue alphanumerics that flashed at just the right frequency to inspire nausea.

Breathe . . .

She lay back her head and studied the ceiling. The edges of the tiles shimmered, like tarmac on a hot day.

Breathe . . .

"Feeling better?"

Jani opened her eyes and found a familiar pale visage regarding her sideways. "I won't be dashing up and down the beach anytime soon."

"Not for a day or two, at least." John raised her shoulders, then sat down and lowered her so she rested on his lap. "You nicked a vein. You only lost a little over half a liter, but you lost it fast, which explains your weakness. Just your body's way of telling you to put your feet up." He plucked one of her curls, then worked his fingers down to her scalp and commenced therapeutic massage. "Then there's your

idomeni nature. Funny how your rages drain you as much as
your augmentation did."

"Hilarious." Jani yawned. "What's happening out in the
land of the fully sanguinated?"

John laughed, sending a pleasant vibration along Jani's
shoulders. "Things are bustling. I've ordered everyone to let
you rest, otherwise the procession of those wanting to pay
their respects would bury you. Wola and friends have departed. Feyó summoned a couple of her suborns to come re-
trieve them and escort them back to the Elyan enclave. She
used the hospital comroom to make the call. Apparently this
was seen as some sort of breakthrough in Thalassa-Elyas relations—thought they'd break out the champagne there for a
minute."

"If you think it will help, break it out." Jani tilted her head
so she could look John in the face. "This house of cards
needs all the adhesive it can get."

"Don't underestimate yourself—you always do, you
know." John relocated his attention from the top of Jani's
head to the back. "I'll have you know that Bon and Torin
spent the last hour tearing strips from old table linens and using them to wipe your blood from the courtyard floor. Those
strips have become the souvenir of the moment—everyone
I've seen has one tied around their right wrist, including
Feyó herself." He halted his ministrations long enough to allow Jani a peek at his own band of red-stained cloth.

"You're kidding." Jani reached up and tugged one end of
the tie, already stiff with dried blood. "You're not kidding."

"You are well, ná Kièrshia?" Gisa edged within Jani's
sightline. She had changed into one of her usual crisp out-
fits, a trouser suit in pale blue that darkened her grey eyes to
gunmetal. "You do not yet appear yourself."

"I feel quite fine, ná Gisa." Apparent ally though the hybrid dominant now was, Jani didn't feel comfortable revealing the extent of her weakness to her. "But my physician
compels me to rest, so I must follow his direction."

"I'm writing *that* down," John said.

"There is still much to discuss." Gisa sat in a chair opposite Jani and took care to rest her right hand atop her knee so her strip of blooded cloth was fully exposed. "Details of responsibility. Contingencies. What will happen to us if Feyó loses a challenge—"

Jani held up her hand, then waited for Gisa to lapse into grudging silence. "I'm officially indisposed, and I believe ná Feyó has been battered enough for one day. Tomorrow, ná Gisa, will be time enough. The important thing is that Thalassa now has official standing within the Trade Board, and the cracks in the Outer Circle Haárin's united front have been repaired." She sniffed the air, as much to annoy the impatient Gisa as to confirm that she really did smell what she thought she smelled. "Food?"

"Mid-evening sacrament is at hand, ná Kièrshia." Gisa rose, her attention fixed on the transfuser. "You will sit at table, of course."

"Of course, ná Gisa." Jani pushed her legs off the couch and let their momentum pull her into a sitting position. "I will join you in a moment." She nodded acceptance of the female's gesture of esteem, and watched her cut through the darkened room to the bustling courtyard beyond.

"Do you trust her?" John followed Gisa's progress as well, while he scratched at the dried blood that still stained his cheek. "I sure as hell don't." He turned back to Jani and started disconnecting the transfuser.

"She wants to be Elyan dominant. In a few years, depending on how well Thalassa integrates into the Haárin network and how much the hybrid population grows, she might build sufficient status to have a shot." Jani straightened her arm and rubbed the reddened crook of her elbow where the transfuser injector had attached itself, gasping as her fatigued shoulder cramped.

"You're more qualified to be dominant than she is," John said as he brought his viselike grip to bear on Jani's tightened muscles.

"No, thanks. This priest thing has its advantages." Jani tilted her head to one side and rubbed her cheek against John's hand. "I can do my job without constantly having to worry whether someone's gearing up to knock me off my perch." She savored a final few moments of John's attention, but just as she made ready to work to her feet, the entry chimes sounded.

"If that's the cheery ná Wola come back because she forgot something, the food odors are going to send her screaming into the rain." John stood and turned to the door. "Torin's getting it. Kid's a little lightning bolt—everywhere you look, there he is with a shit-eating grin and that handheld of his."

Jani smiled. "He's my historian."

"He's a pain in the ass. I feel like I've got the *Tribune-Times* tailing me for one of those 'how so-and-so spends his day' stories." John stilled, his eyes narrowing. "Hello. Company."

Jani turned in time to see Torin lead Niall around an obstacle course of furniture. The man wore fresh desertweights, and had a documents case tucked under his arm. He wasn't alone, either. A female captain shadowed him, also in desertweights, documents case also in hand.

"Evenin'." Niall stopped beside Jani's couch and sniffed the air, a picture in studied informality, his Sheridan persona in full force. "Bracing. The aromas alone are enough to make my eyes water. I can imagine the taste."

"You're welcome to join us," Jani replied. "We offer food to please every palate. Even humanish." She hadn't meant the remark as an insult, but if Niall's reddening face served as indication, he chose to take it that way.

"Those are Haárin." The captain looked toward the courtyard at the assembling diners, her eyes widening. "Eating together? In public?"

"They're not full Haárin. They're hybrid, like me." Jani met the young woman's stare head-on, and was treated to the sight of a blond complexion flaring to bright peach. *A blushing bunch, our officers be*. She glanced at Niall just as he reached reflexively for his shirt pocket. "Feel free to light up, Colonel—this is Thalassa." As soon as she spoke, she wished she'd kept her mouth shut—*Colonel* had much the same effect on Niall's complexion as had *humanish*. "Damn it, Niall," she muttered under her breath, "give the A-G's hatchet man gig a rest."

Niall stared down at his shoes for a time. Then he edged around the low table and lowered into the same chair Gisa had recently vacated. "Sit down, Captain," he said to his companion. "If past history is any indication, you're going to need to take good notes." He set his case atop the table, then made a show of looking toward the courtyard. "Are Major Thomas Hamil or Colonel Dieter Brondt here at the enclave currently?"

"I don't know." Jani looked to the collecting diners in time to see Torin dart into the lift. *Off to sound the alarm, I'll be bound*. "I haven't seen them for a while." She looked back at Niall, to find him regarding her with humorless resolve.

"Jan, they're mine." He tilted his head in the direction of his note-taking captain. "I have enough evidence to request a Board of Inquiry as a Friend of the Service. If they decline to talk to me now, it will only get worse for them."

Jani felt John's hand enclose hers. He squeezed—she squeezed back. "This enclave is currently under the jurisdiction of the Elyan Haárin, as are all its inhabitants. If you wish to question either Hamil or Brondt, you will need to submit the appropriate request to ná Feyó Tal's offices at the Trade Board in Karistos." *Where it will be filed appropriately, if I have anything to say about it.*

"Request! They're still Service!"

"Only until their next physicals. At that point they'd have been medicalled out. If I hadn't shown up, that's exactly what would have happened. Why not skip a few steps and dump them now?"

Niall held out a fist as though he meant to shake it in Jani's face, then raised one finger. "Dereliction of duty." He raised a second finger. "Desertion." A third. "Treason, if I can swing it."

"Heavy charges, Colonel."

"Not to mention warranted—Brondt's been feeding the Elyan Haárin information about sealed bid projects and dock restrictions for the past eighteen months, at least."

"Anything detrimental to the Service?"

Niall hesitated. "I'm working on it."

Jani rested her head against the couchback. Her stomach grumbled as the food odors grew stronger and more complex and inviting. "The Service guidelines regarding detriment are fairly malleable, as I recall. A whack of the jeweler's hammer here and there, and they can be reformed to suit the occasion. I need them here, Niall. Brondt especially."

"I am not going to let you rework the Service Code for your own convenience."

"Why not? The Service reworks it for theirs. If they didn't, I wouldn't be alive today." *And neither would you.* Jani kept that to herself, but she could tell from the flicker in Niall's eyes that he heard it anyway. "A good attorney might argue that the bioemotional changes wrought by their hybridization rendered them incapable of proper Service behavior." She looked to John, who eyed her with something dangerously close to cold-blooded admiration.

"That's why you made sure Thalassa fell in under Feyó's control," he said. "To protect them."

"I was thinking of Tsecha, but the same principle applies to them." Jani pondered for a moment. "Do you know any good lawyers?"

John smiled. "A few."

Niall glared at Jani, the hunter's light in his eye returned. "I will say that I expected to have to go to round two on that one." He nodded, and dragged his documents case onto his lap. "Heard much news lately?"

"From Chicago?" Jani shook her head. "I didn't trust the security of the lines for anything important."

"How about public?"

"The 'sheets? Haven't had the chance to dig around much lately." Jani felt her stomach tighten. "Why?"

Niall reached into his documents case and removed a newssheet. "Fort Karistos edition of *Blue and Grey*. Front page." He unrolled the display parchment and handed it to Jani. "One of Elon's security suborns challenged Pretty Boy. Depending on when the details can be worked out, the bout will be scheduled for the end of next month." He reached into his shirt pocket and removed his nicstick case, shook out a cylinder, and bit down on the ignition tip with a decisive crunch. "If we leave now," he said through a haze of smoke, "we just might get to Chicago in time for the show."

CHAPTER 25

"This story isn't very detailed." Jani bit into a piece of flatbread, then brushed the crumbs from the newssheet surface. "Lots of extraneous garbage about Lucien's personal life, but very little about why nìRau Ghos challenged him in the first place."

"Everyone I talk to who knows Pascal thinks the 'general principles' argument covers the 'why' pretty well." Niall set aside a glass of iced tea, then stirred and dredged the contents of his soup bowl. "We're more interested in what he was doing at the Shèráin embassy in the first place. Granted, he does occasionally field for the home team, but most of the time, when he goes there, he goes there for you." He sniffed at the contents of his spoon, then sipped. Paused to roll the broth around in his mouth, then swallowed with a shrug. "Tastes like good old chicken vegetable to me." He picked up a slice of flatbread and crumbled it atop the soup. "He's not talking, and he's been pulling in various markers to avoid being pressed. The thought occurred that this might have something to do with Tsecha's problem. What do you think?"

I think that either you already know, and you want to see if what I say matches, or Lucien is holding something back about the mine investigation. Jani played for time by picking at her food and looking around the half-deserted courtyard. The rain had stopped sometime before, and many of the Thalassans had dispersed to various parts of the enclave to check for storm damage. The few who remained bustled about on various errands, casting not so surreptitious glances at Jani, Niall, and John each time they passed their table. Of the regular residents, only Eamon had yet to show his face. John said that he was still clearing up after the postaccident onslaught, but Jani wondered. Gisa was Eamon's horse, after all, and she had emerged in fine shape from a messy situation. A little gloating on his part wouldn't have been out of character.

"Lucien spends a lot of his off-time at the Haárin enclave. He tends to travel with Dathim and Tsecha as though he's a natural member of the entourage—he doesn't always stop to think about what some humanish and idomeni think of that." Jani pushed aside the newssheet and worked on finishing her supper—the chicken that hadn't wound up in the soup, laced with a hot, dark brown sauce that tasted the way John's voice sounded. "Add to that the fact that, as you say, he isn't universally admired. It's a miracle that something like this didn't happen sooner." She picked up a spice dispenser and shook more ground pepper atop her food. *Lucien, of all the damned times—why now*? "Dathim is training him. That's something, anyway."

"So you're not worried. It's just one of those things, and you see no reason to return to Chicago to check into it." Niall shrugged. "Fine. After I finish this, Captain Eglin and I"—he nodded to his blond cohort, who sat downtable rooting through the bread basket—"will take ourselves off and leave you in peace." He tossed back a swallow of tea, then started back in on his soup, hybrid-watching in between spoonfuls. "What are those things everyone has tied around their wrists?"

"Strips of cloth dipped in my blood." Jani hid her smile at the sound of Captain Eglin's fork hitting her plate. "We had a little excitement here a couple of hours ago."

Niall looked from Jani to John, then back again. "Uh-huh." Alarm warred with irritation on his face—his news about Lucien had been one-upped, and it was obvious from his twitchy expression that the curiosity was killing him. "Cutlery accident?" He raised a butter spreader point up and tipped it back and forth as he eyed the bandage on Jani's arm.

"More a case of pied piper diplomacy." John tossed his napkin atop his plate and pushed back from the table. "And on that note"—" He bent down and kissed Jani. "—I shall hie off to the clinic and see what Eamon's up to."

"Get him to look at your cheek." Jani watched him walk to the lift, his only response to her concern a backhand wave. *Brushing me off already, are you?* The spice residue from his lips had left an enticing sting behind. *Just you wait, Doctor.* She licked it off, then turned back to the table to find Niall eyeing her with annoyance.

"OK, point to you." He pushed away his bowl, then sat back and took his nicstick case from his pocket. "Do you care about this challenge to Pascal or don't you?"

"Of course I care." *Damn it.* Jani scrubbed her hands over her face and stifled a yawn. She needed sleep, and it didn't look like she'd be getting it anytime soon. "Revenge for the Vynshàrau killed in the mine accident crosses one's mind."

"That was the first thing that occurred to us, too, but it's never that simple these days, is it?" Niall took a 'stick from his case, but instead of igniting it, he held it lengthwise and tapped it on the table so it slid through his fingers, then turned it over and started again. "The only direct experience Burkett at Diplo has with challenges was what he picked up with yours last summer. His folks have studied, but you know as well as I do that it's not the same thing. Tsecha's problems have made him persona non grata at his embassy and have also compounded our difficulties in trying to work with him."

"So he's still in Chicago?" Jani hoped the relief in her voice wasn't as obvious as it sounded.

"Yes, he is, for all the good he's doing anyone." Niall took a deep breath. "Not to put too fine a point on it, but we're scrambling here, time is short, and tempers on both sides are just looking for an excuse. We need your help, and I'm authorized to deal to get it." He spoke in a voice so low that even Eglin had to sit forward to hear him. "What do you want?"

Jani sat silent, conscious of Niall's worried glower, Eglin's more goggle-eyed assessment, the fidgeting of a group of younger hybrids who stood off to one side and waited for them to leave so they could clear the table. *All they have to do is ask.* Yes, sometimes it really was that simple. She glanced across the table at Niall, a move sufficient to set him fidgeting. *So that's how a friendship ends.* When what once would have been a request, an appeal, turns to an act of barter. *Fine.* "I note the fact that you made this proposal after you tried to get your hands on Brondt and Hamil."

"I really wanted them, Jan. Brondt especially." Niall shrugged. "Can't blame a man for trying."

"Whyever not?" Jani cradled her right arm—the transfuser site ached and her wound stung every time she moved. "Leave them be. You want them out, medical them. I doubt Mako wants the news of Elyan Haárin dock infiltration to get out, anyway."

Niall tapped the 'stick through his fingers one last time, then stared at it. "Is that all?"

"If I've any consideration left, I'll bank it. If I can." Jani looked to the skylight, the railed walkways, the gardens that surrounded them. Her color-coded dishes and the aromas that fed her just by inhaling. "When were you planning on leaving?" She tried not to think of the view from her bedroom window, the warmth, the sounds of the sea. *I can ask John to come back with me.* That idea, at least, gave her mood a boost.

"Tomorrow early afternoon. I would come here to get you late morning, to allow time for all those last minute complications that always seem to arise." Niall nodded once, a shaky lowering of his chin. "Thank you. I'm gathering the impression that you really don't want to leave right now."

"It's not a good time, no." Jani wondered if despite earlier signs, Feyó's concussion was severe enough to incapacitate her, and if she would still be able to ride herd on the Outer Circle Haárin and maintain the newly mended union. If Gisa would make trouble again. If Niall's word regarding Brondt and Hamil meant anything. "I might ask John to come."

Niall brightened, which indicated how uncomfortable he felt at the prospect of spending over five weeks alone with her. "That would be fine. Whatever you want."

"Yes." Jani dragged her napkin off her lap and tossed it on the table. "Tomorrow, then."

Niall stiffened as the fact of the dismissal soaked in. "Tomorrow." He stood, his chair tottering as he pushed it back with force. "And tomorrow, and tomorrow." He headed for the door, leaving Eglin to hustle to catch him up. "Not an appropriate quote for the moment, but it is still from the Scottish play, and anything with knives in it seems befitting now." The door slid open and he vanished into the night, Eglin closing in behind him like a flustered shadow.

"We confirm Colonel Pierce's information. Ní Tsecha is still in Chicago." Ná Feyó lay atop the scanbed in the clinic's largest examining room, holding a court of sorts, surrounded by suborns and a few of the hybrid Haárin that had come from her enclave. "His movements have been restricted more and more. It is feared and truly that he will simply disappear one day, and that the next we hear of him will be when we learn that Cèel has him." The skin around her eye shone slick with anti-inflammatories, and the swelling had receded enough that she could partially open her eye. "This is not a time I ever believed I would see."

"Ní Tsecha has changed. It's as though he hybridized in the mind instead of the body." Jani sat on a lab chair, which was situated high enough so she could rest her feet atop one of the lab benches. "He's been delving into university libraries, reading of humanish religions and histories. I'm guessing his views would rattle any Haárin, much less a bornsect."

"I wish to meet him, and truly." Gisa sat in the far corner of the room, Bon as usual at her side. "You must bring him back with you, ná Kièrshia, so he may glory in his words come to life."

Jani nodded as the tension ramped. Feyó lay her head back in an attention-getting swoon that drew two of her suborns to her side, an act that brought smiles from Bon and Gisa. *This place is starting to remind me of Cabinet Row.* She huddled in the medcoat one of the techs had given her to cover her bare arms. *Maybe I need a vacation after all.* Not that the trip to Chicago would count. *Please let those damned wristbands keep working after I break orbit, Lord Ganesh, I pray.* "My doctor must see to my injuries—please excuse me, ná Feyó." She slipped off the chair and out the door before anyone had the chance to reply.

Chamberlain, where are you? Jani stalked the halls, shoved aside doors and searched empty labs and offices, on the hunt for Brondt. She had just completed a circuit of the basement and made ready to enter the lift when she sensed a presence behind her and turned.

"Ná Kièrshia." Brondt first bowed in the humanish fashion, then stood as straight as he could in a posture of idomeni regard. A look of uncharacteristic puzzlement suffused his broad features, as though he couldn't decide which protocol stated his feelings better. "I understand I owe you more than I can ever repay." He finally settled for a variation of Service at-ease—feet shoulders-width apart, hands clasped loosely behind his back—which seemed to fit him best of all. "My thanks. Thanks from Hamil as well—he's repairing a leaky roof at one of the greenhouses or he'd tell you himself."

"You're not in the clear yet." Jani stepped away from the

lift and started down the hall, pausing to allow Brondt to precede her. "Niall wants your hide—he believes your informing Feyó of station issues constitutes treason against the Commonwealth."

Brondt stopped in mid-stride and looked at Jani over his shoulder. "Do you feel that way?"

"By his standards, I'm a traitor as well. Our friendship kept him from seeing it."

"But you're not friends anymore." Brondt's usually composed gaze softened. "I'm sorry." He hung his head and resumed walking. "I should compliment you on your display this evening." He raised his right hand in a mailfist salute, exposing the strip of bloodstained cloth tied around his wrist. "I knew blood would be shed, but I never thought it would be yours alone."

"I couldn't cut Gisa—that would have signified declaration, which in turn would have led to a permanent schism here." Jani passed a lab and wondered if John worked there, or Eamon. Whether they labored together or kept their distance from one another. "While Haárin are used to dealing with that sort of public animosity, humanish feel the need to escalate. Every drop of blood Gisa shed would have meant a corpse later on, of that I am most sure, and truly." They came upon a small break area, and she herded Brondt inside. "Does Feyó still expect you to provide her information of what goes on here?"

"I believe that now more than ever she will expect such." Brondt waved Jani toward the lone table in the alcove, and poured coffee from the community brewer that dominated one corner of the space. "You've granted Gisa her own power base and ordained it with the blood of the priest." He grinned in memory as he trudged to the table, steaming dispos in hand. "Feyó's not happy with you right now, I'm guessing. She's hoping that if you bring ní Tsecha here, she can work her influence through him to keep you at bay."

"This place is Chicago with palm trees." Jani hunched over her cup. "What are you going to tell her?"

Brondt stared into his coffee. "What do you want me to say?"

Jani leaned forward, elbows on table, and propped her chin in her hands. "We need to strike a balance—if we look too strong, we'll panic the Haárin. If we look too weak, they'll leave us to twist in the wind." She held up three fingers. "I'll be gone three months Common, minimum. Repeated reminders that the one who started it all is coming should keep the lid on the place."

Brondt sipped the coffee and made a face. "So, you are going to try to bring ní Tsecha here?"

"I have to. Chicago's become too inhospitable, and he can never return to the worldskein." Jani tried her own coffee, found it rather good, and felt pity for the soul responsible for making a brew that tasted reasonable to palates at multiple stages of hybridization.

They stood in silence for a time, lost in thought and subdued by fatigue. Then one of Eamon's techs entered, her face brightening when she saw Jani. "Ná Kièrshia!" She held up her right hand, exposing the ubiquitous wristband. "Such a great thing, and truly. It is all we speak of—Doctor Eamon grew quite sick of our talk and bade us all leave his laboratory."

"So Eamon *is* working." Jani finished her coffee and returned to the brewer for more. "The accident took a great deal of his time, I understand.

"The accident?" The tech shrugged, an exaggerated lift of the shoulders that implied she had just learned the gesture. "All who were hurt have been treated. Basic injuries, and truly. Nothing complex." She joined Jani by the brewer. "Doctor Eamon blends skin spray. He must balance the proteins properly, and eliminate those that would cause reaction. Otherwise, mess. Vast mess. Skin like ground meat, he says. So he tests and blends, a different spray for each who is injured."

Jani leaned against the brewer case, enjoying the warmth on her back. "There weren't any hybrids injured tonight, were there? During the storm clean-up?" She looked to Brondt, who shook his head. "John needs to get his cheek fixed, but he's not—" Her mind blanked, and no brewer on Elyas would have been warm enough to ease her sudden chill.

"Ná Kièrshia?" Brondt took a step toward her. "Are you all right?"

"Where is John?" Jani had already left the alcove by the time the tech made it to the exit and called out the room number.

Jani stood before the laboratory door. Hit the entry buzzer. Heard the achingly familiar voice intone, "Come in."

John sat at a desk, bowed over a notebook entry pad. He looked up when she entered, his face lightening. "Hello." He smiled. Sometime after his departure from supper, he had found time to shower and change clothes. He wore med-whites now, the same outfit he had lived in during their Rauta Shèràa basement days, the neckline flecked with damp spots courtesy of his dripping hair.

"I never asked you about the message you sent Val." Jani walked into the room and tried to examine John without seeming to. *Still so pale*. Still a snow wraith, untouched by the sun. *I'm just jumpy*. Letting her nerves get the best of her. *I'm a damned fool*.

"I asked him some business questions, with a few of your carefully worded concerns mixed in. I know it seems like ages, but it was only yesterday. If we're lucky, Val will receive the transmit tomorrow. That's assuming all transfer points are hitting optimally, though, and that's seldom the case." John held a stylus by the ends, and stared at it as though transfixed. "You'll be gone by then, won't you?"

"Yes." Jani lowered into a nearby lab chair, taking care to avoid sitting on the dispenser nestled in her pocket. "You didn't seem concerned upstairs."

"Public air of nonchalance—I've gotten quite good at it over the years." John looked up. "I had to leave the table. I knew Niall was going to ask you to return to Chicago, and you were going to agree, and I'm afraid I just didn't want to hear it."

"I was going to ask you to come along."

"Eamon needs help here. The realization of what he's done has settled around his shoulders over the past few days—his drinking is getting worse and his mood swings are scaring his patients." John sat back and started tossing the stylus into the air. "We all need his brain, but he needs to keep his mouth shut and his hands in his pockets for the next few weeks."

"He's just figured out now what he did?" Jani took a dispo cloth from the bench next to her and started tearing the edge to a fringe. Her mind had turned to a jumble, and she felt the urge to keep her hands busy. "Where the hell has he been?"

"You know us ivory tower types. Heads in the clouds. Refusing to consider the realities of what we do, committed to the art and the art alone." John stopped tossing the stylus and moved on to doodling invisible patterns on a piece of scrap parchment. "It never really hit me what I had done to you until the day we disembarked at Elyas. I had known on an intellectual level, of course. I know your MedRec by heart. But I didn't feel the change in my bones until I saw you walk down that corridor, wearing one of Tsecha's old overrobes." His hands stilled. "Your carriage, your . . . presence, your life, all changed, irrevocably and completely." He hung his head. "Did you ever hate me?"

"Yes." Jani looked away as John's head came up, so that she didn't have to see the pain in his eyes. "I . . . moved on. You used to remind me of the advantages of the situation on a regular basis—I finally started to realize what they were."

"But you hated being the only one. I never knew that."

"I didn't know it either until I saw Torin's image that first time. I've been in a state of befuddlement ever since."

That brought back the smile. "If this is befuddled, I'd hate to have to deal with you when you're on the ball." The expression faded. "When do you leave?"

"Tomorrow morning, late. Niall will meet me here." Jani tore off a corner of the dispo, shredding it to snow that fluttered to the floor at her feet. "Tsecha's troubles were bad enough. Now Lucien. I have to go—I have no choice."

John nodded. "I know."

Jani paused in mid-rip. Then she wadded the remains of the dispo and tossed them atop the bench. "You still haven't fixed that gash." She rose, reaching into her pocket as she approached John's desk. "Hours have passed. You should treat it now."

John sat back, his gaze locked on her hands. "Don't you think a scar would add a certain piratical aspect to the enterprise?"

Jani stopped in front of him and held out the dispenser of humanish skin spray that she'd taken from a first aid tray. "Here. I brought this for you. Humanish skin repair, ready to go."

John took the dispenser from her hand, holding it by the ends as he had the stylus, turning it over and over. "I—" He removed the cover, spritzed some of the solution into the air, then capped it. "Jani—"

"John—"

"Don't look at me like that."

"What the hell do you expect?"

"I—wanted it to be a surprise." He stared at the dispenser as though he read his fortune in it, tipping it at every angle. "Weeks would pass. Then one day you'd look at me, and you'd know."

"You decide to turn your life inside out because you watched me walk down a hallway!" Jani wheeled and paced the perimeter of the room. She usually felt better when she moved, but this time it didn't help. Not at all. "You've just begun." She stopped to swallow, her throat aching. "You can't be that far along yet, no matter how well Eamon's refined the process. Go back."

John's head came up. "To what?" His voice dropped, like a stone into cold, still water. "To what?" He reached out and placed a hand atop his notebook. "I'm recording any changes I feel, as they happen. No one has done this yet—imagine. It will prove an invaluable record." He shifted the notebook back and forth, as though he couldn't find the right position. "I remember what you said, that every day you're as much yourself as you will ever be again. There's another way to look at that, and that is that every day you change a little more. Meanwhile, I stay the same, and watch you move further and further away." His voice darkened. "You're not the only one who's grown to hate the idea of being alone." He tilted his head to one side, as though the notebook emitted a sound that only he could hear. "Then there's the fact that I love you—do I need to say that again? I've said it so often, but I never did anything about it." He finally looked up at her. "Now I have."

Jani sat transfixed by a gaze that had savored her every expression over the past months, that had just reacquainted itself with her every line and curve. *John . . .* She felt stricken enough to weep, frightened enough to tremble, even as that bastard part of her that had survived almost two decades of a gutter existence sent up a barely detectable murmur of delight. *Friend . . . lover . . . not alone . . .*

Not alone. Ever again.

"Say something." John forced disinterested lightness into his tone, his usual shield against rejection. "Love you. Bless you. Go away. Go to hell." He exhaled with a rumble. *"Something."*

Jani sat quietly, listening as a laughing group passed close by the door, their voices coming from nowhere, then fading to nothing. She slid off her chair and walked over to John. He drew up straight as she approached, shifting in his chair so he faced her as she circled around, one hand on the edge of the desk, the other on the edge of his chair, braced for whatever he feared she would tell him.

She took his upturned face in her hands and bent close, taking care to avoid his angry wound, savoring the clean scent of soap and the fine roughness of his skin as she brushed her lips over his before pressing down and kissing him harder than she ever had.

They broke apart once to breathe, then joined again. John pulled her onto his lap, holding her hacked arm as lightly as spun glass before snaking his arms around her waist and pulling her close.

"Well," he said, his voice muffled, "if you're not going to speak, I suppose this is an acceptable substitute." He positioned her so he could rest his head upon her shoulder.

"So?" Jani stopped to clear her throat. "That first time I walked in on you and Eamon—"

"I had already proposed the deal. If he hybridized me, I would let him keep his stake in Neoclona." John's face hardened. "Someone like Niall would have appreciated watching him battle through that decision, I think. Very operatic. Greed versus whatever sense of kinship he still felt for me." He looked away, jaw muscles tensed. "Greed won, of course. As if there was ever any doubt."

"I wondered why his disgust with me had moved to a higher level." Jani put her arm around his shoulder. "Does Val know?"

John shook his head eventually. "Not yet. I tried to drop some hints in my message. About how much I enjoyed it here. The fact that you and I were . . . together again." He grinned halfheartedly. "I'll think of something. Val is my best friend. But some things are harder to explain than others."

Jani ruffled John's hair—the air in the office was cool but very dry, and the white strands had already dried. "How do you feel now?"

John shrugged. "Not much different. Yet. Eamon's data show that it takes a few weeks before the mutated enzymes really kick in and the diet needs adjusting." His eyes clouded. "I would have liked one last late supper at Gaetan's. In the rear garden, under the spring stars. Ah, well." He glanced shyly at Jani. "There are stars here, too." He pulled back from her with a sigh. "I need to get dosed." He laced one hand with hers. "Come with me?"

Jani stood and followed him out of the room. "Is it true that doctors make the worst patients?"

"Oh yes—we're big babies. Eamon tells me that I complain about the treatments more than anybody here and nothing's even happened yet." John examined the pale whiteness of the back of his hand. "Not that I can tell, anyway."

They entered one of the busier hallways, then passed through a double-wide panel into a gleaming laboratory. Cushioned scanchairs lined one wall, each one backed by a thin-branched metal tree suitable for hanging drip bags and other insertion devices.

Eamon stood in front of a lab bench, next to the chair farthest from the door. He'd already set out a pair of small metal canisters that contained the gene broth, and now occupied himself with calibrating the injector. When he heard sounds behind him, he turned. His heavy face softened with something like pity when he looked at John, then hardened when he shifted to Jani. "And she shall sow chaos wherever she goes."

"Belt it, Eamon." John took the injector from him, then picked up the cartridges and shoved them into the slotted housing. "So." He held the device out to Jani. "Care to do the honors?"

Jani held her breath as John placed the injector in her hands, then sat in the nearest chair. Avoided his eye as she bent over him and slid the device along his lower arm until it nestled in the crook. The injector was shaped like a scanpack with a curved notch on the end, and had much the same control layout—she intuited the switches for the grips that clasped John's arm just above the elbow, as well as the preinjector that numbed the skin.

"Well well." John examined her handiwork, then lay back his head. "We'll make a medico of you yet."

Jani ran a hand along the injector casing, which grew warm to the touch as the device heated the broth to body temperature. "How long does it take?"

"Ten minutes. Fifteen, if I develop irritation at the site and the thing needs to pump out anti-inflammatory." He watched her as though she undressed, breath quickening, eyes locked on her every move. "Chance to get a little of your own back, isn't it?"

Jani pulled back from the control pad. "Revenge has nothing to do with this."

"Not even a little?" John looked quickly away, his face reddening. "Poetic justice, then. Patient, heal thy physician." He turned back to her. "Whenever you're ready."

Jani placed her hand atop the injector. Behind her, she could hear Eamon curse and stalk off to the other side of the lab. She gazed into John's dark-filmed eyes and tried to imagine what color they'd turn as he hybridized. What shade his hair would darken to. His skin. Whether his voice would alter, and how.

Then she moved her thumb over the injector switch and pressed it.

CHAPTER 26

Jani opened her eyes. She could sense morning through the coated window wall, even though the glass shone dull and the bedroom itself was as dark as a cave. *Niall will be here soon*. She worked out from beneath the covers, moving carefully to avoid waking John.

She showered, dressed in her remaining coverall, then tossed her scanpack, overrobe, and other odds and ends into her duffel and pronounced herself packed. Slung the bag over her shoulder and tiptoed out of the room into the day-bright walkway. There, she paused, leaning against the wall and inhaling the flower odors from the gardens below. Orange smells. Red smells. Purple. Yellow. White. She breathed them all in, and filed them away for future reference. *Tomorrow morning at this time I'll be heading out toward Amsun GateWay*. Bound in a diplomatic marriage of convenience to a man she had once called a friend, who was now merely someone she knew well enough to fear more completely than anyone she knew. "Damn." She pushed away from the wall and headed for the lift down to the courtyard.

Early morning sacrament seemed to have caught the Thalassans by surprise—some set out food, plates, and cutlery, while others assembled the table and laid out the linens. They turned as one toward her when she entered the courtyard. Most smiled, waved, or held their wristbands in the air. A few, Jani noted, merely eyed her steadily, as though she were a stranger. *Well well—looks like not everyone buys into my brilliance.* She found that reassuring, in an odd way. After the rough and tumble of life in Chicago, complete and total acceptance would have felt too bizarre for words.

"Glories of this morning to you, ná Kièrshia." Gisa stood near her usual spot at the low head of the table, waiting for her place to be set. She had dressed in uncharacteristically jarring pink and yellow, and had twisted her hair into a loose topknot from which stray strands escaped. "Such a time we have had here."

"Glories of the morning to you, as well, ná Gisa." Jani felt herself slipping into the professional politeness she had employed for her dealings with Cabinet Row. "Everyone seems a little flustered."

"We all stayed awake too long. Hybrid and Haárin who had not spoken since the beginnings of this place spoke together once more. It was a great thing, and truly." Gisa took her seat as the young hybrid who set her place moved on, then motioned for Jani to sit next to her. "And now you must leave. Such sadness."

You are desolation itself, Gisa. Jani concentrated on serving herself, and decided to keep her mouth shut and not explore the idomeni grasp of sarcasm before coffee.

"While you are not here, I will petition Feyó to allow a Thalassan representative to the Trade Board," Gisa continued. "We do not own transports or shuttles." An unspoken *yet* hung in the air. "But many here own businesses or practice skilled trades. They merit one who speaks for them just as do those who own the ships that convey their products."

"That would be a change in Board membership philosophy—they haven't considered that aspect before." Jani glanced up and saw John looking down at her from the walkway. "If this proposal comes from you alone, Feyó may block it. If you go to the other enclaves and find members who wish the same as you, you would stand a better chance of gaining Feyó's approval."

"Such takes time, ná Kièrshia."

"That which is worthwhile often does."

"The Thalassans merit such representation now."

"Do the Thalassans know this?" Jani backtracked as Gisa's puzzled look slowly sharpened. "Which trades are practiced here?" She found herself eating as she always did when she was forced to mix business with mealtime—small bites chewed quickly and swallowed, their taste barely detected.

Gisa thought for a moment, then shook her head. "Too many to name."

"Well, name them as best you are able, then find their counterparts in the other enclaves." Jani felt a hand on her shoulder, and turned in time to catch a wink and a roll of the eyes from John as he sat down beside her. "Feyó will have a more difficult time rejecting a request from multiple enclaves, especially if the larger ones such as Amsun are represented. In addition, it would give you the opportunity to build a reputation as a consensus builder." *Which would be a nice change of pace.*

Gisa poked at her food with her fork, then let the utensil fall with a clatter. "Ná Kièr—"

"Thalassa is an official enclave now, Gisa, and you are an acknowledged dominant. What this means is that you now fall under the rules—you know that as well as I. You cannot act as you will and push these rules aside, and then expect to be treated according to your standing. The conservatives will not stand for it, and at present they are the majority." Jani speared slices of kettle ham onto a slice of soft flatbread. "Unless you want ná Wola poking her finger in your face at every turn, you have to think beyond the boundaries of Thalassa to how you fit into the whole, for this place is too small to act on its own." She stood, makeshift sandwich in hand, and felt a tug on the knee of her pants leg. John, offering encouragement. Or prompting her to quiet down. "In deference to ní Tsecha, the Elyan Haárin gave this place enclave status," she continued, letting the tug go unheeded. "Ponder that. Would any humanish colony have allowed us to declare our sovereignty? Would they even have considered such? What about the worldskein—what part do you imagine Cèel would have allowed us in that?"

Gisa sat still, her head down, shoulders bowed in the age-old posture. *"Gratitude."* She twisted her neck to look up at Jani, her eyes metal. "One tires of gratitude."

"But one must provide it when it is due, or one is as the greedy youngish who knows only to take. Such is not what we want to be." Jani reached behind with her free hand and tugged at John's shirt, then let go. "Now, I am going to take one last walk on this beach. We will have plenty of time in the future, ná Gisa, to argue of gratitude. For today, I think, let us concentrate on deactivating the tripbeam arrays you have set on the Thalassa road." She shouldered her duffel, then circled around the end of the table, making the demi-rooms in a few easy strides, and was out the door before anyone had the chance to say a word.

"I don't think you can eat this." Jani stood at the water's edge, a fingernail-sized bit of ham in hand. "Wrong proteins—you'll get sick."

The crab-thing she addressed responded by waving its pincers at the toe of her boot. It may or may not have been the same one Torin had chased about the beach the previous day. It seemed more ornery than that one had; on the other hand, there didn't seem to be any others around.

"You probably chased them away." She tossed the fleck of meat onto the sand and watched the crab-thing scuttle over to it and scoop it up, then hop to the solitude of a nearby pile of rocks. "I think I'll name you Gisa." She tossed another bit of ham into the water, followed by the last morsel of bread.

"I've never seen you flee before."

Jani turned to find John standing on the dry region of the

beach on the far side of the rocks. "I didn't flee. I just . . ." She bent low to pick up a rock, then flung it into the water. "Gisa wants to build a nation in a day. She won't listen to anyone who tells her that's not how it works." Another bend, another rock, another toss. "We just got over one crisis, and having her push now for a seat on the Trade Board just might precipitate another one."

"You told her what to do." John joined her at the water's edge. He wore light grey trousers and short-sleeve shirt—the sun turned the hair on his arms to silver wire. "She'll gripe, but she'll do it. For one thing, you've already shown her that you're capable of handling whatever ná Wola dishes out. For another, you're the star—she's the understudy. That may grate her, but too damned bad. I didn't see anyone here wearing her blood as a talisman."

"Expert in the ways of the stage, are we?"

"I've known a few actresses. Does that count?" John drew closer and slipped his arm around her. "I'm not used to hearing you argue for the long view. You've mellowed."

"I've seen too much waste. Dealt with too many whose only thought was what they could take." Jani looked to the opposite side of the bay and saw the bright domes of Karistos flicker in the sun like pinpoint gems. "I'm not going to let that happen here."

"Beware the wanderer who decides to stay." John looked out over the water as well, but Jani couldn't tell from his expression how he felt. "What was it about this place that touched you?" He sounded genuinely puzzled.

Jani gave a half shrug. "I don't know. Sometimes, you walk about a place, and everywhere you look says 'home.' This is the first time since my youth that I've felt this way, and I'm not going to let anyone screw that up for me— how's that for mellowing?" She felt a frisson of panic. "You do like it here, don't you?"

"You're here." John smiled, then paused to tug at his shirt-front. "It's a little too hot for me at the moment." He pondered the view for a time. "It reminds me of the Greek islands. That's a bit of a turnabout for a rain-forest boy like me." He toed an arc in the sand. "I may miss the nightlife more than anything, although Karistos does have an opera company. Two symphony orchestras—wait—make that one symphony orchestra and one chamber music consort. And there's a theater company—"

"When did you find this out?"

"I do talk to people when I'm treating them, you know. The symphony's second violin is a hybrid."

Patron of the arts—yes, I think John may have found a hobby. And the artists of Karistos, a financial wellspring they never dared hope for. Jani nodded, biting the inside of her cheek to avoid smiling. "Not to change the subject," she said, changing the subject, "but should you be exposing your skin like that?"

John held out his free arm in front of him. "I want to see how much I can tolerate. Monitoring the process, remember?" He tilted his arm this way and that, as though he examined a cut of meat at the end of a fork. "A couple more minutes, then I'll have to go in." He let his arm fall. "We're doing a first-rate job of avoiding the issue, aren't we?"

Jani felt his grip around her waist tighten. "I wish I didn't have to go." She put her arm around him and hugged back even harder.

"And I wish I didn't have to stay. Slaves to duty, aren't we?" John seemed to be avoiding her eye now, staring down at the sand while maintaining his hold on her. "I'll have plenty of work to do, at any rate. And if there are any less than attractive aspects to this change, you won't have to see them."

"I don't care about that."

"I do. Some things are better learned about in MedRecs."

They lapsed into silence. John pulled Jani closer, until she had no choice but to turn to face him. He had filmed his eyes pale blue, mismatching his clothes for the first time she could recall, and she wondered whether he guessed what his hybrid eye color might be, and if he did this as some sort of preparation for the future.

Then he bent down and pressed his lips to hers, and she stopped wondering about much of anything.

"Ná Kièrshia!"

Jani pulled back, and felt as well as heard John's muttered *"Damn."* She looked around him toward the cliffside road that led up to the houses, and saw Brondt standing near the bottom, Torin at his side.

"Colonel Pierce is here. So soon." Brondt avoided looking at John as he shrugged.

"Tell him I'm on my way." Jani took one last look at the bay before starting her trudge toward the road.

"I tried to avoid him, but he saw me. I don't believe I am his favorite person at the moment." Brondt stood in place, one hand in his pocket, his demeanor singularly stiff for one usually so unruffled. "I want to—" He stopped, then took a deep breath. "You said that your parents would take something of Acadia with them when they left, then restore it when they returned." He pulled his hand from his pocket and held it out to her. "Take this with you to remember us by. When you return, you may put it back, and make this place whole once more."

Jani held out her hand, and felt the sudden weight as Brondt dropped the stone onto her palm. It was one of the countless water-smoothed shapes she had seen gathered in long sweeps along the shore, a round-edged triangle in banded brown and black.

"Thank you." She coughed to clear her tightening throat, but before she could say more, Brondt turned his back and started up the road, which saved them both. She followed, John at her side, and mounted the incline as hybrids gathered at the top and waited. Then she was among them, and they closed in around her and walked with her to the main house.

Niall stood in the skimmer circle beside a vehicle pool

sedan. He had switched out his desertweights for civvies, tan trousers and a white shirt that reflected the sun like a shield, battering the eye like the bright center of a flame. "I know I'm early, but if we make Elyas Station by local noon, we can head out right away." He eyed John, then the rest of her escort, and his demeanor grew formal. "This way, please." He popped the passenger-side gullwing, stood by solemnly as she got in, then slammed the door closed and circled to his side.

Jani lowered her window and held out her hand to John, who stepped forward to take it as he knelt beside the vehicle. "Keep an eye on things."

"Of course."

"Take . . . care of yourself." Jani placed her hand over his, and wondered at the contrast in their skins, as always. *How much darker will he be when I return*? How much closer would they have become?

"I look on it as a great adventure." John exhaled shakily. Then he leaned through the window and kissed her until Niall's not so subtle throat-clearing signaled that it was time to go. He broke away eventually, then glared in Niall's direction. "Pierce."

Niall nodded once. "Shroud," he said, keeping his gaze fixed on the view through the windscreen as he pressed the charge-through.

The skimmer pulled away. At first Jani watched the hybrids recede in her passenger mirror. Brondt. Torin. Bon. Gisa.

Then she fixed on John. When Niall veered the skimmer so she could no longer see him, she lowered the window and boosted herself through, hanging out the door from the waist up, balancing on the frame. The morning air, scented by the sea, flowed around her. She blamed it for the way her eyes stung as she watched John's grey-clad form grow smaller and smaller until they turned the final corner and he disappeared entirely.

* * *

Micah sat at his desk and tried to concentrate on his work. A new device. A new manual to read. A new something that he prayed would divert his attention yet never seemed to for long.

Weeks had passed since Veles had picked his pocket outside Forrestal, and his every waking moment since had been consumed by the *waiting*. For the visitors to his flat, the gym where he worked out, the bullpen. *Pairs*. He flipped through one display screen after the other. *They always work in pairs*. That's what he'd heard, at any rate. In case the suspect tried to make a break for it, and they needed to use force to subdue him.

"Hey, scholar?"

Micah closed his eyes. The more things changed, the more Cashman remained the same. "What?"

"I got a call—I can't take it." Cashman's head poked over the cubicle divider. "An *interview* at the Dahlberg Annex. Second floor. Two five five."

Interview. Micah prayed he looked relaxed as his stomach roiled. *Make that interrogation*. He sat back and folded his arms. *No—I don't think so*. Too close to his possible future for comfort. "You don't look busy."

"Not this split second, no." Cashman rolled his eyes. "But I've got to record the insurance talk this afternoon, and I need to be here when the Benefits crew stops by to take them to the room, and before that I need to set up." He held out a soft, fat hand. "Come on, man. I see what's on your display when you don't think anyone is looking. This is right up your alley. All that psych stuff—brain changes during stress and shit."

You noticed. Micah hung his head, then stood and gathered his gearbag. If nothing else, he'd get away from Cashman for the afternoon. That had to be worth something.

"Thinking of changing your spec or something?"

"Yeah." Micah stepped out into the corridor, looking both ways first to make sure it was clear.

The Dahlberg Annex was a three-story white box located

just west of the Far North buildings. A poured cement coffin of a place, it contained offices for base auditors and temporary staff. The second floor, windowless and with coded doors throughout, was reserved for miscellaneous "questioning," the sort of discussions that often lead to a date with the counsel of one's choosing and an extended stay at Camp Brigstone.

The rooms are soundshielded. Micah keyed into the stairwell, trudged up the short flight of steps, then keyed out onto the floor itself. *That way, no one can hear the screams.* Not strictly true. He had recorded several interrogations, and in only one had the tension escalated to violence. But they had the guy dead to rights for murder, and he didn't have anything left to lose . . .

Micah walked the corridor and scanned the doorplates. *Two fifty-one . . . 253 . . . 255 . . .* He stopped, keyed in his passcode, pressed his hand to the doorpad. Watched as the door panel slid open, and found himself staring into a damnably familiar face.

"Come in, Faber." Pascal stepped aside and motioned him through. "Always room for one more."

Micah backed away from the door. Then he ran, down the hallway toward the stairwell, only to have one of the doorway shadows move, and change into Veles, who stood at the hallway's end, shooter drawn.

They work in pairs . . . Micah slid to a stop. Held his hands out in front of him to show he wasn't armed. Bit back a howl as Veles grabbed his wrist and spun him against the wall, then kicked at his ankles to spread his legs.

*Shit—shit—*He felt hands. Yanking his gearbag from his shoulder. Patting down his thighs, his ass, his waist and chest. Knew they didn't belong to Veles, because Veles stood off to one side, shooter aimed at his head. *Keep your goddamn hands off of me, you freak-fucker!* But he pressed his face to the wall and kept his mouth shut because if he said anything like that, well, then they'd have him. If they didn't already.

"Just walk to the room, Micah." Pascal stood too damned close and whispered too damned low.

Micah pushed off the wall and walked, his hands over his head. *They know.* If they didn't know, why Dahlberg? The place was official. It had a reputation. *Why did they set it up through Cashman?* How did they know Cashman was busy, and would bounce the call to him? *Maybe Cashman isn't busy.* Maybe he worked with Pascal and Veles. Maybe he helped with the setup. *Bastard.* He should have killed the loudmouth creep when he had the chance.

He entered the room. White walls and ceiling, cut at regular intervals with inset lighting. Grey floor. All smooth surfaces, suitable for hosing down if necessary. A table and three chairs.

"Have a seat, Micah." Pascal dragged one of the chairs away from the table and sat. He wore dress blue-greys, as did Veles, who declined a seat, preferring to lean against the far wall.

Micah sat. Wiped his hands on his trousers once, then again. Watched Pascal, who pulled his gearbag onto his lap and examined the scuffed exterior.

"This has seen some use." Pascal cracked the fasteners, then began rummaging through the pouches and pockets.

Keep your goddamned hands off my—Micah choked back his silent scream.—*stuff.* He didn't stash anything unofficial in his gearbag anyway—it wasn't as though they'd find anything—

"What do these go with?" Pascal held up a set of earbugs, then placed them on the table.

No. Micah sat back. *They only look like the ones I use for the sims—they* aren't *the ones I use for the sims, so what difference does it make?* "They're all-purpose earbugs, sir. I use them when I need to jack into systems during setups." There. Easy as you please. *I'm supposed to have those, so shove it up your ass, freak-fucker!*

"Air all clear?"

Micah froze. It had to have been Veles who spoke—his

voice was unmistakable. *Why does it sound familiar?* Then he remembered. *Chrivet. Something she said.* As they coursed over the water to the embassy, the spray tossing around them.

They cracked the wafer. Well, they must have. Else why was he here? *They know everything.* So why question him here—why wasn't he under arrest and sitting under barred windows at Camp Brigstone? *Because they don't know anything.* But that didn't make sense—

"You have some interesting tastes in pornography, Micah." Pascal looked up from his exploration of the gearbag. "*Tessa's Tempting Offer*—quite a story. What did you think about the scene in the back of the skimbus?"

Micah swallowed. His head felt as though it might explode. He didn't want to talk, didn't want to answer Pascal's disgusting question. *They searched my flat, found the porn wafer.* But he'd set out traps, flecks of paper and such—he'd have known. *They went to the place where I rented it.* That made sense, too, maybe more sense. Everyone knew what kind of place it was. "Skimbus?" He shook his head. "There's no—no scene like that, sir." He heard Veles's ragged snicker, and imagined his face smashed and bloody.

Pascal shrugged. "Perhaps I'm thinking of another story." He gave one last look through the gearbag, closed the fasteners, and dropped it to the floor beside his chair. Then he reached inside his tunic and removed a small imager. The silver cylinder glinted, the only spot of life in the room.

"I thought you might find this interesting. It's a scene from another wafer." Pascal twisted the imager's activator ring, then set it atop the table. The top of the cylinder flickered. Then the image sprang up, life-size and in full color.

Micah sat, his hands on his knees, his mind a white-hot blank. But he stood astride the table as well, in full exoskeletal kit, mid-range in hand, his helmet faceplate a semitransparency that revealed his identity for all to see.

He remembered the moment captured before him, felt the weight of the exo, the heft of his mid-range. The battle had ended, the last regions of the embassy secured. They had won. *We won!*

"Different sort of fantasy, this. Yes?" Pascal cocked his head to one side as he regarded the image.

"We won! We won!" Veles's singsong raked like sandpaper.

Micah looked to the image and wrung the last drop of pride from it. *We won that one.* They hadn't won many since. The room changed as he stared at himself, from white and bare to darker and centered by concentric rings of chairs. Chrivet in the middle, stalking and talking.

Take 'em down!

Micah felt the room shift as part of him stepped atop the table and entered the image while the rest of him remained seated. He turned from his tabletop vantage point, reactivating his mid-range as he swung toward Veles. He rose from his chair as well, raised his arm and sighted down as he took the first room-spanning step—

Then Pascal moved toward him. The bastard should have fallen, blitzed by the mid-range, but he charged forward, grabbing Micah and spinning him around and down.

Micah yelled as he slammed against the floor. Felt the cold tile—*why!*—the weight of a body atop him—*how!*

Invincible. Invincible! *"We won! We won!"*

"He's hallucinating! Why did you push . . . !" Pascal, angry, yelling in English, then slipping into a language Micah didn't understand. Veles, just as angry, answering in kind.

Micah tried to break loose as Pascal tore open the cuff fastener of his sleeve, then pushed it up past his elbow. Let loose his howl as he felt a sting in the crook of his arm. Felt the cry stop in his throat as the warmth filled him, flowing with his blood to his shoulder, across his chest, into his gut and below.

Quiet. So long since he'd enjoyed . . . quiet. Peace.

"What's your name?" asked a voice in the distance.

"Faber." His lips felt numbed, his tongue thick. Every

scrap of pain left him—he felt light enough to lift off the floor and float away. "Micah. Lance Corporal. Cee number—"

"What is today's date?"

Micah told him.

"Tell me about 'we won.' "

Micah told him that, too.

My head. Pounding. *My mouth*. Dry. Infested.

Micah opened his eyes.

Dream? He'd had a number of those lately, each worse than the last. None with Pascal, though. A few with Veles. The same, over and over. Veles had the wafer, and he had chased Veles.

Wafer? Micah turned over on his back. Regarded his room shadows, his dresser and armoire, flush against the wall like—

—Veles.

Micah blinked. *We won! We won!* A cry in his head, over and over and over. He turned back on his stomach and buried his head in his pillow.

White room. Bare but for a table and three chairs. Pascal was there. Veles.

"Crappy dream." Micah rose in stages—sat up, pushed his legs off the bed, stood. He didn't recall the walk home from work, yet here he was. He knew he had been at work, because he remembered Cashman hanging over the divider, asking him to cover the interview at—

—Dahlberg.

He stopped halfway to the bathroom. Looked down at himself, naked but for shorts. Worked his arms, and felt a stiff ache everywhere, a soreness in the bend of his right elbow.

A scene flashed. Pascal, dragging him down.

Micah raised his arm and forced himself to examine the spot. Nothing. Walked over to the freestanding lamp, cranked the power to high, and twisted the gooseneck so the source shone full on his arm.

He saw it. Barely, at first, then large and red and pitted after he dug out the microspecs from his gearbag and slapped them on.

A pinprick wound. Like the one an injector would leave behind.

He pushed the lamp away so hard it rattled against the wall. Backpedaled until he hit the bed, then sagged down and clapped his hands over his ears as his brain broke open and the humiliation played again and again. Veles's snicker. The imager. That final takedown, struggling in Pascal's grip.

Pascal.

Micah closed his eyes as other words played through his head, in a soft, accented voice that all the girls loved.

It's quite a game, isn't it? I've played it, too.

Micah bent forward, head between his knees. Covered his head with his hands, and still more words came.

Your story ends after you win, but what comes after? How do you get out? Do they ever tell you how you get out? Seems a bit shortsighted of the designers, don't you think? After all, the game doesn't end when the last shot is fired, but much, much later.

Then came the worst words of all.

If you want to talk about it, you know how to find me.

Micah bounded to his feet. Paced the room. He thought *Flee*. He thought *We're blown*. He thought *They caught us*. "I have to tell—" He needed to warn everyone. In the next wafer. He'd stand up in the middle of class and piss off Chrivet one last time, announce to them all that they needed to run.

Except—

Micah slowed to a walk. Stood still. "Except they might blame me instead." For letting Veles steal the wafer in the first place. For talking to Pascal. For getting caught. *Hough knows Pascal was after me—he'd spill to anyone who asked. The connection was there, had been for months. I didn't tell him anything!* Not willingly anyway. *I just—*

"I just let myself be duped, and drugged, and stripped." Of everything that made him a member of the Group. Of everything that made him a man.

He lowered cross-legged to the floor. Stared at the pattern in the lyno as he imagined the darkness close in around him. He started rocking at some point—didn't remember when. Rocking, as he hugged himself, and stared. *Can't tell— can't—can't—can't tell—can't—can't* . . .

CHAPTER 27

"I wonder what it will be like here tomorrow at this time." Niall looked out the shuttle passenger port as the spacecraft banked for its final approach into O'Hare. "After the challenge."

Jani glanced up from her *Tribune-Times* account of the upcoming "Duel of the Century" just as the city skyline filled the view, backed by cloudless blue. *Vacation's over.* It had proved pleasant, surprisingly enough. Niall's mood had lightened as the distance from Elyas grew, and he had approached Jani with an offer of a truce. By the time they reached Felix, it felt like old times—as long as they avoided any mention of current events, they could almost pretend that nothing had changed between them.

All good things must end. "Chaos, I imagine." She returned to her newssheet. "Bloodsport is, after all, an idomeni invention. Humanish are peace-loving and quite, quite docile."

"Has anyone ever told you that you're sarcastic when you're sarcastic?" Niall tugged at the banded collar of his dress blue-grey tunic, then rested his head against the seatback, his profile blunted to shadow by the brightness outside. "That article you're reading must be great. I can feel the heat from the steam coming out of your ears."

"Echevar, the *Diplomatic Beat* reporter, isn't completely without sense. He understands that it's simply a statement of feeling. No winners. No losers." Jani rolled up the newssheet and tucked it into her duffel, which was secured in the grapple rack at her feet. "The rest make it sound as though a two-being war will be fought, winner take whatever they wish. GateWay rights. Colonial settlements."

Niall tilted his head toward her. "I'd find your sense of outrage more believable if I didn't know for a fact that you're worried sick. On the way here you spent all the time you could in the ship's library gleaning news from every available 'sheet. As soon as we'd dock at a station, you'd disembark and hit every newsstand you could find. You did everything you could to ferret out information except message Pretty Boy himself, which I do confess I found odd. I know you distrust secure lines as much as I do, but I thought nerves would have gotten the better of you eventually."

Jani settled back in her seat. "From what I've pieced together, Ghos is angry with humanish in general—Lucien was just a convenient target." She braced as she felt the shuttle slow into its final descent. "Usually, idomeni anger is more personal, not outrage against an entire race focused on one individual."

Niall pressed his thumb and forefinger to a place above the bridge of his nose, just inside his eye sockets. "Why do I think I'm about to hear something I wish you'd told me earlier." He lowered his hand. "You think Ghos is going to try to kill him, don't you?"

Jani didn't reply, even when Niall's glare threatened to drill a hole in the side of her face. Instead she lay her head back, and counted the minutes to touchdown.

The noise in the Service concourse reached sport stadium proportions, despite the best efforts of the soundshielding. Younger people in civvies made up the bulk of the crowd that filled the glass and metal expanse, along with a smaller proportion of seeming children in dark blue fatigues, duffels large enough to hold bodies slung across their backs.

"Recruits coming in," Niall muttered as he and Jani fled for the quieter reaches of the security wing. "Freshly minted Spacers shipping out. Welcome to Anthill Central." He keyed them through a pair of doors, the silence enveloping them as they passed into a low-ceilinged hallway.

"First and only time I flew in here, I was under arrest." Jani spoke loud enough to draw interested looks from the brace of MPs walking in the opposite direction. "I came in at an off-time—we pretty much had the place to ourselves."

"They try to work it that way." Niall glanced at her over his shoulder. "You've come a long way in a year, my gel." He turned away before Jani could answer, busying himself with the working of another set of doors. "This exit leads outside," he said as he pressed his hand to the touchpad. "Pull should be waiting for us—I got hold of him just before we left Luna." The doormech whined and the panel slid, revealing a short flight of metal-clad stairs that led down to sunlit tarmac.

They clattered down, then stepped out into the face of a cool breeze redolent with machine odors to find Pullman standing beside a dark blue four-door. He looked at Jani, and his somber expression lightened momentarily. "Good to see you, ma'am."

"You, too." Jani thought back to that night months before. Blood in the snow, and a body boosted onto a gurney. "How are you feeling?"

"Everything's been refitted." Pullman patted the spot over his left hip. "Can't complain." He then focused on Niall, nodding toward the silver sportster that floated nearby. "We've got company, sir." He frowned. "Port Security's not happy, but friends in high places made calls, apparently."

Jani set out toward the familiar vehicle just as the gull-wings swept upward. Val emerged from the driver's side, natty in a pale blue daysuit. "God, you're a sight for sore

eyes, Jan!" He slammed down the door and circled around
the front of the vehicle.

The passenger's side door opened more slowly, the passenger emerging with the characteristic stiffness of someone
who'd pushed his body further than normal in the very recent past. Dressed in civvies, brown trousers and a long-
sleeve cream shirt, Lucien walked toward her, taking care to
step in front of Val at just the right time to break the other
man's stride and knock him off course.

"Hello." Jani stopped and watched Lucien's careful approach. "Dathim been pushing you, has he?"

"You could say that, yes." He eased to a halt, gazing at her
with a fixedness he normally reserved for their times alone.
"You look like summer."

Jani felt her face heat. She wore trousers and wrapshirt in
pale melon, an acquisition from a Felix Station shop that she
had meant to save for John until Niall's mutterings convinced her that she needed to give her coverall a rest.
"Thank you."

"Quite a trip, from what I've gathered from Val."

"Yes. You've had quite a time here, too, I believe."

Lucien had the sense to look uncomfortable. For a few
seconds, at any rate. "We'll have to bring one another up to
speed later," he said with a faint smile.

Before Jani could respond, Val cut between them and
threw his arms around her. "Don't. Ask." He spoke in her ear
as he hugged her hard enough to hurt. "I've managed to keep
body and soul together, but so help me he doesn't make it
easy." He backed away, but still held her as though afraid to
let go. He looked older, worn by worry that he didn't bother
to hide. "You do look like summer. Like a lifeline." He
glanced at Niall. "Hello, Colonel—welcome home."

"Parini." Niall nodded. "I was going to take Jani back to
her town house. Is there any reason for me to amend that
plan?"

"No." Val shook his head in that vague way that could

have altered to a nod at any time. "I just wanted to . . . prepare you." He squeezed Jani's shoulders, then let his hands drop. "You have company." He exhaled with a rush. "It's been a time."

Late spring had worked its magic on the town house yard. Bloom-heavy shrubs in rainbow hues lined the front walkway and rear wall, while leafy trees cast shade over the drive. The rest of the street looked much the same, oases of greenery separated by stone walls and wrought metal gates.

Jani remained seated after Pullman switched the skimmer into standby, looking for some exterior hint of the trouble Val had warned her of even as she knew she wouldn't find it. After a few moments, his sportster drifted to a stop alongside—Lucien disembarked first, then walked around to Jani's side of the sedan and popped open her gullwing.

"Let's get going. Faint of heart never won the game," he said as he held his arm out to her.

"They don't get challenged by bornsect security officers, either." Jani shouldered her duffel and climbed out of the skimmer. She caught the discomfort on Lucien's face when she leaned on him too heavily—Dathim must have been knocking the hell out of him during their training sessions. "I've read all the 'sheets. Is what they say reliable?"

"Pretty much." Lucien linked his arm through hers and led her toward the house. "Ghos took exception to my presence at the embassy. He thought I'd come there to spy for the Service. When I tried to explain that I wanted to find out about some hit-and-run raids that had taken place there, he refused to believe me."

"Hit-and-run raids?" Jani tried to extract her arm from Lucien's grip, since Val eyed her strangely, and even Niall arched an eyebrow. Lucien, however, simply placed his hand over hers, encircling her wrist and holding her fast.

"A variation on the attacks that had been occurring at the enclave. Raiders punching through the defenses and leaving tokens of their esteem—food, in these cases—all over the compound." Lucien led Jani up the short flight of steps, then keyed them through the back door. "That's not the biggest problem they're facing, though."

"What is the biggest problem they're facing?" Niall asked as he closed in from behind.

"Can we get inside first?" Jani let Lucien steer her into the entry, noting the care he took to position her between himself and Niall. "I'd like to see what I'm supposed to have prepared for." Then she looked down the narrow hall that led from the back entry to the main rooms of the ground floor, saw a tall, thin form cut through the darkness toward her, and knew.

"Nìa!" Tsecha, a badly dressed vision in clay yellow and green, clapped his hands in an uneven beat. "I feared Dathim would need to return me to the enclave before I could see you!" He took her face between his hands. "See, Dathim, if I place my fingers beneath her jaw just so, she cannot talk."

Jani shook herself loose from Lucien's hold. Then she gripped Tsecha's wrists and yanked down, breaking his hold as well. "What are you doing here?" She looked around him to Dathim. "Does Shai know he's here?"

"You do not think I can answer such, nìa? You look at Dathim to speak for me?" Tsecha sidestepped until he blocked her view of his suborn. "Shai does not know I am here."

"She believes him at the enclave. I have double-set the security array—I must return him in two hours or all will know he has gone." Dathim folded his arms. One sleeve slid up, allowing a view of a nasty contusion that had the long, thin look of a strike with a practice blade. "He is to stay there until the challenge tomorrow. Then he is to prepare to return to Shèrá."

"My ass." Jani grabbed Tsecha by the collar of his shirt and shook him. "First, I must tell you this. I understand your feelings. I comprehend how all you have learned here has affected your thought. But why are you so determined to make my life a living hell!"

Tsecha grabbed the collar of Jani's wrapshirt and shook her in return. *"Feres should have been allowed to live!"* He stopped abruptly, his auric eyes widening when he realized what he did. He released her, smoothing the folds of cloth around her neck before backing away. "They would not listen. They would not think. They are anathema."

Jani reached out and took her old teacher's bony hand in hers. "You will not return to the worldskien. I will talk to Shai and Cao after the challenge tomorrow. After they hear what I have to say, they will allow me to take you to Elyas." She leaned close. "You will see Thalassa, and you will marvel."

"It is warm. So ná Feyó has always said." Tsecha bared his teeth. "She has told me much. You negated the challenge against her, and repaired her standing among the Outer Circle Haárin." He started down the hall, pulling Jani after him. "Tell me of Thalassa. Feyó has finally admitted to facts. Eamon DeVries's involvement—" He shot a look at Val, who flinched in alarm. "—and the life that is lived there. I confess that Feyó's reluctance to deal frankly with me disappointed. I fear she and her suborns require instruction in how to behave in manners not quite so humanish."

"Do not be too angry." Jani tossed her duffel to the floor inside the entry, then pulled Tsecha after her to the couch, drawing him down beside her. "You will enjoy Thalassa so. It is home. They await your arrival. You are their prophet."

"Prophets are all well." Dathim took a seat on Jani's other side, the ergoworks whining as they struggled to support him. "But we must first live through this challenge." He pointed to Lucien, who had dragged a chair into the shaft of sun that streamed through the skylight. "Tell them what you have told us."

Lucien positioned his chair in the natural spotlight, then sat and waited while Niall and Val staked out seats. "Before Jani left for Elyas, she asked me to pull whatever strings necessary to attach myself to the enclave mine investigation." He sat straight, his back barely touching the chair. His white-blond hair shimmered. "I did so, and as I became more involved, I grew aware of a certain lance corporal named Micah Faber, a tech in Supreme Command ComSys. He was present at the enclave the night of the explosion."

"He was the nervy git in our bunker." Niall nodded toward Jani as he patted his tunic above the place where he usually stashed his nicstick case, then let his hand fall with a sigh.

"Yes, sir." Lucien looked to Jani. "Notice anything about him?"

Jani shrugged. "He didn't like me a bit."

"No, he didn't." Lucien paused to lick his lips. In contrast to his usual air of easy competence, he seemed agitated, off-balance. "For the past few months Micah Faber has been undergoing simulation training in some of our most advanced weapons systems, including the V-790 prototype exoskeleton. He has been taking this training in conjunction with others who share his beliefs, namely that the idomeni should be driven from all places of human habitation. They form an organization called the Group. I believe this Group's members may be found at all levels of the Service, and that Faber and his confederates receive their instructions from superiors who are privy to all inner diplomatic and security workings." He glanced at Jani, and shifted in his seat. "I've obtained evidence that I believe shows that Faber and others intend to mount an assault against the idomeni embassy tomorrow morning, during my challenge with nìRau Ghos, in the hope that this will serve to drive the idomeni from Chicago." He leaned forward slightly, one arm braced on his chair arm, the other resting in a not so relaxed manner on his thigh.

Niall sat with his arms crossed in front of his chest, his hand over his chin. "Where is Faber now?"

Lucien drummed his fingers against his chair arm. "I have him under surveillance."

"So why haven't you locked him up so you can sweat names and details out of him and nip this assault at the bud?"

"Because it wouldn't do any good. Sir." Lucien's face darkened. He didn't often lose control, and he had come close. "In the simulation I saw, Faber is referred to as 'Tiebold.' The faces of the other participants change from scene to scene. I believe the trainees are assigned sim names and faces so that no one knows the true identities of the others with whom they're training until the time of the assault."

Jani closed her eyes. *I wonder what John is doing now?* Arguing with Eamon? Discussing music with the hybrid second violin? "How did you find out all this?"

Lucien hesitated again. "During an interrogation of Faber, early last week."

"He spoke freely?"

"No." Lucien hung his head. "Coworkers had commented that Faber had grown moody over the last few weeks. Erratic. I determined that he was buckling under the stress of his training and might prove ready to talk if . . . persuaded." A shadow of anger flickered across his face. "I lured him on a pretext and began to question him. I felt that if I could convince him to think of me as someone he could talk to, he would open up."

Jani glanced at Val and found him staring back, read the same thought in his eyes that she nursed herself. Lucien as brother-confessor. Lucien as friend. The prospect boggled.

If Lucien noticed their silent dismay, he kept it to himself. "Unfortunately, the officer with whom I was working took a more direct approach. Unbeknownst to me, Faber had been teetering in the edge of a sim-psychotic break and the added pressure pushed him over the edge. I was forced to administer Sera—it functions as a tranquilizer as well as a truth drug. Since he was out anyway, I decided to make the best of a bad business and take what I could from him."

Niall rubbed his chin. Patted his pocket again. "And the name of your partner is . . . ?"

Lucien sighed. "Egon Veles—"

"That bastard should be locked up for life!" Niall opened his hand, then closed it in a fist, over and over. "Sera is damned unreliable when used on those prone to sim psychosis, you know that?"

Lucien nodded sharply. "Yes, sir. Sim psychotics lose track of the difference between reality and the sims. What happens to them in the sims is as much truth as anything they experience in real life. However, need I remind you, sir, that both the embassy and the enclave have been infiltrated over these past several months by people with Service-level equipment, and judging by their actions, Service training as well. These groups apparently exist. Is it unreasonable to entertain the possibility that some of them may be training to carry out more deadly assaults?"

"Let me get this straight." Niall sat forward, elbows on knees, his hands hanging between. "You've arrived at the conclusion that a group of anti-idomeni radicals named, vaguely enough, the Group, will attack the embassy tomorrow during your challenge. You've reached this conclusion based on some suspicious behavior evidenced by a nerve-addled desk jockey, along with a few coincidences thrown in for good measure. You haven't shared your findings with your superiors or anyone else's because you're convinced the Group's strings are pulled by some of them, and you don't know who you can trust."

Lucien touched his forehead, where nature's spotlight had caused sweat to bead. "There's more, sir."

Niall covered his face with his hands. "By all means."

"The ones who engaged in the hit-and-runs were the well-trained assault forces having fun. They know how to get in, and more importantly, they know how to get out." Lucien fingered the edge of his collar. "Micah Faber and his cohorts are another story. These people are not trained combat soldiers. They're receiving repetitive training on one exercise only—the attack on the embassy. They're not being taught basic skills or even how to maintain their equipment, and they're too ignorant to know what they're not learning. They're one-offs. I'm convinced they're not meant to survive the assault."

Silence settled. Jani felt Tsecha's and Dathim's presence like weights beside her, pressing.

"I most believed, and truly," Tsecha said, "that humanish liked us, in their way."

Niall glanced at Tsecha, then away. "I have heard some crazy things in my life, Pascal, but you just won the prize."

Jani shot a warning look at Lucien, who had opened his mouth to snap back. "Niall, even if you accept only the fact that some anti-idomeni service personnel are self-training for the Great Someday, is it out of line to consider that one or more of them might try something tomorrow, given the significance of the event, and that heightened security measures are therefore called for?" She shivered, and craved heat. "Someone needs to carry the word to the embassy."

Dathim laughed, a hard, low staccato burst. "Elon will trust nothing you say, ná Kièrshia. Nothing ní Tsecha tells her. Nothing I tell her."

"Will she believe what I tell her?" Niall stood and paced. "Or does it need to come from Admiral-General Mako?"

"Mako, I most believe, Colonel, since he is not seen as a friend of my Jani." Tsecha looked to her and gestured helplessness. "Elon is most blind in that regard."

Niall thumped his fist against the wall. "I probably need to go through Burkett. His ears are still ringing from that mine debacle—he's going to love hearing from me."

"Do you want me to talk to him?" Jani recalled Callum Burkett. A long face and an abrupt manner, but a man who listened eventually.

Niall shook his head. "I can handle Cal, but keep your comlines open just in case." He leaned against the wall, then thumped his head against it. "I wasn't planning on sleeping tonight anyway." He glared at Lucien. "I want that sim wafer of yours, and the transcript of your interrogation."

Lucien reached into his shirt pocket and removed a small wafer folder. Rising stiffly, he walked across the room and handed it to Niall, then paced the room instead of returning to his seat.

"Right." Niall tucked the folder inside his tunic, then pointed to Jani. "You're going to be watched tonight. You will not leave this house. I will send Pullman to collect you in the morning. You're to ride with no one else."

Jani barely restrained the urge to salute. "Yes, Niall."

"Yes, Niall—someone make a note of that." Niall turned to Dathim. "You should head back across the lake now. I will provide an escort. Pullman went through OCS with the men I'm thinking of—if any of them are with this Group—" He pushed a hand over his Service burr, confusion aging him. The thought must have occurred that he had known Thomas Hamil, too. "If any—" He stared down at the floor. "Damn."

Val raised his hand. "I think Neoclona security should watch this house, Colonel, if it's all the same to you. In fact, if you require Lieutenant Pullman for other duties, I will see that Jani gets to the idomeni embassy myself."

Lucien quit his pacing. "I can provide escort for ní Dathim and ní Tsecha."

Dathim shook his head. "You must rest. Prepare."

"Ní Dathim's right, Pascal," Niall agreed grudgingly. "You've got enough on your plate. Lieutenant Pullman will escort you across the lake himself, ní Tsecha. I'm going to head back to the base." He eyed Jani, who took the hint and rose to join him.

Niall lowered his voice as they left the library. "If this assault turns out to be a wet fizzle . . ."

"Considering the mood of the city, are the precautions unreasonable?" Jani followed him back down the hall to the rear door. "I don't think so."

"Glad you came back?" Niall tossed her a sad smile.

Jani shrugged. "All I'd be doing in Thalassa is standing on the beach feeding the crab-things." *Talking to John. Laughing with John. Making love with John.* "Doesn't compare, does it?"

"I'll be glad when tomorrow's over." Niall squinched his eyes shut, then opened them, a sign that a headache had

come to call. "If I had one of those Kilian-special wristbands, I think I'd tie it on about now."

Jani knew it cruel to push the point, given the circumstances, but she did anyway. "Do you want one?" she asked,
rolling up her right sleeve.

Niall started. "I—I'll take the thought and call us even."
He touched the doorpad, then pulled his hand away. "I appreciate it, really. I know what it signifies, it's just . . ."

"It's just not your way." Jani opened the door herself, then
held it aside for him. "Be careful." She remained there as
Tsecha and Dathim passed, their expressions grim and their
steps heavy, then waited until they followed Niall into the
Service skimmer before closing the door and setting the
lock.

"Not much of a homecoming."

Jani turned to find Val standing in the hallway, a dispo of
soft drink in hand.

"I felt so sorry for you and Niall. You both looked like you
wanted to flee back to O'Hare and grab the first flight to anywhere." Val moved to Jani's side and slipped his arm around
her. "I hate to be selfish at a time like this, but how's John?
I've received a few messages. Lots of reassurances, but little
information, which isn't like him."

Jani settled in for the first round of what promised to be
some pointed questioning. *John, it's up to you to tell him,
damn it—he's your best friend.* "Anything lately?"

"Not for two weeks." Val steered her into the kitchen, maneuvering her into a chair, then taking a seat across from her.
"What's going on? You're back together." His face lit, shav-
ing years. "Wonderful. He likes Karistos—all right, what
does that mean? Is he coming back to Chicago in the near
future? Is he coming back *ever*?"

Jani watched Val tap the corners of the dispo against the
tabletop, and wished she had something to worry. "He'll be
staying on Elyas, at least for a while." She settled for the
spice dispenser, opening and closing the slotted lids.

"How are he and Eamon getting along?" Val forced a

laugh. "I've been waiting for the legal knives to start slicing and dicing—*Christ,* sorry. I haven't been able to get knives out of my mind for weeks." He begged the ceiling for mercy, then, slowly, his steady gaze moved down until it locked with Jani's. "You were always a good liar. One could never tell from your face or your manner whether you'd just told the truth or the whopper of a lifetime. Give me a break, Jan. Please."

Damn it, John! Jani breathed in once. Twice. "Do you have any messages waiting for you back at your flat?"

"Not that I'm aware of." Val set the drink dispo aside. "Something's happened, and you think I need to hear it from John." He laced his fingers together and tapped his chin, as though he wanted to pray but needed to work up the nerve. "He didn't *kill* Eamon, did he?"

The image of John standing over Eamon's lumpen body brought a laugh from Jani, which told her how bleak her mood. "*No.* Not to worry."

"Not to worry, she says." Val stood and walked around the table. "Easy for her." His eyes held much the same tenderness they always did, but something else had hitched along for the ride. Resignation, an awareness that one of the people he cared about could hold back from him. "Get some rest—you'll need it." He kissed the top of her head, then slipped out the door.

Jani concentrated on the sound of his receding footsteps, then waited. *One still left unaccounted for.* One more colony left to be heard from.

Then she heard movement behind her, so soft it might not have been sound at all. Felt the grip around her arm, dragging her to her feet and spinning her around.

Lucien pulled her close, his grasp tight enough to bruise. "Like summer." He buried his face in her neck. "A warm, warm place." He moved to the hollow of her throat, his lips tracing lines that burned, that left a growing ache behind.

Jani fought every building sensation even as her back arched and her knees went weak. Then she pushed her hands through Lucien's hair, felt the shock of his short stubble instead of John's longer, finger-burying silk, and stopped.

Lucien kept on until it dawned on him that Jani had stopped helping. He lifted his head; clouded eyes met hers. "You're with John now, aren't you?" He shrugged. "Does it make a difference?" When she didn't respond, his gaze slowly sharpened. "I suppose it would with you." He released her gradually, as though she'd change her mind if he lingered. Then he sighed and turned away. "I've been staying here, like a live-in caretaker. I hope you don't mind."

"Not at all." Jani leaned against the table and slowly recovered her bearings. "Thank you again."

"'Not at all.' 'Thank you.' You're so polite. Makes me wonder what I did wrong." Lucien opened cupboard doors one after the other, then closed them, a mindless circuit of movement.

Jani watched him, sensed his growing agitation, and damned herself for needing to add to it. "I think Ghos might try to kill you."

Lucien wheeled. "You're too late." His voice came too harsh. "Dathim informed me of that right after the bastard challenged me. I'm the focus. The symbol. All idomeni hatred for humanity, done up in one blue and grey bundle. Lucky me, huh?" He laughed as he opened and closed more doors, his movements growing more jerky, the slams louder.

"You're—" Jani thought of her duffel, tossed aside in the library, and of her shooter, nestled in its usual hiding place. "You're welcome to stay, if you don't want to be alone tonight."

"So you'll hold my hand?" Lucien rooted through a drawer, lifting out a bread slicer. "Ice my bruises? Tell me bedtime stories?" He tilted the crimped blade one way, then the other, then tossed it back in its place. "I need something more than that, I'm afraid." He exhaled with a shudder, then turned on his heel and blew through the door into the hallway.

"Lucien?" Jani hurried after him, torn between wanting

him to stay and hoping that he'd leave. "Where are you going?"

"None of your business." He pulled a battered field coat out of the entry closet and dragged it on. "Veles might be able to give you a few possibilities, if you need to get hold of me." He keyed open the door and walked outside.

"Don't—" Jani reached the open door to find he had already neared the end of the walkway. *"Lucien."*

He stopped, then slowly turned back to her. Late afternoon had come—the sky had lost its crystal brightness and the first wisp of cloud had formed in the east. He watched her as dogs barked and children ran past, a variation of life that had never touched him. Then he turned away and resumed walking, through the front gate and down the sidewalk, hands in pockets and shoulders hunched, finally disappearing in other houses' shadows.

Jani stood in the open doorway for a time. Then she closed the door and locked it. She worked for a few hours, sorting the paper mail that Lucien had collected, then culling her comport messages. Tried to contact both Prime Minister Cao and Ambassador Shai, and found herself relegated to the same second deputy assistants who dealt with the interview requests from prep school newssheets. Wandered from room to room like a haunt, wondering whether she should toss Niall's caution to the wind and search the city darkside for Lucien, bring him back to this empty house, and meet her growing edge with his.

"Welcome back to Chicago." She stood in front of her bedroom window until the sky darkened and the night took hold.

CHAPTER 28

Elon sat at her worktable and monitored the embassy security array from her display. The function of utilities had always been of little interest to her, but the lines that ferried pink throughout the buildings were closely aligned with those systems, and she needed to acquire Dathim's skill in little time if she was to shut them down prior to the beginning of the challenge.

Her mind felt most godly. Her soul. She had thought they might wait seasons, she and Ghos, to join their paths along the Way. But Admiral-General Mako had scheduled an emergency conclave with the Interior Minister, the Exterior Deputy, and Ambassador Shai, and to Elon's surprise had confirmed all that Pascal had told them weeks before. *Elements in the Service . . . radical . . . intentions to attack . . .* He had requested that the challenge be postponed, and Shai refused to consider such because the humanish Service had already delayed enough, and declaration needed to be made so that one and all could, as she said, *get on with matters*.

"Whatever such meant." Elon's shoulders curved in the first stages of anger. Shai's speech and gestures had grown more humanish since she had come to this damned cold place, though she most strongly denied such when confronted. "It is fitting that she should die here." As she had come to think as humanish, so let her die with them.

Elon continued to scroll through the screens. When she heard her door open, she did not turn to see who visited, for there was only one who it could be at this late time.

"Did you believe him?" Ghos dragged a chair to the side of Elon's table and sat. "Mako. The small one. Do you believe his tales of upcoming attack?"

"His suborn is the scarred colonel, who knows ná Kièrshia." Elon reached out and plucked a dried grass blade from Ghos's braids—he had spent the day examining border systems, and no matter how well he laved, he never removed all that attached to him. "But Mako himself despises her. He would not act for her." She gestured inconsequence. "Such does not matter. Whether what he says is truth or lie, our systems will still be disabled. The new-form pink will not flow in the lines. And whoever will come, will come."

"So." Ghos's breathing grew heavy as he moved in his chair. He had labored much in recent days to increase his blade skill, and his body ached from the exertion. "But the scarred colonel himself will attend tomorrow. He will demand to know of our preparations."

"Then we lie." Elon looked him in the eye and bared her teeth. Such familiarity was not as seemly since their pairing had accomplished its godly purpose, but the glory of their deaths would surely override such. "Then we lie." She felt a surge of kinship unlike any other she had experienced when Ghos bared his teeth in reply, and she felt the warmth of Rauta Shèràa in her bones as she resumed her disabling of the security array.

The call had come that morning, in Micah's latest wafer. The time, the place, what to bring, what to wear.

Now, twelve hours later, he sat on the floor in the cargo bay of a truck parked in the middle of some unknown woods, cradling his left arm, studying the faces around him as best he could through a haze of pain. *They all look like they did in the sims*. Even though their faces had changed, he'd have known them anywhere. Bevan with his perpetual sneer. O'Shae with her arched eyebrows and startled expression. Manda with her coltish walk, all knees and elbows like a twelve-year-old boy.

Except that now they'd left their sneers and starts and gangly walks behind and sat with him on the floor, their positions mimicking his as the bone-deep pain of blitzed ID chips made them partners in misery.

Micah heard a thud and looked up to find Foley sprawled across the table that centered the bare room. He barely stifled his cry as Chrivet pressed the IDscan to the place on his inside lower arm and activated it. His left arm spasmed just as theirs had. He pressed the side of his face against the cool polywood just as they had, clenching the edge with his free hand, biting his lower lip until the blood came. Chrivet, for her part, displayed a remarkable lack of emotion as she bore down on the device charge-through, delivering that little extra burst of energy that would ensure that Foley's Service ID chip, like the rest, had been rendered untraceable in every way.

Shared agony. One way to bond those for whom the sim exercises hadn't been enough. Micah caught the looks that passed between Manda and Bevan, the way O'Shae scooted along the floor to make room for Foley as he slid down the wall, arms folded, eyes clamped shut. The way she stroked his right arm with her fingertips, sympathy softening the rough planes of her face. O'Shae, who howled for idomeni blood and slaughtered with glee in every scenario.

They all looked up to watch as Patel, the last of their crew to be zapped, walked to the table. Even Foley pried open his lids so that the barest glitter of eyes shown. Fear set Patel's face like stone, but Foley caught her eye and held up a clenched fist. The left one, hand tremoring from the pain. That drew a smile from the stone, a raised fist in return. Then

Patel lowered to the tabletop and held out her arm. Got the jolt. Moved to the floor.

Micah studied his compatriots. They all dressed alike, in blue and grey springweights stripped of all designators and badges, anything that identified the clothing as Service. After entering the room, they'd all disrobed to their underwear and submitted to scanning by the focused Chrivet, modesty discarded in the interest of self-preservation, another humiliation designed to bond. *Can't be too careful, boys and girls*, Chrivet had said as she waved the scanning wands over their bodies. *There are a lot of people out there who would like to know who you are.* She had seemed to stare at Micah for an unduly long time when she said it, but she didn't like him, after all. She probably wished someone had found him before he showed up at the truck.

Micah stretched out his arm, slowly worked it back and forth. The pain had eased, but when he tried to pick up a wadded dispo on the floor beside him, he couldn't close his fingers to grip.

"It will take you until morning to regain your strength."

Micah looked up to find Chrivet looming straight above him, her breasts like a ledge she peeked over. "Yes, ma'am." He tried not to stare at her for too long—just as she did on the sims, she unnerved him. As it turned out, she most closely resembled her sim image—the razored hair and downturned face, the muscular build and barking voice. "Looking forward to it."

"Are you?" Chrivet smiled. As always, when she smiled she looked as though she was the only one who got the joke, and it was being played on someone else. "Get some sleep, Tiebold. You're going to need it." Then she walked to the bay controls and lowered the lights.

CHAPTER 29

"Did you get any sleep last night?" Val steered the sedan through the early morning traffic. "I sure as hell didn't."

Jani stifled a yawn. "Neither did I." She caught sight of the *Trib-Times* headline in a kiosk window—TODAY'S THE DAY!—and decided she didn't need to read any further. "Not that it's any of my business, but did Lucien stop by your place last night?"

"*No.*" Val graced her with a fish-eyed stare as he turned onto the Boul artery that would take them to the embassy. "Not that he didn't show up at the occasional odd hour over the course of your absence—that young man doesn't take 'Go to hell' for an answer, does he—but after the challenge, his focus changed. He spent most of his time at the enclave, training. Why?"

Jani folded her arms and hugged herself, shivering despite her long-sleeve tunic and coat. It was a hard sun that shone, highlighting the pedestrians, the other skimmers, the occasional NO BLOODSPORT sign that hung in a store window. "He seemed tense yesterday, is all. Destructive."

"My guess is that he wanted to break John over the head." Val frowned as another No Bloodsport sign came into view. "You were his ticket, Jan. Now you've moved on, and he's angry. Given all the other things that have been going on in his life, I'd say 'destructive' might describe his feelings pretty well." He veered off onto the embassy access road, which was already lined with news vans and buses. "Isn't that how he should feel, considering the circumstances?"

"No. Counterintuitive as it sounds, you really need to go into a challenge with a cool head. Helps prevent accidents." Jani watched as a group of humanish carrying anti-challenge signs trudged up the road. "I'm surprised Niall's letting all these people get this close."

"I doubt he has much choice." Val slowed as he reached the end of the vehicle check-in line. "Face it, Jan, Lucien's story is pretty farfetched. All he has is his gut feeling, some odd wafer recordings, and one name. For all we know, Micah Faber is a one-man fighting force, getting his rocks off killing simulated idomeni on nights and weekends." He let his hands drop to his lap as, up ahead, Vynshàrau and Interior security searched and checked vehicles one by one. "I think we have enough to worry about without throwing a hypothetical attack into the mix."

"Yeah." Jani watched the protestors wave signs, the lettering showing in reverse in her side mirror. "TROPSDOOLB ON." She lay her head back, thought of a black and brown stone nestled in the bottom of her duffel, which she'd left behind at Val's, and muttered a prayer to her Lord Ganesh, as she had so often that morning.

The challenge room was filling by the time Jani and Val entered. A sprawling space, it was furnished at opposing ends with banked rows of seats to accommodate spectators of both species. While some humanish and idomeni still wandered the floor, they stuck with their own for the most part, with little mixing. Jani spotted Tsecha on the idomeni side, gesturing roughly at something Ambassador Shai said while Elon looked on. She caught his eye and raised a hand in greeting; he nodded in return, his expression grim.

Val tugged at his shirtfront. Experience in Rauta Shèràa

had taught him the value of cool clothes—he wore a short-sleeve shirt and trousers in white desertweave. "God, this brings back memories, and not all of them happy ones." He took a pale yellow scarf from his pocket and tied it around his forehead to catch the sweat. "My heart's pounding."

"Yours and mine both, Doctor."

Jani turned to find Niall standing behind them, kitted out in desertweights, shooter holster uncapped, an earbug with mouthpiece hugging one side of his head. "What's wrong?"

"No one can find Micah Faber, that's what's wrong." Niall leaned close and lowered his voice. "As soon as I walked out your door yesterday, I called ahead to Sheridan and sent someone to back up Veles. She gets to Faber's building, no Veles, and Faber is nowhere to be found."

Jani surveyed the crowd, which eyed the entry doors in anticipation. "Has Veles shown up?"

"No." Niall brushed his hand over his damp brow. "He was either in on it with Faber, which doesn't make sense, or he's moved on to more interesting pastures, as he has done in the past. Or . . ." He hesitated. "Or he's dead." He paced a tight circle, his eyes on the attendees. "V-790 detection specs have been programmed into everyone's systems. I've got Exterior security on the north border, Interior monitoring the south, with my folks mixed in for good measure. The Vynshàrau are handling the lake and the air—they were pretty insistent, and Burkett couldn't sway them." His eyes were bloodshot, his remark about not getting any sleep the night before seemingly fulfilled. "I didn't like this before, but I really don't like it now."

"The perimeter of the embassy compound is most closely monitored, and truly." Elon straightened in respect before Shai, then gestured to one of the many humanish ministers who had come to attend the challenge. "Admiral-General Mako's suborns have been most precise with their information. We do not anticipate assault, but we are most prepared for it." She hesitated when she noticed the Kièrshia, who stood beside Colonel Pierce in a far corner of the room, speaking to another humanish male she did not recognize.

"You are not assisting Ghos in his preparations, Elon?" Shai's words came rough, so much like Vynshàrau Haárin even when it was English she spoke. "You have left him to pray alone?"

"It is his right to ready himself in his own way, nìRauta." Elon felt a surge of anger that Shai would question her in front of the humanish. So much she spoke of the "united front" they were to project at all times, yet when it suited her, she ignored her own dictum most readily. "He requested I depart so that he could contemplate the blade Captain Pascal chose with which to fight."

"The knight marking vigil over his sword." The minister, Abascal, moved his head up and down. The humanish nod, which could mean nothing or everything.

"Ghos is not contemplative." Shai jerked her left hand in a gesture of dismissal. "It is a wonder to me that on this day he divines the meaning of calm. I regret he did not do so on the day he offered challenge to Pascal."

Elon felt her shoulders curve, and fought them straight. Beneath her overrobe, the weight of three blades provided her the same calm that Ghos sought with his prayers. "It has always been Pascal's desire to learn of our ways. Did you not say yourself, nìaRanta, that it is thus our place to instruct him?" She offered a gesture of parting, then walked away before Shai gave voice to the anger that bowed her own back.

Elon relaxed as she walked from one side of the meeting room to the other then back, her blades bumping softly against her thigh with every step. According to the perimeter guard, the morning sun offered its usual cold light. She knew that if she walked outside, the wind off the lake would flay her as a hundred knives. *I will never feel that wind again.* The thought filled her with such joy that she wanted to step into the circle and offer thanks to the gods, unsheath one of her blades and bleed herself in their honor. She considered such, striding to the center of the room and stepping up to the painted edge that would soon enclose Ghos and Pascal in combat, ignoring the questioning postures of the Vynshàrau who wondered at her seemliness—

"Elon?"

—but stopping at the sound of the voice. She felt Caith's hand on her heart, as chill as the wind. "Tsecha."

"Such an oddness here. A sense of tension. One would think that neither we nor the humanish understood the concept of fighting." Tsecha's shirt and trousers pained the eye with their colors, the blue of indicator illumins and a yellow seen only if one shone ultraviolet light on certain types of seaweed. "The outer perimeter scan sometimes malfunctioned here. Something to do with the acidity of the soil."

"The soil has been dredged and replaced since you left, ní Tsecha."

"The guardposts near the border with Exterior—the trees impair their ability to sight—"

"Those trees have been cut, ní Tsecha. Exterior Minister Ulanova proved quite accommodating to our request, and truly."

"You are so confident, Elon, and truly." Tsecha positioned the toes of his boots as close to the red-ring edge of the circle as he could without touching. No one expressed surprise at this action, but then, he was Tsecha, was he not, and thus expected to behave as he would, even as the justice of Temple awaited him. "Do you possess such faith in the order of Shiou, or in the quality of your security?"

Elon turned away from the circle and looked her old teacher, her esteemed enemy, in the face. "Security is a most sound thing, and truly. But order is all, nìRau." She gloried in his anger at her use of his former title. It would prove a fitting end to their conflict as the time for their journey to the Star grew closer.

She left Tsecha by the circle and found a quiet corner where she could monitor her scanset in private. She entered the codes for various points about the compound, and received only machine responses. No guards remained in the perimeter—Ghos had ordered them to one of the meeting rooms to watch the challenge via holoremote. He had also reduced the settings of the field arrays to standby status—no autoweaponry would discharge, even if one of the humanish invaders fired at it first. Structural systems announced the same quiet state. The doors of the embassy would open to all who wished to enter.

"Thus and so." Elon deactivated the scanset and returned it to her beltpouch, and offered a prayer to Shiou that the humanish would arrive soon.

"They'll be starting any minute," Jani said as the doors to the challenge room opened and Vynshàrau attendants entered bearing the weapons of choice. "We should choose our seats." She watched Tsecha speak with Elon, the security dominant. Elon ended their conversation abruptly, leaving Tsecha to cut through the crowd on the opposite side of the room and make his way to Shai, whose back bowed as soon as she saw him. "That's my old teacher—sowing disorder wherever he goes."

"Like I said, the memories." Val inhaled deeply as he fell in behind Jani. "The heat. The nerves. The underlying sense of panic."

"They didn't get this fancy when you fought Hantìa last summer." General Callum Burkett, head of Service Diplomatic, followed them to the second row of seats on the humanish side of the room. "If I recall correctly, it was pretty much a case of throwing the blades at you and getting out of the way." He had dressed in the latest Service weapon against Vynshàrau room temperatures, desertweights equipped with cooling cells. His tan shirt still appeared crisp and dry. Sweat already sheened his horsey face, though, and he cast an envious glance at Val's headband as he took his seat.

"The level of formality can vary. Anything from the equivalent of a corner brawl to a three-day event." Jani sat, mindful of the stares, not all of them friendly, that greeted her arrival. "I think the Vynshàrau realize how uncomfortable most of the Service brass feel about this, so they're doing their best to play it up."

As if on cue, the door mechanisms hummed and the panels opened wide. "Remove all obstacles in Lucien's path, my Lord Ganesh, I pray," Jani whispered once, then again.

To an overwhelming press of silence, Dathim and Elon entered. In contrast to his usual attire, Dathim's brown trousers and tan wrapshirt appeared staid—his appearance complemented that of Elon, who wore the dull brown overshirt and trousers favored by diplomatic suborns, topped with an off-white overrobe.

Jani watched as Dathim's amber gaze searched the human side of the room before settling on her. *He's been prowling about his old territory, I bet.* She sensed the question in his stare, noted the tension in his bearing, and felt the long, slow clench of her stomach. *He's found something.* Her legs tensed—she almost stood up, but forced herself still. *He'll tell me when he can.* The challenge had begun— any disruption at this point would be considered unseemly in the extreme.

After a slow ten-count, Lucien and Ghos entered side by side. Lucien looked at home in grey base casual trousers and steel-blue T-shirt; the harsh light thrown by the chandeliers reflected off his muscled arms, accentuating the rough blend of fresh and healing contusions that hashed his skin. He made a quick scan of the crowd as he strode to the place outside the circle that Dathim had chosen, a momentary pause as his eyes met Jani's his only acknowledgment of her presence.

Ghos, for his part, carried with him the odd calm that most idomeni did as they prepared for violence. He moved as though he walked through a garden, eyes fixed straight ahead, snake face in repose. He wore a sleeveless tunic and trousers in off-white, and had bound his fringed braids in a loose napeknot, tying them with a strip of cloth.

Then Dathim bent to Lucien's ear and spoke. Lucien looked to Jani again, then slowly nodded once. Dathim left his side and headed in Jani's direction.

"Ná Kièrshia?" The occupants of the front row scooted in either direction to allow him room. "You must act in my place."

Jani heard the gasps and mutters around her. Everyone had read the 'sheets and learned the challenge drill, and knew what rule Dathim was about to break. "Why?"

"Yes," Niall echoed. "Why?"

Dathim bent close. "I initiated my check of systems, and they did not respond properly." He spoke without gesture, his hands clenched by his sides. "I will go to primary control and evaluate. When I do this, ná Kièrshia must take my place as Pascal's second."

"I'm sending one of mine with him." Niall started muttering into his earbug mouthpiece, but before he could get out one sentence, Jani silenced him with a tug on his arm.

"You can't send a humanish into the secure heart of the embassy, Niall—you'll stop the challenge—"

"That's not a bad idea."

"—and initiate an incident that will make the Night of the Mine look like a belch at a garden party by comparison." Jani placed a hand on his arm. "Only an idomeni can enter that space, all right?" She waited for Niall's brusque nod before she stood and followed Dathim to the circle. "The neighbors will wonder what happened."

"I do not understand you, Kièrshia."

"Everyone will ask what is going on." The air seemed to press around Jani as the tension in the room ramped. She followed Dathim around the edge of the ring to join Lucien by the weapons rack.

Dathim positioned himself on one side of Lucien and motioned for Jani to stand on the other. "He will attempt to kill you, Pascal. Before I only believed. Now, I know."

Lucien's bland expression never altered. Some of his sangfroid could be explained by his augmentation, but whatever he had indulged in the previous night to ease his tension, it seemed to have worked. "What do I do?"

"Watch his hands. If he strikes at your body, strike at his to let him know that you are aware of what he does. If he cuts you, cut him harder. If the physician-priests protest, let them end it. Otherwise, do as you must to protect your life." The three of them regarded their bornsect opponents on the other side of the circle as Sànalàn uttered an invocation. Ghos, who seemed so serene as to be drugged. Elon, who stood beside him, watching them like a cat sensing movement in the weeds.

"If it goes to hell, I'll be right behind you." Jani picked up one of the short blades from the rack and examined it before returning it to its place. Her temper had risen, spurred by the heat and the shine of metal. The self-inflicted gash on her arm, long healed, tingled. *This is my place—I know my way here.*

Lucien jerked his chin in Elon's direction. "She has a shooter."

"What makes you think I don't?" Jani patted the familiar heft, concealed by her tunic. "I'm Tsecha's suborn—they don't scan me anymore."

"I must go." Agitation surrounded Dathim like an aura—Jani expected him to crackle when he walked.

"Take Fa with you." She looked to the high seats on the idomeni side of the room, where the enclave Haárin had gathered to watch the challenge. "He was your suborn when you worked embassy utilities. He can help you."

"He must stay here and watch. So I have told him. More to worry of here, with so many humanish." Dathim gestured to Lucien. "Fight well, Pascal. Maybe for your next challenge, I will be able to act as I pledged." He straightened and gestured regret to Shai, but before she could beckon him to come and inform her exactly what the hell was going on, he had slipped out the door.

Lucien eyed the silent gathering. "Do we need to announce you as the understudy?"

"Not if no one asks." Jani gestured their readiness to Elon, who responded slowly. "I'd suggest keeping to this side of the circle, and not exposing your back to Elon."

The first crack formed in Lucien's blasé facade, a slight widening of the eyes that spoke of rising temper. "That's going to limit my ability to defend myself against Ghos."

"Not as much as a knife under the ribs." Jani looked to Shai, who gestured wary permission. To Tsecha, who clenched his hand and shook it once. Then, finally, to Sànalàn, who completed her prayer and gestured toward the circle. "It's time."

Lucien walked to the weapons rack and removed his blade of choice, a mid-length curved sword. He entered the circle, back straight, weapon held out to the side. *"We will begin now,"* he said, his High Vynshàrau smooth and free of accent.

"Yes." Ghos collected his blade and entered the circle. *"We will begin now,"* he responded as he lowered into *hain*, the Stance of Welcome.

Lucien bent his knees and started to spread his arms wide in mirror of Ghos, but before he could fully attain the position, Ghos darted forward, sweeping his blade in a wide arc before him. Lucien leapt back, but not before the Vynshàrau's blade raked him, slicing his T-shirt. Blood welled from a gash the width of his torso.

"Ghos!" Tsecha struggled to his feet while Shai tried to drag him back down to his low seat. *"Fight as the gods demand, or I will strike you myself!"*

Ghos ignored him, following his blade in. But Lucien followed Dathim's orders like a physical law, catching Ghos' weapon with the side of his own, pushing it aside, then drawing his sword in and striking the Vynshàrau in the stomach with the point. Ghos gasped and doubled over, his hand pressed to the front of his tunic. He stilled, looking down as he eased his hand away from the wound. Then he bared his teeth and wiped his hand over his tunicfront, smearing the welling red across the off-white cloth in a wide slash. "Only skin, Pascal." Then he raised his sword over his head and strode in.

Lucien's strike should have slowed Ghos, but it didn't. He brought his blade down, his greater height forcing Lucien to hold his blade up higher to block him, force his arm straighter to maintain the distance between them. Lucien's arm shook from the strain, sweat already coursing down his face, his arms. He broke contact and leapt back, dodging Ghos's downward stroke by a handsbreadth.

Jani checked the temperature of the human side of the room. Everyone, civvie and Service alike, sat forward, hands on their knees or the edges of their seats, ready to push to their feet and storm the circle. She caught Niall's eye and held up one hand in a "back down" gesture. Niall nodded, then slowly sat back—some of the Service personnel took his lead, but not all—they watched the battle as if hypnotized by the ring of the blades and the flash of light off polished metal.

Jani felt the same pull, but forced herself to look outside the circle in time to see Elon slip out of the room. *I should follow.* But the challenge already teetered on the brink of collapse, and she had pledged Lucien she'd remain at his back.

Shit. She looked to the idomeni side of the room once more, and motioned to ní Fa once, then again, cursing under her breath when he hesitated.

Then he finally stepped down from his seat, head forward and shoulders rounded in the slump he employed whether angry or not. "Ná Kièrshia?"

Jani backed as far away from the edge of the circle as she dared. "Ní Dathim is in primary control. Go to him."

Fa gestured in the negative. "He said I am to remain here."

"Go to Dathim." Jani lowered her voice when Lucien half turned toward the sound and barely dodged a blow from Ghos. *"Now."* She waited until the door closed after him. Then she reached beneath her tunic and activated her shooter.

"Like Jesus Christ himself, boys and girls!" Chrivet led them in the now familiar charge, lake spray hosing around her with every impact of her exo boots on the water's surface.

Micah declined to rebuke the sergeant this time. *Four minutes to landfall.* He checked his readouts, comparing the heat-emitting rainbow blobs that filled his display with the occasional soft shimmer in the air that marked the location of a sheathed exo. "Walking in Jesus' footsteps." He quickened his pace, his physical params—heartbeat, respiration—edging into orange or red for all categories.

"Slow down, Tiebold." Chrivet's tinny growl filled his head. "Time enough to top out when we hit 'em."

"Ma'am." Micah eased off, trying to shake the wonder that gripped him as he compared the sims to the real thing. The same water beaded on his faceplate in the same perfect spheres, then ran down like weird rain, leaving the same dry surface behind. The same shoreline spanned before him. The same Exterior Ministry lights marked their progress.

Someone should have seen us disembark. But no one had been walking on the private stretch of beach five kees north of the embassy when the truck parked and disgorged them onto the rocky sand. No one spotted them from shore. No one marked them from overhead. They passed through the most heavily patrolled stretch of lakefront bordering the most populous urbanscape on Earth, and no one detected their presence.

The shielding is that good. Micah swallowed a nervous laugh. *All of Chicago belongs to the Group—they know we're here but they're pretending they don't see, pretending they don't realize what we're doing.* He heard the click of his exo intercom, Chrivet's voice again.

"*Target at eleven, distance zero point two four two kilometers.*"

One and a half minutes to landfall. Micah swallowed hard as the first outbuildings of the idomeni embassy came into view.

Elon crept to the entry of the primary utility chase, then paused. She heard nothing for some time, and made ready to turn away and search elsewhere.

Then she heard the scrape of boots on bare concrete, the slow, measured step of someone monitoring the readouts of the embassy systems.

"Ní Dathim?" She stepped inside the chase. "You have no right to work here. You are an Haárin of the enclave now." She squinted into the half-light, and felt the press of systems array structures on either side like a closing in of walls. Saw the blink and flutter of blue and green indicators, the air and water and heat of the embassy.

A motion in front of her, a shadow from behind an array. A head. Dathim, looking around the corner to see who interrupted him. "The embassy defenses have been inactivated." He vanished behind the array once more. "You know your scanset codes, Elon? Enter them, and save me time."

"Why are you not at the challenge?" Elon reached beneath her overrobe, felt the knives, then released them reluctantly and probed for her shooter holster. "Why are you not assisting your Pascal to defend himself?"

Dathim looked around the corner once more. He may have even looked her in the face, but thanks to the gods for the dimness of the light, that she did not need to suffer the knowledge of his unseemliness.

He did not move for a long time. Then he stirred. *"Why did you inactivate the defenses?"*

"This ungodly place must be cleansed with blood." Elon took one step farther down the chase. Another. "Humanish. Bornsect. Haárin. One godly event. The end of this unclean place."

Dathim stepped away from the array that sheltered him. Then he reached to his belt and slipped a blade from its sheath.

Elon's shoulders curved. "No blood here, Dathim." She unholstered her shooter and disengaged the safety in a single smooth motion. "You do not merit a godly death."

CHAPTER 30

Blood streamed from the wounds on Lucien's arms and dripped to the coated floor, smearing and streaking beneath his trainers. He panted as though he'd run kilometers. Sweat soaked his T-shirt and the upper portion of his trousers, flattened his hair, darkening it to yellow. He stood by the edge of the circle now, grabbing a few seconds' respite as he waited for Ghos to initiate the next round.

Ghos didn't look any better. He had settled down since the initial exchange, concentrating on the proper *à lérine* form, confining his cuts to Lucien's arms only. But the need to rein himself in hadn't tempered the fight in him. He moved like the snake he resembled, with no wasted motion, striking after one or two parries before backing away. Lucien had slowed him down by inflicting a deep gash to the outside of his right elbow that hampered his ability to grip his blade. It forced Ghos to switch the weapon to his left hand, but even in that circumstance, his skill and experience showed. For every cut Lucien had managed to inflict on him, he repaid with three.

Lucien's going to sport an impressive set of scars. Jani looked to the human side of the room. *I wonder how Appearances & Standards will fit that into the Officer's Guide.* The officers themselves had been swept up in the tension—

they stood, fists clenched, punching the air in silent applause each time Lucien landed a hit. Only Niall stood quietly, muttering occasional comments into his earbug mouthpiece as he monitored the proceedings.

A moment of stasis. Neither challenger breathed. Then Ghos hurtled forward, blade at waist level. Lucien struck it aside, then stepped in with a counterstrike of his own. But he'd had to reach across his body to parry Ghos's attack, and his blow had been weak—the Vynshàrau was able to bring his blade back in, delivering a gash to Lucien's upper thigh.

"Enough!" Jani walked the rim of the circle and considered breaking the plane even though it meant the challenge would end without declaration being made. "This isn't combat. There are no winners and losers. Declaration is made, and the fight ends. You have traded enough blows to declare."

"I have seen challenges that lasted day into night," Shai called out. "So have you, Kièrshia."

"Not when one of the combatants had something else on his mind." Jani pointed at Ghos, goading him by looking him in the eye. *"I know that which you are thinking,"* she said in High Vynshàrau.

Ghos's shoulders rounded as he cocked his head to the side. *"Do you, Kièrshia?"*

Jani looked at Lucien, who eyed her uncertainly. "The purpose of this exercise is to declare your hatred for one another. You've both made your point. Lay down your weapons. Declaration is—"

A sound echoed through the cavernous room, like a distant roll of thunder. Then came a shorter, sharper burst.

Jani looked across the room to Niall—the expression on his face mirrored her thought. *Oh hell—*

"Secure the doors!" Niall pulled out his shooter and jammed home the powerpack. "No one enters or leaves until further orders." He drove the point home by advancing on a gaggle of deputy ministers who tried to push toward the entry. It was anyone's guess what compelled them to return to their seats, the look on his face or the weapon in his hand.

"Ghos?" Shai struggled to her feet, the rest of the idomeni in her row following her lead. "What I hear now—these are our defenses?"

"No." Ghos bared his teeth and held up his sword. "These are our defenses, nìaRauta. Our godly blades. No other are required. Choose one, and fight the humanish as the gods intended."

Another blast. The Sìah chandeliers rattled. Screams and cries sounded.

"We must get to the armory." Tsecha bounded from his seat and across the room, skirting the edge of the circle before stopping at Niall's side. "It is three corridors over." He hesitated as he worked out the translation of directions. "Toward the lake, then left. There is armor there, short and long-range weaponry—"

"*Tsecha!*" Shai rose and started toward him, two of the security suborns falling in behind. "Silence!"

"We have no choice, Shai!" Tsecha's bowed shoulders stopped the security contingent in its tracks. "The attack Mako warned you of—it has started."

"This challenge is over." Niall stalked across the room to the blade rack. "Everyone with a weapon—a shooter, not a blade—over here. Burkett!" He pointed to the general, who stood and beckoned to a couple of subordinates. "You're handling the home team. Station them by the doors. Keep everyone back." He gestured toward the group of agitated civilians braced against the far wall. "After the away team pulls out, no one gets in without a password." He pointed to two Vynshàrau security and a Service major. "Make it 'crimson'—"

"Not a good word, Niall—the accents." Jani gestured to the three guards. "'Hana'! *The password is 'Hana'!*" she said once in English, then again in High Vynshàrau. "It's the Pathen dominant city—I doubt any of the Group knows it, and it's easy for everyone to say."

"Hana." Niall nodded. "All right, away team . . ."

While Niall culled the chosen few to storm the armory and hammered out the hallway layouts with Tsecha, Jani kept her eye on Ghos. He had lowered his sword, but he stood on the balls of his feet, ready to move in any direction, the tension radiating from him like scent.

"What have you done, Ghos?" Shai gestured for a pair of Haárin to guard him. "Where is Elon?"

"Dathim knew of the assault Mako told you of. He initiated his own check of embassy systems as a precaution, and did not receive the responses he expected." Jani monitored Ghos's reaction to her words, but saw only the tension. "He's down in the primary control chase evaluating the systems. I do not know if Elon has gone to him, but I sent Fa to check."

"He believes systems are compromised?" Shai's shoulders rounded. "Why did not he tell me this himself?"

"You must ask him such yourself, nìaRauta." Jani still watched Ghos. Their eyes locked once more, and the Vynshàrau's grip on his sword tightened.

"Pierce!" Burkett stepped away from his huddle with the ministers. "Service codes are blocked." He held up an earbug and shook it. "Are Vynshàrau communications blocked as well?" The gestures he received from some of Elon's suborns gave him the answer he needed. "We can't call out. So far, no one's called in."

"All right!" Niall backed away from Tsecha, who walked to the weapons rack and removed a knife and short sword to add to his shooter. "Away team." He waved for the mixed group of Service, Vynshàrau, and Haárin to follow as he headed for the door. "Let's go!"

As Jani headed for the door, she caught movement from the corner of her eye and turned to the circle. *"Lucien!"*

Ghos shook off the two Haárin as they grabbed for him—Lucien turned just as he closed in, blade raised. He brought up his own blade and pushed the Vynshàrau back, then moved in as Ghos swept his blade in a wide, backhand arc that left his body open. Lucien stepped in and plunged his blade into Ghos's abdomen, then tilted it up. Under the rib cage to the heart. Ghos slumped and fell into his arms as blood poured from his mouth, spread across his tunic. Lucien shook him off and let him fall to the floor.

Jani entered the circle and moved to Lucien's side.

"Instinct took over." He stepped closer to her, out of the path of Ghos's streaming blood.

"I know." Jani looked from the gore-drenched front of his T-shirt to his spattered face. "Given the shape you're in, you better stay here."

"How much trouble am I in?"

"I don't think that's our biggest problem right now." Jani took her shooter from beneath her tunic, then grabbed a short blade from the rack and rushed for the door.

Niall moved to block her before she could break through to the hall. "Give someone your shooter and stay put."

"I speak every language you've got here—you need me." Jani pushed past him to the Vynshàrau-Haárin contingent charged with leading them to the armory. Tsecha moved at the head of the group, coding into doors, then covering as his people secured the rooms.

"The old bird has teeth," Niall rasped as he shoved a serrated-edge blade into his belt. "Elon and Ghos lowered the building defenses, didn't they?" He swore under his breath when Jani nodded. "I hope humans can use whatever the hell they've got in that armory." A rumble sounded from behind, and he exhaled with a growl. "That's one exterior wall gone."

Micah blew through the gap in the outer wall that O'Shae had punched. *Where are the fuckin' screamers?* The boundary alarms, notifying the idomeni of the breach in their defenses. "Breach?" He laughed, acid searing his throat. "Fuckin' canyon!" He pounded up the hallway behind O'Shae as he had so many times, swinging his mid-range into place as she blew the first door. Pulled back on his charge-through, braced for the kick, and spun back on one heel as it smacked him. *"Ha-hah!"*

The chatter sounded in his ears, whoops and shouts of laughter from the rest of the Group as the reality of the moment drove home, backed by the incessant batter and rumble of disintegrating structure.

"Who's out there! Who's out there!" A lilting female voice, breathless with glee.

Micah slipstreamed behind O'Shae as she blew another door. "Patel!"

"Tiebold, is that you? This is for real! This is—"

A crazed flash shot across Micah's display. He unloaded into another room, then fell in behind O'Shae again. "Patel?" Not her signals going down, couldn't have been. The noise from the mid-range must have drowned her out. Must have. "Patel!" Must have. *"Patel!"*

O'Shae blew another door. Micah unloaded. Felt the recoil, but not as much. Stride made a difference. Stride, and how he set. He hadn't noticed that as much in the sims.

Patel?

They neared an open area—the first of the large meeting rooms.

"Let's go!" O'Shae blew through the double-wide panels like paper, then—

Micah's display blitzed as the floor shook. The walls. Plaster rained down as blue flame licked through the gap O'Shae had punched in the doors.

Micah braked, slamming against the wall in his effort to stop. His display came up—suit sensors, smelling . . . what did they smell? Burned—burned—

Stronger than in the sims. Did they realize? It was all stronger—the recoils, the emotions.

The display histogram of the stink of charred flesh.

"O'Shae?" No response, only a distant rumble, which grew louder.

Patel's words. Her last words.

This is for real.

"Where is everybody?" He raised his display, looking for signals.

Instead he got flashes. More than one. A dozen. More. Different signals. Live bodies, but not the Group's.

Micah upped his sensor. Heard the sound. The steady *whoosh whoosh* of exo legs pumping. Coming from behind.

He turned and looked down the hall.

Elon raised her shooter just as Dathim ducked back behind the array—

—and staggered forward as a blow shook the back of her head. Black fog closed in. She dropped to her knees, fell to her side, and turned behind her in time to see Fa, Dathim's suborn, lurch toward her, a length of sheathing in his hand.

"*Fa!* She is armed!" Dathim's voice. Hated English.

Elon propped her elbow against the floor, felt the cold through her overrobe, the black fog ebb and flow. Squeezed her hand. Fell back as the force of the shot shook through her.

"*Fa!*" Dathim's voice as an echo in a cave. The caves of Rauta Shèràa, that opened onto the sea. The sound of booted footsteps. First distant, then near her head.

Elon forced open her eyes. Saw an orb of gold amid the black that sharpened to a face. Dathim, daring to look her in the eye.

"Fa is dead," he said.

English. That hated sound. "Speak your own language, Dathim." She heard her voice, her beloved High Vynshàrau, rise and fall within the chamber of her skull.

"I am, Elon," Dathim replied in English as he placed a hand over her face.

Tsecha stood still as the armory array scanned his biometrics. Mechanics hissed and clicked, then the door opened.

Niall stood against the wall, monitoring the rumbles as he tried to raise a signal on his earbug. "Funny they didn't wipe him from the system when he made outcast."

"They did." Jani checked the view down the hall, then fell in line to enter the armory. "Dathim kept reloading him."

"I thought they wiped Dathim from the system."

"They tried."

"Good old Dathim." Niall tapped his mouthpiece with his thumb, then frowned. "The occasional hiss or part of a word, then nothing."

The armory contained all the equipment necessary to outfit embassy security and then some—Tsecha took charge of rooting through all the shelves and cabinets and doling out the minimum required gear. Armor. Helmets. Short-range shooters.

"There's a whole line of exos here," someone called out from the back.

"You cannot use them—they are not typed to humanish."

"Keep it simple, folks—body armor and small arms." Niall had already kitted out in upper body armor and leg shields. "If Dathim gets the pink flowing, all these pretty toys are so much ballast."

"I thought the idomeni had fine-tuned their latest pink so it didn't attack their systems." That came from another of the Service officers. "We won't mention that they shouldn't have it here in the first place."

"And we will not discuss the fact that humanish are exploding holes in my embassy!" Tsecha shoved a helmet under the man's nose. As if in counterpoint, more bursts and rumbles sounded in the distance.

Jani fastened her armor, then added another shooter to her weapon belt. She felt as she did when her augmentation functioned—dry hands, slow heartbeat. Only the undercurrent of anger seemed as different. A desire to break and shatter that she had never known before. *Control yourself, Kilian.*

"Work in teams of three." Niall donned his helmet, faceplate up. "Clear rooms, keep pushing out. You run into something you can't handle, fall back fast. Keep your comlines open—when the works come back on, I want to know where you are." He lowered his faceplate. "Let's go."

"Oh boy, we're having fun now," someone said as they streamed back into the hall.

Pinlights through the dust and smoke. Red needle eyes. Growing bigger. Bigger.

Whoosh whoosh.

Micah looked ahead of him, toward the hole O'Shae disappeared through. Noise came from there as well. Thuds. Crackles.

"Which way?" He didn't realize he'd spoken until his display fired up. Hallways, marked and mapped. The one he stood in now, capped at both ends by moving blobs converging on him.

Whoosh whoosh.

"Shit!" Micah pushed off the wall. Headed for O'Shae's last hole. "There's an offshoot hallway here." Didn't know where it led. Not a dead end—all he cared about. *Move!* He swung down his mid-range and barreled ahead. Fired.

Smoke. A waist-level cloud. Sense display—chemical fire. Toxic. Filters working.

Micah held to the wall, edged forward, hit something with the tip of his boot. Waved smoke away. Looked down.

O'Shae. Part of her, anyway.

"What the hell hit her?" Micah kept moving. Not like the sims—no Vynshàrau, pieces of bodies out of nowhere and *whoosh whoosh* getting louder and louder from behind—

—walls shook. Floor. Blast. Blitzed display.

Micah ran, bouncing off walls as the exo took him farther than the hallway allowed. His mid-range swung like a crazy third arm, jerking up then down, banging the walls, whacking the side of his helmet.

He broke around a corner. Fresh hallway. No smoke, no shatter, no bodies. "Display." He pulled up the hallway, saw the blinking close from all around.

Micah ran as new sounds converged from all directions. High-pitched whines. The unmistakable static crack of shooters.

He ran faster, careened around a corner, bounced off walls like a bead in a box, pushing straight on as a hiss filled his ears and a—

—sea of pink flooded around him. Found openings he shouldn't have had and poured into his exo, like feathered silk against his skin. Shot down his arms and legs, rattling them until they shook like seizure.

"What the fu—" Ragged chirps stung Micah's ears as his sensors went mad, flashes of red and blue zinging before his eyes. The pink—mist—gas—*what!*—flowed around his face. He inhaled, tasted it sweet in the back of his throat—

"Aghhhh!"

—then dragged himself into the shelter of a doorway as something huge and dark spun like a dervish down the center of the hall. The sleek lines of the V-790, encasing a thing gone mad, loose mid-range swinging back and forth, flashes of white light bursting through the joints of the exo.

Then came . . . the scream. Low at first, then thinning and rising in pitch like a siren as the flares grew brighter and brighter and thick strands of grey smoke emerged from the exo and intertwined with the pink.

Micah held his breath and watched as the jerking and twisting slowed, the wail ceased. Then the exo turned, a graceful heel-toe spin, arms floating away from its sides, weaving like a dancer's, shreds of pink mist streaming from gaps in the exo and dancing around its hands.

The mid-range ceased its yardarm swing, its standby hum ramping in pitch.

"Oh shit." Micah bolted down the hall in the direction opposite the singing exo. Cooked like a spud in its skin. Whoever they were. He choked back a laugh that veered to a sob and kept running, legs pumping in an exo that didn't want to go where he told it, its joints stiffening, whiffs of that fucking weird mist puffing out of the gaps with every stride.

Dove around a corner into another hall as the heavy whine hit its peak. Tripped over his boots. Somersaulted and spun to a stop against a wall and prayed he'd run far enough—

—and buried his face in his arms just as the explosion ripped. Saw the flash through the pink-eaten gaps in his exo sleeves. Felt the rumble through the floor, the walls, heard the crash of the ceiling as it collapsed.

He looked up as the sound died away, in time to see the last whispers of pink mist flame to blue and vanish. Fragments of ceiling fell atop him. Cracked, buckled wall bowed over him.

Micah stared out at the clear quiet. Then he scooted to his knees and tore at his exo, battling jammed fasteners and tremoring limbs. Unlatched his helmet and flung it away. Tore at the coverall, the boots. Safety joints came apart in his hands—he tossed piece after piece of his suit after the helmet, as far as he could, trying to decoy the last wisps of pink fog that dogged every move of his hands and flurried before his eyes like dust devils.

He checked every flap and fold of his T-shirt, his pull-on trousers. Worked to his feet, testing his every move. "Not gonna take me over—not—no—no—no—" He danced in place, kicked out, did a jumping jack, his overhand clap ringing through the still air.

"All me." He ran down the hall, turned and headed in the direction opposite the dervish's scant remains. Found himself in a hallway still flooded with pink, held his breath as he cut through it, thought *Hell with it* and breathed, then hugged the wall as another rumbling blast sounded.

"Oh—God." Who had cooked in their suit this time? Who? "Manda?" He ran, the layout of the embassy unfurling in his head.

CHAPTER 31

"Hey hey!" Niall gave Jani a thumbs-up sign. "Pull, talk to me!"

Jani smiled as Pullman's dry tones filled her helmet.

"—embassy systems coming up in fits and starts." A pause. Thumps and whines in the background. "Still piecing together what happened. Damned Exterior missed 'em coming in, apparently, and then they blew right through the embassy shields."

"That's because the embassy shields weren't up." Niall's helmet moved in a slow headshake.

"Well, that explains that." More thumps. "We're pulling out bodies. Fifteen in V-790s, so far. Give or take. Hartman's crew is clearing out the south wing. Some of Vynshàrau security were holed up in a meeting room there—bunch of them took it when the roof came down."

Jani glanced to her right, where the third member of their team, a Vynshàrau security suborn named Pashé, stood straight as a statue against the wall.

"Bessard's gang has the west and the outbuildings," Pullman continued. "They're reporting all clear. Jamil's crew has north and east. I don't hear a thing but she's not happy and they're going through again to make sure. She doesn't

like that we don't know how many of these people we're
dealing with. Any ideas?"

"No." Niall sighed. "Burkett's holding down the challenge room—I've got a team pushing out from there right
now. Nothing so far but empty rooms."

A pause. "Jamil just called in, sir. They're at the challenge
room. Some Haárin won't let them in without the password."

"I'll go." Jani headed back down the hall. "The sooner we
get them out of there, the better."

"We'll all go back." Niall fell in behind Jani. "Pull, I'm
calling my team back to the challenge room—I want Jamil's
crew to take over."

"Yes, sir. We've got a few Vynshàrau out here now—they
said that once they get their systems back up, we'll be able
to run a heat scan and nail down the stragglers." More
thumps, then a muttered "damn." "Sir, the PM's holed up in
the Exterior Annex. She wants a report."

"Tell her to put on a goddamned headset!" Niall quickened his pace. "This place is not yet nailed down."

"No, sir."

"Damn it." Niall moved ahead of Jani and around the corner. "Ministers . . ."

Jani slowed, then looked back to find Pashé still standing
in place. "NìaRauta?" She moved back toward her. *"We are
going back,"* she said in High Vynshàrau. *"Others will take
over."*

"Speak your own language," Pashé replied in English.
Then she turned and started walking in the direction opposite, vanishing around a corner in a few long strides.

"Shit!" Jani took one last look in the direction Niall had
gone, then hurried after the Vynshàrau. "Can't have gone
far—" She rounded the corner and found the female getting
ready to boost over a pile of rubble that blocked an entry to
another wing. *"NìaRauta! We are going back!"*

"You go back! Humanish!" Pashé flipped up her faceplate—she shared Ghos's stark, snakelike features, and radi-
ated the same tension he had. "Not even humanish. Worse.

You go back. Back, and farther back. This is a Vynshàrau place!" She raised her shooter over her head, then set her free hand on the pile of rubble and clambered over the top.

"NìaRauta!" Jani sprinted down the hall toward the blocked entry. "Hate me later—we have to move now!" She boosted atop the rubble and tried to see into the semidarkness beyond. Cracked and buckled walls. Shattered columns. The flow from ruptured plumbing dripped from ceilings, pooled in corners. She strained to discern any movement, but saw only half-dark and shadows, heard only the drip and trickle of running water.

Then a sound reached her. A sharp intake of breath on the cusp of a cry.

She strained to hear more, heard nothing but water, and with a swallowed curse clambered over the rubble pile to the other side.

The air on the closed side of the barrier already felt chilled compared to that on the side that had been secured, its former warmth victim to disrupted air handling and the initial impacts that had broken through from the outside. "Pashé?" Jani reached the end of the hallway and debated her next move. "Right? Left?" She looked down the quiet, broken passages, back over her shoulder to the comparative comfort of the rubble boundary, then started down the corridor. Shooter in hand, creeping with her back to the wall.

First room. The safety illumins in the walls had lighted, revealing a sparse arrangement of soaked furniture and nothing else. *Second room.* Across the corridor. A tricky L-shaped entry with shadows in all the wrong places.

"Hell with this." Jani backed away to return to the safe side, and caught sight of the mound of darkness in the corner of the room. She ducked inside, shooter at the ready, and found Pashé.

Jani knelt beside the Vynshàrau. Cracked the faceplate of her helmet, and caught a whiff of the choking stench of burned flesh. Turned her over, and saw what was left of her face.

The hissing started then, from points along the ceiling. The slow billow of pink. The candy cloud, tumbling through the room.

"Oh, hell!" Jani straightened, turned, pushed through the thickening rose fog toward the door. Lifted her head in time to see a darker form appear in the doorway, blocking her.

An older woman. Broad-shouldered and muscular with a Service burr. Burned face and arms, charred to black in places. One ear was gone. She strode forward, shooter at the ready. She didn't speak—her eyes said it all.

Jani raised her shooter, made to fire, then felt the room shift as her left knee buckled, animandroid muscles cramping. The woman fired at where she had been, the shot grazing her helmet. The display flared in multicolor chaos, then blanked.

Jani tried to boost to her feet, to see what had tripped her even as she kept her eyes on the woman. *I don't see anything . . .* The pink continued its slow-motion tumble throughout the room. She inhaled through her mouth and felt its sweet taste on her lips. She tried once more to rise, almost straightened, tried to sight down once more through the fog—

—and fell again, left leg cramping, the pain like fire, left arm tremoring. Tried to sight down once more. Fired. Saw her shot go wide as both left siders spasmed at once.

"Having a problem?" The woman lowered her shooter and stepped closer. "Whatever you are." She kicked out, caught Jani's shooter with her booted foot, sent it flying.

Damn! Jani tried to tuck and roll as she reached for the blade in her weapon belt, but her left side fought her every move.

The woman tossed her shooter aside and fell on Jani, left hand gripping her right wrist and holding her blade back as she pushed up the faceplate of her helmet.

"Do my eyes deceive me?" She crimped Jani's right wrist until the pain sang, plucked the knife from her grasp.

Jani smelled the woman's scorched flesh as a blistered smile filled her field of vision.

"Cat eyes." The woman held her knife so the point dangled above Jani's left eye. "Mutant eyes." Her voice came thick, smoke-damaged and raw. "Glass eyes—watch them shatter."

Jani tried to will her left limbs steady. Felt them twitch instead, refuse to respond. "You have the look of a sergeant about you. I'll bet you were involved in the training." She watched the woman's smile freeze. "They told you they'd get you out, didn't they? They lied."

The smile vanished. The knife dangled.

Micah edged out of the blasted room, strained for any sound. He thought he'd heard the *whoosh whoosh* of exos again, but the noise had come from reactivated airflow pushing its way through a crumpled outlet grating.

"Walkin' in Jesus' footsteps." This part of the embassy had been hit the hardest—Micah stepped over rubble, fallen sections of wall, pieces of furniture. Splashed through the flooding caused by damaged pipes. He'd found an idomeni clock in one of the blown rooms and tried to figure out how long he'd been inside the embassy, but he couldn't make heads or tails of the display and smashed it as the anger took him.

Walkin' . . . one, two, three. . . . Counting his steps.

"Fifteen minutes? Twenty?" Had it been that long since he'd sent the lakespray flying? Felt that first gorgeous recoil of his mid-range?

He turned the corner, pausing first to look around and check if anyone was in the hall. He hadn't seen anyone for a time, but that didn't mean they weren't there. He heard them through the walls, with their whines, hisses, tremors. They'd find him eventually, since no one had taught him how to get out. It was like Pascal said, damn him.

Walkin'. . . . Four . . . five . . . six. . . .

He walked past one empty, blasted room. Another. Then he heard voices as he neared the third, and his step slowed.

"They promised they'd take care of you." Jani tried to will her limbs calm. The pink had dissipated, and she sensed that the twitching had lessened. The spasms. "Train these nonessentials, give them just enough skill to be dangerous, but not enough to do the job right. We don't want to make it look like the real Service wants the idomeni out, after all. But an offshoot? A submerged couple of percent? We can explain that away to Cabinet Row. Not our fault. Nothing we could control."

The knife shook. "Filth. You should have died years ago."

I did, in theory. Jani tried to bend her leg, jam her right knee into the woman's side. But she couldn't find the leverage, and the woman's body weighted her like stone. "You may as well talk, because they aren't going to help you. They'll probably kill you, in fact, when they find out you lived through the assault."

The woman's eyes were small, mud brown, bright as if with fever. They clouded momentarily, as though she actually heard what Jani told her. But it didn't last. She hadn't come to the embassy to talk.

She raised the knife and her upper body at the same time. Pushed off Jani's helmet, then grabbed a fistful of hair and forced her head still.

"'Night, kitty." The woman's smile widened as she brought her blade up.

Jani felt her left arm still for just long enough. Curled her fingers and brought up the heel of her hand, jamming it against the woman's chin, pushing her head back, pushing, pushing. The woman struck, the blade came down—once—twice—hitting Jani's left wrist, slipping between skin and the edge of armor. Pink carrier spattered—the more that flowed, the more the arm steadied.

Jani kept pushing up, until she felt the weight atop her ease. Brought up her right leg, then kicked out, pushing the woman off. *"Niall!"* She tried to roll over to her hands and knees, tried to stand, but her animandroid limbs still betrayed. They trembled as she put weight on them. Buckled. She fell back to the floor, made slick with rose-pink carrier.

The woman careened backwards, then rolled into a

crouch like a cat. She still held the blade. "No one can hear you." She tensed as she made to spring.

"Walkin' in Jesus' footsteps."

They both stilled, and looked to the entry.

"That's what you said." A young man walked into the room. He wore base casuals, sweat-stained and torn, and held the woman's discarded shooter in a loose grip.

Jani fixed on the pointed, pale face. *I've seen him before.* The lance from the bunker, whose coat she'd worn. Faber.

"That's what you said, Sergeant." Faber's voice came quiet, like he spoke to a child. "You trained us and drilled us and told us how special we were, and every time we stormed the embassy in the sims, you said the same thing. Walkin'." His eyes, in contrast to his voice, looked stone-carved. There was a disconnect between how he looked and sounded, what he said and the way he said it. "Well, where is he?"

The woman's breathing had gone shaky, as though she tried to hoist a weight that was too heavy for her. She held out a hand to Faber. "At ease, Tiebold. Stand down."

"That's not my name," Faber responded, "just like Chrivet isn't yours." He raised the shooter, and sighted down. *"Where is he?"*

"I said—" The woman's voice stopped in her throat as the shooter crack sounded. The impact knocked her backwards, sending her sprawling, her limbs jerking as the pulse packet dissipated throughout her body.

"Lance Corporal." Jani had worked into a sitting position, left limbs still twitching. "Stand down."

Faber paused to look at her. Then he turned back to Chrivet, and sighted down once more.

"Drop the shooter, then raise your arms. Above your head. Slowly." Niall entered, shooter fixed on Faber. *"Now!"* The young man slowly lowered the weapon—Niall stepped forward and plucked it from his grasp. *"Pull! Get the hell in here!"* He powered down the shooter and holstered it, then flipped up his faceplate and looked to Jani. "You're bleeding."

"It's just carrier—I'm all right." Jani watched Faber, who

still stood in front of Chrivet's body, his eyes fixed on nothing.

Pullman blew in, followed by a mixed bag of human and idomeni equipped with scanners and gurneys. Niall stepped out of the way of a pair of humanish medics who headed toward Chrivet, and came to a halt next to Faber. "Pull, this is Lance Corporal Micah Faber. It was his late buddy made mincemeat out your left kidney."

"Is that a fact, sir?" Pullman flipped up his faceplate. "I'll bear that in mind." He closed in behind Faber, yanking back his arms and binding his wrists with restraints he'd pulled from his weapons belt.

"All right." Niall walked to Jani's side, and crouched down. "What happened?"

Jani raised her shaky left hand. "The pink blitzed my animandroid limbs—"

"*Before that.*" Niall reached down and detached the armor plate that covered her left forearm, then examined her wound. "I order you back to the challenge room, look around two seconds later and find you gone."

Jani jerked her chin toward the place where two physician-priests administered to Pashé's corpse. "She was on our team. When you ordered us to pull back, she didn't want to go. She didn't want anything to do with humanish."

"So you went after her?" Niall dragged off his helmet, revealing sweat-flattened hair and a reddened groove across his forehead where the stabilizer band had rested. "You want to play on my team, you follow my rules. Stick that in your documents case for future reference." He straightened, then turned back to Pull. "Get him out of here," he said, pointing at Faber.

Pullman took Faber by the elbow and steered him toward the entry, only to stop as they reached the door. "Sir."

Jani looked up in time to see Lucien walk in. He still wore the slashed and bloody casuals from his challenge, to which he'd added a stripped-down assortment of body armor and a packed weapons holster. He looked around the room, gaze fixing first on the two teams of medics before coming to rest on Jani. "You're hurt?"

Jani shook her head. "The pink took out my left side."

Niall grimaced. "I told you to report to Medical, Pascal."

"I'm afraid you were superceded, sir." Lucien approached Faber, a change coming over him as he drew close to the young man. His voice lightened. He even managed a smile. "Good morning, Lance Corporal."

"Good morning, sir." Faber drew up straight, his shoulders working as though he tried to salute. "You were right. You said they didn't show us how to get out. You were right." He fell silent. "You said—" His expression lightened again. It did so only when he spoke, fading to blankness as he quieted. "You said that anytime I wanted to talk, I'd be able to find you."

Lucien moved in front of him. Someone had wrapped his *à lérine* wounds in light gauze through which the blood had managed to seep. "Yes, Faber. You are correct."

"You're not—" Faber hesitated. "You're not the Jesus Sergeant Chrivet told us about."

Niall emitted a harsh laugh. "Not even close, boyo."

Faber looked down at the floor. "Maybe . . ." This time when he spoke, his face remained blank. "Maybe you're the only one I get."

Lucien looked to Niall—the two men fought a stare-down until Niall gave in with a grumble and a sharp nod. Lucien motioned for Pullman to back away, then took his place at Faber's side. "Let's go, Micah. Anything you want to talk about, I'm ready to listen." He ushered the young man into the hallway, Pullman bringing up the rear. Then the medics departed, gurneys in tow—first the humanish, then the Vynshàrau, leaving Jani and Niall alone.

"Let's get you out of here." Niall dragged a gurney over to Jani, shaking his head as he stepped into a wet patch of carrier. "Now I know for a fact that both John and Val have been after you for months to trade in those half-mechanical limbs of yours for full-tissue replacements, but you always put them off." He glared down at her. "This is what you get for sticking with outdated technology."

Jani felt the anger rise, then bit back her retort when she caught the light flash in Niall's eyes. She smiled—he grinned back. Then the laughter took them both, and wouldn't let go.

"*Niall.*" Jani finally gasped, her stomach aching. "They're going to come in here and see the blood and us laughing and lock us both up."

Niall wiped his eyes with the back of his hand. "They tried that. More than once. Never worked, did it? Never did, and never will." He straightened slowly. "We're immune in that regard."

Jani held her good hand out to him. "Please get me out of here."

"As my Captain wishes." Niall bent to her, positioning himself so she could drape her right arm around his neck for balance, and lifted her up.

"Bird bones." He lay her atop the gurney like and infant, then escorted her out of the room.

CHAPTER 32

Jani sat silent as Niall drove them past the shattered midsection of the embassy. He'd seconded a wheeled scoot from one of the damage survey teams, but could only approach within a few meters before the shrub-strewn rubble that had been the walled garden made further exploration impossible.

"They came in off the lake, sheathed to the gills thanks to the latest masking technology, and punched through here." He pointed to the gaping hole where there'd once been a set of triple-width doors. "Exterior scan picked up something big coursing over the water's surface, but before they could analyze the image, it vanished. They chalked it up to an artifact. Morons." He shook his head, then glanced at Jani. "You feeling better?"

"Fine." She forced a smile.

"Fine." Niall reversed the scoot, jerking it into a tight turn. They rumbled over the churned-up lawns and past the smoking outbuildings into the stretch of wilderness that marked the boundary between the idomeni and Exterior lands.

As soon as they passed through the eyescan and were cleared to cross the border into humanish territory, Niall reached into his shirt pocket and pulled out his nicstick case. He shook out a 'stick and with careful one-handed maneu-

vering bit the bulbed ignition tip, then turned it around, leaning forward so he could put it in his mouth.

He steered across the Exterior lawns and rimmed the edge
of the main charge-lot, on the lookout for an empty space
amid the triple-lengths of a dozen ministries. "They're all inside," he said. "Cao, every other minister on the block, Shai,
Mako."

"Tsecha?" Jani had been on the lookout for her old
teacher since Niall floated her out of the blasted office, but
she hadn't seen him anywhere.

"They dragged him over first of all," Niall said through a
haze of smoke. "Some of the ministers would still rather
deal with him than Shai, especially under the circumstances,
and don't think that didn't go over like a lead balloon."

They trundled around the ministry building to the lakeside enclosed terrace, which, judging from the various
medblanket-covered shapes that filled the area, had been
designated the temporary morgue. As they drew close, Jani
caught sight of Val sitting on the terrace outer railing, head
hanging, hands braced in his knees. He glanced up when he
heard their approach, but he didn't smile.

"Doctor Parini." Niall braked to a stop. "So far . . . ?"

"Forty-four dead. Ten Vynshàrau, the rest humanish." Val
jerked his chin toward Niall's nicstick. "Can you spare one
of those?" Niall tossed him the case; he shook out a stick and
ignited it, then drew on it as though it was his last breath.

Jani watched her friend raise the 'stick to his lips. Did his
hand shake or was it simply a trick of the breeze? "When
was the last time you smoked?"

"The last time I saw something like this." Val glanced at
Niall. "Inform your weapons designers, Colonel, that the V-
790 leaves something to be desired. After we cracked the
third charred corpse out of the remains of their smoking exo,
we christened it the 'Lobster.'" He took another drag. "I'll
be fine, it's just been a while is all." He looked at Jani again,
and something of the old kindness returned to his face.
"How are you?"

"The new-gen pink took out my left side." Jani raised her shaking left hand. "Walking is quite the adventure."

"New limbs coming up. As soon as I see whether they need me anymore here." Val stood. "Vehicles . . . ?"

"You can't get into the embassy lot." Niall struggled out of the scoot's tight cabin. "Stake out a spot here, and I'll find you something."

As he strode off, Val walked to the scoot and inserted himself as replacement driver. "I never imagined this." He took a last pull on the 'stick, then tossed it. "Not in a hundred years could I have."

"Not even after that last night in Rauta Shèràa?" Jani watched two orderlies bear another blanketed form onto the terrace. "The Night of the Blade?" She studied her hands, then flexed her fingers, the steady and the trembling. She looked toward the lake and imagined a line of exo-clad forms coursing toward her over the chop, a pale, pointed face among them. Walking. Walking.

Jani and Val arrived at Neoclona Chicago to find the level of tension ramped to warning levels. Jani sensed the looks that followed her as they navigated the hospital halls. Some held curiosity, others concern. But there were enough hostile glares scattered about to drive the two of them to use the stairs instead of lifts when possible, and to avoid telling anyone where they went. They arrived at Orthopedics to find a pair of doctors standing by. Val dismissed them and switched out Jani's animandroid limbs himself, running through the post-installation examination in record time. They then departed the hospital by a different, circuitous route.

"Think the lid will stay on for a week?" Val steered his Service loaner out of the underground garage and blended into the evening traffic.

"I think I'm glad my parents aren't here to see this." Jani saw a group of people standing around a storefront, watching a holoVee display. As the skimmer passed, she could see what they watched—the sweep of the embassy grounds, the shattered main building, the gurneys laden with blanketed mounds that it seemed couldn't possibly be entire bodies but were.

"The idomeni are going to leave." Val edged around a disabled skimmer and drove on. "My prediction. Their embassy is a shambles—they can't stay there. The Haárin are no longer safe at the enclave. Cèel wants them back in the worldskein, so back in the worldskein they will go."

"Except for Tsecha," Jani said, "And the other Haárin. They're going to Elyas."

"How the hell are you going to swing that?" Val slowed as they approached his apartment building, then floated down the ramp to the parking garage. "I remember Cèel—I dealt with him often enough. He was bad enough when he was younger, and by all accounts he's gotten worse." As he approached his private bay, he stiffened, then struck the steering mech with the flat of his hand. "I'll be—"

Jani followed his gaze and felt her own flavor of wonderment when she saw Lucien sitting atop a skimmer charge station console, his duffel on the floor beside him. "I've been ordered to remain under medical supervision, so I thought . . . ?" He tried to shrug, but injury forced him to settle for a borderline flinch. "I'll leave, if you want me to."

Jani felt Val's stare, willing her to look in his direction. "Of course you can stay." She heard him sigh, and pretended she didn't.

"Sheridan's a war zone." Lucien broke eggs into a bowl, then whisked in various spices. "I had to get the hell out. Medical put me on two weeks' leave, so I thought, why not decamp to someplace sane?"

Val sat up and craned his neck as he tried to see what Lucien mixed. "Omelets again?"

"Crepes." Lucien smiled. "There are plenty of fillers in your cooler—fresh fruit, whipping cream, mushrooms. Your kitchen's much better stocked than Jani's."

"You're too cruel." Jani took a lemon slice from a garni plate and bit one end. "You mentioned a war zone?"

Lucien nodded as he ladled batter onto a flat pan. "The wafer Veles lifted from Micah Faber contained a lot more than the training scenarios. There was some background coding that revealed where some of the scenarios were constructed. The first round of arrests took place about three hours ago."

What timing. Jani chewed the lemon slice to the rind. "What happened to Veles?"

Lucien hesitated. "He's dead. They found his body in the garage of Faber's building. A professional kill—Faber wasn't capable. Someone simply wanted to make sure that he got to his outfit."

Val sat back and crossed his arms. "Now, I'm no expert in these sorts of assaults—I've only lived through a few. But the question that occurs is, why? I'm trying to follow all the convolutions, and I just don't get it."

Jani cradled her chin in her hand and regarded him solemnly. "I'm more cynical than you are—correct?" She waited until he shrugged agreement. "Assume the Service wants the idomeni out, even the factions that claim to want to get along. Now look at what happened today." She held up her hand, index finger extended, and earned a matching response from Val. "One, the idomeni will be off Earth within the month, at the latest." Second finger. "Two, the Service learned more about Vynshàrau weapons systems and building defenses in the space of a couple of hours than they could have in months or years of hunt and peck spying." She glanced at Lucien, who had the sense to keep his eyes on his crepe pan, then extended her ring finger. "Three, they've tested a prototype exo in the field against the enemy that they designed it for, and found it wanting. Is that enough, or do you need more?"

Val exhaled with a shudder. "Quite a few people died, some horribly."

Jani studied the plate of mushroom crepes Lucien set before her, and reached for the spice dispenser. "Quite a few of them hated beings like me. They would have to a person cheerfully cut my throat given half a chance." Food aromas filled her nose—she swallowed hard as her throat tightened. "Any man's death diminishes me . . . but be that as it may."

"Micah Faber didn't hurt you." Lucien reached across the table to set out Val's plate—the long sleeve of his pullover rode up his arm, revealing a fresh gauze dressing. "He had more than half a chance, too."

"I think he hated Chrivet more than he hated me. She lied to him." Jani picked up a knife to slice her crepes, then set it down with a clatter as the room light flashed off the glinting point. "Where is he now?"

"Neuro Isolation." Lucien sat down at the table. Up close, the strain of the day showed in his drawn face and ashen skin. "Under guard. He's the only survivor who could do some talking anytime soon."

Jani tried to pick up the knife again, then set it aside for good and settled for slicing her food with the side of her fork. "What are they worried about more, suicide or murder?"

Before Lucien could respond, the kitchen door swung aside. One of Val's admins entered carrying a documents pouch in Neoclona's trademark purple. Val took the packet with a shaky hand, taking a deep breath before opening the flap. "Misty." He pulled a small wafer folder out of the bag. "From John." He flipped open the cover and removed the silvery disc. "Clean up first. I'll be waiting in the view room."

Jani showered and dressed in some of Val's castoffs, a sweater and pull-on trousers in his favorite dark green. She met Lucien by the kitchen, and together they adjourned to Val's viewing room, a plush alcove furnished with lounge seats and a portable bar. Jani sat next to Val, while Lucien hedged his bets by choosing a seat in the row behind theirs that was staggered directly between them. Val, she noted, had availed himself of the bar's contents—a half-filled tumbler of something clear and frosty sat at his elbow.

"And so we begin." Val raised his glass to the display, then fingered the control pad set in his chair arm.

The room darkened, the display lightening in turn. The Neoclona *N* unfurled across the panel, followed by a security warning. Then an emptiness, followed by a face.

"*John.*" Val sank back in his seat. "Oh God."

Lucien just stared.

Jani felt her heart catch, and smiled.

John sat at a desk, most likely his office at Neoclona Karistos, judging from the security flags that continued to scroll along the bottom of the display. He'd forsaken medwhites for a dark blue shirt, to which he'd added a gold and blue length of cloth looped and draped like a scarf.

Almost two months had passed since he'd begun the hybridization process. His skin, once milk tinged with blue, had darkened to the cream-gold of the palest Oà. His eyes, once pink, had changed to dull silver centered with clear grey.

"Hello, Val. I'm guessing words are a waste at this point, aren't they?" His voice rumbled as ever, changes in inflection and phrasing not yet apparent. "Before you fall on anyone here, the first they knew of it was when I walked through the entry ten minutes ago. They seemed . . . shocked, but not altogether surprised. This is Karistos, after all. They look at things differently here."

Jani savored the sight and sound of him, and wondered at the touch. His hair was now the same palest wheat shade as his skin. Did it still feel like silk? Would she have been able to feel it at all, considering that he had cut it into a Service burr so sheared as to make Niall's short back and sides appear mussed?

"I know." John passed a hand over his scalp, as if he had predicted her response. "Too damned short, and I'm too tall for it. So help me, from a distance, I look like a pin. But when it started growing out . . . the half-white just looked too strange. So I let Brondt go at it with the clippers. I told him this wasn't the second day of Boot Camp, but as soon as the first few hairs hit the floor, he became a man possessed. Or should I say 'hybrid possessed'?" He tilted his head to the side. "Brondt. Right. You don't know who he is." His eyes softened, from metal to the underside of a cloud. "Is Jani there? She can explain it to you. The short form is that he's her suborn. He's managing the place while she's away." A smile teased a corner of his mouth, brightened his argent eyes. "I'm the staff physician of the Thalassan enclave. Physician-priest, really—I've been undergoing some training. It's a new universe, Val. A life so different I could never have imagined it. Part of me thinks I should have taken the plunge years ago. But then again, perhaps it was better that I waited until now."

Jani glanced to the side to find that Val had drained his glass and now stared at the display over the rim.

"I'll be staying here. For a while, at any rate." John continued to talk easily, as though he sat across the desk from them instead of five GateWays distant. "I've gone over matters with our legal team here—they're sending the usual stuff and nonsense your way. I've also sent along another Misty that's more official. I'm afraid you're stuck on Earth as long as both Eamon and I remain here. Eamon would like to flee immediately, frankly, but he's too afraid of you to risk returning to Chicago even though he misses the place. He's still in, by the way. I've explained it in the other Misty." He rested his elbow atop the desk and propped his chin atop his fist. "I don't miss Earth at all—isn't that odd? I thought Seattle might be calling my name by now, but I haven't heard a thing. Not even a whisper." He looked into the display. "I miss you, though, old friend. The decent thing would have been to tell you in person, but I couldn't leave, and . . . I thought if you saw me before I was too far along, you might try to talk me out of it." He hung his head. "Perhaps that was a mistake."

Then his head came up. "Is Jani there? Tell her that I miss her. In ways I can't begin to express." His look grew weighty. "And in ways I can express quite well. Tell her I love her." He sighed. "So long, Val. We will talk in person, as soon as we can." The image stilled, then faded. The display darkened.

Val remained motionless, even as the lights came up, fingers laced around the empty glass. "He loves you," he said finally, setting the glass down with a clatter, then boosting to his feet and leaving the room.

Jani found Val in a chair by the window, his head in his hands. He looked up when he heard her approach. His cheeks were flushed, either from alcohol or because he fought back anger, or maybe a combination of both.

"Why didn't you tell me?" His voice emerged rough, as though his throat ached. "You knew. You knew!"

Jani walked to the window. "I believed that it should come from him. You two have been friends for so long . . . I thought he'd tell you in the way he felt best." Out of seeming nowhere, rain had come. Drops spattered the window, then tracked downward like tears. "If it helps at all, he didn't tell me, either. Not until after he'd started. He wanted to surprise me. Boy, did he ever."

A trace of a smile crossed Val's face. "How did Eamon take it?"

"Outraged that John had lowered himself to research subject. Scared, in case someone decided to arrest him. The usual Eamonesque self-interest."

"I hate to break this to you, but I can see his point." Val scrubbed a hand through his hair and sat up. "Once this news gets out, Neoclona is going to quake to its core."

"Don't you think you're exaggerating a little?"

"Do you think Earth's ready for a human-idomeni hybrid heading up the largest single business entity in the Commonwealth? Especially after what happened today?" Val stood and started to pace. "It's going to take every arm I can twist to keep Li Cao and friends from stripping John of everything he owns." His pace quickened. "He's already talked to the lawyers, which means they're working on it, I

hope. Not that it will matter much when your anti-idomeni
friends start bombing our facilities." He stopped in front of
Jani, his face set with a sternness that wasn't entirely an act.
"You do like to complicate a man's life, don't you?" He
reached out and touched her arm. "Then there's the fact . . ."
He raised his hand to the line of her jaw. "Not to sound like
a whiner, but do you have any idea how lonely I feel right
now?"

Jani looked into Val's hazel eyes, glassy with pent-up an-
guish. She reached for him and pulled him close—he held
her as though she was the last person he would ever embrace, and released her reluctantly.

"When do you think you'll be leaving?" he asked.

Jani shook her head. "Depending on when I get in to see
Shai and Cao, sometime in the next few days. Assuming I'm
not arrested or shot in the street by then."

Val turned away from her, staking out his own place at the
window. "Back in Rauta Shèràa, John used to refer to the
two of you as Pygmalion and Galatea. The sculptor who
carved a woman so beautiful he begged the gods to give her
life. In the official story they answer his prayers. One day,
she steps down from the pedestal into his arms." He turned
to her. "You've given the story a new ending. In this one,
Galatea lifts up Pygmalion to join her." His eyes widened.
"And how the gods will react, one cannot begin to imagine."

Jani left Val in the sitting room and set out to find a spot in
the vast penthouse where she could find refuge, at least for a
little while. After a search, she came upon a small bedroom
decorated in the same blues and corals as her room in Thalassa. She hunted through drawers until she found a sheet of
parchment and a stylus. Then she sat at the narrow desk and
composed a letter to Prime Minister Cao. *I am not political . . . unless I have to be.* She affixed her signature to the
bottom, tucked the missive into a documents pouch, then
summoned one of Val's admins and asked them to deliver it.
That task completed, she walked to the narrow window, took

in the view of the rainswept lake, and tried to imagine bare rock cliffs, the palms, and the sun.

"You're really leaving?"

Jani turned to find Lucien standing in the doorway, looked into a face drawn with pain and exhaustion, eyes deadened by a devil's marriage of nature and technology. "I prefer to call it, 'going home.'"

"What about me?" He stepped inside far enough for the door to sweep closed. "If you leave, what happens?"

"At the rate you're going, you may find yourself with a place here, if only as a cook." Jani set her hand on the sill. The wood was coated white, a blued shade that brought out the yellow in her skin by contrast. "We both knew it would come to this eventually. You're incapable of love, and I'm incapable of loving you. We . . . enjoyed one another. Took what the other offered. It's the sort of thing that's nice while it lasts, but it never lasts. Not for long enough."

Lucien cocked his head to one side, as though he couldn't hear her, or didn't understand what he heard. He walked to her, let his hands slip down her arms until he held her hands in his, and traced his fingers over hers.

Then he unfastened the cuff of her right sleeve and pushed it to her elbow, revealing the long, wealed scar she'd inflicted upon herself at Thalassa. "Tsecha told me about this." He ran the edge of his thumb from one end of the scar to the other and back again. "He said you always inflict the worst wounds upon yourself." He rolled up his right sleeve. "I could argue that." Slipping his thumbnail beneath the edges of the gauze, he peeled it away, revealing the fresh wounds that crisscrossed his forearm, some scabbed, some glistening as though fresh. "My first time. It's been a while since I could say that about anything."

He took Jani's right arm in his left hand, cradling it near the elbow. Then he took his right arm and rested it atop hers so their scars overlaid.

Jani flinched as the warmth of his blood touched her skin, felt his grip tighten to keep her close.

"You lead, I follow. You show the way, I walk in your footsteps. That's the way it is." He looked over her shoulder, his eyes locked on some middle distance. "Today, you acted as my second. You backed me up. You warned me when Ghos tried to strike. You were there." His eyes met hers, unfocused. Then he looked down at their arms. "I don't remember my dreams. Everyone dreams, you dream or you go mad. Well, I don't remember mine." He shook his head slowly, then he stilled. "After takedowns, something disconnects for a while. I come the closest to feeling like I'm in an imagined place." His voice had fallen to a murmur. "When I arrived here this afternoon, I entered through the garage. It was dark. I walked to the foot of that short flight of stairs and looked up into the darkness. My sightline closed in—all I could see was a long, empty tunnel of black. And I knew there was no one at the other end. I was completely alone, and I knew it. I always would be, and I knew that, too." He looked at her again, eyes no longer dead but clouded by something that for him marked a place worse than any he had ever been. "That's the way I feel now."

Jani reached up with her free hand and touched Lucien's face. *Liar*. She brushed her fingers over his lips. *Broken boy, who'll say anything to get what he needs*. Hers to see through to the end, because no one else could. "You'll never be alone as long as I'm alive."

"And you're going to live a good, long time, right?" Lucien's face brightened with a smile. You had to look hard to see that it didn't reach his eyes. "Hybrids are supposed to live a long time. That means I will, too." He rested his head on her shoulder, his skin hot as fever. "Although doing what, I have no idea. I always assumed I'd make it to full colonel. Find some general who needed a second right hand, put in my twenty years—"

"Then retire to the country and keep bees?" Jani tried to edge her arm away from Lucien's, stopping when he raised his head to look at her.

"Retire with you." The deadness had left his eyes, replaced by the usual cold, jewel light.

This time, Jani couldn't hold back. "Liar."

"If it makes you feel better to think that," Lucien said as he kissed her.

Jani lay atop the bed as Lucien undressed her—when she reached for his shirt, he pushed her hands away. This was his night to manage, his to prove she needed him as much as he needed her, no matter how she tried to deny it. She could feel it in the way he held her, the way he concentrated on every part of her as though no one else had ever entered this strange land before and only he knew the way. She sensed his desperation, tried to slow him, and felt his need overpower them both. She realized then that he was trying to change her mind, trying to convince her to stay in the only way he could, and told herself that if she was focused enough to think about it at a time like this, he had lost whatever hold he had on her, and their only connection now was the hold she had on him.

Then his hair caught the light, the pale washed gold of it, and she saw John's sheared head and heard his laugh. Felt his wiry weight on top of her and the insistent rhythm inside her, and closed her eyes, and used that sweetest memory to guide her home.

She slept. She dreamed. Unlike Lucien, she remembered. The point of a blade. A charred smile.

"Jani. Jani, wake up."

She opened her eyes to find Lucien leaning over her, steaming cup of coffee in hand.

"The PM's aide called. She's sending a skimmer. It will be here in thirty minutes. You need to get out of bed, shower, and dress. I've laid out clothes. I'm going to the kitchen to make breakfast. Val says to tell you he's got his fingers crossed."

Jani took the cup and struggled into a sitting position. "Do I look that helpless that I need step by step instructions?"

Lucien folded down the bedclothes. "You look like I do. We need downtime, and we won't get it." He headed for the door. "If you're not dressed and in the kitchen in fifteen minutes, I'm sending in Val."

Jani watched him leave. It broke through the daze that he'd donned his dress blue-greys.

She stumbled out of bed and made for the bathroom, cup in hand.

CHAPTER 33

Prime Minister Li Cao's Family estate cut an enviable swath through the Bluffs. Bordered on one side by the lake and on the other three sides by ravine-sliced woodland, it rolled for square kilometer after square kilometer.

The house itself lacked the immensity of the land that surrounded it. A single story built of stone and wood, flat expanses and arches in grey and brown. A house built for the needs of those who lived there, not to impress those who didn't.

Jani followed Cao's aide down a long white hallway as stripped-down as a Vynshàrau corridor, capped at the end by a set of hinged double doors. The aide turned the knob on one side and pushed the panel open, revealing a long, narrow sunroom framed by glass and wood beams. Jani took a deep breath and stepped inside.

The Prime Minister stood at the far end of the room, wearing a floor-length skirt and pullover in the signature cream color of her ministry. "Good morning." She held a cup by its underside like a bowl. "I trust you have recovered from yesterday's . . . episode." The contents of the cup steamed—she held the vessel to her nose to sniff, but didn't drink.

"I am quite well, Your Excellency. Thank you for inquiring." Jani paused just inside the doorway, shifting her weight from real leg to animandroid. She hadn't yet adjusted to her new limb's quirks, and she didn't want to risk a stumble at such a delicate time.

"I admit that I am not sure what to call you." Cao smiled. "Jani or Kilian or Kièrshia. To which name are you answering today?"

Jani walked slowly to the middle of the room. Lucien had chosen a trouser suit in dark green that he always said matched her eyes—she felt like a tree compared to the more diminutive Cao. "Jani or Kilian, Your Excellency, if you don't mind. You're mangling Kièrshia."

Cao had been ferrying the cup-bowl to her nose for another sniff—it stopped in mid-transit. "You never change. Even when you have no room to maneuver, that neck doesn't bend, does it? Kilian?" She walked toward the far windowed wall, where a pair of chairs bracketed a low, round table. "However, in this particular instance, you do have some room. But you knew that, didn't you?" She gestured for Jani to join her. "I decided it would be better if we discussed this matter in private." She sat, the cup still cradled in her hand. "Shai becomes too difficult to deal with when you're present—you bring out her stubbornness. As for ní Tsecha . . ." She shook her head. "I can only take so much torment with my morning tea. Even without you, he's problem enough. Many thought his outcast would eliminate his powerbase, and it did to a point. He lost the bornsect, but they don't count for much anymore next to the Haárin, do they, and he hasn't lost a one of them." She graced Jani with a look of quiet accusation. "You made sure of that." She sat back, and once more held the cup to her nose. "Jasmine. The scent reminds me that summer will come, even though now it is still too cold to enjoy my garden. Tell me about Thalassa."

Read Niall's report. Jani swallowed that response and counted a long pause. When the aide returned with a beverage tray, she asked for coffee, and remained silent until the young woman prepared her cup and departed. "Thalassa is a community of fifty-seven hybrids." *Fifty-nine, after John and I settle in.* "The number is fairly equally distributed between those who were Haárin originally and those who were—"

"I know all that." Cao reached into a pocket in her skirt and removed a data wafer. "Courtesy of Niall Pierce, whose . . . regard for you tended to color some of his more politically significant conclusions." She paused to drink, taking a long draught that betrayed how much she needed the energy and the comfort the tea provided. "Let me rephrase the question. Tell me about Thalassa's influence."

"That's a more difficult quantity to define at present." Jani looked through the window to the garden beyond, arrangements of stone set amid hybrid shrubs blooming yellow and orange. *If I make us appear too strong, she'll hold back whatever she is offering out of fear, and if I make us appear too weak, she'll hold back because there's no need to give anything up.* "We are the physical manifestation of ní Tsecha's beliefs. There is a fervor about the place you could describe as religious." She flashed back to the day she met Gisa in the circle, and the sight of cloths dipped in her blood. "Our official status at the moment is as a subsidiary offshoot of the Elyan Haárin, who already possess a formidable power base in their own right. We are a responsibility to them more than an asset at this point."

"You say subsidiary, not suborn."

You would catch that, wouldn't you? "When I left Thalassa, Your Excellency, we were still laying down plumbing in the houses. We are still finding our place."

"Which means you are open to influence, suasion, lobbying, and all the other sins that politics is heir to?" Cao concentrated on the garden view as well. "Or that you are waiting to see which way the wind blows." She glanced at Jani out of the corner of her eye. "You've learned to keep your mouth shut at least part of the time, Kilian. Yet another thing for the rest of us to worry about."

Jani finished her coffee and set down the cup. "I'm sure I don't know what you mean, Your Excellency."

"Of course you don't." Cao sighed. "The bornsect have once more been shaken by life outside their worldskein, and like an injured crab into its shell, they will retreat. The word came today, from Shai, the embassy to be razed, and the enclave as well. They could extract so much more from us if they cared to, but they have lost their resolve. I doubt seriously that they will emerge again under the current regime."

"Cèel will have to if he wants to keep open any lines of communication with the colonial Haárin."

"Cèel, for all his talk of modernity, is still too much of an ideologue. He will die before he changes. I expect another bornsect to ascend to *rau* before too long, as I'm sure you do." Cao ran a finger along the rim of her cup. "I hear other names bandied about by my idomeni-watchers. Doches, the Oà's Chief Propitiator. The Pathen dominant, Aolun. Do either of them strike a responsive chord?"

"I have heard both names mentioned, Your Excellency, but I don't know enough about either to hazard a guess."

"Indeed." Cao tapped an enameled fingernail against the arm of her chair. "John Shroud. Yet another unknown quantity. If I could toss both him and Eamon DeVries into a Luna prison and lose the code, I would do so and gladly." Her tone hardened. "He's backing you financially. Shroud."

"The houses in which the hybrids live as well as the surrounding property are part of Eamon DeVries's personal holdings. John didn't know what Eamon had done until he arrived on site almost two months ago."

"But he didn't respond by kicking DeVries out of Neoclona, as their contract demands, and evicting the hybrids, did he? DeVries is still a member of Neoclona, and the hybrids live there still." Cao's voice held petulance, as though she considered his decision a personal affront. "Why did he decide to hybridize?"

Jani smiled—she couldn't help herself. "He loves me." She looked up to find Cao regarding her with narrow-eyed annoyance, and felt the heat flood her face.

"Love is a marvelous thing, and in and of itself, not as complicating an issue as one might think. Adjustments can be made regarding love." Cao set her cup down, then stood and walked to the window. "It's the money and power that one or the other parties brings to the table that confound matters. John Shroud's personal fortune dwarfs the Gross Domestic Product of any number of colonies. If he chooses to use it in support of the Thalassans, and through them the Elyan Haárin, he will upset the balance of power for the entire Outer Circle."

"The balance of power is already upset. The Outer Circle Haárin control transportation and shipping for the region. At this point, John's money doesn't make a great deal of difference."

"At this point." Cao placed a hand on the window. "The medical aspects of the issue also concern me. The control of Neoclona—"

"You need to discuss that with Val Parini."

"He has scheduled an appointment for this afternoon." The hand dropped. "I had hoped it a social call, but I fear now it will be a negotiating session." Cao remained at the window, gaze fixed on a trio of yard workers digging around the browned skeleton of a shrub.

"The pressing issue at the moment is keeping the Outer Circle Haárin settled." Jani felt her idomeni anger rise. She was hungry and tired. She missed John with a physical ache, and the half-emerged buds in the trees outside the window would emerge into full leaf by the time she saw him again. "The accompanying issues are distance, perceived reliability of the native population, and the military and financial clubs you can wield. At this point, neither you nor Cèel have all those issues weighted in your favor. Therefore, you have to deal."

Cao's shoulders shook in soundless mirth. "The Kilian Tongue of Lead wins out after all." She stilled. "This aborted challenge-cum-murder involving Captain Pascal and the security suborn, Ghos—it complicates matters."

"Ghos and his dominant Elon lowered the embassy defenses to permit attack. Humans died as a result." Jani tried to project a calm she didn't feel. "I've seen the 'Vee reports. Shai has no recourse where that's concerned."

"Except ideology, which is the one great unknown." Cao tapped the window one last time, then returned to her seat. "If the Outer Circle Haárin are placated, what can they offer in return?"

"I cannot speak for them. The Thalassan hybrids are beholden to the Elyan Haárin for protection; in turn, we owe them obedience *to a point*. I can speak *to* them regarding matters of mutual interest." Jani looked out toward the garden—the workers had hacked down the shrub with cutters in preparation for digging out the root remains. "We have the right to protect ourselves—that is paramount. But I can pledge that I will do my utmost to prevent the Elyan Haárin from taking aggressive actions against the humanish colonists."

Cao's voice perked. "Aggressive, militarily speaking? Politically? Economically?"

"Militarily. Politically."

"In other words, you won't persuade the Elyan Haárin away from my docks?"

"They are not your docks, Cao. Your representatives signed contracts in your name. We've dealt with the matter of Sìah Haárin and contracts before—do you really want to revisit such?"

Cao's brow arched—her expression turned thoughtful. "Your speech changes when you become emotional. It becomes harsher, more idomeni-like. I also hear Shai's stubbornness. Is it a Vynshàrau trait, I wonder?" She sat forward, hands folded. The light from the window highlighted the fine lines that grooved the corners of her eyes. When she first took office, the power of the Commonwealth seemed bound to rise ever higher. Now, she seemed to be contemplating the opposite trajectory. "I will lend my support to your request that ní Tsecha Egri and the other Chicago Haárin be allowed to resettle on Elyas." She reached into a pocket hidden in the folds of her skirt, and removed Jani's letter, setting it on the table in front of her. "I cannot guarantee that Shai will agree, but she has shown herself more willing to listen to the hard realities than has Cèel." She regarded her hands, heavy with rings. "You should leave tomorrow, I think. That will most likely force Shai to acquiesce to the decision, then explain it to Cèel. She works better under pressure."

Jani waited for Cao to say more, but the woman simply poured herself another cup of tea. *That's it?* She wondered at what they had discussed, and what little had been decided. So what was the point of the exercise? To feel her out? Impress upon her the possibility of alliance? Roust her out of bed in the early morning?

I got what I wanted. Barring any exercise in stubbornness on Shai's part. *Maybe I shouldn't complain too loudly.*

Then she realized the silence. Like suborns of every species, she knew a dismissal when she didn't hear it. "Thank you, Your Excellency." She rose and headed for the door.

Cao remained seated, her gaze fixed on the workers. "Farewell, Captain Jani Moragh Kilian. Kièrshia nìaRauta Haárin. Tsecha vo Kièrshia. Tsecha's toxin come to life, to plague us forever." She paused to hold the cup to her nose. "We will meet again, I am sure. Across one bargaining table or another."

Jani left the room to find a different aide waiting to escort her to the skimmer. The ride back to Val's seemed shorter than had the drive to Cao's house, as was usual with those sorts of visits. When the vehicle drifted to a stop in front of Val's building, Lucien clipped down the steps to meet her.

"We leave tomorrow," she said as soon as they moved out of earshot of the driver.

The barest shadow crossed his perfect face. "I'll alert the enclave."

Micah lay still, listening for any sounds from the hallway outside. When anyone looked through the narrow window, he faked sleep, or talked to himself *with intent*, as though he actually held a conversation with voices in his head. *This isn't going to work forever*. Eventually, they'd drag him out of bed and subject him to a neuroscan. He knew they suspected trauma disorder, along with a laundry list of other problems. He knew that if he told them that he felt sure someone wanted to kill him, they'd add that problem to the list.

"I've seen people in the hall, you understand. Men, mostly, although they sent a woman this morning who could have been Chrivet's twin." He wished he'd had the wit to demand Chrivet tell him her real name before he shot her. He would have liked to know, to compare it with that of the woman who had stood outside his door, staring at him through the window until the day nurse spooked her.

He would have liked to know Manda's real name as well, but he tried not to think about that.

He fell asleep. Dreamed quiet dreams for a change. Awoke with a lighter heart, and had his hopes dashed as soon as he opened his eyes.

"Hello, Micah." Pascal had dragged a visitor's chair to the bedside and sat. He wore civvies, which was surprising, a blue shirt and tan trousers. An outpatient ID bracelet encircled one bandaged wrist. "How are you feeling?" He waited for an answer, then shrugged when one didn't prove forthcoming. "I was in the area—" He raised his braceleted wrist. "—thought I'd stop by to see how you're doing." He smiled. "Veles is dead—did you kill him?"

Micah gripped a handful of sheet as the remembered voice rasped in his ear. He tried to imagine the man's face, but the effort made his head swim. "No."

"You're sure? Didn't have another one of your moments, like you did during our last meeting?"

Micah closed his eyes, then opened them. Unfortunately, Pascal didn't prove a moment. "No. I didn't kill him."

Pascal studied him as though he was a not particularly interesting piece of furniture. "You're the only one left—did they tell you that? They couldn't save Chrivet."

Micah replayed a curtain of brown hair. A coffee-flavored kiss. "No. They didn't tell me."

"And now they have you locked away. No press, no interviews, no lawyers. May as well have fallen down a hole—"

"What do you want!" Micah pushed himself into a sitting position hugging the bed's guardrails as the room tilted. "What the hell do you want?"

"To fix you in my mind." Pascal cocked his head. "In case someone changes your face, your build, your coloring. Mannerisms are the hardest thing to unlearn, and you have a few interesting ones. I won't tell you what they are, of course, because . . . well, then you'd know."

"My face?" Micah leaned forward slowly, and tried to stretch. His muscles felt stiff from inactivity. Flabby. He knew that if he could only work out that ache, his head would clear. He'd stop thinking about advocates and courts martial and prison cells, what the Service wanted to do to him and how quickly they planned to do it. Stop thinking about goddamned Pascal, sitting in his room as though he owned it, all arrogance and alien scars.

He pressed his hands to his head. With all the watchers who had monitored him since his arrival, he'd have thought someone would check on him now. Intervene. Ask Pascal to leave. "I don't know what you're talking about."

"No, I don't think you do." Pascal raised a hand to his forehead, revealing a thin line of blood that marred his shirtsleeve. "If you consider cities as beasts, Chicago qualifies as a predator of sorts. Dangerous, yes, but also shrewd. Adaptable. It moves quickly when it senses the hunter close in." He sat back, hands folded in his lap. "Change is the hunter, in this case. Fear of what the future holds." He smiled. "You are in for an interesting next few months, I expect. I advise you to relax and observe. Take good notes. Remember what is said and who says it. You will witness feats of denial, chicanery, and outright criminality the likes of which you'll never see again. I'd look forward to it if I were you."

"You're crazy." Micah leaned forward and hugged his

aching stomach. "Chrivet's dead. I killed her." He relived the scene at times. Dreamed it. Saw the fear in Chrivet's eyes as she faced her own shooter. Heard Kilian call to him to stand down. Wondered if he should have listened. "They're going to execute me."

Pascal shook his head. "No. Not if they want to maintain the support of the ultraconservative anti-idomeni factions, which I think they do. They're scared, you see. They know she won't rest until they're nailed." He looked down at his hands, then fingered his bloodstained sleeve.

"You'll be medicalled out, I'm guessing. That's how the Service usually buries their mistakes." He brushed some imaginary blemish from his trousers, then stood. "I shall follow your career with interest, Micah, whatever it happens to be. I'm quite confident that we shall meet again." He left the room as quietly as he'd entered, the door closing behind him with a sigh.

CHAPTER 34

It was possible to arrange the transport of an enclave's worth of Haárin from a standing start in a day's time, Jani found, if one went without sleep and had the entire Prime Ministry at one's beck and call in the bargain.

And if one has Lucien. She tried not to notice that his labors to that end contained the same undercurrents of desperation as had his lovemaking. *See what I can do,* his every action whispered. *You don't want to leave me behind.*

"I'll handle the cancellation of the town-house lease." He sat beside her in the isolated corner of the idomeni shuttle-port that was open to humanish. "The office supply company will pick up the combooth equipment and workstation this afternoon."

"Wipe the boards first." Jani pressed her palms against the sides of her throbbing head. "Erase all the inputs."

"I did that this morning while you were in the shower, after I made breakfast and packed your luggage, such as it was." Lucien stifled a yawn. "It's good to know that I'm still officially on leave and under orders to take it easy." He lay his head against the seatback and closed his eyes.

Jani turned to study his resting profile, as she had so many times that morning. "Thank you."

One side of Lucien's mouth twitched. "I'm being completely self-serving, of course. That's always the reason behind everything I do."

"I know." Jani lay her head back and closed her eyes as well. The old Service rule—sleep whenever the opportunity presented itself, because you never knew when you'd get the chance again.

She felt herself relax, heard Lucien emit a barely audible snore—

"Nìa!"

—until that familiar voice rattled around in her skull and jerked her upright.

Lucien groaned and struggled to his feet. "I knew the silence was too good to last."

"Shai is mad, I have decided." Tsecha swept through the concourse behind Dathim, his coat flapping around his ankles. "To agree to my leaving with you. Cèel will recall her, of this I have no doubt. Kill her, most likely." He stepped to the edge of the barrier that separated the concourse from the humanish section, then shrugged, hoisted his coat to his knees and stepped over it. "We leave in less than an hour. Every Haárin finds that they now have more to pack than they ever brought with them. All is madness." He slumped into a seat.

Jani glanced over at Dathim. "You can arrange to have things shipped."

"Pascal and I have already done such. We are the only two sane ones left." Dathim turned to Lucien. "You will come to Elyas. From what I hear, there is much to organize there as well."

Lucien opened his mouth to speak, then closed it. He looked to each of them in turn, his eyes finally coming to rest on the strapping Haárin. "When I can." He wiped a hand across his mouth. "Excuse me." He hurried from the waiting area, pushing through the entry door before it had a chance to open completely.

Tsecha watched Lucien depart. "Humanish leave-taking. If you have never experienced such, Dathim, you must prepare." He turned back to Jani. "All that will meet again, will meet again. All that will separate, will separate. Such is as it is." He gestured uncertainty. "And yet, I understand . . ." He turned back to look out through the windows to the rolling spring green outside. "Such dreams I had for this damned cold place."

Dathim walked to his side and placed a hand on his shoulder. "Then we should go outside, ní Tsecha, and bid this damned cold place a proper good-bye."

"Yes." Tsecha rose and followed Dathim outside.

Jani looked around the empty area. The other Haárin waited in a separate wing of the port. The shuttles had all arrived, and were being loaded even now. "Nothing to do but wait." She sat down and wondered if she had time to grab a nap.

"Jan?"

She turned.

Lucien stood in the entry. He pressed his thumb and first two fingers together and held them to his lips, as if he held a nicstick. "You have a visitor."

Jani cut across the front of the port and around to the charge lot reserved for humanish skimmers, to find Niall standing beside a dark blue sedan. He couldn't smoke on the premises, so he made do with tapping an irregular beat on the skimmer roof.

"Niall." Jani stopped short of the lot's edge.

Niall stopped in mid-tap, then stepped back from the skimmer. "Hello." He looked up at the sky. "Clear. Not much crosswind. PM kept the reporters away. Good day to fly." He turned to her. "What time do you leave?"

Jani checked her timepiece. "The shuttle dominant wants us aboard in a half hour."

"Can't the idomeni even call their pilots 'pilots'?" Niall paused for a time over that bit of annoyance. "So, I understand the PM herself is providing the ships."

Jani nodded. "They've been in emergency drydock at

Luna Station getting retrofitted to transport idomeni. Amazing how quickly things can get done when a Prime Minister wants you out of the way." She sighed, which precipitated a yawn. "It's all gotten very complicated."

"Well, you're involved. Stands to reason." Niall grinned, then scuffed his feet. "Faber's going to be medicalled out. That's the latest buzz, at any rate. Someone in Service Investigative started a death pool—pick the day we find his body washed up on the lakeshore."

Jani recalled the slight figure Lucien led away. Lost. Broken. "I thought I had no pity left, but I pity him. He didn't belong in that sort of operation—he didn't have the mind-set for it. Now all he has left are memories of the dead and a shattered career."

"There but for the grace of God . . . ?" Niall shook his head. "I don't buy it, sorry. It's very simple—there are people who have what it takes and people who don't, and whether you're one or the other is determined at birth." He pushed his hands into his pockets, then pulled them out immediately. "For example, I'd trust you at my back anytime, even when you don't follow orders. But then, you're worth any number of Micah Fabers."

"Don't let any of your friends at Supreme Command hear you say that." Jani smiled. "What about Lucien?"

"You're worth any number of him as well. But I'm not in Intelligence, so I have no say in the matter." Niall shrugged. "What time is it?"

Jani glanced at her timepiece. "Twenty minutes."

"Right." Niall cleared his throat. "I'm . . . going to miss you, now the hurly-burly's done."

Jani's eyes stung. She looked around to see if Tsecha and Dathim were in sight, then walked up to Niall. "I'm going to miss you, too." She slipped her arms around his waist and hugged him.

Niall stiffened at first. Then he hugged back, his hands tentative on her shoulders, as if he never expected to touch her and didn't know what to do.

"Farewell, too little and too lately known, whom I began to think and call my own." His tunic felt rough against Jani's cheek, the cloth scented with fresh air and the sharp undercurrent of smoke. " 'For sure our souls were near allied, and thine cast in the same poetic mould with mine.' " He stopped, inhaled shakily. " 'One common note on either lyre did strike, and knaves and fools we both abhorred alike—' " His voice cracked. He released her abruptly and stepped back, eyes fixed on the ground. "John Dryden. Poet. Critic. Playwright. Restoration period, old England." He turned away, took a long, slow step toward his skimmer, then stopped. "He wrote the poem for a friend who died. 'To the Memory of Mr. Oldham.' John Oldham, a satirist and poet . . ." His voice dwindled once more. He reached into his trouser pocket and removed a folded sheet of parchment. "I've written the rest out, in case you want to read it later. I know how much you love when I give you things to read." He walked back to Jani and handed her the sheet, pale blue with charcoal trim, courtesy of Supreme Command HQ. "Speaking of men named John." He still didn't raise his eyes to look her in the face. "You love him. He loves you. You're happy."

"Yes." Jani nodded carefully. A sudden move on her part and the tears would spill, and once they started, she doubted they'd stop.

"Good. You deserve to be." Niall nodded, then pointed to the sheet of parchment. "It's not that I believe this to be an epitaph or a eulogy, or that we've reached the end of our friendship. I know things have changed between us, and will continue to change, and that . . . a time may come when we find ourselves on opposite sides. But whatever happens, whatever events transpire, I just wanted you to know that . . . I consider you my best and closest friend."

Jani closed her eyes and stood as still as she could. "I feel the same way." She breathed, concentrated on the air pulling in and pushing out. "I have to go." She turned and hurried back to the terminal.

"I may be out your way in the autumn," Niall called after her. "Possibly earlier. Sorting out Fort Karistos."

Jani stopped and turned around. "Mako's sending the right man."

"Yeah." Niall patted his pockets again, then stilled. "Think there's any neutral ground where we can meet for dinner?"

"I'm sure something can be arranged."

"You can still eat in a restaurant?"

"I still eat in a restaurant." Jani regarded Niall for a time. Then she drew to attention and snapped a salute. "Colonel."

Niall saluted back. "Captain."

Jani turned and walked back into the terminal. The place was deserted now—her footsteps echoed within the space, the dull rasp of boot soles against rough tile.

She returned to the humanish side of the concourse and took a seat by the window, waiting for the final call to board. Three shuttles had already departed for Luna, leaving the runways bare and her sightlines clear. She could see Tsecha and Dathim strolling toward the far end of the tarmac, as well as the shuttle dominant who paced around the remaining craft that abutted the concourse's Haárin gangway, executing her preflight walk-around.

Not shuttle dominant. Pilot. Jani replayed Niall's grumble, and smiled.

"And the time dwindles down."

Jani looked around to find Lucien standing at the end of the row of seats. *It's just the two of us.* She'd had a feeling that when the time came for good-byes, his would be the last. Unfortunately, that hadn't helped her prepare. Forewarned and forearmed never did much good when it came to Lucien Pascal. "I was just thinking of something Niall said." She stifled a cough. She loved John more than her life, saw aspects of him in the sun-bright surface of a cloud or the sweep of a shuttle's wing, had only to close her eyes to imagine his smile, his touch.

And yet . . .

"Dathim says I'm not allowed on the tarmac." Lucien

walked to the window and watched the pilot circle. "Anything we say needs to be said here."

Jani's hand went to the neck of her coverall, which felt constricting despite its usual baggy fit. "Such as?"

Lucien stood up straight and clasped his hands behind his back. He wore civvies, shirt and trousers in shades of blue that managed to look like a uniform. "I've put in for a spot on Pierce's Karistos audit team. He doesn't know it yet, of course. I can't wait to hear the howls of agony."

Jani grinned. "I'll just bet you can't." She tugged at her cuffs. Checked her timepiece. Then she looked up to find Lucien had turned his back to the window, and watched her.

"You'll miss me, won't you?" He smiled his brilliant smile.

Jani nodded. "Yes, I think I will."

"You think." Lucien stood still for a time. Then he started toward her, walking so slowly, as though he knew she'd wait forever.

Jani's heart pounded as he pulled her to her feet, his hands roaming over her body before locking around her waist. He drew her in slowly, his lips tracing heat over her face, her neck and throat before finally settling over hers. She savored his taste for what she told herself would be the last time. Pepper with a hint of bitter orange, flavors he knew she enjoyed.

He released her just as gradually, hands drifting along her neck, her shoulders, over her breasts before finally falling away. He backed off, fingers curled as though he held onto her still, his eyes locked with hers. Then he turned on his heel and walked to the entry, through the doors and away.

Jani watched the space where Lucien had been as the last sense of him faded. Then she detected motion out of the corner of her eye, and looked out the window in time to see Dathim and Tsecha hurrying toward the terminal.

"It is time, nìa," Tsecha called as he bustled through the entry, his step slowing as he drew close. "Time to leave this damned cold place." He stopped and looked around the terminal as though lost. "So strange. I thought, and truly, that I would die here."

"You might have." Dathim cut in front of Tsecha, then waved him and Jani both toward the gangway. "As we all might have. Now we shall go someplace else, and live." He looked to the window, then away. In his way, he had wanted to live on Earth as much as had Tsecha, but if he felt any regret at leaving, he kept it to himself. "Now we shall go," he said again.

They boarded the shuttle. Jani strapped herself into her seat, then sat back. Studied the other Haárin who had already boarded. Wondered at how far she had come in a year and a half, and where she still needed to go.

Then came the rumble of the engines. The acceleration. The lift and bank of flight.

"Nìa?" Tsecha loosened his seat brake and spun around to face her. "What is that on the water?"

Jani loosened her safety harness and edged closer to the porthole until she could see the lake below.

The skimmers flitted side by side over the water like low-flying seabirds, their rings of emergency lights blazing yellow-white. At first they darted to the left, then to the right, like glowing waterbugs. Then their paths straightened as they sped up to race the shuttle, their lights flashing on then off in flickering patterns.

"Humanish leave-taking, nìRau." Jani leaned close to the window and watched the display until the shuttle banked and the skimmers disappeared from view.

EPILOGUE

"Who is that youngish, nìa?" Tsecha leaned forward so he could look around Jani, but not so far that he couldn't pretend he looked somewhere else in case someone caught him.

Jani glanced back toward the enclave road, saw the familiar figure sitting atop a nearby rock, and hid a smile. "You did meet him, inshah. Torin Clase—he's the historian."

"Ah." Tsecha nodded as he drew up straight. "He appears most as different when he writes."

"He does get a rather pointed look, yes."

"He is *everywhere*, nìa."

"He believes that recording the history of Thalassa is his born duty. He believes it must be done at the time things happen so that the facts don't get muddled."

"So." Tsecha sniffed. "Can he hear us if we whisper?"

"*No.*" Jani fought to stifle a laugh. "But then he'll try to get you to commit to once-a-week interviews."

"He has done such already, nìa—everywhere I turn—" Tsecha shook his head. "The price I must pay, I most suppose, for this blessed sun."

Jani closed her eyes and felt the heat on her face. Winter was almost upon them, and she could still walk about without a coat in the afternoons. Yet still, at times, she thought

436

about what had been. "I am sorry that Chicago didn't work out. I know how much it meant to you." She hesitated. "It meant a lot to me as well."

"The gods did not mean for me to die in such a cold place." Tsecha bared his teeth. "They meant for us to labor where we were wanted in the first place, where we did not have to spend so much energy asserting our right to *be*." He glanced at Jani, then away. "I speak as one of you. I am not, however—this I know and truly. I do not presume."

Since when? "If you wanted to hybridize, all you'd have to do is go to John and say the word."

"He would enjoy it too much, I believe."

"There would be something rather circular about it, yes." Jani watched a sailracer's rainbow-hued craft swoop in the distance. "It is a good place."

"It is." Tsecha nodded. "It is *warm*, which is a wonder. I did not believe that I would ever enjoy such again." He started down the beach. "Come, nìa. We must speak of ná Gisa again. I fear and truly that she will drive me most as mad."

"In a minute, inshah." Jani stretched her arms over her head, as though she could reach the few wisps of cloud that coursed the sky if she tried hard enough. After a few moments she let them fall to her sides. Rocked back and forth, heel to toe to heel, inhaling the sea air and listening to the birds screech. Then . . .

. . . *she reached into her pocket and removed a stone, one of the banded triangles that are so numerous here. She looked out over the water, as she has done so often since her return. Bending low, she tossed the stone atop the curved mass of them that had washed up over the years past. Then she started down the beach after ní Tsecha, running until she caught up to him, and they talked until sunset.*